DISCARD

PRETTY MONSTERS

OTHER COLLECTIONS BY

KELLY LINK

Stranger Things Happen

Magic for Beginners

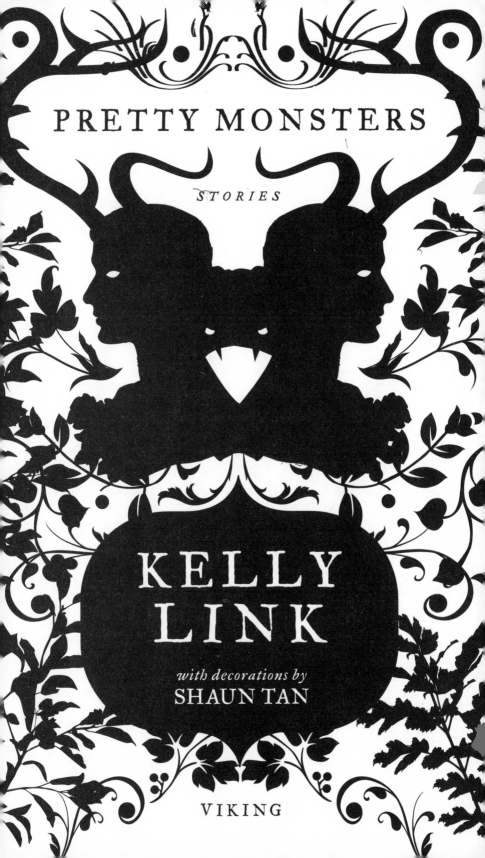

PRETTY MONSTERS

STORIES

KELLY LINK

with decorations by
SHAUN TAN

VIKING

VIKING
Published by Penguin Group
Penguin Group (USA) Inc., 345 Hudson Street, New York, New York 10014, U.S.A.
Penguin Group (Canada), 90 Eglinton Avenue East, Suite 700, Toronto, Ontario, Canada M4P 2Y3
(a division of Pearson Penguin Canada Inc.)

Penguin Books Ltd, Registered Offices: 80 Strand, London WC2R 0RL, England

First published in 2008 by Viking, a member of Penguin Group (USA) Inc.

10   9   8   7   6   5   4   3   2   1

"The Wrong Grave" first appeared in *The Restless Dead: Ten Original Stories of the Supernatural*,
edited by Deborah Noyes, published by Candlewick Press, 2007.

"Monster" first appeared in *Noisy Outlaws, Unfriendly Blobs, and Some Other Things That Aren't as Scary, Maybe, Depending on How You Feel About Lost Lands, Stray Cellphones, Creatures from the Sky, Parents Who Disappear in Peru, a Man Named Lars Farf, and One Other Story We Couldn't Quite Finish, So Maybe You Could Help Us Out*, edited by Ted Thompson, published by McSweeney's, 2005.

"The Faery Handbag" originally appeared in *The Faery Reel: Tales from the Twilight Realm*, edited by Ellen Datlow and Terri Windling, published by Viking, a division of Penguin Young Readers Group, 2004.

"The Wizards of Perfil" originally appeared in *Firebirds Rising: An Anthology of Original Science Fiction and Fantasy*, edited by Sharyn November, published by Firebird, an imprint of Penguin Group (USA) Inc., 2006.

"The Specialist's Hat" first appeared in *Event Horizon* in 1998; reprinted by permission of Small Beer Press, 2001.

"The Surfer" originally appeared in *The Starry Rift: Tales of New Tomorrows*, edited by Jonathan Strahan, published by Viking, a member of Penguin Group (USA) Inc., 2008.

"The Constable of Abal" originally appeared in *The Coyote Road: Trickster Tales*, edited by Ellen Datlow and Terri Windling, published by Viking, a member of Penguin Group (USA) Inc., 2007.

"Magic For Beginners" originally appeared in *Magic for Beginners*, published by Small Beer Press, 2005.

"Pretty Monsters" is original to this collection.

LIBRARY OF CONGRESS CATALOGING-IN-PUBLICATION DATA IS AVAILABLE
ISBN: 978-0-670-01090-5

Printed in U.S.A.   Set in Cochin   Book design by Jim Hoover

for **Annabel** *Jones* **Link**

ACKNOWLEDGMENTS

Thanks to my funny, forgiving, and unfailingly inspirational family—especially my cousin Bryan Jones who told me to write him into a story, my sister Holly Link who read many of these in early drafts, and my mother, Annabel Jones Link, who was my co-worker at B. Dolphin, a children's bookstore run by Mimi Levin and Janis Fields. Thanks to Elke and Penelope, who aren't old enough to read these yet. Thanks to the editors who originally published these stories: Ellen Datlow, Terri Windling, Jonathan Strahan, Eli Horowitz, Deborah Noyes, and, finally, my editor at Viking, Sharyn November, for her sharp eyes, her patience, her persistence. Inadequate thanks to Holly Black, Karen Joy Fowler, Molly Gloss, Leslie What, Betty Husted, Cassandra Clare, Gwenda Bond, Delia Sherman, Ellen Kushner, Sarah Smith, Jedediah Berry, Walter Jon Williams and the Rio Hondo Workshop, Richard Butner and John Kessel and the Sycamore Hill Workshop. Eternal thanks to my agent, Renee Zuckerbrot, and to Whitney Lee and Jenny Meyer. Thanks to Jim Hoover, for designing such a beautiful book. Thanks to Shaun Tan, whose illustrations have let me see some of these stories for the first time. Partial inspiration for "The Specialist's Hat" came from an exhibit at the Peabody Museum in Cambridge, MA: the longest poem in that story begins with a passage stuck up beside an empty exhibit case. Also adapted, for the same story, is a passage about snake whiskey from an outdoor folklore exhibit I visited in Raleigh, North Carolina. While working on this collection, I was supported by a grant from the National Endowment for the Arts. The stories in this collection owe a particular debt to the short stories and novels of Joan Aiken, Diana Wynne Jones, Robert Westall, Ursula K. Le Guin, and to the anthologies of Helen Hoke. Finally, thanks to my husband, Gavin, for the window display and everything since then.

CONTENTS

Anyone might accidentally dig up the wrong grave.

THE WRONG GRAVE

ALL OF THIS happened because a boy I once knew named Miles Sperry decided to go into the resurrectionist business and dig up the grave of his girlfriend, Bethany Baldwin, who had been dead for not quite a year. Miles planned to do this in order to recover the sheaf of poems he had, in what he'd felt was a beautiful and romantic gesture, put into her casket. Or possibly it had just been a really dumb thing to do. He hadn't made copies. Miles had always been impulsive. I think you should know that right up front.

He'd tucked the poems, handwritten, tear-stained and with cross-outs, under Bethany's hands. Her fingers had felt like candles, fat and waxy and pleasantly cool, until you remembered that they were fingers. And he couldn't help noticing that there was something wrong about her breasts, they seemed larger. If Bethany had known that she was going to die, would she have gone all the way with him? One of his poems was about that, about how now they never would, how it was too late now. Carpe diem before you run out of diem.

Bethany's eyes were closed, someone had done that, too, just like they'd arranged her hands, and even her smile looked composed, in the wrong sense of the word. Miles wasn't sure how you made someone smile after they were dead. Bethany didn't look much like she had when she'd been alive. That had been only a few days ago. Now she seemed smaller, and also, oddly, larger. It was the nearest Miles had ever been to a dead person, and he stood there, looking at Bethany, wishing two things: that he was dead, too, and also that it had seemed appropriate to bring along his notebook and a pen. He felt he should be taking notes. After all, this was the most significant thing that had ever happened to Miles. A great change was occurring within him, moment by singular moment.

Poets were supposed to be in the moment, and also stand outside the moment, looking in. For example, Miles had never noticed before, but Bethany's ears were slightly lopsided. One was smaller and slightly higher up. Not that he would have cared, or written a poem about it, or even mentioned it to her, ever, in case it made her self-conscious, but it was a fact and now that he'd noticed it he thought it might have driven him crazy, not mentioning it: he bent over and kissed Bethany's forehead, breathing in. She smelled like a new car. Miles's mind was full of poetic thoughts. Every cloud had a silver lining, except there was probably a more interesting and meaningful way to say that, and death wasn't really a cloud. He thought about what it was: more like an earthquake, maybe, or falling from a great height and smacking into the ground, really hard, which knocked the wind out of you and made it hard to sleep or wake up or eat or care about things like homework or whether there was anything good on TV. And death was foggy, too, but also prickly, so maybe instead of a cloud, a fog made of little sharp things. Needles. Every death fog has a lot of silver needles. Did that make sense? Did it scan?

Then the thought came to Miles like the tolling of a large and leaden bell that Bethany was dead. This may sound strange, but in my experience it's strange and it's also just how it works. You wake up and you remember that the person you loved is dead. And then you think: really?

Then you think how strange it is, how you have to remind yourself that the person you loved is dead, and even while you're thinking about that, the thought comes to you again that the person you loved is dead. And it's the same stupid fog, the same needles or mallet to the intestines or whatever worse thing you want to call it, all over again. But you'll see for yourself someday.

Miles stood there, remembering, until Bethany's mother, Mrs. Baldwin, came up beside him. Her eyes were dry, but her hair was a mess. She'd only managed to put eye shadow on one eyelid. She was wearing jeans and one of Bethany's old T-shirts. Not even one of Bethany's favorite T-shirts. Miles felt embarrassed for her, and for Bethany, too.

"What's that?" Mrs. Baldwin said. Her voice sounded rusty and outlandish, as if she were translating from some other language. Something Indo-Germanic, perhaps.

"My poems. Poems I wrote for her," Miles said. He felt very solemn. This was a historic moment. One day Miles's biographers would write about this. "Three haikus, a sestina, and two villanelles. Some longer pieces. No one else will ever read them."

Mrs. Baldwin looked into Miles's face with her terrible, dry eyes. "I see," she said. "She said you were a lousy poet." She put her hand down into the casket, smoothed Bethany's favorite dress, the one with spider webs, and several holes through which you could see Bethany's itchy black tights. She patted Bethany's hands, and said, "Well, good-bye, old girl. Don't forget to send a postcard."

Don't ask me what she meant by this. Sometimes Bethany's mother said strange things. She was a lapsed Buddhist and a substitute math teacher. Once she'd caught Miles cheating on an algebra quiz. Relations between Miles and Mrs. Baldwin had not improved during the time that Bethany and Miles were dating, and Miles couldn't decide whether or not to believe her about Bethany not liking his poetry. Substitute teachers had strange senses of humor when they had them at all.

He almost reached into the casket and took his poetry back. But Mrs. Baldwin would have thought that she'd proved something; that she'd won. Not that this was a situation where anyone was going to win anything. This was a funeral, not a game show. Nobody was going to get to take Bethany home.

Mrs. Baldwin looked at Miles and Miles looked back. Bethany wasn't looking at anyone. The two people that Bethany had loved most in the world could see, through that dull hateful fog, what the other was thinking, just for a minute, and although you weren't there and even if you had been you wouldn't have known what they were thinking anyway, I'll tell you. I wish it had been me, Miles thought. And Mrs. Baldwin thought, I wish it had been you, too.

Miles put his hands into the pockets of his new suit, turned, and left Mrs. Baldwin standing there. He went and sat next to his own mother, who was trying very hard not to cry. She'd liked Bethany. Everyone had liked Bethany. A few rows in front, a girl named April Lamb was picking her nose in some kind of frenzy of grief. When they got to the cemetery, there was another funeral service going on, the burial of the girl who had been in the other car, and the two groups of mourners glared at each other as they parked their cars and tried to figure out which grave site to gather around.

Two florists had misspelled Bethany's name on the ugly wreaths, BERTHANY and also BETHONY, just like tribe members did when they were voting each other out on the television show *Survivor*, which had always been Bethany's favorite thing about *Survivor*. Bethany had been an excellent speller, although the Lutheran minister who was conducting the sermon didn't mention that.

Miles had an uncomfortable feeling: he became aware that he couldn't wait to get home and call Bethany, to tell her all about this, about everything that had happened since she'd died. He sat and waited until the feeling wore off. It was a feeling he was getting used to.

Bethany had liked Miles because he made her laugh. He makes me laugh, too. Miles figured that digging up Bethany's grave, even that would have made her laugh. Bethany had had a great laugh, which went up and up like a clarinetist on an escalator. It wasn't annoying. It had been delightful, if you liked that kind of laugh. It would have made Bethany laugh that Miles Googled grave digging in order to educate himself. He read an Edgar Allan Poe story, he watched several relevant episodes of *Buffy the Vampire Slayer*, and he bought Vicks VapoRub, which you were supposed to apply under your nose. He bought equipment at Target: a special, battery-operated, telescoping shovel, a set of wire cutters, a flashlight, extra batteries for the shovel and flashlight, and even a Velcro headband with a headlamp that came with a special red lens filter, so that you were less likely to be noticed.

Miles printed out a map of the cemetery so that he could find his way to Bethany's grave off Weeping Fish Lane, even—as an acquaintance of mine once remarked—"in the dead of night when naught can be seen, so pitch is the dark." (Not that the dark would be very pitch. Miles had picked a night when the moon would be full.) The map was also just in case, because he'd seen movies where the dead rose from their graves. You wanted to have all the exits marked in a situation like that.

He told his mother that he was spending the night at his friend John's house. He told his friend John not to tell his mother anything.

If Miles had Googled "poetry" as well as "digging up graves," he would have discovered that his situation was not without precedent. The poet and painter Dante Gabriel Rossetti also buried his poetry with his dead lover. Rossetti, too, had regretted this gesture, had eventually decided to dig up his lover to get back his poems. I'm telling you this so that you never make the same mistake.

I can't tell you whether Dante Gabriel Rossetti was a better poet than Miles, although Rossetti had a sister, Christina Rossetti, who was really something. But you're not interested in my views on poetry. I know you better than that, even if you don't know me. You're waiting for me to get to the part about grave digging.

Miles had a couple of friends and he thought about asking someone to come along on the expedition. But no one except for Bethany knew that Miles wrote poetry. And Bethany had been dead for a while. Eleven months, in fact, which was one month longer than Bethany had been Miles's girlfriend. Long enough that Miles was beginning to make his way out of the fog and the needles. Long enough that he could listen to certain songs on the radio again. Long enough that sometimes there was something dreamlike about his memories of Bethany, as if she'd been a movie that he'd seen a long time ago, late at night on television. Long enough that when he tried to reconstruct the poems he'd written her, especially the villanelle, which had been, in his opinion, really quite good, he couldn't. It was as if when he'd put those poems into the casket, he hadn't just given Bethany the only copies of some poems, but had instead given away those shining, perfect lines, given them away so thoroughly that he'd never be able to write them out again. Miles knew that Bethany was dead. There was nothing to do about that. But the poetry was different. You have to salvage what you can, even if you're the one who buried it in the first place.

You might think at certain points in this story that I'm being hard on Miles, that I'm not sympathetic to his situation. This isn't true. I'm as fond of Miles as I am of anyone else. I don't think he's any stupider or any bit less special or remarkable than—for example—you. Anyone might accidentally dig up the wrong grave. It's a mistake anyone could make.

The moon was full and the map was easy to read even without the aid of the flashlight. The cemetery was full of cats. Don't ask me why. Miles was not afraid. He was resolute. The battery-operated telescoping shovel at first refused to untelescope. He'd tested it in his own backyard, but here, in the cemetery, it seemed unbearably loud. It scared off the cats for a while, but it didn't draw any unwelcome attention. The cats came back. Miles set aside the moldering wreaths and bouquets, and then he used his wire cutters to trace a rectangle. He stuck the telescoping shovel under and pried up fat squares of sod above Bethany's grave. He stacked them up like carpet samples and got to work.

By two A.M., Miles had knotted a length of rope at short, regular intervals for footholds, and then looped it around a tree, so he'd be able to climb out of the grave again, once he'd retrieved his poetry. He was waist-deep in the hole he'd made. The night was warm and he was sweating. It was hard work, directing the shovel. Every once in a while it telescoped while he was using it. He'd borrowed his mother's gardening gloves to keep from getting blisters, but still his hands were getting tired. The gloves were too big. His arms ached.

By three thirty, Miles could no longer see out of the grave in any direction except up. A large white cat came and peered down at Miles, grew bored and left again. The moon moved over Miles's head like a spotlight. He began to wield the shovel more carefully. He didn't want to damage Bethany's casket. When the shovel struck something that was not dirt, Miles remembered that he'd left the Vicks VapoRub on his bed at home. He improvised with a cherry ChapStick he found in his pocket. Now he used his garden-gloved hands to dig and to smooth dirt away. The bloody light emanating from his Velcro headband picked out the ingenious telescoping ridges of the discarded shovel, the little rocks and worms and worm-like roots that poked out of the dirt walls of Miles's excavation, the smoother lid of Bethany's casket.

Miles realized he was standing on the lid. Perhaps he should have made the hole a bit wider. It would be difficult to get the lid open while standing on it. He needed to pee: there was that as well. When he came back, he shone his flashlight into the grave. It seemed to him that the lid of the coffin was slightly ajar. Was that possible? Had he damaged the hinges with the telescoping shovel, or kicked the lid askew somehow when he was shimmying up the rope? He essayed a slow, judicious sniff, but all he smelled was dirt and cherry ChapStick. He applied more cherry ChapStick. Then he lowered himself down into the grave.

The lid wobbled when he tested it with his feet. He decided that if he kept hold of the rope, and slid his foot down and under the lid, like so, then perhaps he could cantilever the lid up—

It was very strange. It felt as if something had hold of his foot. He tried to tug it free, but no, his foot was stuck, caught in some kind of vise or grip. He lowered the toe of his other hiking boot down into the black gap between the coffin and its lid, and tentatively poked it forward, but this produced no result. He'd have to let go of the rope and lift the lid with his hands. Balance like so, carefully, carefully, on the thin rim of the casket. Figure out how he was caught.

It was hard work, balancing and lifting at the same time, although the one foot was still firmly wedged in its accidental toehold. Miles became aware of his own breathing, the furtive scuffling noise of his other boot against the coffin lid. Even the red beam of his lamp as it pitched and swung, back and forth, up and down in the narrow space, seemed unutterably noisy. "Shit, shit, shit," Miles whispered. It was either that or else scream. He got his fingers under the lid of the coffin on either side of his feet and bent his wobbly knees so he wouldn't hurt his back, lifting. Something touched the fingers of his right hand.

No, his fingers had touched something. *Don't be ridiculous, Miles.* He yanked the lid up as fast and hard as he could, the way you would rip off a bandage if you suspected there were baby spiders hatching under it. "Shit, shit, shit, shit, shit!"

He yanked and someone else pushed. The lid shot up and fell back against the opposite embankment of dirt. The dead girl who had hold of Miles's boot let go.

This was the first of the many unexpected and unpleasant shocks that Miles was to endure for the sake of poetry. The second was the sickening—no, shocking—shock that he had dug up the wrong grave, the wrong dead girl.

The wrong dead girl was lying there, smiling up at him, and her eyes were open. She was several years older than Bethany. She was taller and had a significantly more developed rack. She even had a tattoo.

The smile of the wrong dead girl was white and orthodontically perfected. Bethany had had braces that turned kissing into a heroic feat. You had to kiss around braces, slide your tongue up or sideways or under, like navigating through barbed wire: a delicious, tricky trip through No Man's Land. Bethany pursed her mouth forward when she kissed. If Miles forgot and mashed his lips down too hard on hers, she whacked him on the back of his head. This was one of the things about his relationship with Bethany that Miles remembered vividly, looking down at the wrong dead girl.

The wrong dead girl spoke first. "Knock knock," she said.

"What?" Miles said.

"Knock knock," the wrong dead girl said again.

"Who's there?" Miles said.

"Gloria," the wrong dead girl said. "Gloria Palnick. Who are you and what are you doing in my grave?"

"This isn't your grave," Miles said, aware that he was arguing with a dead girl, and the wrong dead girl at that. "This is

Bethany's grave. What are you doing in Bethany's grave?"

"Oh no," Gloria Palnick said. "This is my grave and I get to ask the questions."

A notion crept, like little dead cat feet, over Miles. Possibly he had made a dangerous and deeply embarrassing mistake. "Poetry," he managed to say. "There was some poetry that I, ah, that I accidentally left in my girlfriend's casket. And there's a deadline for a poetry contest coming up, and so I really, really needed to get it back."

The dead girl stared at him. There was something about her hair that Miles didn't like.

"Excuse me, but are you for real?" she said. "This sounds like one of those lame excuses. The dog ate my homework. I accidentally buried my poetry with my dead girlfriend."

"Look," Miles said, "I checked the tombstone and everything. This is supposed to be Bethany's grave. Bethany Baldwin. I'm really sorry I bothered you and everything, but this isn't really my fault." The dead girl just stared at him thoughtfully. He wished that she would blink. She wasn't smiling anymore. Her hair, lank and black, where Bethany's had been brownish and frizzy in summer, was writhing a little, like snakes. Miles thought of centipedes. Inky midnight tentacles.

"Maybe I should just go away," Miles said. "Leave you to, ah, rest in peace or whatever."

"I don't think sorry cuts the mustard here," Gloria Palnick said. She barely moved her mouth when she spoke, Miles noticed. And yet her enunciation was fine. "Besides, I'm sick of this place. It's boring. Maybe I'll just come along with."

"What?" Miles said. He felt behind himself, surreptitiously, for the knotted rope.

"I said, maybe I'll come with you," Gloria Palnick said. She sat up. Her hair was really coiling around, really seething now. Miles thought he could hear hissing noises.

"You can't do that!" he said. "I'm sorry, but no. Just no."

"Well then, you stay here and keep me company," Gloria Palnick said. Her hair was really something.

"I can't do that either," Miles said, trying to explain quickly, before the dead girl's hair decided to strangle him. "I'm going to be a poet. It would be a great loss to the world if I never got a chance to publish my poetry."

"I see," Gloria Palnick said, as if she did, in fact, see a great deal. Her hair settled back down on her shoulders and began to act a lot more like hair. "You don't want me to come home with you. You don't want to stay here with me. Then how about this? If you're such a great poet, then write me a poem. Write something about me so that everyone will be sad that I died."

"I could do that," Miles said. Relief bubbled up through his middle like tiny doughnuts in an industrial deep-fat fryer. "Let's do that. You lie down and make yourself comfortable and I'll rebury you. Today I've got a quiz in American History, and I was going to study for it during my free period after lunch, but I could write a poem for you instead."

"Today is Saturday," the dead girl said.

"Oh, hey," Miles said. "Then no problem. I'll go straight home and work on your poem. Should be done by Monday."

"Not so fast," Gloria Palnick said. "You need to know all about my life and about me, if you're going to write a poem about me, right? And how do I know you'll write a poem if I let you bury me again? How will I know if the poem's any good? No dice. I'm coming home with you and I'm sticking around until I get my poem. 'Kay?"

She stood up. She was several inches taller than Miles. "Do

you have any ChapStick?" she said. "My lips are really dry."

"Here," Miles said. Then, "You can keep it."

"Oh, afraid of dead girl cooties," Gloria Palnick said. She smacked her lips at him in an upsetting way.

"I'll climb up first," Miles said. He had the idea that if he could just get up the rope, if he could yank the rope up after himself fast enough, he might be able to run away, get to the fence where he'd chained up his bike, before Gloria managed to get out. It wasn't like she knew where he lived. She didn't even know his name.

"Fine," Gloria said. She looked like she knew what Miles was thinking and didn't really care. By the time Miles had bolted up the rope, yanking it up out of the grave, abandoning the telescoping shovel, the wire cutters, the wronged dead girl, and had unlocked his road bike and was racing down the empty 5 A.M. road, the little red dot of light from his headlamp falling into potholes, he'd almost managed to persuade himself that it had all been a grisly hallucination. Except for the fact that the dead girl's cold dead arms were around his waist, suddenly, and her cold dead face was pressed against his back, her damp hair coiling around his head and tapping at his mouth, burrowing down his filthy shirt.

"Don't leave me like that again," she said.

"No," Miles said. "I won't. Sorry."

He couldn't take the dead girl home. He couldn't think of how to explain it to his parents. No, no, no. He didn't want to take her over to John's house either. It was far too complicated. Not just the girl, but he was covered in dirt. John wouldn't be able to keep his big mouth shut.

"Where are we going?" the dead girl said.

"I know a place," Miles said. "Could you please not put your hands under my shirt? They're really cold. And your fingernails are kind of sharp."

"Sorry," the dead girl said.

They rode along in silence until they were passing the 7-Eleven at the corner of Eighth and Walnut, and the dead girl said, "Could we stop for a minute? I'd like some beef jerky. And a Diet Coke."

Miles braked. "Beef jerky?" he said. "Is that what dead people eat?"

"It's the preservatives," the dead girl said, somewhat obscurely.

Miles gave up. He steered the bike into the parking lot. "Let go, please," he said. The dead girl let go. He got off the bike and turned around. He'd been wondering just exactly how she'd managed to sit behind him on the bike, and he saw that she was sitting above the rear tire on a cushion of her horrible, shiny hair. Her legs were stretched out on either side, toes in black combat boots floating just above the asphalt, and yet the bike didn't fall over. It just hung there under her. For the first time in almost a month, Miles found himself thinking about Bethany as if she were still alive: Bethany is never going to believe this. But then, Bethany had never believed in anything like ghosts. She'd hardly believed in the school dress code. She definitely wouldn't have believed in a dead girl who could float around on her hair like it was an anti-gravity device.

"I can also speak fluent Spanish," Gloria Palnick said.

Miles reached into his back pocket for his wallet, and discovered that the pocket was full of dirt. "I can't go in there," he said. "For one thing, I'm a kid and it's five in the morning. Also I look like I just escaped from a gang of naked mole rats. I'm filthy."

The dead girl just looked at him. He said, coaxingly, *"You* should go in. You're older. I'll give you all the money I've got. You go in and I'll stay out here and work on the poem."

"You'll ride off and leave me here," the dead girl said. She didn't sound angry, just matter of fact. But her hair was beginning to float up. It lifted her up off Miles's bike in a kind of hairy cloud and then plaited itself down her back in a long, business-like rope.

"I won't," Miles promised. "Here. Take this. Buy whatever you want."

Gloria Palnick took the money. "How very generous of you," she said.

"No problem," Miles told her. "I'll wait here." And he did wait. He waited until Gloria Palnick went into the 7-Eleven. Then he counted to thirty, waited one second more, got back on his bike and rode away. By the time he'd made it to the meditation cabin in the woods back behind Bethany's mother's house, where he and Bethany had liked to sit and play Monopoly, Miles felt as if things were under control again, more or less. There is nothing so calming as a meditation cabin where long, boring games of Monopoly have taken place. He'd clean up in the cabin sink, and maybe take a nap. Bethany's mother never went out there. Her ex-husband's meditation clothes, his scratchy prayer mat, all his Buddhas and scrolls and incense holders and posters of Che Guevara were still out here. Miles had snuck into the cabin a few times since Bethany's death, to sit in the dark and listen to the plink-plink of the meditation fountain and think about things. He was sure Bethany's mother wouldn't have minded if she knew, although he hadn't ever asked, just in case. Which had been wise of him.

The key to the cabin was on the beam just above the door, but he didn't need it after all. The door stood open. There was a smell of incense, and of other things: cherry ChapStick and dirt and beef jerky. There was a pair of black combat boots beside the door.

Miles squared his shoulders. I have to admit that he was behaving sensibly here, finally. Finally. Because—and Miles and I are in agreement for once—if the dead girl could follow him somewhere before he even knew exactly where he was going, then there was no point in running away. Anywhere he went she'd already be there. Miles took off his shoes, because you were supposed to take off your shoes when you went into the cabin. It was a gesture of respect. He put them down beside the combat boots and went inside. The waxed pine floor felt silky under his bare feet. He looked down and saw that he was walking on Gloria Palnick's hair.

"Sorry!" Miles said. He meant several things by that. He meant sorry for walking on your hair. Sorry for riding off and leaving you in the 7-Eleven after promising that I wouldn't. Sorry for the grave wrong I've done you. But most of all he meant sorry, dead girl, that I ever dug you up in the first place.

"Don't mention it," the dead girl said. "Want some jerky?"

"Sure," he said. He felt he had no other choice.

He was beginning to feel he would have liked this dead girl under other circumstances, despite her annoying, bullying hair. She had poise. A sense of humor. She seemed to have what his mother called stick-to-itiveness; what the AP English Exam prefers to call tenacity. Miles recognized the quality. He had it in no small degree himself. The dead girl was also extremely pretty, if you ignored the hair. You might think less of Miles that he thought so well of the dead girl, that this was a betrayal of Bethany. *Miles* felt it was a betrayal. But he thought that Bethany might have liked the dead girl too. She would certainly have liked her tattoo.

"How is the poem coming?" the dead girl said.

"There's not a lot that rhymes with Gloria," Miles said. "Or Palnick."

"Toothpick," said the dead girl. There was a fragment of jerky caught in her teeth. "Euphoria."

"Maybe *you* should write the stupid poem," Miles said. There was an awkward pause, broken only by the almost-noiseless glide of hair retreating across a pine floor. Miles sat down, sweeping the floor with his hand, just in case.

"You were going to tell me something about your life," he said.

"Boring," Gloria Palnick said. "Short. Over."

"That's not much to work with. Unless you want a haiku."

"Tell me about this girl you were trying to dig up," Gloria said. "The one you wrote the poetry for."

"Her name was Bethany," Miles said. "She died in a car crash."

"Was she pretty?" Gloria said.

"Yeah," Miles said.

"You liked her a lot," Gloria said.

"Yeah," Miles said.

"Are you sure you're a poet?" Gloria asked.

Miles was silent. He gnawed his jerky ferociously. It tasted like dirt. Maybe he'd write a poem about it. That would show Gloria Palnick.

He swallowed and said, "Why were you in Bethany's grave?"

"How should I know?" she said. She was sitting across from him, leaning against a concrete Buddha the size of a three-year-old, but much fatter and holier. Her hair hung down over her face, just like a Japanese horror movie. "What do you think, that Bethany and I swapped coffins, just for fun?"

"Is Bethany like you?" Miles said. "Does she have weird hair and follow people around and scare them just for fun?"

"No," the dead girl said through her hair. "Not for fun. But what's wrong with having a little fun? It gets dull. And why should we stop having fun, just because we're dead? It's not all demon cocktails and Scrabble down in the old bardo, you know?"

"You know what's weird?" Miles said. "You sound like her. Bethany. You say the same kind of stuff."

"It was dumb to try to get your poems back," said the dead girl. "You can't just give something to somebody and then take it back again."

"I just miss her," Miles said. He began to cry.

After a while, the dead girl got up and came over to him. She took a big handful of her hair and wiped his face with it. It was soft and absorbent and it made Miles's skin crawl. He stopped crying, which might have been what the dead girl was hoping. "Go home," she said.

Miles shook his head. "No," he finally managed to say. He was shivering like crazy.

"Why not?" the dead girl said.

"Because I'll go home and you'll be there, waiting for me."

"I won't," the dead girl said. "I promise."

"Really?" Miles said.

"I really promise," said the dead girl. "I'm sorry I teased you, Miles."

"That's okay," Miles said. He got up and then he just stood there, looking down at her. He seemed to be about to ask her something, and then he changed his mind. She could see this happen, and she could see why, too. He knew he ought to leave now, while she was willing to let him go. He didn't want to fuck up by asking something impossible and obvious and stupid. That was okay by her. She couldn't be sure that he wouldn't say something that would rile up her hair. Not to mention the tattoo. She didn't think he'd noticed when her tattoo had started getting annoyed.

"Good-bye," Miles said at last. It almost looked as if he wanted her to shake his hand, but when she sent out a length of her hair, he turned and ran. It was a little disappointing. And the dead girl couldn't help but notice that he'd left his shoes and his bike behind.

The dead girl walked around the cabin, picking things up and putting them down again. She kicked the Monopoly box, which was a game that she'd always hated. That was one of the okay things about being dead, that nobody ever wanted to play Monopoly.

At last she came to the statue of St. Francis, whose head had been knocked right off during an indoor game of croquet a long time ago. Bethany Baldwin had made St. Francis a lumpy substitute Ganesh head out of modeling clay. You could lift that clay elephant head off, and there was a hollow space where Miles and Bethany had left secret things for each other. The dead girl reached down her shirt and into the cavity where her more interesting and useful organs had once been (she had been an organ donor). She'd put Miles's poetry in there for safekeeping.

She folded up the poetry, wedged it inside St. Francis, and fixed the Ganesh head back on. Maybe Miles would find it someday. She would have liked to see the look on his face.

We don't often get a chance to see our dead. Still less often do we know them when we see them. Mrs. Baldwin's eyes opened. She looked up and saw the dead girl and smiled. She said, "Bethany."

Bethany sat down on her mother's bed. She took her mother's hand. If Mrs. Baldwin thought Bethany's hand was cold, she didn't say so. She held on tightly. "I was dreaming about you," she told Bethany. "You were in an Andrew Lloyd Webber musical."

"It was just a dream," Bethany said.

Mrs. Baldwin reached up and touched a piece of Bethany's hair with her other hand. "You've changed your hair," she said. "I like it."

They were both silent. Bethany's hair stayed very still. Perhaps it felt flattered.

"Thank you for coming back," Mrs. Baldwin said at last.

"I can't stay," Bethany said.

Mrs. Baldwin held her daughter's hand tighter. "I'll go with you. That's why you've come, isn't it? Because I'm dead too?"

Bethany shook her head. "No. Sorry. You're not dead. It's Miles's fault. He dug me up."

"He did what?" Mrs. Baldwin said. She forgot the small, lowering unhappiness of discovering that she was not dead after all.

"He wanted his poetry back," Bethany said. "The poems he gave me."

"That idiot," Mrs. Baldwin said. It was exactly the sort of thing she expected of Miles, but only with the advantage of hindsight, because how could you really expect such a thing. "What did you do to him?"

"I played a good joke on him," Bethany said. She'd never really tried to explain her relationship with Miles to her mother. It seemed especially pointless now. She wriggled her fingers, and her mother instantly let go of Bethany's hand.

Being a former Buddhist, Mrs. Baldwin had always understood that when you hold onto your children too tightly, you end up pushing them away instead. Except that after Bethany had died, she wished she'd held on a little tighter. She drank up Bethany with her eyes. She noted the tattoo on Bethany's arm with both disapproval and delight. Disapproval, because one day Bethany might regret getting a tattoo of a cobra that wrapped all the way around her bicep. Delight, because something about the tattoo suggested Bethany was really here. That this wasn't just a dream. Andrew Lloyd Webber musicals were one thing. But she would never have dreamed that her daughter was alive again and tattooed and wearing long, writhing, midnight tails of hair.

"I have to go," Bethany said. She had turned her head a little, towards the window, as if she were listening for something far away.

"Oh," her mother said, trying to sound as if she didn't mind. She didn't want to ask: Will you come back? She was a lapsed Buddhist, but not so very lapsed, after all. She was still working to relinquish all desire, all hope, all self. When a person like Mrs. Baldwin suddenly finds that her life has been dismantled by a great catastrophe, she may then hold on to her belief as if to a life raft, even if the belief is this: that one should hold on to nothing. Mrs. Baldwin had taken her Buddhism very seriously, once, before substitute teaching had knocked it out of her.

Bethany stood up. "I'm sorry I wrecked the car," she said, although this wasn't completely true. If she'd still been alive, she would have been sorry. But she was dead. She didn't know how to be sorry anymore. And the longer she stayed, the more likely it seemed that her hair would do something truly terrible. Her hair was not good Buddhist hair. It did not love the living world or the things in the living world, and it *did not love them* in an utterly unenlightened way. There was nothing of light or enlightenment about Bethany's hair. It knew nothing of hope, but it had desires and ambitions. It's best not to speak of those ambitions. As for the tattoo, it wanted to be left alone. And to be allowed to eat people, just every once in a while.

When Bethany stood up, Mrs. Baldwin said suddenly, "I've been thinking I might give up substitute teaching."

Bethany waited.

"I might go to Japan to teach English," Mrs. Baldwin said. "Sell the house, just pack up and go. Is that okay with you? Do you mind?"

Bethany didn't mind. She bent over and kissed her mother on her forehead. She left a smear of cherry ChapStick. When she had gone, Mrs. Baldwin got up and put on her bathrobe, the one with white cranes and frogs. She went downstairs and made coffee and sat at the kitchen table for a long time, staring at nothing. Her coffee got cold and she never even noticed.

The dead girl left town as the sun was coming up. I won't tell you where she went. Maybe she joined the circus and took part in daring trapeze acts that put her hair to good use, kept it from getting bored and plotting the destruction of all that is good and pure and lovely. Maybe she shaved her head and went on a pilgrimage to some remote lamasery and came back as a superhero with a dark past and some kick-ass martial-arts moves. Maybe she sent her mother postcards from time to time. Maybe she wrote them as part of her circus act, using the tips of her hair, dipping them into an inkwell. These postcards, not to mention her calligraphic scrolls, are highly sought after by collectors nowadays. I have two.

Miles stopped writing poetry for several years. He never went back to get his bike. He stayed away from graveyards and also from girls with long hair. The last I heard, he had a job writing topical haikus for the Weather Channel. One of his best-known haikus is the one about tropical storm Suzy. It goes something like this:

A young girl passes
in a hurry. Hair uncombed.
Full of black devils.

Wizards are always hungry.

The Wizards of Perfil

THE WOMAN WHO sold leech grass baskets and pickled beets in the Perfil market took pity on Onion's aunt. "On your own, my love?"

Onion's aunt nodded. She was still holding out the earrings which she'd hoped someone would buy. There was a train leaving in the morning for Qual, but the tickets were dear. Her daughter Halsa, Onion's cousin, was sulking. She'd wanted the earrings for herself. The twins held hands and stared about the market.

Onion thought the beets were more beautiful than the earrings, which had belonged to his mother. The beets were rich and velvety and mysterious as pickled stars in shining jars. Onion had had nothing to eat all day. His stomach was empty, and his head was full of the thoughts of the people in the market: Halsa thinking of the earrings, the market woman's disinterested kindness, his aunt's dull worry. There was a man at another stall whose wife was sick. She was coughing up blood. A girl went by. She was thinking about a man who had gone to the war. The man wouldn't come back. Onion went back to thinking about the beets.

"Just you to look after all these children," the market woman said. "These are bad times. Where's your lot from?"

"Come from Labbit, and Larch before that," Onion's aunt said. "We're trying to get to Qual. My husband had family there. I have these earrings and these candlesticks."

The woman shook her head. "No one will buy these," she said. "Not for any good price. The market is full of refugees selling off their bits and pieces."

Onion's aunt said, "Then what should I do?" She didn't seem to expect an answer, but the woman said, "There's a man who comes to the market today, who buys children for the wizards of Perfil. He pays good money and they say that the children are treated well."

All wizards are strange, but the wizards of Perfil are strangest of all. They build tall towers in the marshes of Perfil, and there they live like anchorites in lonely little rooms at the top of their towers. They rarely come down at all, and no one is sure what their magic is good for. There are balls of sickly green fire that dash around the marshes at night, hunting for who knows what, and sometimes a tower tumbles down and then the prickly reeds and marsh lilies that look like ghostly white hands grow up over the tumbled stones and the marsh mud sucks the rubble down.

Everyone knows that there are wizard bones under the marsh mud and that the fish and the birds that live in the marsh are strange creatures. They have got magic in them. Children dare each other to go into the marsh and catch fish. Sometimes when a brave child catches a fish in the murky, muddy marsh pools, the fish will call the child by name and beg to be released. And if you don't let that fish go, it will tell you, gasping for air, when and how you will die. And if you cook the fish and eat it, you will dream wizard dreams. But if you let your fish go, it will tell you a secret.

This is what the people of Perfil say about the wizards of Perfil.

Everyone knows that the wizards of Perfil talk to demons and hate sunlight and have long twitching noses like rats. They never bathe.

Everyone knows that the wizards of Perfil are hundreds and hundreds of years old. They sit and dangle their fishing lines out of the windows of their towers and they use magic to bait their hooks. They eat their fish raw and they throw the fish bones out of the window the same way that they empty their chamber pots. The wizards of Perfil have filthy habits and no manners at all.

Everyone knows that the wizards of Perfil eat children when they grow tired of fish.

This is what Halsa told her brothers and Onion while Onion's aunt bargained in the Perfil markets with the wizard's secretary.

The wizard's secretary was a man named Tolcet and he wore a sword in his belt. He was a black man with white-pink spatters on his face and across the backs of his hands. Onion had never seen a man who was two colors.

Tolcet gave Onion and his cousins pieces of candy. He said to Onion's aunt, "Can any of them sing?"

Onion's aunt indicated that the children should sing. The

twins, Mik and Bonti, had strong, clear soprano voices, and when Halsa sang, everyone in the market fell silent and listened. Halsa's voice was like honey and sunlight and sweet water.

Onion loved to sing, but no one loved to hear it. When it was his turn and he opened his mouth to sing, he thought of his mother and tears came to his eyes. The song that came out of his mouth wasn't one he knew. It wasn't even in a proper language and Halsa crossed her eyes and stuck out her tongue. Onion went on singing.

"Enough," Tolcet said. He pointed at Onion. "You sing like a toad, boy. Do you know when to be quiet?"

"He's quiet," Onion's aunt said. "His parents are dead. He doesn't eat much, and he's strong enough. We walked here from Larch. And he's not afraid of witchy folk, begging your pardon. There were no wizards in Larch, but his mother could find things when you lost them. She could charm your cows so that they always came home."

"How old is he?" Tolcet said.

"Eleven," Onion's aunt said, and Tolcet grunted.

"Small for his age." Tolcet looked at Onion. He looked at Halsa, who crossed her arms and scowled hard. "Will you come with me, boy?"

Onion's aunt nudged him. He nodded.

"I'm sorry for it," his aunt said to Onion, "but it can't be helped. I promised your mother I'd see you were taken care of. This is the best I can do."

Onion said nothing. He knew his aunt would have sold Halsa to the wizard's secretary and hoped it was a piece of luck for her daughter. But there was also a part of his aunt that was glad that Tolcet wanted Onion instead. Onion could see it in her mind.

Tolcet paid Onion's aunt twenty-four brass fish, which was

slightly more than it had cost to bury Onion's parents, but slightly less than Onion's father had paid for their best milk cow, two years before. It was important to know how much things were worth. The cow was dead and so was Onion's father.

"Be *good*," Onion's aunt said. "Here. Take this." She gave Onion one of the earrings that had belonged to his mother. It was shaped like a snake. Its writhing tail hooked into its narrow mouth, and Onion had always wondered if the snake was surprised about that, to end up with a mouthful of itself like that, for all eternity. Or maybe it was eternally furious, like Halsa.

Halsa's mouth was screwed up like a button. When she hugged Onion good-bye, she said, "Brat. Give it to me." Halsa had already taken the wooden horse that Onion's father had carved, and Onion's knife, the one with the bone handle.

Onion tried to pull away, but she held him tightly, as if she couldn't bear to let him go. "He wants to eat you," she said. "The wizard will put you in an oven and roast you like a suckling pig. So give me the earring. Suckling pigs don't need earrings."

Onion wriggled away. The wizard's secretary was watching, and Onion wondered if he'd heard Halsa. Of course, anyone who wanted a child to eat would have taken Halsa, not Onion. Halsa was older and bigger and plumper. Then again, anyone who looked hard at Halsa would suspect she would taste sour and unpleasant. The only sweetness in Halsa was in her singing. Even Onion loved to listen to Halsa when she sang.

Mik and Bonti gave Onion shy little kisses on his cheek. He knew they wished the wizard's secretary had bought Halsa instead. Now that Onion was gone, it would be the twins that Halsa pinched and bullied and teased.

Tolcet swung a long leg over his horse. Then he leaned down.

"Come on, boy," he said, and held his speckled hand out to Onion. Onion took it.

The horse was warm and its back was broad and high. There was no saddle and no reins, only a kind of woven harness with a basket on either flank, filled with goods from the market. Tolcet held the horse quiet with his knees, and Onion held on tight to Tolcet's belt.

"That song you sang," Tolcet said. "Where did you learn it?"

"I don't know," Onion said. It came to him that the song had been a song that Tolcet's mother had sung to her son, when Tolcet was a child. Onion wasn't sure what the words meant because Tolcet wasn't sure either. There was something about a lake and a boat, something about a girl who had eaten the moon.

The marketplace was full of people selling things. From his vantage point Onion felt like a prince: as if he could afford to buy anything he saw. He looked down at a stall selling apples and potatoes and hot leek pies. His mouth watered. Over here was an incense seller's stall, and there was a woman telling fortunes. At the train station, people were lining up to buy tickets for Qual. In the morning a train would leave and Onion's aunt and Halsa and the twins would be on it. It was a dangerous passage. There were unfriendly armies between here and Qual. When Onion looked back at his aunt, he knew it would do no good, she would only think he was begging her not to leave him with the wizard's secretary, but he said it all the same: "Don't go to Qual."

But he knew even as he said it that she would go anyway. No one ever listened to Onion.

The horse tossed its head. The wizard's secretary made a *tch-tch* sound and then leaned back in the saddle. He seemed undecided about something. Onion looked back one more time at his aunt. He had never seen her smile once in the two years he'd lived with her, and she did not smile now, even though twenty-four brass fish was not a small sum of money and even though she'd kept her promise to Onion's mother. Onion's mother had smiled often, despite the fact that her teeth were not particularly good.

"He'll eat you," Halsa called to Onion. "Or he'll drown you in the marsh! He'll cut you up into little pieces and bait his fishing line with your fingers!" She stamped her foot.

"Halsa!" her mother said.

"On second thought," Tolcet said, "I'll take the girl. Will you sell her to me instead?"

"What?" Halsa said.

"What?" Onion's aunt said.

"No!" Onion said, but Tolcet drew out his purse again. Halsa, it seemed, was worth more than a small boy with a bad voice. And Onion's aunt needed money badly. So Halsa got up on the horse behind Tolcet, and Onion watched as his bad-tempered cousin rode away with the wizard's servant.

There was a voice in Onion's head. It said, "Don't worry, boy. All will be well and all manner of things will be well." It sounded like Tolcet, a little amused, a little sad.

There is a story about the wizards of Perfil and how one fell in love with a church bell. First he tried to buy it with gold and then, when the church refused his money, he stole it by magic. As the wizard flew back across the marshes, carrying the bell in his arms, he flew too low and the devil reached up and grabbed his heel. The wizard dropped the church bell into the marshes and it sank and was lost forever. Its voice is clappered with mud and moss, and although the wizard never gave up searching for it and calling its name, the bell never answered and the wizard grew thin and died of grief. Fishermen say that the dead wizard still flies over the marsh, crying out for the lost bell.

Everyone knows that wizards are pigheaded and come to bad ends. No wizard has ever made himself useful by magic, or, if they've tried, they've only made matters worse. No wizard has ever stopped a war or mended a fence. It's better that they stay in their marshes, out of the way of worldly folk like farmers and soldiers and merchants and kings.

"Well," Onion's aunt said. She sagged. They could no longer see Tolcet or Halsa. "Come along, then."

They went back through the market and Onion's aunt bought cakes of sweetened rice for the three children. Onion ate his without knowing that he did so: since the wizard's servant had taken away Halsa instead, it felt as if there were two Onions, one Onion here in the market and one Onion riding along with Tolcet and Halsa. He stood and was carried along at the same time and it made him feel terribly dizzy. Market-Onion stumbled, his mouth full of rice, and his aunt caught him by the elbow.

"We don't eat children," Tolcet was saying. "There are plenty of fish and birds in the marshes."

"I know," Halsa said. She sounded sulky. "And the wizards live in houses with lots of stairs. Towers. Because they think they're so much better than anybody else. So above the rest of the world."

"And how do you know about the wizards of Perfil?" Tolcet said.

"The woman in the market," Halsa said. "And the other people in the market. Some are afraid of the wizards and some think that there are no wizards. That they're a story for children. That the marshes are full of runaway slaves and deserters. Nobody knows why wizards would come and build towers in the Perfil marsh, where the ground is like cheese and no one can find them. Why do the wizards live in the marshes?"

"Because the marsh is full of magic," Tolcet said.

"Then why do they build the towers so high?" Halsa said.

"Because wizards are curious," Tolcet said. "They like to be able to see things that are far off. They like to be as close as possible to the stars. And they don't like to be bothered by people who ask lots of questions."

"Why do the wizards buy children?" Halsa said.

"To run up and down the stairs," Tolcet said, "to fetch them water for bathing and to carry messages and to bring them breakfasts and dinners and lunches and suppers. Wizards are always hungry."

"So am I," Halsa said.

"Here," Tolcet said. He gave Halsa an apple. "You see things that are in people's heads. You can see things that are going to happen."

"Yes," Halsa said. "Sometimes." The apple was wrinkled but sweet.

"Your cousin has a gift, too," Tolcet said.

"Onion?" Halsa said scornfully. Onion saw that it had never felt like a gift to Halsa. No wonder she'd hidden it.

"Can you see what is in my head right now?" Tolcet said.

Halsa looked and Onion looked, too. There was no curiosity or fear about in Tolcet's head. There was nothing. There was no Tolcet, no wizard's servant. Only brackish water and lonely white birds flying above it.

It's beautiful, Onion said.

"What?" his aunt said in the market. "Onion? Sit down, child."

"Some people find it so," Tolcet said, answering Onion. Halsa said nothing, but she frowned.

Tolcet and Halsa rode through the town and out of the town gates onto the road that led back toward Labbit and east, where there were more refugees coming and going, day and night. They were mostly women and children and they were afraid. There were rumors of armies behind them. There was a story that, in a fit of madness, the king had killed his youngest son. Onion saw a chess game, a thin-faced, anxious, yellow-haired boy Onion's age moving a black queen across the board, and then the chess pieces scattered across a stone floor. A woman was saying something. The boy bent down to pick up the scattered pieces. The king was laughing. He had a sword in his hand and he brought it down and then there was blood on it. Onion had never seen a king before, although he had seen men with swords. He had seen men with blood on their swords.

Tolcet and Halsa went away from the road, following a wide river, which was less a river than a series of wide, shallow pools. On the other side of the river, muddy paths disappeared into thick stands of rushes and bushes full of berries. There was a feeling of watchfulness, and the cunning, curious stillness of something alive, something half-asleep and half-waiting, a hidden, invisible humming, as if even the air were saturated with magic.

"Berries! Ripe and sweet!" a girl was singing out, over and over again in the market. Onion wished she would be quiet. His aunt bought bread and salt and hard cheese. She piled them into Onion's arms.

"It will be uncomfortable at first," Tolcet was saying. "The marshes of Perfil are so full of magic that they drink up all other kinds of magic. The only ones who work magic in the marshes of Perfil are the wizards of Perfil. And there are bugs."

"I don't want anything to do with magic," Halsa said primly.

Again Onion tried to look in Tolcet's mind, but again all he saw was the marshes. Fat-petaled, waxy, white flowers and crouching trees that dangled their long brown fingers as if fishing. Tolcet laughed. "I can feel you looking," he said. "Don't look too long or you'll fall in and drown."

"I'm not looking!" Halsa said. But she *was* looking. Onion could feel her looking, as if she were turning a key in a door.

The marshes smelled salty and rich, like a bowl of broth. Tolcet's horse ambled along, its hooves sinking into the path. Behind them, water welled up and filled the depressions. Fat jeweled flies clung, vibrating, to the rushes, and once, in a clear pool of water, Onion saw a snake curling like a green ribbon through water weeds soft as a cloud of hair.

"Wait here and watch Bonti and Mik for me," Onion's aunt said. "I'll go to the train station. Onion? Are you all right?"

Onion nodded dreamily.

Tolcet and Halsa rode farther into the marsh, away from the road and the Perfil market and Onion. It was very different from the journey to Perfil, which had been hurried and dusty and dry and on foot. Whenever Onion or one of the twins stumbled or lagged behind, Halsa had rounded them up like a dog chasing sheep, pinching and slapping. It was hard to imagine cruel, greedy, unhappy Halsa being able to pick things out of other people's minds, although she had always seemed to know when Mik or Bonti had found something edible; where there might be a soft piece of ground to sleep; when they should duck off the road because soldiers were coming.

Halsa was thinking of her mother and her brothers. She was thinking about the look on her father's face when the soldiers had shot him behind the barn; the earrings shaped like snakes; how the train to Qual would be blown up by saboteurs. She meant to be on that train, she knew it. She was furious at Tolcet for taking her away; at Onion, because Tolcet had changed his mind about Onion.

Every now and then, while he waited in the market for his aunt to come back, Onion could see the pointy roofs of the wizards' towers leaning against the sky as if they were waiting for him, just beyond the Perfil market, and then the towers would recede, and he would go with them, and find himself again with Tolcet and Halsa. Their path ran up along a canal of tarry water, angled off into thickets of bushes bent down with bright yellow berries, and then returned. It cut across other paths, these narrower and crookeder, overgrown and secret looking. At last they rode through a stand of sweet-smelling trees and came out into a grassy meadow that seemed not much larger than the Perfil market. Up close, the towers were not particularly splendid. They were tumbledown and so close together one might have strung a line for laundry from tower to tower, if wizards had been concerned with such things as laundry. Efforts had been made to buttress the towers; some had long, eccentrically curving fins of strategically piled rocks. There were twelve standing towers that looked as if they might be occupied. Others were half in ruins or were only piles of lichen-encrusted rocks that had already been scavenged for useful building materials.

Around the meadow were more paths: worn, dirt paths and canals that sank into branchy, briary tangles, some so low that a boat would never have passed without catching. Even a swimmer would have to duck her head. Children sat on the ruined walls of toppled towers and watched Tolcet and Halsa ride up. There was a fire with a thin man stirring something in a pot. Two women were winding up a ball of rough-looking twine.

They were dressed like Tolcet. More wizards' servants, Halsa and Onion thought. Clearly wizards were very lazy.

"Down you go," Tolcet said, and Halsa gladly slid off the horse's back. Then Tolcet got down and lifted off the harness and the horse suddenly became a naked, brown girl of about fourteen years. She straightened her back and wiped her muddy hands on her legs. She didn't seem to care that she was naked. Halsa gaped at her.

The girl frowned. She said, "You be good, now, or they'll turn you into something even worse."

"Who?" Halsa said.

"The wizards of Perfil," the girl said, and laughed. It was a neighing, horsey laugh. All of the other children began to giggle.

"Oooh, Essa gave Tolcet a ride."

"Essa, did you bring me back a present?"

"Essa makes a prettier horse than she does a girl."

"Oh, shut up," Essa said. She picked up a rock and threw it. Halsa admired her economy of motion, and her accuracy.

"Oi!" her target said, putting her hand up to her ear. "That hurt, Essa."

"Thank you, Essa," Tolcet said. She made a remarkably graceful curtsy, considering that until a moment ago she had had four legs and no waist to speak of. There was a shirt and a pair of leggings folded and lying on a rock. Essa put them on. "This is Halsa," Tolcet said to the others. "I bought her in the market."

There was silence. Halsa's face was bright red. For once she was speechless. She looked at the ground and then up at the towers, and Onion looked, too, trying to catch a glimpse of a wizard. All the windows of the towers were empty, but he could feel the wizards of Perfil, feel the weight of their watching. The boggy ground under his feet was full of wizards' magic and the towers threw magic out like waves of heat from a stove. Magic clung even to the children and servants of the wizards of Perfil, as if they had been marinated in it.

"Come get something to eat," Tolcet said, and Halsa stumbled after him. There was a flat bread, and onions and fish. Halsa drank water that had the faint, slightly metallic taste of magic. Onion could taste it in his own mouth.

"Onion," someone said. "Bonti, Mik." Onion looked up. He was back in the market and his aunt stood there. "There's a church nearby where they'll let us sleep. The train leaves early tomorrow morning."

After she had eaten, Tolcet took Halsa into one of the towers, where there was a small cubby under the stairs. There was a pallet of reeds and a mothy wool blanket. The sun was still in the sky. Onion and his aunt and his cousins went to the church, where there was a yard where refugees might curl up and sleep a few hours. Halsa lay awake, thinking of the wizard in the room above the stairs where she was sleeping. The tower was so full of wizards' magic that she could hardly breathe. She imagined a wizard of Perfil creeping, creeping down the stairs above her cubby, and although the pallet was soft, she pinched her arms to stay awake. But Onion fell asleep immediately, as if drugged. He dreamed of wizards flying above the marshes like white lonely birds.

In the morning, Tolcet came and shook Halsa awake. "Go and fetch water for the wizard," he said. He was holding an empty bucket.

Halsa would have liked to say *go and fetch it yourself,* but she was not a stupid girl. She was a slave now. Onion was in her head again, telling her to be careful. "Oh, go away," Halsa said. She realized she had said this aloud, and flinched. But Tolcet only laughed.

Halsa rubbed her eyes and took the bucket and followed him. Outside, the air was full of biting bugs too small to see. They seemed to like the taste of Halsa. That seemed funny to Onion, for no reason that she could understand.

The other children were standing around the fire pit and eating porridge. "Are you hungry?" Tolcet said. Halsa nodded. "Bring the water up and then get yourself something to eat. It's not a good idea to keep a wizard waiting."

He led her along a well-trodden path that quickly sloped down into a small pool and disappeared. "The water is sweet here," he said. "Fill your bucket and bring it up to the top of the wizard's tower. I have an errand to run. I'll return before nightfall. Don't be afraid, Halsa."

"I'm not afraid," Halsa said. She knelt down and filled the bucket. She was almost back to the tower before she realized that the bucket was half empty again. There was a split in the wooden bottom. The other children were watching her and she straightened her back. *So it's a test,* she said in her head, to Onion.

You could ask them for a bucket without a hole in it, he said.

I don't need anyone's help, Halsa said. She went back down the path and scooped up a handful of clayey mud where the path ran into the pool. She packed this into the bottom of the bucket and then pressed moss down on top of the mud. This time the bucket held water.

There were three windows lined with red tiles on Halsa's wizard's tower, and a nest that some bird had built on an outcropping of stone. The roof was round and red and shaped like a bishop's hat. The stairs inside were narrow. The steps had been worn down, smooth and slippery as wax. The higher she went, the heavier the pail of water became. Finally she set it down on a step and sat down beside it. *Four hundred and twenty-two steps,* Onion said. Halsa had counted five hundred and ninety-eight. There seemed to be many more steps on the inside than one would have thought, looking at the tower from outside. "Wizardly tricks," Halsa said in disgust, as if she'd expected nothing better. "You would think they'd make it fewer steps rather than more steps. What's the use of more steps?"

When she stood and picked up the bucket, the handle broke in her hand. The water spilled down the steps and Halsa threw the bucket after it as hard as she could. Then she marched down the stairs and went to mend the bucket and fetch more water. It didn't do to keep wizards waiting.

At the top of the steps in the wizard's tower there was a door. Halsa set the bucket down and knocked. No one answered and so she knocked again. She tried the latch: the door was locked. Up here, the smell of magic was so thick that Halsa's eyes watered. She tried to look *through* the door. This is what she saw: a room, a window, a bed, a mirror, a table. The mirror was full of rushes and light and water. A bright-eyed fox was curled up on the bed, sleeping. A white bird flew through the unshuttered window, and then another and another. They circled around and around the room and then they began to mass on the table. One flung itself at the door where Halsa stood, peering in. She recoiled. The door vibrated with peck and blows.

She turned and ran down the stairs, leaving the bucket, leaving Onion behind her. There were even more steps on the way down. And there was no porridge left in the pot beside the fire.

Someone tapped her on the shoulder and she jumped. "Here," Essa said, handing her a piece of bread.

"Thanks," Halsa said. The bread was stale and hard. It was the most delicious thing she'd ever eaten.

"So your mother sold you," Essa said.

Halsa swallowed hard. It was strange, not being able to see inside Essa's head, but it was also restful. As if Essa might be anyone at all. As if Halsa herself might become anyone she wished to be. "I didn't care," she said. "Who sold you?"

"No one," Essa said. "I ran away from home. I didn't want to be a soldier's whore like my sisters."

"Are the wizards better than soldiers?" Halsa said.

Essa gave her a strange look. "What do you think? Did you meet your wizard?"

"He was old and ugly, of course," Halsa said. "I didn't like the way he looked at me."

Essa put her hand over her mouth as if she were trying not to laugh. "Oh dear," she said.

"What must I do?" Halsa said. "I've never been a wizard's servant before."

"Didn't your wizard tell you?" Essa said. "What did he tell you to do?"

Halsa blew out an irritated breath. "I asked what he needed, but he said nothing. I think he was hard of hearing."

Essa laughed long and hard, exactly like a horse, Halsa thought. There were three or four other children, now, watching them. They were all laughing at Halsa. "Admit it," Essa said. "You didn't talk to the wizard."

"So?" Halsa said. "I knocked, but no one answered. So obviously he's hard of hearing."

"Of course," a boy said.

"Or maybe the wizard is shy," said another boy. He had green eyes like Bonti and Mik. "Or asleep. Wizards like to take naps."

Everyone was laughing again.

"Stop making fun of me," Halsa said. She tried to look fierce and dangerous. Onion and her brothers would have quailed. "Tell me what my duties are. What does a wizard's servant do?"

Someone said, "You carry things up the stairs. Food. Firewood. Kaffa, when Tolcet brings it back from the market. Wizards like unusual things. Old things. So you go out in the marsh and look for things."

"Things?" Halsa said.

"Glass bottles," Essa said. "Petrified imps. Strange things, things out of the ordinary. Or ordinary things like plants or stones or animals or anything that feels right. Do you know what I mean?"

"No," Halsa said, but she did know. Some things felt more magic-soaked than other things. Her father had found an arrowhead in his field. He'd put it aside to take to the schoolmaster, but that night while everyone was sleeping, Halsa had wrapped it in a rag and taken it back to the field and buried it. Bonti got the blame. Sometimes Halsa wondered if that was what had brought the soldiers to kill her father, the malicious, evil luck of that arrowhead. But you couldn't blame a whole war on one arrowhead.

"Here," a boy said. "Go and catch fish if you're too stupid to know magic when you see it. Have you ever caught fish?"

Halsa took the fishing pole. "Take that path," Essa said. "The muddiest one. And stay on it. There's a pier out that way where the fishing is good."

When Halsa looked back at the wizards' towers, she thought she saw Onion looking down at her, out of a high window. But that was ridiculous. It was only a bird.

The train was so crowded that some passengers gave up and went and sat on top of the cars. Vendors sold umbrellas to keep the sun off. Onion's aunt had found two seats, and she and Onion sat with one twin on each lap. Two rich women sat across from them. You could tell they were rich because their shoes were green leather. They held filmy pink handkerchiefs like embroidered rose petals up to their rabbity noses. Bonti looked at them from under his eyelashes. Bonti was a terrible flirt.

Onion had never been on a train before. He could smell the furnace room of the train, rich with coal and magic. Passengers stumbled up and down the aisles, drinking and laughing as if they were at a festival. Men and women stood beside the train windows, sticking their heads in. They shouted messages. A woman leaning against the seats fell against Onion and Mik when someone shoved past her. "Pardon, sweet," she said, and smiled brilliantly. Her teeth were studded with gemstones. She was wearing at least four silk dresses, one on top of the other. A man across the aisle coughed wetly. There was a bandage wrapped around his throat, stained with red. Babies were crying.

"I hear they'll reach Perfil in three days or less," a man in the next row said.

"The king's men won't sack Perfil," said his companion. "They're coming to defend it."

"The king is mad," the man said. "God has told him all men are his enemies. He hasn't paid his army in two years. When they rebel, he just conscripts another army and sends them off to fight the first one. We're safer leaving."

"Oooh," a woman said, somewhere behind Onion. "At last we're off. Isn't this fun! What a pleasant outing!"

Onion tried to think of the marshes of Perfil, of the wizards. But Halsa was suddenly there on the train, instead. *You have to tell them*, she said.

Tell them what? Onion asked her, although he knew. When the train was in the mountains, there would be an explosion. There would be soldiers, riding down at the train. No one would reach Qual. *Nobody will believe me,* he said.

You should tell them anyway, Halsa said.

Onion's legs were falling asleep. He shifted Mik. *Why do you care?* he said. *You hate everyone.*

I don't! Halsa said. But she did. She hated her mother. Her mother had watched her husband die, and done nothing. Halsa had been screaming and her mother slapped her across the face. She hated the twins because they weren't like her, they didn't *see* things the way Halsa had to. Because they were little and they got tired and it had been so much work keeping them safe. Halsa had hated Onion, too, because he *was* like her. Because he'd been afraid of Halsa, and because the day he'd come to live with her family, she'd known that one day she would be like him, alone and without a family. Magic was bad luck, people like Onion and Halsa were bad luck. The only person who'd ever looked at Halsa and really seen her, really known her, had been Onion's mother. Onion's mother was kind and good and she'd known she was going to die. *Take care of my son,* she'd said to Halsa's mother and father, but she'd been looking at Halsa when she said it. But Onion would have to take care of himself. Halsa would make him.

Tell them, Halsa said. There was a fish jerking on her line. She ignored it. *Tell them, tell them, tell them.* She and Onion were in the marsh and on the train at the same time. Everything smelled like coal and salt and ferment. Onion ignored her the way she was ignoring the fish. He sat and dangled his feet in the water, even though he wasn't really there.

Halsa caught five fish. She cleaned them and wrapped them in leaves and brought them back to the cooking fire. She also brought back the greeny-copper key that had caught on her fishing line. "I found this," she said to Tolcet.

"Ah," Tolcet said. "May I see it?" It looked even smaller and more ordinary in Tolcet's hand.

"Burd," Tolcet said. "Where is the box you found, the one we couldn't open?"

The boy with green eyes got up and disappeared into one of the towers. He came out after a few minutes and gave Tolcet a metal box no bigger than a pickle jar. The key fit. Tolcet unlocked it, although it seemed to Halsa that she ought to have been the one to unlock it, not Tolcet.

"A doll," Halsa said, disappointed. But it was a strange-looking doll. It was carved out of a greasy black wood, and when Tolcet turned it over, it had no back, only two fronts, so it was always looking backward and forward at the same time.

"What do you think, Burd?" Tolcet said.

Burd shrugged. "It's not mine."

"It's yours," Tolcet said to Halsa. "Take it up the stairs and give it to your wizard. And refill the bucket with fresh water and bring some dinner, too. Did you think to take up lunch?"

"No," Halsa said. She hadn't had any lunch herself. She cooked the fish along with some greens Tolcet gave her, and ate two. The other three fish and the rest of the greens she carried up to the top of the stairs in the tower. She had to stop to rest twice, there were so many stairs this time. The door was still closed and the bucket on the top step was empty. She thought that maybe all the water had leaked away, slowly. But she left the fish and she went and drew more water and carried the bucket back up.

"I've brought you dinner," Halsa said, when she'd caught her breath. "And something else. Something I found in the marsh. Tolcet said I should give it to you."

Silence.

She felt silly, talking to the wizard's door. "It's a doll," she said. "Perhaps it's a magic doll."

Silence again. Not even Onion was there. She hadn't noticed when he went away. She thought of the train. "If I give you the doll," she said, "will you do something for me? You're a wizard, so you ought to be able to do anything, right? Will you help the people on the train? They're going to Qual. Something bad is going to happen if you won't stop it. You know about the soldiers? Can you stop them?"

Halsa waited for a long time, but the wizard behind the door never said anything. She put the doll down on the steps and then she picked it up again and put it in her pocket. She was furious. "I think you're a coward," she said. "That's why you hide up here, isn't it? I would have got on that train and I know what's going to happen. Onion got on that train. And you could stop it, but you won't. Well, if you won't stop it, then I won't give you the doll."

She spat in the bucket of water and then immediately wished she hadn't. "You keep the train safe," she said, "and I'll give you the doll. I promise. I'll bring you other things, too. And I'm sorry I spit in your water. I'll go and get more."

She took the bucket and went back down the stairs. Her legs ached and there were welts where the little biting bugs had drawn blood.

"Mud," Essa said. She was standing in the meadow, smoking a pipe. "The flies are only bad in the morning and at twilight. If you put mud on your face and arms, they leave you alone."

"It smells," Halsa said.

"So do you," Essa said. She snapped her clay pipe in two,

which seemed extravagant to Halsa, and wandered over to where some of the other children were playing a complicated-looking game of pickup sticks and dice. Under a night-flowering tree, Tolcet sat in a battered, oaken throne that looked as if it had been spat up by the marsh. He was smoking a pipe, too, with a clay stem even longer than Essa's had been. It was ridiculously long. "Did you give the poppet to the wizard?" he said.

"Oh yes," Halsa said.

"What did she say?"

"Well," Halsa said. "I'm not sure. She's young and quite lovely. But she had a horrible stutter. I could hardly understand her. I think she said something about the moon, how she wanted me to go cut her a slice of it. I'm to bake it into a pie."

"Wizards are very fond of pie," Tolcet said.

"Of course they are," Halsa said. "And I'm fond of my arse."

"Better watch your mouth," Burd, the boy with green eyes, said. He was standing on his head, for no good reason that Halsa could see. His legs waved in the air languidly, semaphoring. "Or the wizards will make you sorry."

"I'm already sorry," Halsa said. But she didn't say anything else. She carried the bucket of water up to the closed door. Then she ran back down the stairs to the cubbyhole and this time she fell straight asleep. She dreamed a fox came and looked at her. It stuck its muzzle in her face. Then it trotted up the stairs and ate the three fish Halsa had left there. *You'll be sorry*, Halsa thought. *The wizards will turn you into a one-legged crow*. But then she was chasing the fox up the aisle of a train to Qual, where her mother and her brothers and Onion were sleeping uncomfortably in their two seats, their legs tucked under them, their arms hanging down as if they were dead—the stink of coal and magic was even stronger than it had been in the morning. The train was laboring hard. It panted like a fox with a pack of dogs after it, dragging itself along. There was no way it would reach all the way to the top of the wizard of Perfil's stairs. And if it did, the wizard wouldn't be there, anyway, just the moon, rising up over the mountains, round and fat as a lardy bone.

The wizards of Perfil don't write poetry, as a general rule. As far as anyone knows, they don't marry, or plow fields, or have much use for polite speech. It is said that the wizards of Perfil appreciate a good joke, but telling a joke to a wizard is dangerous business. What if the wizard doesn't find the joke funny? Wizards are sly, greedy, absentminded, obsessed with stars and bugs, parsimonious, frivolous, invisible, tyrannous, untrustworthy, secretive, inquisitive, meddlesome, long-lived, dangerous, useless, and have far too good an opinion of themselves. Kings go mad, the land is blighted, children starve or get sick or die spitted on the pointy end of a pike, and it's all beneath the notice of the wizards of Perfil. The wizards of Perfil don't fight wars.

It was like having a stone in his shoe. Halsa was always there, nagging. *Tell them, tell them. Tell them.* They had been on the train for a day and a night. Halsa was in the swamp, getting farther and farther away. Why wouldn't she leave him alone? Mik and Bonti had seduced the two rich women who sat across from them. There were no more frowns or handkerchiefs, only smiles and tidbits of food and love, love, love all around. On went the train through burned fields and towns that had been put to the sword by one army or another. The train and its passengers overtook people on foot, or fleeing in wagons piled high with goods: mattresses, wardrobes, a pianoforte once, stoves and skillets and butter churns and pigs and angry-looking geese. Sometimes the train stopped while men got out and examined the tracks and made repairs. They did not stop at any stations, although there were people waiting, sometimes, who yelled and ran after the train. No one got off. There were fewer people up in the mountains, when they got there. Instead there was snow. Once Onion saw a wolf.

"When we get to Qual," one of the rich women, the older one, said to Onion's aunt, "my sister and I will set up our establishment. We'll need someone to keep house for us. Are you thrifty?" She had Bonti on her lap. He was half-asleep.

"Yes, ma'am," Onion's aunt said.

"Well, we'll see," said the woman. She was half in love with Bonti. Onion had never had much opportunity to see what the rich thought about. He was a little disappointed to find out that it was much the same as other people. The only difference seemed to be that the rich woman, like the wizard's secretary, seemed to think that all of this would end up all right. Money, it seemed, was like luck, or magic. All manner of things would be well, except they wouldn't. If it weren't for the thing that was going to happen to the train, perhaps Onion's aunt could have sold more of her children.

Why won't you tell them? Halsa said. *Soon it will be too late.*

You tell them, Onion thought back at her. Having an invisible Halsa around, always telling him things that he already knew, was far worse than the real Halsa had been. The real Halsa was safe, asleep, on the pallet under the wizard's stairs. Onion should have been there instead. Onion bet the wizards of Perfil were sorry that Tolcet had ever bought a girl like Halsa.

Halsa shoved past Onion. She put her invisible hands on her mother's shoulders and looked into her face. Her mother didn't look up. *You have to get off the train,* Halsa said. She yelled. *GET OFF THE TRAIN!*

But it was like talking to the door at the top of the wizard's tower. There was something in Halsa's pocket, pressing into her stomach so hard it almost felt like a bruise. Halsa wasn't on the train, she was sleeping on something with a sharp little face.

"Oh, stop yelling. Go away. How am I supposed to stop a train?" Onion said.

"Onion?" his aunt said. Onion realized he'd said it aloud. Halsa looked smug.

"Something bad is going to happen," Onion said, capitulating. "We have to stop the train and get off." The two rich women stared at him as if he were a lunatic. Onion's aunt patted his shoulder. "Onion," she said. "You were asleep. You were having a bad dream."

"But—" Onion protested.

"Here," his aunt said, glancing at the two women. "Take Mik for a walk. Shake off your dream."

Onion gave up. The rich women were thinking that perhaps they would be better off looking for a housekeeper in Qual. Halsa was tapping her foot, standing in the aisle with her arms folded.

Come on, she said. *No point talking to* them. *They just think you're crazy. Come talk to the conductor instead.*

"Sorry," Onion said to his aunt. "I had a bad dream. I'll go for a walk." He took Mik's hand.

They went up the aisle, stepping over sleeping people and people stupid or quarrelsome with drink, people slapping down playing cards. Halsa always in front of them: *Hurry up, hurry, hurry. We're almost there. You've left it too late. That useless wizard, I should have known not to bother asking for help. I should have known not to expect you to take care of things. You're as useless as they are. Stupid good-for-nothing wizards of Perfil.*

Up ahead of the train, Onion could feel the gunpowder

charges, little bundles wedged between the ties of the track. It was like there was a stone in his shoe. He wasn't afraid, he was merely irritated: at Halsa, at the people on the train who didn't even know enough to be afraid, at the wizards and the rich women who thought that they could just buy children, just like that. He was angry, too. He was angry at his parents, for dying, for leaving him stuck here. He was angry at the king, who had gone mad; at the soldiers, who wouldn't stay home with their own families, who went around stabbing and shooting and blowing up other people's families.

They were at the front of the train. Halsa led Onion right into the cab, where two men were throwing enormous scoops of coal into a red-black, boiling furnace. They were filthy as devils. Their arms bulged with muscles and their eyes were red. One turned and saw Onion. "Oi!" he said. "What's he doing here? You, kid, what are you doing?"

"You have to stop the train," Onion said. "Something is going to happen. I saw soldiers. They're going to make the train blow up."

"Soldiers? Back there? How long ago?"

"They're up ahead of us," Onion said. "We have to stop now."

Mik was looking up at him.

"He saw soldiers?" the other man said.

"Naw," said the first man. Onion could see he didn't know whether to be angry or whether to laugh. "The fucking kid's making things up. Pretending he sees things. Hey, maybe he's a wizard of Perfil! Lucky us, we got a wizard on the train!"

"I'm not a wizard," Onion said. Halsa snorted in agreement. "But I know things. If you don't stop the train, everyone will die."

Both men stared at him. Then the first said, angrily, "Get out of here, you. And don't go talking to people like that or we'll throw you in the boiler."

"Okay," Onion said "Come on, Mik."

Wait, Halsa said. *What are you doing? You have to make them understand. Do you want to be dead? Do you think you can prove something to me by being dead?*

Onion put Mik on his shoulders. *I'm sorry,* he said to Halsa. *But it's no good. Maybe you should just go away. Wake up. Catch fish. Fetch water for the wizards of Perfil.*

The pain in Halsa's stomach was sharper, as if someone were stabbing her. When she put her hand down, she had hold of the wooden doll.

What's that? Onion said.

Nothing, Halsa said. *Something I found in the swamp. I said I would give it to the wizard, but I won't! Here, you take it!*

She thrust it at Onion. It went all the way through him. It was an uncomfortable feeling, even though it wasn't really there. *Halsa,* he said. He put Mik down.

Take it! she said. *Here! Take it now!*

The train was roaring. Onion knew where they were; he recognized the way the light looked. Someone was telling a joke in the front of the train, and in a minute a woman would laugh. It would be a lot brighter in a minute. He put his hand up to stop the thing that Halsa was stabbing him with and something smacked against his palm. His fingers brushed Halsa's fingers.

It was a wooden doll with a sharp little nose. There was a nose on the back of its head, too. *Oh, take it!* Halsa said. Something was pouring out of her, through the doll, into Onion. Onion fell back against a woman holding a birdcage on her lap. "Get off!" the woman said. It *hurt.* The stuff pouring out of Halsa felt like *life*, as if the doll were pulling out her life like a skein of heavy, sodden, black wool. It hurt Onion, too. Black stuff poured and poured through the doll, into him, until there was no space for Onion, no space to breathe or think or see. The black stuff welled up in his throat, pressed behind his eyes. "Halsa," he said, "let go!"

The woman with the birdcage said, "What's wrong with him?"

Mik said, "What's wrong? What's wrong?"

The light changed. *Onion,* Halsa said, and let go of the doll. He staggered backward. The tracks beneath the train were singing *tara-ta tara-ta ta-rata-ta.* Onion's nose was full of swamp water and coal and metal and magic. "No," Onion said. He threw the doll at the woman holding the birdcage and pushed Mik down on the floor. "No," Onion said again, louder. People were staring at him. The woman who'd been laughing at the joke had stopped laughing. Onion covered Mik with his body. The light grew brighter and blacker, all at once.

Onion! Halsa said. But she couldn't see him anymore. She was awake in the cubby beneath the stair. The doll was gone.

Halsa had seen men coming home from the war. Some of them had been blinded. Some had lost a hand or an arm. She'd seen one man wrapped in lengths of cloth and propped up in a dog cart that his young daughter pulled on a rope. He'd had no legs, no arms. When people looked at him, he cursed them. There was another man who ran a cockpit in Larch. He came back from the war and paid a man to carve him a leg out of knotty pine. At first he was unsteady on the pine leg, trying to find his balance again. It had been funny to watch him chase after his cocks, like watching a windup toy. By the time the army came through Larch again, though, he could run as fast as anyone.

It felt as if half of her had died on the train in the mountains. Her ears rang. She couldn't find her balance. It was as if a part of her had been cut away, as if she were blind. The part of her that *knew* things, *saw* things, wasn't there anymore. She went about all day in a miserable deafening fog.

She brought water up the stairs and she put mud on her arms and legs. She caught fish, because Onion had said that she ought to catch fish. Late in the afternoon, she looked and saw Tolcet sitting beside her on the pier.

"You shouldn't have bought me," she said. "You should have bought Onion. He wanted to come with you. I'm bad-tempered and unkind and I have no good opinion of the wizards of Perfil."

"Of whom do you have a low opinion? Yourself or the wizards of Perfil?" Tolcet asked.

"How can you serve them?" Halsa said. "How can you serve men and women who hide in towers and do nothing to help people who need help? What good is magic if it doesn't serve anyone?"

"These are dangerous times," Tolcet said. "For wizards as well as for children."

"Dangerous times! Hard times! Bad times," Halsa said. "Things have been bad since the day I was born. Why do I see things and know things, when there's nothing I can do to stop them? When will there be better times?"

"What do you see?" Tolcet said. He took Halsa's chin in his hand and tilted her head this way and that, as if her head were a glass ball that he could see inside. He put his hand on her head and smoothed her hair as if she were his own child. Halsa closed her eyes. Misery welled up inside her.

"I don't see anything," she said. "It feels like someone wrapped me in a wool blanket and beat me and left me in the dark. Is this what it feels like not to see anything? Did the wizards of Perfil do this to me?"

"Is it better or worse?" Tolcet said.

"Worse," Halsa said. "No. Better. I don't know. What am I to do? What am I to be?"

"You are a servant of the wizards of Perfil," Tolcet said. "Be patient. All things may yet be well."

Halsa said nothing. What was there to say?

She climbed up and down the stairs of the wizard's tower, carrying water, toasted bread and cheese, little things that she found in the swamp. The door at the top of the stairs was never open. She couldn't see through it. No one spoke to her, although she sat there sometimes, holding her breath so that the wizard would think she had gone away again. But the wizard wouldn't be fooled so easily. Tolcet went up the stairs, too, and perhaps the wizard admitted him. Halsa didn't know.

Essa and Burd and the other children were kind to her, as if they knew that she had been broken. She knew that she wouldn't have been kind to them if their situations had been reversed. But perhaps they knew that, too. The two women and the skinny man kept their distance. She didn't even know their names. They disappeared on errands and came back again and disappeared into the towers.

Once, when she was coming back from the pier with a bucket of fish, there was a dragon on the path. It wasn't very big, only the size of a mastiff. But it gazed at her with wicked, jeweled eyes. She couldn't get past it. It would eat her, and that would be that. It was almost a relief. She put the bucket down and stood waiting to be eaten. But then Essa was there, holding a stick. She hit the dragon on its head, once, twice, and then gave it a kick for good measure. "Go on, you!" Essa said. The dragon went, giving Halsa one last reproachful look. Essa picked up the bucket of fish. "You have to be firm with them," she said. "Otherwise they get inside your head and make you feel as if you deserve to be eaten. They're too lazy to eat anything that puts up a fight."

Halsa shook off a last, wistful regret, almost sorry not to have been eaten. It was like waking up from a dream, something beautiful and noble and sad and utterly untrue. "Thank you," she said to Essa. Her knees were trembling.

"The bigger ones stay away from the meadow," Essa said. "It's the smaller ones who get curious about the wizards of Perfil. And by 'curious,' what I really mean is hungry. Dragons eat the things that they're curious about. Come on, let's go for a swim."

Sometimes Essa or one of the others would tell Halsa stories about the wizards of Perfil. Most of the stories were silly, or plainly untrue. The children sounded almost indulgent, as if they found their masters more amusing than frightful. There were other stories, sad stories about long-ago wizards who had fought great battles or gone on long journeys. Wizards who had perished by treachery or been imprisoned by ones they'd thought friends.

Tolcet carved her a comb. Halsa found frogs whose backs were marked with strange mathematical formulas, and put them in a bucket and took them to the top of the tower. She caught a mole with eyes like pinpricks and a nose like a fleshy pink hand. She found the hilt of a sword, a coin with a hole in it, the outgrown carapace of a dragon, small as a badger and almost weightless, but hard, too. When she cleaned off the mud that covered it, it shone dully, like a candlestick. She took all of these up the stairs. She couldn't tell whether the things she found had any meaning. But she took a small, private pleasure in finding them nevertheless.

The mole had come back down the stairs again, fast, wriggly, and furtive. The frogs were still in the bucket, making their gloomy pronouncements, when she returned with the wizard's dinner. But other things disappeared behind the wizard of Perfil's door.

The thing that Tolcet had called Halsa's gift came back, a little at a time. Once again, she became aware of the wizards in their towers, and of how they watched her. There was something else, too. It sat beside her, sometimes, while she was fishing, or when she rowed out in the abandoned coracle Tolcet helped her to repair. She thought she knew who, or what, it was. It was the part of Onion that he'd learned to send out. It was what was left of him: shadowy, thin, and silent. It wouldn't talk to her. It only watched. At night, it stood beside her pallet and watched her sleep. She was glad it was there. To be haunted was a kind of comfort.

She helped Tolcet repair a part of the wizard's tower where the stones were loose in their mortar. She learned how to make paper out of rushes and bark. Apparently wizards needed a great deal of paper. Tolcet began to teach her how to read.

One afternoon when she came back from fishing, all of the wizards' servants were standing in a circle. There was a leveret motionless as a stone in the middle of the circle. Onion's ghost crouched down with the other children. So Halsa stood and watched, too. Something was pouring back and forth between the leveret and the servants of the wizards of Perfil. It was the same as it had been for Halsa and Onion, when she'd given him the two-faced doll. The leveret's sides rose and fell.

Its eyes were glassy and dark and knowing. Its fur bristled with magic.

"Who is it?" Halsa said to Burd. "Is it a wizard of Perfil?"

"Who?" Burd said. He didn't take his eyes off the leveret. "No, not a wizard. It's a hare. Just a hare. It came out of the marsh."

"But," Halsa said. "But I can feel it. I can almost hear what it's saying."

Burd looked at her. Essa looked too. "Everything speaks," he said, speaking slowly, as if to a child. "Listen, Halsa."

There was something about the way Burd and Essa were looking at her, as if it were an invitation, as if they were asking her to look inside their heads, to see what they were thinking. The others were watching, too, watching Halsa now, instead of the leveret. Halsa took a step back. "I can't," she said. "I can't hear anything."

She went to fetch water. When she came out of the tower, Burd and Essa and the other children weren't there. Leverets dashed between towers, leaping over one another, tussling in midair. Onion sat on Tolcet's throne, watching and laughing silently. She didn't think she'd seen Onion laugh since the death of his mother. It made her feel strange to know that a dead boy could be so joyful.

The next day Halsa found an injured fox kit in the briar. It snapped at her when she tried to free it and the briars tore her hand. There was a tear in its belly and she could see a shiny gray loop of intestine. She tore off a piece of her shirt and wrapped it around the fox kit. She put the kit in her pocket. She ran all the way back to the wizard's tower, all the way up the steps. She didn't count them. She didn't stop to rest. Onion followed her, quick as a shadow.

When she reached the door at the top of the stairs, she knocked hard. No one answered.

"Wizard!" she said.

No one answered.

"Please help me," she said. She lifted the fox kit out of her pocket and sat down on the steps with it swaddled in her lap. It didn't try to bite her. It needed all its energy for dying. Onion sat next to her. He stroked the kit's throat.

"Please," Halsa said again. "Please don't let it die. Please do something."

She could feel the wizard of Perfil, standing next to the door. The wizard put a hand out, as if—at last—the door might open. She saw that the wizard loved foxes and all the wild marsh things. But the wizard said nothing. The wizard didn't love Halsa. The door didn't open.

"Help me," Halsa said one more time. She felt that dreadful black pull again, just as it had been on the train with Onion. It was as if the wizard were yanking at her shoulder, shaking her in a stony, black rage. How dare someone like Halsa ask a wizard for help. Onion was shaking her, too. Where Onion's hand gripped her, Halsa could feel stuff pouring through her and out of her. She could feel the kit, feel the place where its stomach had torn open. She could feel its heart pumping blood, its panic and fear and the life that was spilling out of it. Magic flowed up and down the stairs of the tower. The wizard of Perfil was winding it up like a skein of black, tarry wool, and then letting it go again. It poured through Halsa and Onion and the fox kit until Halsa thought she would die.

"Please," she said, and what she meant this time was *stop*. It would kill her. And then she was empty again. The magic had gone through her and there was nothing left of it or her. Her bones had been turned into jelly. The fox kit began to struggle, clawing at her. When she unwrapped it, it sank its teeth into her wrist and then ran down the stairs as if it had never been dying at all.

Halsa stood up. Onion was gone, but she could still feel the wizard standing there on the other side of the door. "Thank you," she said. She followed the fox kit down the stairs.

The next morning she woke and found Onion lying on the pallet beside her. He seemed nearer, somehow, this time. As if he weren't entirely dead. Halsa felt that if she tried to speak to him, he would answer. But she was afraid of what he would say.

Essa saw Onion too. "You have a shadow," she said.

"His name is Onion," Halsa said.

"Help me with this," Essa said. Someone had cut lengths of bamboo. Essa was fixing them in the ground, using a mixture of rocks and mud to keep them upright. Burd and some of the other children wove rushes through the bamboo, making walls, Halsa saw.

"What are we doing?" Halsa asked.

"There is an army coming," Burd said. "To burn down the town of Perfil. Tolcet went to warn them."

"What will happen?" Halsa said. "Will the wizards protect the town?"

Essa laid another bamboo pole across the tops of the two upright poles. She said, "They can come to the marshes, if they want to, and take refuge. The army won't come here. They're afraid of the wizards."

"Afraid of the wizards!" Halsa said. "Why? The wizards are cowards and fools. Why won't they save Perfil?"

"Go ask them yourself," Essa said. "If you're brave enough."

"Halsa?" Onion said. Halsa looked away from Essa's steady

gaze. For a moment there were two Onions. One was the shadowy ghost from the train, close enough to touch. The second Onion stood beside the cooking fire. He was filthy, skinny, and real. Shadow-Onion guttered and then was gone.

"Onion?" Halsa said.

"I came out of the mountains," Onion said. "Five days ago, I think. I didn't know where I was going, except that I could see you. Here. I walked and walked and you were with me and I was with you."

"Where are Mik and Bonti?" Halsa said. "Where's Mother?"

"There were two women on the train with us. They were rich. They've promised to take care of Mik and Bonti. They will. I know they will. They were going to Qual. When you gave me the doll, Halsa, you saved the train. We could see the explosion, but we passed through it. The tracks were destroyed and there were clouds and clouds of black smoke and fire, but nothing touched the train. We saved everyone."

"Where's Mother?" Halsa said again. But she already knew. Onion was silent. The train stopped beside a narrow stream to take on water. There was an ambush. Soldiers. There was a bottle with water leaking out of it. Halsa's mother had dropped it. There was an arrow sticking out of her back.

Onion said, "I'm sorry, Halsa. Everyone was afraid of me, because of how the train had been saved. Because I knew that there was going to be an explosion. Because I didn't know about the ambush and people died. So I got off the train."

"Here," Burd said to Onion. He gave him a bowl of porridge. "No, eat it slowly. There's plenty more."

Onion said with his mouth full, "Where are the wizards of Perfil?"

Halsa began to laugh. She laughed until her sides ached and

until Onion stared at her and until Essa came over and shook her. "We don't have time for this," Essa said. "Take that boy and find him somewhere to lie down. He's exhausted."

"Come on," Halsa said to Onion. "You can sleep in my bed. Or if you'd rather, you can go knock on the door at the top of the tower and ask the wizard of Perfil if you can have his bed."

She showed Onion the cubby under the stairs and he lay down on it. "You're dirty," she said. "You'll get the sheets dirty."

"I'm sorry," Onion said.

"It's fine," Halsa said. "We can wash them later. There's plenty of water here. Are you still hungry? Do you need anything?"

"I brought something for you," Onion said. He held out his hand and there were the earrings that had belonged to his mother.

"No," Halsa said.

Halsa hated herself. She was scratching at her own arm, ferociously, not as if she had an insect bite, but as if she wanted to dig beneath the skin. Onion saw something that he hadn't known before, something astonishing and terrible, that Halsa was no kinder to herself than to anyone else. No wonder Halsa had wanted the earrings—just like the snakes, Halsa would gnaw on herself if there was nothing else to gnaw on. How Halsa wished that she'd been kind to her mother.

Onion said, "Take them. Your mother was kind to me, Halsa. So I want to give them to you. My mother would have wanted you to have them, too."

"All right," Halsa said. She wanted to weep, but she scratched and scratched instead. Her arm was white and red from scratching. She took the earrings and put them in her pocket. "Go to sleep now."

"I came here because you were here," Onion said. "I wanted to tell you what had happened. What should I do now?"

"Sleep," Halsa said.

"Will you tell the wizards that I'm here? How we saved the train?" Onion said. He yawned so wide that Halsa thought his head would split in two. "Can I be a servant of the wizards of Perfil?"

"We'll see," Halsa said. "You go to sleep. I'll go climb the stairs and tell them that you've come."

"It's funny," Onion said. "I can feel them all around us. I'm glad you're here. I feel safe."

Halsa sat on the bed. She didn't know what to do. Onion was quiet for a while and then he said, "Halsa?"

"What?" Halsa said.

"I can't sleep," he said, apologetically.

"Shhh," Halsa said. She stroked his filthy hair. She sang a song her father had liked to sing. She held Onion's hand until his breathing became slower and she was sure that he was sleeping. Then she went up the stairs to tell the wizard about Onion. "I don't understand you," she said to the door. "Why do you hide away from the world? Don't you get tired of hiding?"

The wizard didn't say anything.

"Onion is braver than you are," Halsa told the door. "Essa is braver. My mother was—"

She swallowed and said, "She was braver than you. Stop ignoring me. What good are you, up here? You won't talk to me, and you won't help the town of Perfil, and Onion's going to be very disappointed when he realizes that all you do is skulk around in your room, waiting for someone to bring you breakfast. If you like waiting so much, then you can wait as long as you like. I'm not going to bring you any food or any water or anything that I find in the swamp. If you want anything, you can magic it. Or you can come get it yourself. Or you can turn me into a toad."

She waited to see if the wizard would turn her into a toad. "All right," she said at last. "Well, good-bye then." She went back down the stairs.

The wizards of Perfil are lazy and useless. They hate to climb stairs and they never listen when you talk. They don't answer questions because their ears are full of beetles and wax and their faces are wrinkled and hideous. Marsh fairies live deep in the wrinkles of the faces of the wizards of Perfil and the marsh fairies ride around in the bottomless canyons of the wrinkles on saddle-broken fleas who grow fat grazing on magical, wizardly blood. The wizards of Perfil spend all night scratching their fleabites and sleep all day. I'd rather be a scullery maid than a servant of the invisible, doddering, nearly blind, flea-bitten, mildewy, clammy-fingered, conceited marsh-wizards of Perfil.

Halsa checked Onion, to make sure that he was still asleep. Then she went and found Essa. "Will you pierce my ears for me?" she said.

Essa shrugged. "It will hurt," she said.

"Good," said Halsa. So Essa boiled water and put her needle in it. Then she pierced Halsa's ears. It did hurt, and Halsa was glad. She put on Onion's mother's earrings, and then she helped Essa and the others dig latrines for the townspeople of Perfil.

Tolcet came back before sunset. There were half a dozen women and their children with him.

"Where are the others?" Essa said.

Tolcet said, "Some don't believe me. They don't trust wizardly folk. There are some that want to stay and defend the town. Others are striking out on foot for Qual, along the tracks."

"Where is the army now?" Burd said.

"Close," Halsa said. Tolcet nodded.

The women from the town had brought food and bedding. They seemed subdued and anxious, and it was hard to tell whether it was the approaching army or the wizards of Perfil that scared them most. The women stared at the ground. They didn't look up at the towers. If they caught their children looking up, they scolded them in low voices.

"Don't be silly," Halsa said crossly to a woman whose child had been digging a hole near a tumbled tower. The woman shook him until he cried and cried and wouldn't stop. What was she thinking? That wizards liked to eat mucky children who dug holes? "The wizards are lazy and unsociable and harmless. They keep to themselves and don't bother anyone."

The woman only stared at Halsa, and Halsa realized that she was as afraid of Halsa as she was of the wizards of Perfil. Halsa was amazed. Was she that terrible? Mik and Bonti and Onion had always been afraid of her, but they'd had good reason to be. And she'd changed. She was as mild and meek as butter now.

Tolcet, who was helping with dinner, snorted as if he'd caught her thought. The woman grabbed up her child and rushed away, as if Halsa might open her mouth again and eat them both.

"Halsa, look." It was Onion, awake and so filthy that you could smell him from two yards away. They would need to burn his clothes. Joy poured through Halsa, because Onion had come to find her and because he was here and because he was alive. He'd come out of Halsa's tower, where he'd gotten her cubby bed grimy and smelly, how wonderful to think of it, and he was pointing east, toward the town of Perfil. There was a red glow hanging over the marsh, as if the sun were rising instead of setting. Everyone was silent, looking east as if they might be able to see what was happening in Perfil. Presently the wind carried an ashy, desolate smoke over the marsh. "The war has come to Perfil," a woman said.

"Which army is it?" another woman said, as if the first woman might know.

"Does it matter?" said the first woman. "They're all the same. My eldest went off to join the king's army and my youngest joined General Balder's men. They've set fire to plenty of towns, and killed other mothers' sons and maybe one day they'll kill each other, and never think of me. What difference does it make to the town that's being attacked, to know what army is attacking them? Does it matter to a cow who kills her?"

"They'll follow us," someone else said in a resigned voice. "They'll find us here and they'll kill us all!"

"They won't," Tolcet said. He spoke loudly. His voice was calm and reassuring. "They won't follow you and they won't find you here. Be brave for your children. All will be well."

"Oh, please," Halsa said, under her breath. She stood and glared up at the towers of the wizards of Perfil, her hands on her hips. But as usual, the wizards of Perfil were up to nothing. They didn't strike her dead for glaring. They didn't stand at their windows to look out over the marshes to see the town of Perfil and how it was burning while they only stood and watched. Perhaps they were already asleep in their beds, dreaming about breakfast, lunch, and dinner. She went and helped Burd and Essa and the others make up beds for the refugees from Perfil. Onion cut up wild onions for the stew pot. He was going to have to have a bath soon, Halsa thought. Clearly he needed someone like Halsa to tell him what to do.

None of the servants of the wizards of Perfil slept. There was too much work to do. The latrines weren't finished. A child wandered off into the marshes and had to be found before it drowned or met a dragon. A little girl fell into the well and had to be hauled up.

Before the sun came up again, more refugees from the town of Perfil arrived. They came into the camp in groups of twos or threes, until there were almost a hundred townspeople in the wizards' meadow. Some of the newcomers were wounded or badly burned or deep in shock. Essa and Tolcet took charge. There were compresses to apply, clothes that had already been cut up for bandages, hot drinks that smelled bitter and medicinal and not particularly magical. People went rushing around, trying to discover news of family members or friends who had stayed behind. Young children who had been asleep woke up and began to cry.

"They put the mayor and his wife to the sword," a man was saying.

"They'll march on the king's city next," an old woman said. "But our army will stop them."

"It *was* our army—I saw the butcher's boy and Philpot's middle son. They said that we'd been trading with the enemies of our country. The king sent them. It was to teach us a lesson. They burned down the market church and they hung the pastor from the bell tower."

There was a girl lying on the ground who looked Mik and Bonti's age. Her face was gray. Tolcet touched her stomach lightly and she emitted a thin, high scream, not a human noise at all, Onion thought. The marshes were so noisy with magic that he couldn't hear what she was thinking, and he was glad.

"What happened?" Tolcet said to the man who'd carried her into the camp.

"She fell," the man said. "She was trampled underfoot."

Onion watched the girl, breathing slowly and steadily, as if he could somehow breathe for her. Halsa watched Onion. Then: "That's enough," she said. "Come on, Onion."

She marched away from Tolcet and the girl, shoving through the refugees.

"Where are we going?" Onion said.

"To make the wizards come down," Halsa said. "I'm sick and tired of doing all their work for them. Their cooking and fetching. I'm going to knock down that stupid door. I'm going to drag them down their stupid stairs. I'm going to make them help that girl."

There were a lot of stairs this time. Of course the accursed wizards of Perfil would know what she was up to. This was their favorite kind of wizardly joke, making her climb and climb and climb. They'd wait until she and Onion got to the top and then they'd turn them into lizards. Well, maybe it wouldn't be so bad, being a small poisonous lizard. She could slip under the door and bite one of the damned wizards of Perfil. She went up and up and up, half running and half stumbling, until it seemed she and Onion must have climbed right up into the sky. When the stairs abruptly ended, she was still running. She crashed into the door so hard that she saw stars.

"Halsa?" Onion said. He bent over her. He looked so worried that she almost laughed.

"I'm fine," she said. "Just wizards playing tricks." She hammered on the door, then kicked it for good measure. "Open up!"

"What are you doing?" Onion said.

"It never does any good," Halsa said. "I should have brought an ax."

"Let me try," Onion said.

Halsa shrugged. *Stupid boy*, she thought, and Onion could hear her perfectly. "Go ahead," she said.

Onion put his hand on the door and pushed. It swung open. He looked up at Halsa and flinched. "Sorry," he said.

Halsa went in.

There was a desk in the room, and a single candle, which was burning. There was a bed, neatly made, and a mirror on the wall over the desk. There was no wizard of Perfil, not even hiding under the bed. Halsa checked, just in case.

She went to the empty window and looked out. There was the meadow and the makeshift camp, below them, and the marsh. The canals, shining like silver. There was the sun, coming up, the way it always did. It was strange to see all the windows of the other towers from up here, so far above, all empty. White birds were floating over the marsh. She wondered if they were wizards; she wished she had a bow and arrows.

"Where is the wizard?" Onion said. He poked the bed. Maybe the wizard had turned himself into a bed. Or the desk. Maybe the wizard was a desk.

"There are no wizards," Halsa said.

"But I can feel them!" Onion sniffed, then sniffed harder. He could practically smell the wizard, as if the wizard of Perfil had turned himself into a mist or a vapor that Onion was inhaling. He sneezed violently.

Someone was coming up the stairs. He and Halsa waited to see if it was a wizard of Perfil. But it was only Tolcet. He looked tired and cross, as if he'd had to climb many, many stairs.

"Where are the wizards of Perfil?" Halsa said.

Tolcet held up a finger. "A minute to catch my breath," he said.

Halsa stamped her foot. Onion sat down on the bed. He apologized to it silently, just in case it was the wizard. Or maybe the candle was the wizard. He wondered what happened if you tried to blow a wizard out. Halsa was so angry he thought she might explode.

Tolcet sat down on the bed beside Onion. "A long time ago," he said, "the father of the present king visited the wizards of Perfil. He'd had certain dreams about his son, who was only a baby. He was afraid of these dreams. The wizards told him that he was right to be afraid. His son would go mad. There would be war and famine and more war and his son would be to blame. The old king went into a rage. He sent his men to throw the wizards of Perfil down from their towers. They did."

"Wait," Onion said. "Wait. What happened to the wizards? Did they turn into white birds and fly away?"

"No," Tolcet said. "The king's men slit their throats and threw them out of the towers. I was away. When I came back, the towers had been ransacked. The wizards were dead."

"No!" Halsa said. "Why are you lying? I know the wizards are here. They're hiding somehow. They're cowards."

"I can feel them too," Onion said.

"Come and see," Tolcet said. He went to the window. When they looked down, they saw Essa and the other servants of the wizards of Perfil moving among the refugees. The two old women who never spoke were sorting through bundles of clothes and blankets. The thin man was staking down someone's cow. Children were chasing chickens as Burd held open the gate of a makeshift pen. One of the younger girls, Perla, was singing a lullaby to some mother's baby. Her voice, rough and sweet at the same time, rose straight up to the window of the tower, where Halsa and Onion and Tolcet stood looking down. It was a song they all knew. It was a song that said all would be well.

"Don't you understand?" Tolcet, the wizard of Perfil, said to Halsa and Onion. "There are the wizards of Perfil. They are young, most of them. They haven't come into their full powers yet. But all may yet be well."

"Essa is a wizard of Perfil?" Halsa said. Essa, a shovel in her hand, looked up at the tower, as if she'd heard Halsa. She smiled and shrugged, as if to say, *Perhaps I am, perhaps not, but isn't it a good joke? Didn't you ever wonder?*

Tolcet turned Halsa and Onion around so that they faced the mirror that hung on the wall. He rested his strong, speckled hands on their shoulders for a minute, as if to give them courage. Then he pointed to the mirror, to the reflected Halsa and Onion who stood there staring back at themselves, astonished. Tolcet began to laugh. Despite everything, he laughed so hard that tears came from his eyes. He snorted. Onion and Halsa began to laugh, too. They couldn't help it. The wizard's room was full of magic, and so were the marshes and Tolcet and the mirror where the children and Tolcet stood reflected, and the children were full of magic, too.

Tolcet pointed again at the mirror, and his reflection pointed its finger straight back at Halsa and Onion. Tolcet said, "Here they are in front of you! Ha! Do you know them? Here are the wizards of Perfil!"

It's night in The Free People's World-Tree Library.
All the librarians are asleep, tucked into their coffins, their
scabbards, priest-holes, button holes, pockets, hidden cupboards, between the pages of their enchanted novels.

MAGIC FOR BEGINNERS

FOX IS A television character, and she isn't dead yet. But she will be, soon. She's a character on a television show called *The Library*. You've never seen *The Library* on TV, but I bet you wish you had.

In one episode of *The Library*, a boy named Jeremy Mars, fifteen years old, sits on the roof of his house in Plantagenet, Vermont. It's eight o'clock at night, a school night, and he and his friend Elizabeth should be studying for the math quiz which their teacher, Mr. Cliff, has been hinting at all week long. Instead, they've sneaked out onto the roof. It's cold. They don't know everything they should know about X, when X is the square root of Y. They don't even know Y. They ought to go in.

But there's nothing good on TV and the sky is very beautiful. They have jackets on, and up in the corners where the sky begins are patches of white in the darkness, still, where there's snow, up on the mountains. Down in the trees around the house, some animal is making a small, anxious sound: "Why cry? Why cry?"

"What's that one?" Elizabeth says, pointing at a squarish configuration of stars.

"That's The Parking Structure," Jeremy says. "And right next to that is The Big Shopping Mall and The Lesser Shopping Mall."

"And that's Orion, right? Orion the Bargain Hunter?"

Jeremy squints up. "No, Orion is over there. That's The Austrian Bodybuilder. That thing that's sort of wrapped around his lower leg is The Amorous Cephalopod. The Hungry, Hungry Octopus. It can't make up its mind whether it should eat him or make crazy, eight-legged love to him. You know that myth, right?"

"Of course," Elizabeth says. "Is Karl going to be pissed off that we didn't invite him over to study?"

"Karl's always pissed off about something," Jeremy says. Jeremy is resolutely resisting a notion about Elizabeth. Why are they sitting up here? Was it his idea or was it hers? Are they friends, are they just two friends sitting on the roof and talking? Or is Jeremy supposed to try to kiss her? He thinks maybe he's supposed to kiss her. If he kisses her, will they still be friends? He can't ask Karl about this. Karl doesn't believe in being helpful. Karl believes in mocking.

Jeremy doesn't even know if he wants to kiss Elizabeth. He's never thought about it until right now.

"I should go home," Elizabeth says. "There could be a new episode on right now, and we wouldn't even know."

"Someone would call and tell us," Jeremy says. "My mom would come up and yell for us." His mother is something else Jeremy doesn't want to worry about, but he does, he does.

Jeremy Mars knows a lot about the planet Mars, although he's never been there. He knows some girls, and yet he doesn't know much about them. He wishes there were books about girls, the way there are books about Mars, that you could observe the orbits and brightness of girls through telescopes without appearing to be perverted. Once Jeremy read a book about Mars out loud to Karl, except he kept replacing the word Mars with the word "girls." ("It was in the seventeenth century that girls at last came under serious scrutiny." "Girls have virtually no surface liquid water: their temperatures are too cold and the air is too thin." And so on.) Karl cracked up every time.

Jeremy's mother is a librarian. His father writes books. Jeremy reads biographies. He plays trombone in a marching band. He jumps hurdles while wearing a school tracksuit. Jeremy is also passionately addicted to a television show in which a renegade librarian and magician named Fox is trying to save her world from thieves, murderers, cabalists, and pirates. Jeremy is a geek, although he's a telegenic geek. Somebody should make a TV show about him.

Jeremy's friends call him Germ, although he would rather be called Mars. His parents haven't spoken to each other in a week.

Jeremy doesn't kiss Elizabeth. The stars don't fall out of the sky, and Jeremy and Elizabeth don't fall off the roof either. They go inside and finish their homework.

Someone that Jeremy has never met, never even heard of—a woman named Cleo Baldrick—has died. Lots of people, so far, have managed to live and die without making the acquaintance of Jeremy Mars, but Cleo Baldrick has left Jeremy Mars and his mother something strange in her will: a phone booth on a state highway, some forty miles outside of Las Vegas, and a Las Vegas wedding chapel. The wedding chapel is called Hell's Bells. Jeremy isn't sure what kind of people get married there. Bikers, maybe. Supervillains, freaks, and Satanists.

Jeremy's mother wants to tell him something. It's probably something about Las Vegas and about Cleo Baldrick, who—it turns out—was his mother's great-aunt. (Jeremy never knew his mother had a great-aunt. His mother is a mysterious person.) But it may be, on the other hand, something concerning Jeremy's father. For a week and a half now, Jeremy has managed to avoid finding out what his mother is worrying about. It's easy not to find out things, if you try hard enough. There's band practice. He has overslept on weekdays in order to rule out conversations at breakfast, and at night he climbs up on the roof with his telescope to look at stars, to look at Mars. His mother is afraid of heights. She grew up in L.A.

It's clear that whatever it is she has to tell Jeremy is not something she wants to tell him. As long as he avoids being alone with her, he's safe.

But it's hard to keep your guard up at all times. Jeremy comes home from school, feeling as if he has passed the math test, after all. Jeremy is an optimist. Maybe there's something good on TV. He settles down with the remote control on one of his father's pet couches: oversized and reupholstered in an orange-juice-colored corduroy that makes it appear as if the couch has just escaped from a maximum security prison for criminally insane furniture. This couch looks as if its hobby is devouring interior decorators. Jeremy's father is a horror writer, so no one should be surprised if some of the couches he reupholsters are hideous and eldritch.

Jeremy's mother comes into the room and stands above the couch, looking down at him. "Germ?" she says. She looks absolutely miserable, which is more or less how she has looked all week.

The phone rings and Jeremy jumps up.

As soon as he hears Elizabeth's voice, he knows. She says, "Germ, it's on. Channel forty-two. I'm taping it." She hangs up.

"It's on!" Jeremy says. "Channel forty-two! Now!"

His mother has the television on by the time he sits down. Being a librarian, she has a particular fondness for *The Library*. "I should go tell your dad," she says, but instead she sits down beside Jeremy. And of course it's now all the more clear something is wrong between Jeremy's parents. But *The Library* is on and Fox is about to rescue Prince Wing.

When the episode ends, he can tell without looking over that his mother is crying. "Don't mind me," she says and wipes her nose on her sleeve. "Do you think she's really dead?"

But Jeremy can't stay around and talk.

Jeremy has always wondered about what kind of television shows the characters *in* television shows watch. Television characters almost always have better haircuts, funnier friends, simpler attitudes toward sex. They marry magicians, win lotteries, have affairs with women who carry guns in their purses. Curious things happen to them on an hourly basis. Jeremy and I can forgive their haircuts. We just want to ask them about their television shows.

Just like always, it's Elizabeth who worked out in the nick of time that the new episode was on. Everyone will show up at Elizabeth's house afterwards, for the postmortem. This time, it really is a postmortem. Why did Prince Wing kill Fox? How could Fox let him do it? Fox is ten times stronger.

Jeremy runs all the way, slapping his old track shoes against the sidewalk for the pleasure of the jar, for the sweetness of the sting. He likes the rough, cottony ache in his lungs. His coach says you have to be part masochist to enjoy something like running. It's nothing to be ashamed of. It's something to exploit.

Talis opens the door. She grins at him, although he can tell that she's been crying, too. She's wearing a T-shirt that says I'M SO GOTH I SHIT TINY VAMPIRES.

"Hey," Jeremy says. Talis nods. Talis isn't so Goth, at least not as far as Jeremy or anyone else knows. Talis just has a lot of T-shirts. She's an enigma wrapped in a mysterious T-shirt. A woman once said to Calvin Coolidge, "Mr. President, I bet my husband that I could get you to say more than two words." Coolidge said, "You lose." Jeremy can imagine Talis as Calvin Coolidge in a former life. Or maybe she was one of those dogs that don't bark. A basenji. Or a rock. A dolmen. There was an episode of *The Library*, once, with some sinister dancing dolmens in it.

Elizabeth comes up behind Talis. If Talis is unGoth, then Elizabeth is Ballerina Goth. She likes hearts and skulls and black pen-ink tattoos, pink tulle and Hello Kitty. When the woman who invented Hello Kitty was asked why Hello Kitty was so popular, she said, "Because she has no mouth." Elizabeth's mouth is small. Her lips are chapped.

"That was the most horrible episode ever! I cried and cried," she says. "Hey, Germ, so I was telling Talis about how you inherited a gas station."

"A phone booth," Jeremy says. "In Las Vegas. This great-great aunt died. And there's a wedding chapel, too."

"Hey! Germ!" Karl says, yelling from the living room. "Shut up and get in here! The commercial with the talking cats is on—"

"Shut it, Karl," Jeremy says. He goes in and sits on Karl's head. You have to show Karl who's boss once in a while.

Amy turns up last. She was in the next town over, buying comics. She hasn't seen the new episode and so they all shut it (except for Talis, who has not been saying anything at all), and Elizabeth puts on the tape.

In the previous episode of *The Library*, masked pirate-magicians said they would sell Prince Wing a cure for the spell which infested Faithful Margaret's hair with miniature, wicked, fire-breathing golems. (Faithful Margaret's hair keeps catching fire, but she refuses to shave it off. Her hair is the source of all her magic.)

The pirate-magicians lured Prince Wing into a trap so obvious that it seemed impossible it could really be a trap, on the one-hundred-and-fortieth floor of The Free People's World-Tree Library. The pirate-magicians used finger magic to turn Prince Wing into a porcelain teapot, put two Earl Grey tea bags into the teapot, and poured in boiling water, toasted the Eternally Postponed and Overdue Reign of the Forbidden Books, drained their tea in one gulp, belched, hurled their souvenir pirate mugs to the ground, and then shattered the teapot which had been Prince Wing into hundreds of pieces. Then the wicked pirate-magicians swept the pieces of both Prince Wing and the collectible mugs carelessly into a wooden cigar box, buried the box in the Angela Carter Memorial Park on the seventeenth floor of The World-Tree Library, and erected a statue of George Washington above it.

So then Fox had to go looking for Prince Wing. When she finally discovered the park on the seventeenth floor of

The Library, the George Washington statue stepped down off his plinth and fought her tooth and nail. Literally tooth and nail, and they'd all agreed that there was something especially nightmarish about a biting, scratching, life-sized statue of George Washington with long, pointed metal fangs that threw off sparks when he gnashed them. The statue of George Washington bit Fox's pinky finger right off, just like Gollum biting Frodo's finger off on the top of Mount Doom. But of course, once the statue tasted Fox's magical blood, it fell in love with Fox. It would be her ally from now on.

In the new episode, the actor playing Fox is a young Latina actress whom Jeremy Mars thinks he recognizes. She has been a snotty but well-intentioned fourth-floor librarian in an episode about an epidemic of food-poisoning that triggered bouts of invisibility and/or levitation, and she was also a lovelorn, suicidal Bear Cult priestess in the episode where Prince Wing discovered his mother was one of the Forbidden Books.

This is one of the best things about *The Library*, the way the cast swaps parts, all except for Faithful Margaret and Prince Wing, who are only ever themselves. Faithful Margaret and Prince Wing are the love interests and the main characters, and therefore, inevitably, the most boring characters, although Amy has a crush on Prince Wing.

Fox and the dashing-but-treacherous pirate-magician Two Devils are never played by the same actor twice, although in the twenty-third episode of *The Library*, the same woman played them both. Jeremy supposes that the casting could be perpetually confusing, but instead it makes your brain catch on fire. It's magical.

You always know Fox by her costume (the too-small green T-shirt, the long, full skirts she wears to hide her tail), by her dramatic hand gestures and body language, by the soft, breathy-squeaky voice the actors use when they are Fox. Fox is funny, dangerous, bad-tempered, flirtatious, greedy, untidy, accident-prone, graceful, and has a mysterious past. In some episodes, Fox is played by male actors, but she always sounds like Fox. And she's always beautiful. Every episode you think that this Fox, surely, is the most beautiful Fox there could ever be, and yet the Fox of the next episode will be even more heartbreakingly beautiful.

On television, it's night in The Free People's World-Tree Library. All the librarians are asleep, tucked into their coffins, their scabbards, priest-holes, button holes, pockets, hidden cupboards, between the pages of their enchanted novels. Moonlight pours through the high, arched windows of The Library and between the aisles of shelves, into the park. Fox is on her knees, clawing at the muddy ground with her bare hands. The statue of George Washington kneels beside her, helping.

"So that's Fox, right?" Amy says. Nobody tells her to shut up. It would be pointless. Amy has a large heart and an even larger mouth. When it rains, Amy rescues worms off the sidewalk. When you get tired of having a secret, you tell Amy.

Understand: Amy isn't that much stupider than anyone else in this story. It's just that she thinks out loud.

Elizabeth's mother comes into the living room. "Hey, guys," she says. "Hi, Jeremy. Did I hear something about your mother inheriting a wedding chapel?"

"Yes, ma'am," Jeremy says. "In Las Vegas."

"Las Vegas," Elizabeth's mom says. "I won three hundred bucks once in Las Vegas. Spent it on a helicopter ride over the Grand Canyon. So how many times can you guys watch the same episode in one day?" But she sits down to watch, too. "Do you think she's really dead?"

"Who's dead?" Amy says. Nobody says anything.

Jeremy isn't sure he's ready to see this episode again so soon, anyway, especially not with Amy. He goes upstairs and takes a shower. Elizabeth's family has a large and distracting selection of shampoos. They don't mind when Jeremy uses their bathroom.

Jeremy and Karl and Elizabeth have known each other since the first day of kindergarten. Amy and Talis are a year younger. The five have not always been friends, except for Jeremy and Karl, who have. Talis is, famously, a loner. She doesn't listen to music as far as anyone knows, she doesn't wear significant amounts of black, she isn't particularly good (or bad) at math or English, and she doesn't drink, debate, knit, or refuse to eat meat. If she keeps a blog, she's never admitted it to anyone.

The Library made Jeremy and Karl and Talis and Elizabeth and Amy friends. No one else in school is as passionately devoted. Besides, they are all the children of former hippies, and the town is small. They all live within a few blocks of each other, in run-down Victorians with high ceilings and ranch houses with sunken living rooms. And although they have not always been friends, growing up, they've gone skinny-dipping in lakes on summer nights, and broken bones on each others' trampolines. Once, during an argument about dog names, Elizabeth, who is hot-tempered, tried to run Jeremy over with her tenspeed bicycle, and once, a year ago, Karl got drunk on greenapple schnapps at a party and tried to kiss Talis, and once, for five months in the seventh grade, Karl and Jeremy communicated only through angry e-mails written in all caps. I'm not allowed to tell you what they fought about.

Now the five are inseparable; invincible. They imagine that

life will always be like this—like a television show in eternal syndication—that they will always have each other. They use the same vocabulary. They borrow each other's books and music. They share lunches, and they never say anything when Jeremy comes over and takes a shower. They all know Jeremy's father is eccentric. He's supposed to be eccentric. He's a novelist.

When Jeremy comes back downstairs, Amy is saying, "I've always thought there was something wicked about Prince Wing. He's a dork and he looks like he has bad breath. I never really liked him."

Karl says, "We don't know the whole story yet. Maybe he found out something about Fox while he was a teapot." Elizabeth's mom says, "He's under a spell. I bet you anything." They'll be talking about it all week.

Talis is in the kitchen, making a Velveeta-and-pickle sandwich.

"So what did you think?" Jeremy says. It's like having a hobby, only more pointless, trying to get Talis to talk. "Is Fox really dead?"

"Don't know," Talis says. Then she says, "I had a dream."

Jeremy waits. Talis seems to be waiting, too. She says, "About you." Then she's silent again. There is something dreamlike about the way that she makes a sandwich. As if she is really making something that isn't a sandwich at all; as if she's making something far more meaningful and mysterious. Or as if soon he will wake up and realize that there is no such thing as sandwiches.

"You and Fox," Talis says. "The dream was about the two of you. She told me. To tell you. To call her. She gave me a phone number. She was in trouble. She said you were in trouble. She said *to keep in touch.*"

"Weird," Jeremy says, mulling this over. He's never had a dream about *The Library.* He wonders who was playing Fox in Talis's dream. He had a dream about Talis, once, but it isn't the kind of dream that you'd ever tell anybody about. They were just sitting together, not saying anything. Even Talis's T-shirt hadn't said anything. Talis was holding his hand.

"It didn't feel like a dream," Talis says.

"So what was the phone number?" Jeremy says.

"I forgot," Talis says. "When I woke up, I forgot."

Kurt's mother works in a bank. Talis's father has a karaoke machine in his basement, and he knows all the lyrics to "Like a Virgin" and "Holiday" as well as the lyrics to all the songs from *Godspell* and *Cabaret.* Talis's mother is a licensed therapist who composes multiple-choice personality tests for women's magazines. "Discover Which Television Character You Resemble Most." Etc. Amy's parents met in a commune in Ithaca: her name was Galadriel Moon Shuyler before her parents came to their senses and had it changed legally. Everyone is sworn to secrecy about this, which is ironic, considering that this is Amy.

But Jeremy's father is Gordon Strangle Mars. He writes novels about giant spiders, giant leeches, giant moths, and once, notably, a giant carnivorous rosebush who lives in a mansion in upstate New York, and falls in love with a plucky, teenaged girl with a heart murmur. Saint Bernard–sized spiders chase his characters' cars down dark, bumpy country roads. They fight the spiders off with badminton rackets, lawn tools, and fireworks. The novels with spiders are all bestsellers.

Once a Gordon Strangle Mars fan broke into the Mars house. The fan stole several German first editions of Gordon

Strangle's novels, a hairbrush, and a used mug in which there were two ancient, dehydrated tea bags. The fan left behind a betrayed and abusive letter on a series of Post-It notes, and the manuscript of his own novel, told from the point of view of the iceberg that sank the *Titanic*. Jeremy and his mother read the manuscript out loud to each other. It begins: "The iceberg knew it had a destiny." Jeremy's favorite bit happens when the iceberg sees the doomed ship drawing nearer, and remarks plaintively, "Oh my, does not the Captain know about my large and impenetrable bottom?"

Jeremy discovered, later, that the novel-writing fan had put Gordon Strangle Mars's used tea bags and hairbrush up for sale on eBay, where someone paid forty-two dollars and sixty-eight cents, which was not only deeply creepy, but, Jeremy still feels, somewhat cheap. But of course this is appropriate, as Jeremy's father is famously stingy and just plain weird about money.

Gordon Strangle Mars once spent eight thousand dollars on a Japanese singing toilet. Jeremy's friends love that toilet. Jeremy's mother has a painting of a woman wearing a red dress by some artist, Jeremy can never remember who. Jeremy's father gave her that painting. The woman is beautiful, and she looks right at you as if you're the painting, not her. As if *you're* beautiful. The woman has an apple in one hand and a knife in the other. When Jeremy was little, he used to dream about eating that apple. Apparently it's worth more than the whole house and everything else in the house combined, including the singing toilet. But art and toilets aside, the Marses buy most of their clothes at thrift stores.

Jeremy's father clips coupons.

On the other hand, when Jeremy was twelve and begged

his parents to send him to baseball camp in Florida, his father ponied up. And on Jeremy's last birthday, his father gave him a couch reupholstered in several dozen yards of heavy-duty *Star Wars*–themed fabric. That was a good birthday.

When his writing is going well, Gordon Strangle Mars likes to wake up at 6 A.M. and go out driving. He works out new plot lines about giant spiders and keeps an eye out for abandoned couches, which he wrestles into the back of his pickup truck. Then he writes for the rest of the day. On weekends he reupholsters the thrown-away couches in remaindered, discount fabrics. A few years ago, Jeremy went through his house, counting up fourteen couches, eight love seats, and one rickety chaise longue. That was a few years ago. Once Jeremy had a dream that his father combined his two careers and began reupholstering giant spiders.

All lights in all rooms of the Mars house are on fifteen-minute timers, in case Jeremy or his mother leaves a room and forgets to turn off a lamp. This has caused confusion—and sometimes panic—on the rare occasions that the Marses throw dinner parties.

Everyone thinks that writers are rich, but it seems to Jeremy that his family is only rich some of the time. Some of the time they aren't.

Whenever Gordon Mars gets stuck in a Gordon Strangle Mars novel, he worries about money. He worries that he won't, in fact, manage to finish the current novel. He worries that it will be terrible. He worries that no one will buy it and no one will read it, and that the readers who do read it will demand to be refunded the cost of the book. He's told Jeremy that he imagines these angry readers marching on the Mars house, carrying torches and crowbars.

It would be easier on Jeremy and his mother if Gordon Mars

did not work at home. It's difficult to shower when you know your father is timing you, and thinking dark thoughts about the water bill, instead of concentrating on the scene in the current Gordon Strangle Mars novel, in which the giant spiders have returned to their old haunts in the trees surrounding the ninth hole of the accursed golf course, where they sullenly feast on the pulped entrail-juices of a brace of unlucky poodles and their owner.

During these periods, Jeremy showers at school, after gym, or at his friends' houses, even though it makes his mother unhappy. She says that sometimes you just need to ignore Jeremy's father. She takes especially long showers, lots of baths. She claims that baths are even nicer when you know that Jeremy's father is worried about the water bill. Jeremy's mother has a cruel streak.

What Jeremy likes about showers is the way you can stand there, surrounded by water and yet in absolutely no danger of drowning, and not think about things like whether you fucked up on the Spanish assignment, or why your mother is looking so worried. Instead you can think about things like if there's water on Mars, and whether or not Karl is shaving, and if so, who is he trying to fool, and what the statue of George Washington meant when it said to Fox, during their desperate, bloody fight, "You have a long journey ahead of you," and, "Everything depends on this." And is Fox really dead?

After she dug up the cigar box, and after George Washington helped her carefully separate out the pieces of tea mug from the pieces of teapot, after they glued back together the hundreds of pieces of porcelain, when Fox turned the ramshackle teapot back into Prince Wing, Prince Wing looked about a hundred years old, and as if maybe there were still a few pieces missing. He looked pale. When he saw Fox, he turned even paler, as if he hadn't expected her to be standing there in front of him. He picked up his leviathan sword, which Fox had been keeping safe for him—the one which faithful viewers know was carved out of the tooth of a giant, ancient sea creature that lived happily and peacefully (before Prince Wing was tricked into killing it) in the enchanted underground sea on the third floor—and skewered the statue of George Washington like a kebab, pinning it to a tree. He kicked Fox in the head, knocked her down, and tied her to a card catalog. He stuffed a handful of moss and dirt into her mouth so she couldn't say anything, and then he accused her of plotting to murder Faithful Margaret by magic. He said Fox was more deceitful than a Forbidden Book. He cut off Fox's tail and her ears and he ran her through with the poison-edged, dog-headed knife that he and Fox had stolen from his mother's secret house. Then he left Fox there, tied to the card catalog, limp and bloody, her beautiful head hanging down. He sneezed (Prince Wing is allergic to swordplay) and walked off into the stacks. The librarians crept out of their hiding places. They untied Fox and cleaned off her face. They held a mirror to her mouth, but the mirror stayed clear and unclouded.

When the librarians pulled Prince Wing's leviathan sword out of the tree, the statue of George Washington staggered over and picked up Fox in his arms. He tucked her ears and tail into the capacious pockets of his bird-shit-stained, verdigris riding coat. He carried Fox down seventeen flights of stairs, past the enchanted-and-disagreeable Sphinx on the eighth floor, past the enchanted-and-stormy underground sea on the third floor, past the even-more-enchanted checkout desk on the first floor, and through the hammered-brass doors of the Free People's World-Tree Library. Nobody in *The Library*, not in one single episode, has ever gone outside. *The Library* is full of all the sorts of things that one usually has to go outside to enjoy: trees and lakes and grottoes and fields and mountains and precipices (and full of indoors things as well, like books, of course). Outside The Library, everything is dusty and red and alien, as if George Washington has carried Fox out of The Library and onto the surface of Mars.

"I could really go for a nice cold Euphoria right now," Jeremy says. He and Karl are walking home.

Euphoria is *The Librarian's Tonic—When Watchfulness Is Not Enough.* There are frequently commercials for Euphoria on *The Library.* Although no one is exactly sure what Euphoria is for, whether it is alcoholic or caffeinated, what it tastes like, if it is poisonous or delightful, or even whether or not it's carbonated, everyone, including Jeremy, pines for a glass of Euphoria once in a while.

"Can I ask you a question?" Karl says.

"Why do you always say that?" Jeremy says. "What am I going to say? 'No, you can't ask me a question'?"

"What's up with you and Talis?" Karl says. "What were you talking about in the kitchen?" Jeremy sees that Karl has been Watchful.

"She had this dream about me," he says, uneasily.

"So do you like her?" Karl says. His chin looks raw. Jeremy is sure now that Karl has tried to shave. "Because, remember how I liked her first?"

"We were just talking," Jeremy says. "So did you shave? Because I didn't know you had facial hair. The idea of you shaving is pathetic, Karl. It's like voting Republican if we were old enough to vote. Or farting in Music Appreciation."

"Don't try to change the subject," Karl says. "When have you and Talis ever had a conversation before?"

"One time we talked about a Diana Wynne Jones book that

she'd checked out from the library. She dropped it in the bath accidentally. She wanted to know if I could tell my mother," Jeremy says. "Once we talked about recycling."

"Shut up, Germ," Karl says. "Besides, what about Elizabeth? I thought you liked Elizabeth!"

"Who said that?" Jeremy says. Karl is glaring at him.

"Amy told me," Karl says.

"I never told Amy I liked Elizabeth," Jeremy says. So now Amy is a mind-reader as well as a blabbermouth? What a terrible, deadly combination!

"No," Karl says, grudgingly. "Elizabeth told Amy that she likes you. So I just figured you liked her back."

"Elizabeth likes me?" Jeremy says.

"Apparently everybody likes you," Karl says. He sounds sorry for himself. "What is it about you? It's not like you're all that special. Your nose is funny looking and you have stupid hair."

"Thanks, Karl." Jeremy changes the subject. "Do you think Fox is really dead?" he says. "For good?" He walks faster, so that Karl has to almost-jog to keep up. Presently Jeremy is much taller than Karl, and he intends to enjoy this as long as it lasts. Knowing Karl, he'll either get tall, too, or else chop Jeremy off at the knees.

"They'll use magic," Karl says. "Or maybe it was all a dream. They'll make her alive again. I'll never forgive them if they've killed Fox. And if you like Talis, I'll never forgive you, either. And I know what you're thinking. You're thinking that I think I mean what I say, but if push came to shove, eventually I'd forgive you, and we'd be friends again, like in seventh grade. But I wouldn't, and you're wrong, and we wouldn't be. We wouldn't ever be friends again."

Jeremy doesn't say anything. Of course he likes Talis. He

just hasn't realized how much he likes her, until recently. Until today. Until Karl opened his mouth. Jeremy likes Elizabeth, too, but how can you compare Elizabeth and Talis? You can't. Elizabeth is Elizabeth and Talis is Talis.

"When you tried to kiss Talis, she hit you with a boa constrictor," he says. It had been Amy's boa constrictor. It had probably been an accident. Karl shouldn't have tried to kiss someone while she was holding a boa constrictor.

"Just try to remember what I just said," Karl says. "You're free to like anyone you want to. Anyone except for Talis."

The Library has been on television for two years now. It isn't a regularly scheduled program. Sometimes it's on two times in the same week, and then not on again for another couple of weeks. Often new episodes debut in the middle of the night. There is a large online community who spend hours scanning channels, sending out alarms and false alarms; fans swap theories, tapes, files, write fanfic. Elizabeth has rigged up her computer to shout "Wake up, Elizabeth! The television is on fire!" when reliable *Library*-watch sites discover a new episode.

The Library is a pirate TV show. It's shown up once or twice on most network channels, but usually it's on the kind of channels that Jeremy thinks of as ghost channels. The ones that are just static, unless you're paying for several hundred channels of cable. There are commercial breaks, but the products being advertised are like Euphoria. They never seem to be real brands or things that you can actually buy. Often the commercials aren't even in English, or in any other identifiable language, although the jingles are catchy, nonsense or not. They get stuck in your head.

Episodes of *The Library* have no regular schedule, no credits, and sometimes not even dialogue. One episode of *The Library* takes place inside the top drawer of a card catalog, in pitch dark, and it's all in Morse code with subtitles. Nothing else. No one has ever claimed responsibility for inventing *The Library*. No one has ever interviewed one of the actors, or stumbled across a set, film crew, or script, although in one documentary-style episode, the actors filmed the crew, who all wore paper bags on their heads.

When Jeremy gets home, his father is making upside-down pizza in a casserole dish for dinner.

Meeting writers is usually disappointing, at best. Writers who write sexy thrillers aren't necessarily sexy or thrilling in person. Children's book writers might look more like accountants, or ax murderers for that matter. Horror writers are very rarely scary looking, although they are frequently good cooks.

Though Gordon Strangle Mars *is* scary looking. He has long, thin fingers—currently slimy with pizza sauce—which is why he chose "Strangle" for his fake middle name. He has white-blond hair that he tugs on while he writes until it stands straight up. He has a bad habit of suddenly appearing beside you when you haven't even realized he was in the same part of the house. His eyes are deep-set and he doesn't blink very often. Karl says that when you meet Jeremy's father, he looks at you as if he were imagining you bundled up and stuck away in some giant spider's larder. Which is probably true.

People who read books probably never bother to wonder if their favorite writers are also good parents. Why would they?

Gordon Strangle Mars is a recreational shoplifter. He has a special, complicated, and unspoken arrangement with the local bookstore, where, in exchange for his autographing as many

Gordon Strangle Mars novels as they can possibly sell, the store allows Jeremy's father to shoplift books and doesn't call the police. Jeremy's mother shows up sooner or later and writes a check.

Jeremy's feelings about his father are complicated. His father is a cheapskate and a petty thief, and yet Jeremy likes his father. His father hardly ever loses his temper with Jeremy, he is always interested in Jeremy's life, and he gives interesting (if confusing) advice when Jeremy asks for it. For example, if Jeremy asked his father about kissing Elizabeth, his father might suggest that Jeremy not worry about giant spiders when he kisses Elizabeth. Jeremy's father's advice usually has something to do with giant spiders.

When Jeremy and Karl weren't speaking to each other, it was Jeremy's father who straightened them out. He lured Karl over, and then locked them both into his study. He didn't let them out again until they were on speaking terms.

"I thought of a great idea for your book," Jeremy says. "What if one of the spiders builds a web on a soccer field, across a goal? And what if the goalie doesn't notice until the middle of the game? Could somebody kill one of the spiders with a soccer ball, if they kicked it hard enough? Would it explode? Or even better, the spider could puncture the soccer ball with its massive fangs. That would be cool, too."

"Your mother's out in the garage," Gordon Strangle Mars says to Jeremy. "She wants to talk to you."

"Oh," Jeremy says. All of a sudden, he thinks of Fox in Talis's dream, trying to phone him. Trying to warn him. Unreasonably, he feels that it's his parents' fault that Fox is dead now, as if they have killed her. "Is it about you? Are you getting divorced?"

"I don't know," his father says. He hunches his shoulders. He makes a face. It's a face that Jeremy's father makes frequently, and yet this face is even more pitiful and guilty than usual.

"What did you do?" Jeremy says. "Did you get caught shoplifting at Wal-Mart?"

"No," his father says.

"Did you have an affair?"

"No!" his father says, again. Now he looks disgusted, either with himself or with Jeremy for asking such a horrible question. "I screwed up. Let's leave it at that."

"How's the book coming?" Jeremy says. There is something in his father's voice that makes him feel like kicking something, but there are never giant spiders around when you need them.

"I don't want to talk about that, either," his father says, looking, if possible, even more ashamed. "Go tell your mother dinner will be ready in five minutes. Maybe you and I can watch the new episode of *The Library* after dinner, if you haven't already seen it a thousand times."

"Do you know the end? Did Mom tell you that Fox is —"

"Oh shit," his father interrupts. "They killed Fox?"

That's the problem with being a writer, Jeremy knows. Even the biggest and most startling twists are rarely twists for you. You know how every story goes.

Jeremy's mother is an orphan. Jeremy's father claims that she was raised by feral silent-film stars, and it's true, she looks like a heroine out of a Harold Lloyd movie. She has an appealingly disheveled look to her, as if someone has either just tied her to or untied her from a set of train tracks. She met Gordon Mars (before he added the Strangle and sold his first novel) in the food court of a mall in New Jersey, and fell in love with him before realizing that he was a writer and a recreational shoplifter. She didn't read anything he'd written until after they were married, which was a typically cunning move on Jeremy's father's part.

Jeremy's mother doesn't read horror novels. She doesn't like ghost stories or unexplained phenomena or even the kind of phenomena that require excessively technical explanations. For example: microwaves, airplanes. She doesn't like Halloween, not even Halloween candy. Jeremy's father gives her special editions of his novels, where the scary pages have been glued together.

Jeremy's mother is quiet more often than not. Her name is Alice and sometimes Jeremy thinks about how the two quietest people he knows are named Alice and Talis. But his mother and Talis are quiet in different ways. Jeremy's mother is the kind of person who seems to be keeping something hidden, something secret. Whereas Talis just *is* a secret. Jeremy's mother could easily turn out to be a secret agent. But Talis is the death ray or the key to immortality or whatever it is that secret agents have to keep secret. Hanging out with Talis is like hanging out with a teenaged black hole.

Jeremy's mother is sitting on the floor of the garage, beside a large cardboard box. She has a photo album in her hands. Jeremy sits down beside her.

There are photographs of a cat on a wall, and something blurry that looks like a whale or a zeppelin or a loaf of bread. There's a photograph of a small girl sitting beside a woman. The woman wears a fur collar with a sharp little muzzle, four legs, and a tail, and Jeremy feels a sudden pang. Fox is the first dead person that he's ever cared about, but she's not real. The little girl in the photograph looks utterly blank, as if someone has just hit her with a hammer. Like the person behind the camera has just said, "Smile! Your parents are dead!"

"Cleo," Jeremy's mother says, pointing to the woman. "That's Cleo. She was my mother's aunt. She lived in Los Angeles. I went to live with her when my parents died. I was four. I know I've never talked about her. I've never really known what to say about her."

Jeremy says, "Was she nice?"

His mother says, "She tried to be nice. She didn't expect to be saddled with a little girl. What an odd word. Saddled. As if she were a horse. As if somebody put me on her back and I never got off again. She liked to buy clothes for me. She liked clothes. She hadn't had a happy life. She drank a lot. She liked to go to movies in the afternoon and to séances in the evenings. She had boyfriends. Some of them were jerks. The love of her life was a small-time gangster. He died and she never married. She always said marriage was a joke and that life was a bigger joke, and it was just her bad luck that she didn't have a sense of humor. So it's strange to think that all these years she was running a wedding chapel."

Jeremy looks at his mother. She's half-smiling, half-grimacing, as if her stomach hurts. "I ran away when I was sixteen. And I never saw her again. Once she sent me a letter, care of your father's publishers. She said she'd read all his books, and that was how she found me, I guess, because he kept dedicating them to me. She said she hoped I was happy and that she thought about me. I wrote back. I sent a photograph of you. But she never wrote again. Sounds like an episode of *The Library*, doesn't it?"

Jeremy says, "Is that what you wanted to tell me? Dad said you wanted to tell me something."

"That's part of it," his mother says. "I have to go out to Las Vegas, to check out some things about this wedding chapel. Hell's Bells. I want you to come with me."

"Is that what you wanted to ask me?" Jeremy says, although he knows there's something else. His mother still has that sad half-smile on her face.

"Germ," his mother says. "You know I love your father, right?"

"Why?" Jeremy says. "What did he do?"

His mother flips through the photo album. "Look," she says. "This was when you were born." In the picture, his father holds Jeremy as if someone has just handed him an enchanted porcelain teapot. Jeremy's father grins, but he looks terrified, too. He looks like a kid. A scary, scared kid.

"He wouldn't tell me either," Jeremy says. "So it has to be pretty bad. If you're getting divorced, I think you should go ahead and tell me."

"We're not getting divorced," his mother says, "but it might be a good thing if you and I went out to Las Vegas. We could stay there for a few months while I sort out this inheritance. Take care of Cleo's estate. I'm going to talk to your teachers. I've given notice at the library. Think of it as an adventure."

She sees the look on Jeremy's face. "No, I'm sorry. That was a stupid, stupid thing to say. I know this isn't an adventure."

"I don't want to go," Jeremy says. "All my friends are here! I can't just go away and leave them. That would be terrible!" All this time, he's been preparing himself for the most terrible thing he can imagine. He's imagined a conversation with his mother in which his mother reveals her terrible secret, and in his imagination, he's been calm and reasonable. His imaginary parents have wept and asked for his understanding. The imaginary Jeremy has understood. He has imagined himself understanding everything. But now, as his mother talks, Jeremy's heartbeat speeds up, and his lungs fill with air, as if he is running. He starts to sweat, although the floor of the garage is cold. He wishes he were sitting up on top of the roof with his telescope. There could be meteors, invisible to the naked eye, careening through the sky, hurtling toward Earth. Fox is dead. Everyone he knows is doomed. Even as he thinks this, he knows he's overreacting. But it doesn't help to know this.

"I know it's terrible," his mother says. His mother knows something about terrible.

"So why can't I stay here?" Jeremy says. "You go sort things out in Las Vegas, and I'll stay here with Dad. Why can't I stay here?"

"Because he put you in a book!" his mother says. She spits the words out. He has never heard her sound so angry. His mother never gets angry. "He put you in one of his books! I was in his office, and the manuscript was on his desk. I saw your name, and so I picked it up and started reading."

"So what?" Jeremy says. "He's put me in his books before. Like, stuff I've said. Like when I was eight and I was running a fever and told him the trees were full of dead people wearing party hats. Like when I accidentally set fire to his office."

"It isn't like that," his mother says. "He hasn't even changed your name. The boy in the book, he jumps hurdles and he wants to be a rocket scientist and go to Mars, and he's cute and funny and sweet and his best friend Elizabeth is in love with him and he talks like you and he looks like you and then he dies, Jeremy. He has a brain tumor and he dies. He dies. There aren't any giant spiders. There's just you, and you die."

Jeremy is silent. He imagines his father writing the scene in his book where the kid named Jeremy dies, and crying, just a little. He imagines this Jeremy kid, Jeremy the character who dies. Poor messed-up kid. Now Jeremy and Fox have something in common. They're both made-up people. They're both dead.

"Elizabeth is in love with me?" he says. Just on principle, he never believes anything that Karl says. But if it's in a book, maybe it's true.

"Oh shit," his mother says. "I really didn't want to say that. I'm just so angry at him. We've been married for seventeen years. I was just four years older than you when I met him, Jeremy. I was nineteen. He was only twenty. We were babies. Can you imagine that? I can put up with the singing toilet and the shoplifting and the couches, and I can put up with him being so weird about money. But he killed you, Jeremy. He wrote you into a book and he killed you off. And he knows it was wrong, too. He's ashamed of himself. He didn't want me to tell you. I didn't mean to tell you."

Jeremy sits and thinks. "I still don't want to go to Las Vegas," he says to his mother. "Maybe we could send Dad there instead."

His mother says, "Not a bad idea." But he can tell she's already planning their itinerary.

In one episode of *The Library*, everyone was invisible. You couldn't see the actors: you could only see the books and the bookshelves and the study carrels on the fifth floor where the coin-operated wizards come to flirt and practice their spells. Invisible Forbidden Books were fighting invisible pirate-magicians and the pirate-magicians were fighting Fox and her friends, who were also invisible. The fight was clumsy and full of deadly accidents. You could hear them fighting. Shelves were overturned. Books were thrown. Invisible people tripped over invisible dead bodies, but you didn't find out who'd died until the next episode. Several of the characters—The Accidental Sword, Hairy Pete, and

Ptolemy Krill, who (much like the Vogons in Douglas Adams's *The Hitchhiker's Guide to the Galaxy*) wrote poetry so bad it killed anyone who read it—disappeared for good, and nobody is sure whether they're dead or not.

In another episode, Fox stole a magical drug from The Norns, a prophetic girl band who headline at a cabaret on the mezzanine of The Free People's World-Tree Library. She accidentally injected it, became pregnant, and gave birth to a bunch of snakes who led her to the exact shelf where renegade librarians had misshelved an ancient and terrible book of magic which had never been translated, until Fox asked the snakes for help. The snakes writhed and curled on the ground, spelling out words, letter by letter, with their bodies. As they translated the book for Fox, they hissed and steamed. They became fiery lines on the ground, and then they burnt away entirely. Fox cried. That's the only time anyone has ever seen Fox cry, ever. She isn't like Prince Wing. Prince Wing is a crybaby.

The thing about *The Library* is that characters don't come back when they die. It's as if death is for real. So maybe Fox really is dead and she really isn't coming back. There are a couple of ghosts who hang around The Library looking for blood libations, but they've always been ghosts, all the way back to the beginning of the show. There aren't any evil twins or vampires, either. Although someday, hopefully, there will be evil twins. Who doesn't love evil twins?

"Mom told me about how you wrote about me," Jeremy says. His mother is still in the garage. He feels like a tennis ball in a game where the tennis players love him very, very much, even while they lob and smash and send him back and forth, back and forth.

His father says, "She said she wasn't going to tell you, but I guess I'm glad she did. I'm sorry, Germ. Are you hungry?"

"She's going out to Las Vegas next week. She wants me to go with her," Jeremy says.

"I know," his father says, still holding out a bowl of upside-down pizza. "Try not to worry about all of this, if you can. Think of it as an adventure."

"Mom says that's a stupid thing to say. Are you going to let me read the book with me in it?" Jeremy says.

"No," his father says, looking straight at Jeremy. "I burned it."

"Really?" Jeremy says. "Did you set fire to your computer, too?"

"Well, no," his father says. "But you can't read it. It wasn't any good, anyway. Come watch *The Library* with me. And will you eat some damn pizza, please? I may be a lousy father, but I'm a good cook. And if you love me, you'll eat the damn pizza and be grateful."

So they go sit on the orange couch and Jeremy eats pizza and watches *The Library* for the second-and-a-half time with his father. The lights on the timer in the living room go off, and Prince Wing kills Fox again. And then Jeremy goes to bed. His father goes away to write or to burn stuff. Whatever. His mother is still out in the garage.

On Jeremy's desk is a scrap of paper with a phone number on it. If he wanted to, he could call his phone booth. When he dials the number, it rings for a long time. Jeremy sits on his bed in the dark and listens to it ringing and ringing. When someone picks it up, he almost hangs up. Someone doesn't say anything, so Jeremy says, "Hello? Hello?"

Someone breathes into the phone on the other end of the line. Someone says in a soft, musical, squeaky voice, "Can't talk now, kid. Call back later." Then someone hangs up.

Jeremy dreams that he's sitting beside Fox on a sofa that his father has reupholstered in spider silk. His father has been stealing spiderwebs from the giant-spider superstores. From his own books. Is that shoplifting or is it self-plagiarism? The sofa is soft and gray and a little bit sticky. Fox sits on either side of him. The right-hand-side Fox is being played by Talis. Elizabeth plays the Fox on his left. Both Foxes look at him with enormous compassion.

"Are you dead?" Jeremy says.

"Are you?" the Fox who is being played by Elizabeth says, in that unmistakable Fox voice which, Jeremy's father once said, sounds like a sexy and demented helium balloon. It makes Jeremy's brain hurt, to hear Fox's voice coming out of Elizabeth's mouth.

The Fox who looks like Talis doesn't say anything at all. The writing on her T-shirt is so small and so foreign that Jeremy can't read it without feeling as if he's staring at Fox-Talis's breasts. It's probably something he needs to know, but he'll never be able to read it. He's too polite, and besides he's terrible at foreign languages.

"Hey, look," Jeremy says. "We're on TV!" There he is on television, sitting between two Foxes on a sticky gray couch in a field of red poppies. "Are we in Las Vegas?"

"We're not in Kansas," Fox-Elizabeth says. "There's something I need you to do for me."

"What's that?" Jeremy says.

"If I tell you in the dream," Fox-Elizabeth says, "you won't remember. You have to remember to call me when you're awake. Keep on calling until you get me."

"How will I remember to call you," Jeremy says, "if I don't remember what you tell me in this dream? Why do you need me to help you? Why is Talis here? What does her T-shirt say? Why are you both Fox? Is this Mars?"

Fox-Talis goes on watching TV. Fox-Elizabeth opens her kind and beautiful un-Hello-Kitty-like mouth again. She tells Jeremy the whole story. She explains everything. She translates Fox-Talis's T-shirt, which turns out to explain everything about Talis that Jeremy has ever wondered about. It answers every single question that Jeremy has ever had about girls. And then Jeremy wakes up—

It's dark. Jeremy flips on the light. The dream is moving away from him. There was something about Mars. Elizabeth was asking who he thought was prettier, Talis or Elizabeth. They were laughing. They both had pointy fox ears. They wanted him to do something. There was a telephone number he was supposed to call. There was something he was supposed to do.

In two weeks, on the fifteenth of April, Jeremy and his mother will get in her van and start driving out to Las Vegas. Every morning before school, Jeremy takes long showers and his father doesn't say anything at all. One day it's as if nothing is wrong between his parents. The next day they won't even look at each other. Jeremy's father won't come out of his study. And then the day after that, Jeremy comes home and finds his mother sitting on his father's lap. They're smiling as if they know something stupid and secret. They don't even notice Jeremy when he walks through the room. Even this is preferable, though, to the way they behave when they do notice him. They act guilty and strange and as if they are about to ruin his life. Gordon Mars makes pancakes every morning, and Jeremy's favorite dinner, macaroni and cheese, every night. Jeremy's mother plans out an itinerary for their trip. They will be stopping at libraries across the country, because his mother loves libraries. But she's also bought a new two-man tent and two sleeping bags and a portable stove, so that they can camp, if Jeremy wants to camp. Even though Jeremy's mother hates the outdoors.

Right after she does this, Gordon Mars spends all weekend in the garage. He won't let either of them see what he's doing, and when he does let them in, it turns out that he's removed the seating in the back of the van and bolted down two of his couches, one on each side, both upholstered in electric-blue fake fur.

They have to climb in through the cargo door at the back because one of the couches is blocking the sliding door. Jeremy's father says, looking very pleased with himself, "So now you don't have to camp outside, unless you want to. You can sleep inside. There's space underneath for suitcases. The sofas even have seat belts."

Over the sofas, Jeremy's father has rigged up small wooden shelves that fold down on chains from the walls of the van and become table tops. There's a travel-sized disco ball dangling from the ceiling, and a wooden panel—with Velcro straps and a black, quilted pad—behind the driver's seat, where Jeremy's father explains they can hang up the painting of the woman with the apple and the knife.

The van looks like something out of an episode of *The Library*. Jeremy's mother bursts into tears. She runs back inside the house. Jeremy's father says, helplessly, "I just wanted to make her laugh."

Jeremy wants to say, "I hate both of you." But he doesn't say it, and he doesn't. It would be easier if he did.

When Jeremy told Karl about Las Vegas, Karl punched him in the stomach. Then he said, "Have you told Talis?"

Jeremy said, "You're supposed to be nice to me! You're supposed to tell me not to go and that this sucks and you're not supposed to punch me. Why did you punch me? Is Talis all you ever think about?"

"Kind of," Karl said. "Most of the time. Sorry, Germ, of course I wish you weren't going and yeah, it also pisses me off. We're supposed to be best friends, but you do stuff all the time and I never get to. I've never driven across the country or been to Las Vegas, even though I'd really, really like to. I can't feel sorry for you when I bet you anything that while you're there, you'll sneak into some casino and play slot machines and win like a million bucks. You should feel sorry for me. I'm the one that has to stay here. Can I borrow your dirt bike while you're gone?"

"Sure," Jeremy said.

"How about your telescope?" Karl said.

"I'm taking it with me," Jeremy said.

"Fine. You have to call me every day," Karl said. "You have to e-mail. You have to tell me about Las Vegas show girls. I want to know how tall they really are. Whose phone number is this?"

Karl was holding the scrap of paper with the number of Jeremy's phone booth.

"Mine," Jeremy said. "That's my phone booth. The one I inherited."

"Have you called it?" Karl said.

"No," Jeremy said. He'd called the phone booth a few times. But it wasn't a game. Karl would think it was a game.

"Cool," Karl said and he went ahead and dialed the number. "Hello?" Karl said, "I'd like to speak to the person in charge of Jeremy's life. This is Jeremy's best friend, Karl."

"Not funny," Jeremy said.

"My life is boring," Karl said, into the phone. "I've never inherited anything. This girl I like won't talk to me. So is someone there? Does anybody want to talk to me? Does anyone want to talk to my friend, the Lord of the Phone Booth? Jeremy, they're demanding that you liberate the phone booth from yourself."

"Still not funny," Jeremy said and Karl hung up the phone.

This is how Jeremy told Elizabeth. They were up on the roof of Jeremy's house and he told her the whole thing. Not just the part about Las Vegas, but also the part about his father and how he put Jeremy in a book with no giant spiders in it.

"Have you read it?" Elizabeth said.

"No," Jeremy said. "He won't let me. Don't tell Karl. All I told him is that my mom and I have to go out for a few months to check out the wedding chapel."

"I won't tell Karl," Elizabeth said. She leaned forward and kissed Jeremy and then she wasn't kissing him. It was all very fast and surprising, but they didn't fall off the roof. Nobody falls off the roof in this story. "Talis likes you," Elizabeth said. "That's what Amy says. Maybe you like her back. I don't know. But I thought I should go ahead and kiss you now. Just in case I don't get to kiss you again."

"You can kiss me again," Jeremy said. "Talis probably doesn't like me."

"No," Elizabeth said. "I mean, let's not. I want to stay friends and it's hard enough to be friends, Germ. Look at you and Karl."

"I would never kiss Karl," Jeremy said.

"Funny, Germ. We should have a surprise party for you before you go," Elizabeth said.

"It won't be a surprise party now," Jeremy said. Maybe kissing him once was enough.

"Well, once I tell Amy it can't really be a surprise party,"

Elizabeth said. "She would explode into a million pieces and all the little pieces would start yelling, 'Guess what? Guess what? We're having a surprise party for you, Jeremy!' But just because I'm letting you in on the surprise doesn't mean there won't be surprises."

"I don't actually like surprises," Jeremy said.

"Who does?" Elizabeth said. "Only the people who do the surprising. Can we have the party at your house? I think it should be like Halloween, and it always feels like Halloween here. We could all show up in costumes and watch lots of old episodes of *The Library* and eat ice cream."

"Sure," Jeremy said. And then: "This is terrible! What if there's a new episode of *The Library* while I'm gone? Who am I going to watch it with?"

And he'd said the perfect thing. Elizabeth felt so bad about Jeremy having to watch *The Library* all by himself that she kissed him again.

There has never been a giant spider in any episode of *The Library*, although once Fox got really small and Ptolemy Krill carried her around in his pocket. She had to rip up one of Krill's handkerchiefs and blindfold herself, just in case she accidentally read a draft of Krill's terrible poetry. And then it turned out that, as well as the poetry, Krill's pocket also contained a rare, horned Anubis earwig that hadn't been properly preserved. Ptolemy Krill, it turned out, was careless with his kill jar. The earwig almost ate Fox, but instead it became her friend. It still sends her Christmas cards.

These are the two most important things that Jeremy and his friends have in common: a geographical location, and love of a television show about a library. Jeremy turns on the television as soon as he comes home from school. He flips through the channels, watching reruns of *Star Trek* and *Law & Order*. If there's a new episode of *The Library* before he and his mother leave for Las Vegas, then everything will be fine. Everything will work out. His mother says, "You watch too much television, Jeremy." But he goes on flipping through channels. Then he goes up to his room and makes phone calls.

"The new episode needs to be soon, because we're getting ready to leave. Tonight would be good. You'd tell me if there was going to be a new episode tonight, right?"

Silence.

"Can I take that as a yes? It would be easier if I had a brother," Jeremy tells his telephone booth. "Hello? Are you there? Or a sister. I'm tired of being good all the time. If I had a sibling, then we could take turns being good. If I had an older brother, I might be better at being bad, better at being angry. Karl is really good at being angry. He learned how from his brothers. I wouldn't want brothers like Karl's brothers, of course, but it sucks having to figure out everything all by myself. And the more normal I try to be, the more my parents think that I'm acting out. They think it's a phase that I'll grow out of. They think it isn't normal to be normal. Because there's no such thing as normal.

"And this whole book thing. The whole shoplifting thing, how my dad steals things, it figures that he went and stole my life. It isn't just me being melodramatic, to say that. That's exactly what he did! Did I tell you that once he stole a ferret from a pet store because he felt bad for it, and then he let it loose in our house and it turned out that it was pregnant? There was this woman who came to interview Dad and she sat down on one of the—"

Someone knocks on his bedroom door. "Jeremy?" his mother says.

Jeremy hangs up quickly. He's gotten into the habit of calling his phone booth every day. When he calls, it rings and rings and then it stops ringing, as if someone has picked up. There's just silence on the other end, no squeaky pretend-Fox voice, but it's a peaceful, interested silence. Jeremy complains about all the things there are to complain about, and the silent person on the other end listens and listens. Maybe it is Fox standing there in his phone booth and listening patiently. He wonders what incarnation of Fox is listening. One thing about Fox: she's never sorry for herself. She's always too busy. If it were really Fox, she'd hang up on him.

Jeremy opens his door. "I was on the phone," he says. His mother comes in and sits down on his bed. She's wearing one of his father's old flannel shirts. "All packed up?"

Jeremy shrugs. "I guess," he says. "Why did you cry when you saw what Dad did to the van? Don't you like it?"

"It's that painting," his mother says. "It was the first nice thing he ever gave me. We should have spent the money on health insurance. A new roof. Groceries! And instead he bought a painting. So I got angry. I left him. I took the painting and I moved into a hotel and I stayed there for three days. I was going to sell the painting, but then I decided I liked it instead. I came home."

She puts her hand on Jeremy's head, rubs it. "When I got pregnant with you I was hungry all the time but I couldn't eat. I'd have a dream that someone was going to give me a beautiful apple, like the one she's holding. When I told your father, he said he didn't trust her. He says she's holding out the apple like that as a trick and if you try to take it from her, she'll stab you with the peeling knife. He says that she's a tough old broad and she'll take care of us while we're on the road."

"Do we really have to go?" Jeremy says. "If we go to Las Vegas I might get into trouble. I might start using drugs or gambling or something."

"Oh, Germ. You try so hard to be a good kid," his mother says. "You try so hard to be normal. Sometimes I'd like to be normal, too. Maybe Vegas will be good for us. Are these the books that you're bringing?"

Jeremy shrugs. "I can't decide which ones I should take and which ones I can leave. It feels like whatever I leave behind, I'm leaving behind for good."

"That's silly," his mother says. "We're coming back. I promise. Your father and I will work things out. If you leave something behind that you need, he can mail it to you. Do you think there are slot machines in the libraries in Las Vegas? I talked to a woman at the Hell's Bells chapel and there's something called The Arts and Lovecraft Library where they keep Cleo's special collection of horror novels and gothic romances. You go in and out through a secret, swinging-bookcase door. People get married in it. There's a Dr. Frankenstein's LoveLab, The Masque of the Red Death Ballroom, and also something just called The Crypt. There's also The Vampire's Patio and The Black Lagoon Grotto, where you can get married by moonlight."

"You hate all this stuff," Jeremy says.

"It's not my cup of tea," his mother admits. Then she says, "When is everyone coming over?"

"Around eight," Jeremy says. "Are you going to get dressed up?"

"I don't have to dress up," his mother says. "I'm a librarian, remember?"

Jeremy's father's office is above the garage. In theory, no one is meant to interrupt him while he's working, but in practice Jeremy's father loves nothing better than to be interrupted, as long as the person who interrupts brings him something to eat. When Jeremy and his mother are gone, who will bring Jeremy's father food? Jeremy hardens his heart.

The floor is covered with books and bolts and samples of upholstering fabrics. Jeremy's father is lying facedown on the floor with his feet propped up on a bolt of fabric, which means that he is thinking and also that his back hurts. He claims to think best when he is on the verge of falling asleep.

"I brought you a bowl of Froot Loops," Jeremy says.

His father rolls over and looks up. "Thanks," he says. "What time is it? Is everyone here? Is that your costume? Is that my tuxedo jacket?"

"It's five-ish. Nobody's here yet. Do you like it?" Jeremy says. He's dressed as a Forbidden Book. His father's jacket is too big, but he still feels very elegant. Very sinister. His mother lent him the lipstick and the feathers and the platform heels.

"It's interesting," his father allows. "And a little frightening."

Jeremy feels obscurely pleased, even though he knows that his father is more amused than frightened. "Everyone else will probably come as Fox or Prince Wing. Except for Karl. He's coming as Ptolemy Krill. He even wrote some really bad poetry. I wanted to ask you something, before we leave tomorrow."

"Shoot," his father says.

"Did you really get rid of the novel with me in it?"

"No," his father says. "It felt unlucky. Unlucky to keep it, unlucky not to keep it. I don't know what to do with it."

Jeremy says, "I'm glad you didn't get rid of it."

"It's not any good, you know," his father says. "Which makes all this even worse. At first it was because I was bored with giant spiders. It was going to be something funny to show you. But then I wrote that you had a brain tumor and it wasn't funny any more. I figured I could save you—I'm the author, after all—but you got sicker and sicker. You were going through a rebellious phase. You were sneaking out of the house a lot and you hit your mother. You were a real jerk. But it turned out you had a brain tumor and it was making you behave strangely."

"Can I ask another question?" Jeremy says, deciding to take advantage while his father is still vulnerable.

"Go ahead," says his father.

"Could you not steal things for a while, if I asked you to?" Jeremy says. "Mom isn't going to be around to pay for the books and stuff that you steal. I don't want you to end up in jail because we went to Las Vegas."

His father closes his eyes as if he hopes Jeremy will forget that he asked a question, and go away.

Jeremy says nothing.

"All right," his father says finally. "I won't shoplift anything until you get home again."

Jeremy's mother runs around taking photos of everyone. Talis and Elizabeth have both shown up as Fox, although Talis is dead Fox. She carries her fake fur ears and tail around in a little see-through plastic purse and she also has a sword, which she leaves in the umbrella stand in the kitchen. Jeremy and Talis haven't talked much since she had a dream about him and since he told her that he's going to Las Vegas. She didn't say anything about that. Which is perfectly normal for Talis.

Karl makes an excellent Ptolemy Krill. Jeremy's Forbidden Book disguise is admired.

Amy's Faithful Margaret costume is almost as good as anything Faithful Margaret wears on TV. There are even special effects: Amy has rigged up her hair with red ribbons and wire and spray color and egg whites so that it looks as if it's on fire, and there are tiny papier-mâché golems in it, making horrible faces. She dances a polka with Jeremy's father. Faithful Margaret is mad for polka dancing.

No one has dressed up as Prince Wing.

They watch the episode with the possessed chicken and they watch the episode with the Salt Wife and they watch the episode where Prince Wing and Faithful Margaret fall under a spell and swap bodies and have sex for the first time. They watch the episode where Fox saves Prince Wing's life for the first time.

Jeremy's father makes chocolate/mango/espresso milk shakes for everyone. None of Jeremy's friends, except for Elizabeth, know about the novel. Everyone thinks Jeremy and his mother are just having an adventure. Everyone thinks Jeremy will be back at the end of the summer.

"I wonder how they find the actors," Elizabeth says. "They aren't real actors. They must be regular people. But you'd think that somewhere there would be someone who knows them. That somebody online would say, hey, that's my sister! Or that's the kid I went to school with who threw up in P.E. You know, sometimes someone says something like that or sometimes someone pretends that they know something about *The Library*, but it always turns out to be a hoax. Just somebody wanting to be somebody."

"What about the guy who's writing it?" Karl says.

Talis says, "Who says it's a guy?" and Amy says, "Yeah, Karl, why do you always assume it's a guy writing it?"

"Maybe nobody's writing it," Elizabeth says. "Maybe it's

magic or it's broadcast from outer space. Maybe it's real. Wouldn't that be cool?"

"No," Jeremy says. "Because then Fox would really be dead. That would suck."

"I don't care," Elizabeth says. "I wish it were real, anyway. Maybe it all really happened somewhere, like King Arthur or Robin Hood, and this is just one version of how it happened. Like a magical After School Special."

"Even if it isn't real," Amy says, "parts of it could be real. Like maybe the World-Tree Library is real. Or maybe *The Library* is made up, but Fox is based on somebody that the writer knew. Writers do that all the time, right? Jeremy, I think your dad should write a book about me. I could be eaten by giant spiders. Or have sex with giant spiders and have spider babies. I think that would be so great."

So Amy does have psychic abilities, after all, although hopefully she will never know this. When Jeremy tests his own potential psychic abilities, he can almost sense his father, hovering somewhere just outside the living room, listening to this conversation and maybe even taking notes. Which is what writers do. But Jeremy isn't really psychic. It's just that lurking and hovering and appearing suddenly when you weren't expecting him are what his father does, just like shoplifting and cooking. Jeremy prays to all the dark gods that he never receives the gift of knowing what people are thinking. It's a dark road and it ends up with you trapped on late-night television in front of an invisible audience of depressed insomniacs wearing hats made out of tinfoil, and they all want to pay you nine-ninety-nine per minute to hear you describe in minute, terrible detail what their deceased cat is thinking about, right now. What kind of future is that? He wants to go to Mars. And when will Elizabeth kiss him again?

You can't just kiss someone twice and then never kiss them again. He tries not to think about Elizabeth and kissing, just in case Amy reads his mind. He realizes that he's been staring at Talis's breasts, glares instead at Elizabeth, who is watching TV. Meanwhile, Karl is glaring at him.

On television, Fox is dancing in the Invisible Nightclub with Faithful Margaret, whose hair is about to catch fire again. The Norns are playing their screechy cover of "Come On Eileen." The Norns only know two songs: "Come On Eileen" and "Everybody Wants to Rule the World." They don't play real instruments. They play squeaky dog toys and also a bathtub, which is enchanted, although nobody knows who by, or why or what it was enchanted for.

"If you had to choose one," Jeremy says, "invisibility or the ability to fly, which would you choose?"

Everybody looks at him. "Only perverts want to be invisible," Elizabeth says. "So they can spy on people. Or rob banks. You can't trust invisible people."

"You'd have to be naked if you were invisible," Karl says. "Because otherwise people would see your clothes."

"If you could fly, you'd have to wear thermal underwear because it's cold up there. So it just depends on whether you like to wear long underwear or no underwear at all," Amy says.

It's the kind of conversation that they have all the time. It makes Jeremy feel homesick even though he hasn't left yet.

"Maybe I'll go make brownies," Jeremy says. "Elizabeth, do you want to help me make brownies?"

"Shhh," Elizabeth says. "This is a good part."

On television, Fox and Faithful Margaret are making out. The Faithful part is kind of a joke.

Jeremy's parents go to bed at some point. By three, Amy and Elizabeth are passed out on the couch and Karl has gone upstairs to check his e-mail on Jeremy's iBook. On TV, wolves are roaming the tundra of The Free People's World-Tree Library's fortieth floor. Snow is falling heavily and librarians are burning books to keep warm, but only the most dull and improving works of literature.

Jeremy isn't sure where Talis has gone, so he goes to look for her. She hasn't gone far. She's on the landing, looking at the space on the wall where Alice Mars's painting should be hanging. Talis is carrying her sword with her, and her little plastic purse. In the bathroom off the landing, the singing toilet is still singing away.

"We're taking the painting with us," Jeremy says. "My dad insisted, just in case he accidentally burns down the house while we're gone. Do you want to go see it? I was going to show everybody, but everybody's asleep right now."

"Sure," Talis says.

So Jeremy gets a flashlight and takes her out to the garage and shows her the van. She climbs right inside and sits down on one of the blue-fur couches. She looks around and he wonders what she's thinking. He wonders if the toilet song is stuck in her head.

"My dad did all of this," Jeremy says. He turns on the flashlight and shines it on the disco ball. Light spatters off in anxious, slippery orbits. Jeremy shows Talis how his father has hung up the painting. It looks truly wrong in the van, as if someone demented put it there. Especially with the light reflecting off the disco ball. The woman in the painting looks confused and embarrassed, as if Jeremy's father has accidentally canceled out her protective powers. Maybe the disco ball is her Kryptonite.

"So remember how you had a dream about me?" Jeremy says. Talis nods. "I think I had a dream about you, that you were Fox."

Talis opens up her arms, encompassing her costume, her sword, her plastic purse with poor Fox's ears and tail inside.

"There was something you wanted me to do," Jeremy says. "I was supposed to save you, somehow."

Talis just looks at him.

"How come you never talk?" Jeremy says. All of this is irritating. How he used to feel normal around Elizabeth, like friends, and now everything is peculiar and uncomfortable. How he used to enjoy feeling uncomfortable around Talis, and now, suddenly, he doesn't. This must be what sex is about. Stop thinking about sex, he thinks.

Talis opens her mouth and closes it again. Then she says, "I don't know. Amy talks so much. You all talk a lot. Somebody has to be the person who doesn't. The person who listens."

"Oh," Jeremy says. "I thought maybe you had a tragic secret. Like maybe you used to stutter." Except secrets can't have secrets, they just *are*.

"Nope," Talis says. "It's like being invisible, you know. Not talking. I like it."

"But you're not invisible," Jeremy says. "Not to me. Not to Karl. Karl really likes you. Did you hit him with a boa constrictor on purpose?"

But Talis says, "I wish you weren't leaving." The disco ball spins and spins. It makes Jeremy feel kind of carsick and also, looking down at his arms, as if he has sparkly, disco leprosy. He doesn't say anything back to Talis, just to see how it feels. Except maybe that's rude. Or maybe it's rude the way everybody always talks and doesn't leave any space for Talis to say anything.

"At least you get to miss school," Talis says, at last.

"Yeah," he says. He leaves another space, but Talis doesn't say anything this time. "We're going to stop at all these museums and things on the way across the country. I'm supposed to keep a blog for school and describe stuff in it. I'm going to make a lot of stuff up. So it will be like Creative Writing and not so much like homework."

"You should make a list of all the towns with weird names you drive through," Talis says. "Town of Horseheads. That's a real place."

"Plantagenet," Jeremy says. "That's a real place, too. I had something really weird to tell you."

Talis waits, like she always does.

Jeremy says, "I called my phone booth, the one that I inherited, and someone answered. She sounded just like Fox and she told me—she told me to call back later. So I've called a few more times, but I don't ever get her."

"Fox isn't a real person," Talis says. "*The Library* is just TV." But she sounds uncertain. That's the thing about *The Library*. Nobody knows for sure. Everyone who watches it wishes and hopes that it's not just acting. That it's magic. Real magic.

"I know," Jeremy says.

"I wish Fox was real," Fox-Talis says.

They've been sitting in the van for a long time. If Karl looks for them and can't find them, he's going to think that they've been making out. He'll kill Jeremy. Once Karl tried to strangle another kid for accidentally peeing on his shoes. Jeremy might as well kiss Talis. So he does, even though she's still holding her sword. She doesn't hit him with it. It's dark and he has his eyes closed and he can almost imagine that he's kissing Elizabeth.

Karl has fallen asleep on Jeremy's bed. Talis is downstairs, fast-forwarding through the episode where some librarians drink too much Euphoria and decide to abolish Story Hour. Not just the practice of having a Story Hour, but the whole Hour. Amy and Elizabeth are still sacked out on the couch. It's weird to watch Amy sleep. She doesn't talk in her sleep.

Karl is snoring. Jeremy could go up on the roof and look at stars, except he's already packed up his telescope. He could try to wake up Elizabeth and they could go up on the roof, but Talis is down there. He and Talis could go sit on the roof, but he doesn't want to kiss Talis on the roof. He makes a solemn oath to only ever kiss Elizabeth on the roof.

He picks up his phone. Maybe he can call his phone booth and complain just a little and not wake Karl up. His dad is going to freak out about the phone bill. All these calls to Nevada. It's 4 A.M. Jeremy's plan is not to go to sleep at all. His friends are lame.

The phone rings and rings and rings and then someone picks up. Jeremy recognizes the silence on the other end. "Everybody came over and fell asleep," he whispers. "That's why I'm whispering. I don't even think they care that I'm leaving. And my feet hurt. Remember how I was going to dress up as a Forbidden Book? Platform shoes aren't comfortable. Karl thinks I did it on purpose, to be even taller than him than usual. And I forgot that I was wearing lipstick and I kissed Talis and got lipstick all over her face, so it's a good thing everyone was asleep because otherwise someone would have seen. And my dad says that he won't shoplift at all while Mom and I are gone, but you can't trust him. And that fake-fur upholstery sheds like—"

"Jeremy," that strangely familiar, sweet-and-rusty door-hinge voice says softly. "Shut up, Jeremy. I need your help."

"Wow!" Jeremy says, not in a whisper. "Wow, wow, wow! Is this Fox? Are you really Fox? Is this a joke? Are you real? Are you dead? What are you doing in my phone booth?"

"You know who I am," Fox says, and Jeremy knows with all his heart that it's really Fox. "I need you to do something for me."

"What?" Jeremy says. Karl, on the bed, laughs in his sleep as if the idea of Jeremy doing something is funny to him. "What could I do?"

"I need you to steal three books," Fox says. "From a library in a place called Iowa."

"I know Iowa," Jeremy says. "I mean, I've never been there, but it's a real place. I could go there."

"I'm going to tell you the books you need to steal," Fox says. "Author, title, and the jewelly festival number—"

"Dewey decimal," Jeremy says. "It's actually called the Dewey decimal number in real libraries."

"Real," Fox says, sounding amused. "You need to write this all down and also how to get to the library. You need to steal the three books and bring them to me. It's very important."

"Is it dangerous?" Jeremy says. "Are the Forbidden Books up to something? Are the Forbidden Books real, too? What if I get caught stealing?"

"It's not dangerous to you," Fox says. "Just don't get caught. Remember the episode of *The Library* when I was the old woman with the beehive and I stole the Bishop of Tweedle's false teeth while he was reading the banns for the wedding of Faithful Margaret and Sir Petronella the Younger? Remember how he didn't even notice?"

"I've never seen that episode," Jeremy says, although as far as he knows he's never missed a single episode of *The Library*. He's never even heard of Sir Petronella.

"Oh," Fox says. "Maybe that's a flashback in a later episode or something. That's a great episode. We're depending on you, Jeremy. You have got to steal these books. They contain dreadful secrets. I can't say the titles out loud. I'm going to spell them instead."

So Jeremy gets a pad of paper and Fox spells out the titles of each book twice. (They aren't titles that can be written down here. It's safer not to even think about some books.) "Can I ask you something?" Jeremy says. "Can I tell anybody about this? Not Amy. But could I tell Karl or Elizabeth? Or Talis? Can I tell my mom? If I woke up Karl right now, would you talk to him for a minute?"

"I don't have a lot of time," Fox says. "I have to go now. Please don't tell anyone, Jeremy. I'm sorry."

"Is it the Forbidden Books?" Jeremy says again. What would Fox think if she saw the costume he's still wearing, all except for the platform heels? "Do you think I shouldn't trust my friends? But I've known them my whole life!"

Fox makes a noise, a kind of pained whuff.

"What is it?" Jeremy says. "Are you okay?"

"I have to go," Fox says. "Nobody can know about this. Don't give anybody this number. Don't tell anyone about your phone booth. Or me. Promise, Germ?"

"Only if you promise you won't call me Germ," Jeremy says, feeling really stupid. "I hate when people call me that. Call me Mars instead."

"Mars," Fox says, and it sounds exotic and strange and brave, as if Jeremy has just become a new person, a person named after a whole planet, a person who kisses girls and talks to Foxes.

"I've never stolen anything," Jeremy says.

But Fox has hung up.

Maybe out there, somewhere, is someone who enjoys having to say good-bye, but it isn't anyone that Jeremy knows. All of his friends are grumpy and red-eyed, although not from crying. From lack of sleep. From too much television. There are still faint red stains around Talis's mouth, and if everyone wasn't so tired, they would realize it's Jeremy's lipstick. Karl gives Jeremy a handful of quarters, dimes, nickels, and pennies. "For the slot machines," Karl says. "If you win anything, you can keep a third of what you win."

"Half," Jeremy says, automatically.

"Fine," Karl says. "It's all from your dad's sofas, anyway. Just one more thing. Stop getting taller. Don't get taller while you're gone. Okay." He hugs Jeremy hard: so hard that it's almost like getting punched again. No wonder Talis threw the boa constrictor at Karl.

Talis and Elizabeth both hug Jeremy good-bye. Talis looks even more mysterious now that he's sat with her under a disco ball and made out. Later on, Jeremy will discover that Talis has left her sword under the blue-fur couch and he'll wonder if she left it on purpose.

Talis doesn't say anything and Amy, of course, doesn't shut up, not even when she kisses him. It feels weird to be kissed by someone who goes right on talking while they kiss you, and yet it shouldn't be a surprise that Amy kisses him. He imagines that later Amy and Talis and Elizabeth will all compare notes.

Elizabeth says, "So I promise to tape every episode of *The Library* while you're gone so we can all watch them together when you get back. And I promise I'll call you in Vegas, no matter what time it is there, when there's a new episode."

Her hair is a mess and her breath is faintly sour. Jeremy

wishes he could tell her how beautiful she looks. "I'll write bad poetry and send it to you," he says.

Jeremy's mother is looking hideously cheerful as she goes in and out of the house, making sure that she hasn't left anything behind. She loves long car trips. It doesn't seem to bother her one bit that she and her son are abandoning their entire lives. She passes Jeremy a folder full of maps. "You're in charge of not getting lost," she says. "Put these somewhere safe."

Jeremy says, "I found a library online that I want to go visit. Out in Iowa. They have a corn mosaic on the façade of the building, with a lot of naked goddesses and gods dancing around in a field of corn. Someone wants to take it down. Can we go see it first?"

His mother gives him a pleased, conspiratorial look. "Of course," she says.

Jeremy's father has filled a whole grocery bag with sandwiches. His hair is drooping and he looks even more like an ax murderer than usual. If this were a movie, you'd think that Jeremy and his mother were escaping in the nick of time. "You take care of your mother," he says to Jeremy.

"Sure," Jeremy says. "You take care of yourself."

His dad sags. "You take care of yourself, too." So it's settled. They're all supposed to take care of themselves. Why can't they stay home and take care of each other, until Jeremy is good and ready to go off to college? "I've got another bag of sandwiches in the kitchen," his dad says. "I should go get them."

"Wait," Jeremy says. "I have to ask you something before we take off. Suppose I had to steal something. I mean, I don't have to steal anything, of course, and I know stealing is wrong, even when *you* do it, and I would never steal anything. But what if I did? How do you do it? How do you do it and not get caught?"

His father shrugs. He's probably wondering if Jeremy is really his son. Gordon Mars inherited his mutant, long-fingered, ambidextrous hands from a long line of shoplifters and money launderers and petty criminals. They're all deeply ashamed of Jeremy's father. Gordon Mars had a gift and he threw it away to become a writer. "I don't know," he says. He picks up Jeremy's hand and looks at it as if he's never noticed before that Jeremy had something hanging off the end of his wrist. "You just do it. You do it like you're not really doing anything at all. You do it while you're thinking about something else and you forget that you're doing it."

Jeremy takes his hand back. "I'm not planning on stealing anything. I was just curious."

His father looks at him. "Take care of yourself," he says again, as if he really means it, and hugs Jeremy hard.

Then he goes and gets the sandwiches (so many sandwiches that Jeremy and his mother will eat nothing but sandwiches for the first three days, and still have to throw half of them away). Everyone waves. Jeremy and his mother climb in the van. Jeremy's mother turns on the CD player. Bob Dylan is singing about monkeys. His mother loves Bob Dylan. They drive away.

Do you know how, sometimes, during a commercial break in your favorite television shows, your best friend calls and wants to talk about one of her boyfriends, and when you try to hang up, she starts crying and you try to cheer her up and end up missing about half of the episode? And so when you go to work, or to school the next day, you have to get the guy who sits next to you to explain what happened? That's the good thing about a book. You can mark your place in a book. But this isn't really a book. It's an episode of a television show called *The Library*.

In one episode of *The Library*, an adolescent boy drives across the country with his mother. They have to change a tire. The boy practices taking things out of his mother's purse and putting them back again. He steals a sixteen-ounce bottle of Coke from one convenience market and leaves it at another convenience market. The boy and his mother stop at a lot of libraries, and the boy keeps a blog, but he skips the bit about the library in Iowa. He writes in his blog about what he's reading, but he doesn't read the books he stole in Iowa, because Fox told him not to, and because he has to hide them from his mother. Well, he reads just a few pages. Skims, really. He hides them under the blue-fur sofa. They go camping in Utah, and the boy sets up his telescope. He sees three shooting stars and a coyote. He never sees anyone who looks like a Forbidden Book, although he sees a transvestite go into the women's restroom at a rest stop in Indiana. He calls a phone booth just outside Las Vegas twice, but no one ever answers. He has short conversations with his father. He wonders what his father is up to. He wishes he could tell his father about Fox and the books. Once the boy's mother finds a giant spider the size of an Oreo in their tent. She starts laughing hysterically. She takes a picture of it with her digital camera, and the boy puts the picture on his blog. Sometimes the boy asks questions and his mother talks about her parents. Once she cries. The boy doesn't know what to say. They talk about their favorite episodes of *The Library* and the episodes that they really hated, and the mother asks if the boy thinks Fox is really dead. He says he doesn't think so.

Once a man tries to break into the van while they are sleeping in it. But then he goes away. Maybe the painting of the woman with the peeling knife is protecting them.

But you've seen this episode before.

It's Cinco de Mayo. It's almost seven o'clock at night, and the sun is beginning to go down. Jeremy and his mother are in the desert and Las Vegas is somewhere in front of them. Every time they pass a driver coming the other way, Jeremy tries to figure out if that person has just won or lost a lot of money. Everything is flat and sort of tilted here, except off in the distance, where the land goes up abruptly, as if someone started to fold up a map. Somewhere around here is the Grand Canyon, which must have been a surprise when people first saw it.

Jeremy's mother says, "Are you sure we have to do this first? Couldn't we go find your phone booth later?"

"Can we do it now?" Jeremy says. "I said I was going to do it on my blog. It's like a quest that I have to complete."

"Okay," his mother says. "It should be around here some-where. It's supposed to be four and a half miles after the turn-off, and here's the turn-off."

It isn't hard to find the phone booth. There isn't much else around. Jeremy should feel excited when he sees it, but it's a disappointment, really. He's seen phone booths before. He was expecting something to be different. Mostly he feels tired of road trips and tired of roads and just tired, tired, tired. He looks around to see if Fox is somewhere nearby, but there's just a hiker off in the distance.

"Okay, Germ," his mother says. "Make this quick."

"I need to get my backpack out of the back," Jeremy says.

"Do you want me to come, too?" his mother says.

"No," Jeremy says. "This is kind of personal."

His mother looks like she's trying not to laugh. "Just hurry up. I have to pee."

When Jeremy gets to the phone booth, he turns around. His

mother has the light on in the van. It looks like she's singing along to the radio. His mother has a terrible voice.

When he steps inside the phone booth, it isn't magical. The phone booth smells rank, as if an animal has been living in it. The windows are smudgy. He takes the stolen books out of his backpack and puts them in the little shelf where someone has stolen a phone book. Then he waits. Maybe Fox is going to call him. Maybe he's supposed to wait until she calls. But she doesn't call. He feels lonely. There's no one he can tell about this. He feels like an idiot and he also feels kind of proud. Because he did it. He drove cross-country with his mother and saved an imaginary person.

"So how's your phone booth?" his mother says.

"Great!" he says, and they're both silent again. Las Vegas is in front of them and then all around them and everything is lit up like they're inside a pinball game. All of the trees look fake. Like someone read too much Dr. Seuss and got ideas. People are walking up and down the sidewalks. Some of them look normal. Others look like they just escaped from a fancy-dress ball at a lunatic asylum. Jeremy hopes they've just won lots of money and that's why they look so startled, so strange. Or maybe they're all vampires.

"Left," he tells his mother. "Go left here. Look out for the vampires on the crosswalk. And then it's an immediate right." Four times his mother let him drive the van: once in Utah, twice in South Dakota, once in Pennsylvania. The van smells like old burger wrappers and fake fur, and it doesn't help that Jeremy's gotten used to the smell. The woman in the painting has had a pained expression on her face for the last few nights, and the disco ball has lost some of its pieces of mirror because Jeremy kept knocking his head on it in the morning. Jeremy and his mother haven't showered in three days.

Here is the wedding chapel, in front of them, at the end of a long driveway. Electric purple light shines on a sign that spells out HELL'S BELLS. There's a wrought-iron fence and a yard full of trees dripping Spanish moss. Under the trees, tombstones and miniature mausoleums.

"Do you think those are real?" his mother says. She sounds slightly worried.

"'Harry East, Recently Deceased,'" Jeremy says. "No, I don't."

There's a white hearse in the driveway with a little plaque on the back. *Recently ~~Buried~~ Married.* The chapel is a Victorian house with a bell tower. Perhaps it's full of bats. Or giant spiders. Jeremy's father would love this place. His mother is going to hate it.

Someone stands at the threshold of the chapel, door open, looking out at them. But as Jeremy and his mother get out of the van, he turns and goes inside and shuts the door. His mother says, "They've probably gone to put the boiling oil in the microwave."

She rings the doorbell determinedly. Instead of ringing, there's a recording of a crow. *Caw, caw, caw.* All the lights in the Victorian house go out. Then they turn on again. The door swings open and Jeremy tightens his grip on his backpack, just in case. "Good evening, Madam. Young man," a man says and Jeremy looks up and up and up. The man at the door has to lower his head to look out. His hands are large as toaster ovens. He looks like he's wearing Chihuahua coffins on his feet. Two realistic-looking bolts stick out on either side of his head. He wears green pancake makeup and glittery green eye shadow, and his lashes are as long and thick and green as AstroTurf. "We weren't expecting you so soon."

"We should have called ahead," Jeremy's mother says. "I'm so sorry."

"Great costume," Jeremy says.

The Frankenstein curls his lip in a somber way. "Thank you," he says. "Call me Miss Thing, please."

"I'm Jeremy," Jeremy says. "This is my mother."

"Oh please," Miss Thing says. Even his wink is somehow lugubrious. "You tease me. She isn't old enough to be your mother."

"Oh please, yourself," Jeremy's mother says.

"Quick, the two of you," someone yells from somewhere inside Hell's Bells. "While you zthtand there gabbing, the devil ithz prowling around like a lion, looking for a way to get in. Are you juthzt going to zthtand there and hold the door wide open for him?"

So they all step inside. "Iz that Jeremy Marthz at lathzt?" the voice says. "Earth to Marthz, Earth to Marthz. Marthzzz, Jeremy Marthzzz, there'thz zthomeone on the phone for Jeremy Marthz. She'thz called three timethz in the lathzt ten minutethz, Jeremy Marthzzzz."

It's Fox, Jeremy knows. Of course, it's Fox! She's in the phone booth. She's got the books and she's going to tell me that I saved whatever it is that I was saving. He walks toward the buzzing voice while Miss Thing and his mother go back out to the van.

He hurries past a room full of artfully draped spider webs and candelabras drooping with drippy candles. Someone is playing the organ behind a wooden screen. He goes down the hall and up a long staircase. The banisters are carved with little faces. Owls and foxes and ugly children. The voice goes on talking. "Yoohoo, Jeremy, up the stairthz, that'thz right. Now, come along, come right in! Not in there, in here, in here! Don't mind the dark, we *like* the dark, jutht watch your zthep." Jeremy puts his hand out. He touches something and there's a click and the bookcase in front of him slowly slides back. Now the room is three times as large and there are more bookshelves and there's a young woman wearing dark sunglasses, sitting on a couch. She has a megaphone in one hand and a phone in the other. "For you, Jeremy Marth," she says. She's the palest person Jeremy has ever seen and her two canine teeth are so pointed that she lisps a little when she talks. On the megaphone the lisp was sinister, but now it just makes her sound irritable.

She hands him the phone. "Hello?" he says. He keeps an eye on the vampire.

"Jeremy!" Elizabeth says. "It's on, it's on, it's on! It's just started! We're all just sitting here. Everybody's here. What happened to your cell phone? We kept calling."

"Mom left it at the visitor's center in Zion," Jeremy says.

"Well, you're there. We figured out from your blog that you must be near Vegas. Amy says she had a feeling that you were going to get there in time. She made us keep calling. Stay on the phone, Jeremy. We can all watch it together, okay? Hold on."

Karl grabs the phone. "Hey, Germ, I didn't get any postcards," he says. "You forget how to write or something? Wait a minute. Somebody wants to say something to you." Then he laughs and laughs and passes the phone on to someone else who doesn't say anything at all.

"Talis?" Jeremy says.

Maybe it isn't Talis. Maybe it's Elizabeth again. He thinks about how his mouth is right next to Elizabeth's ear. Or maybe it's Talis's ear.

The vampire on the couch is already flipping through the channels. Jeremy would like to grab the remote away from her, but it's not a good idea to try to take things away from a vampire. His mother and Miss Thing come up the stairs and into the room and suddenly the room seems absolutely full of people, as if Karl and Amy and Elizabeth and Talis have come into the room, too. His hand is getting sweaty around the phone. Miss Thing has a firm hold on Jeremy's mother's painting, as if it might try to escape. Jeremy's mother looks tired. For the past three days her hair has been braided into pigtails. She looks younger to Jeremy, as if they've been traveling backward in time instead of just across the country. She smiles at Jeremy, a giddy, exhausted smile. Jeremy smiles back.

"Is it *The Library?*" Miss Thing says. "Is a new episode on?"

Jeremy sits down on the couch beside the vampire, still holding the phone to his ear. His arm is getting tired.

"I'm here," he says to Talis or Elizabeth or whoever it is on the other end of the phone. "I'm here." And then he sits and doesn't say anything and waits with everyone else for the vampire to find the right channel so they can all find out if he's saved Fox, if Fox is alive, if Fox is still alive.

Faeries live inside it.
I know what that sounds like, but it's true.

THE FAERY HANDBAG

I USED TO go to thrift stores with my friends. We'd take the train into Boston, and go to The Garment District, which is this huge vintage clothing warehouse. Everything is arranged by color, and somehow that makes all of the clothes beautiful. It's kind of like if you went through the wardrobe in the Narnia books, only instead of finding Aslan and the White Witch and horrible Eustace, you found this magic clothing world—instead of talking animals, there were feather boas and wedding dresses and bowling shoes, and paisley shirts and Doc Martens and everything hung up on racks so that first you have black dresses, all together, like the world's largest indoor funeral, and then blue dresses—all the blues you can imagine—and then red dresses and so on. Pink-reds and orangey-reds and purple-reds and exit-light reds and candy reds. Sometimes I'd close my eyes and Natasha and Natalie and Jake would drag me over to a rack, and rub a dress against my hand. "Guess what color this is."

We had this theory that you could learn how to tell, just by feeling, what color something was. For example, if you're sitting on a lawn, you can tell what color green the grass is with your eyes closed, depending on how silky rubbery it feels. With clothing, stretchy velvet stuff always feels red when your eyes are closed, even if it's not red. Natasha was always best at guessing colors, but Natasha is also best at cheating at games and not getting caught.

One time we were looking through kid's T-shirts and we found a Muppets T-shirt that had belonged to Natalie in third grade. We knew it belonged to her, because it still had her name inside, where her mother had written it in permanent marker when Natalie went to summer camp. Jake bought it back for her, because he was the only one who had money that weekend. He was the only one who had a job.

Maybe you're wondering what a guy like Jake is doing in The Garment District with a bunch of girls. The thing about Jake is that he always has a good time, no matter what he's doing. He likes everything, and he likes everyone, but he likes me best of all. Wherever he is now, I bet he's having a great time and wondering when I'm going to show up. I'm always running late. But he knows that.

We had this theory that things have life cycles, the way that people do. The life cycle of wedding dresses and feather boas and T-shirts and shoes and handbags involves The Garment District. If clothes are good, or even if they're bad in an interesting way, The Garment District is where they go when they die. You can tell that they're dead, because of the way that they smell. When you buy them, and wash them, and start wearing them again, and they start to smell like you, that's when they reincarnate. But the point is, if you're looking for a particular thing, you just have to keep looking for it. You have to look hard.

Down in the basement at The Garment District they sell clothing and beat-up suitcases and teacups by the pound. You can get eight pounds worth of prom dresses—a slinky black dress, a poufy lavender dress, a swirly pink dress, a silvery, starry lamé dress so fine you could pass it through a key ring—for eight dollars. I go there every week, hunting for Grandmother Zofia's faery handbag.

The faery handbag: It's huge and black and kind of hairy. Even when your eyes are closed, it feels black. As black as black ever gets, like if you touch it, your hand might get stuck in it, like tar or black quicksand or when you stretch out your hand at night, to turn on a light, but all you feel is darkness.

Faeries live inside it. I know what that sounds like, but it's true.

Grandmother Zofia said it was a family heirloom. She said that it was over two hundred years old. She said that when she died, I had to look after it. Be its guardian. She said that it would be my responsibility.

I said it didn't look that old, and that they didn't have handbags two hundred years ago, but that just made her cross. She said, "So then tell me, Genevieve, darling, where do you think old ladies used to put their reading glasses and their heart medicine and their knitting needles?"

I know no one is going to believe any of this. That's okay. If I thought you would, then I couldn't tell you. Promise me you won't believe a word. That's what Zofia used to say to me when she told me stories. At the funeral, my mother said, half laughing and half crying, that her mother was the world's best liar. I think she thought maybe Zofia wasn't really dead. But I went up to Zofia's coffin, and I looked her right in the eyes. They were closed. The funeral parlor had made her up with blue eye shadow and blue eyeliner. She looked like she was going to be a news anchor on Fox television, instead of dead. It was creepy and it made me even sadder than I already was. But I didn't let that distract me.

"Okay, Zofia," I whispered. "I know you're dead, but this is important. You know exactly how important this is. Where's the handbag? What did you do with it? How do I find it? What am I supposed to do now?"

Of course she didn't say a word. She just lay there, this little smile on her face, as if she thought the whole thing—death, blue eye shadow, Jake, the handbag, fairies, Scrabble, Baldeziwurlekistan, all of it—was a joke. She always did have a weird sense of humor. That's why she and Jake got along so well.

I grew up in a house next door to the house where my mother lived when she was a little girl. Her mother, Zofia Swink, my grandmother, babysat me while my mother and father were at work.

Zofia never looked like a grandmother. She had long black hair which she wore in little braided spiky towers and plaits. She had large blue eyes. She was taller than my father. She looked like a spy or ballerina or a lady pirate or a rock star. She acted like one, too. For example, she never drove anywhere. She rode a bike. It drove my mother crazy. "Why can't you act your age?" she'd say, and Zofia would just laugh.

Zofia and I played Scrabble all the time. Zofia always won, even though her English wasn't all that great, because we'd decided that she was allowed to use Baldeziwurleki vocabulary. Baldeziwurlekistan is where Zofia was born, over two hundred years ago. That's what Zofia said. (My grandmother claimed to be over two hundred years old. Or maybe even older. Sometimes she claimed that she'd even met Genghis Khan. He was much shorter than her. I probably don't have time to tell that story.) Baldeziwurlekistan is also an incredibly valuable word in Scrabble points, even though it doesn't exactly fit on the board. Zofia put it down the first time we played. I was feeling pretty good because I'd gotten forty-one points for "zippery" on my turn.

Zofia kept rearranging her letters on her tray. Then she looked over at me, as if daring me to stop her, and put down "eziwurlekistan," after "bald." She used "delicious," "zippery," "wishes," "kismet," and "needle," and made "to" into "toe." "Baldeziwurlekistan" went all the way across the board and then trailed off down the right-hand side.

I started laughing.

"I used up all my letters," Zofia said. She licked her pencil and started adding up points.

"That's not a word," I said. "Baldeziwurlekistan is not a word. Besides, you can't do that. You can't put an eighteen-letter word on a board that's fifteen squares across."

"Why not? It's a country," Zofia said. "It's where I was born, little darling."

"Challenge," I said. I went and got the dictionary and looked it up. "There's no such place."

"Of course there isn't nowadays," Zofia said. "It wasn't a very big place, even when it was a place. But you've heard of Samarkand, and Uzbekistan and the Silk Road and Genghis Khan. Haven't I told you about meeting Genghis Khan?"

I looked up Samarkand. "Okay," I said. "Samarkand is a real place. A real word. But Baldeziwurlekistan isn't."

"They call it something else now," Zofia said. "But I think it's important to remember where we come from. I think it's only fair that I get to use Baldeziwurleki words. Your English is so much better than me. Promise me something, mouthful of dumpling, a small, small thing. You'll remember its real name. Baldeziwurlekistan. Now when I add it up, I get three hundred and sixty-eight points. Could that be right?"

If you called the faery handbag by its right name, it would be something like "orzipanikanikcz," which means the "bag of skin where the world lives," only Zofia never spelled that word the same way twice. She said you had to spell it a little differently each time. You never wanted to spell it exactly the right way, because that would be dangerous.

I called it the faery handbag because I put "faery" down on the Scrabble board once. Zofia said that you spelled it with an *i* not an *e*. She looked it up in the dictionary, and lost a turn.

Zofia said that in Baldeziwurlekistan they used a board and tiles for divination, prognostication, and sometimes even just for fun. She said it was a little like playing Scrabble. That's probably why she turned out to be so good at Scrabble. The Baldeziwurlekistanians used their tiles and board to communicate with the people who lived under the hill. The people who lived under the hill knew the future. The Baldeziwurlekistanians gave them fermented milk and honey, and the young women of the village used to go and lie out on the hill and sleep under the stars. Apparently the people under the hill were pretty cute. The important thing was that you never went down into the hill and spent the night there, no matter how cute the guy from under the hill was. If you did, even if you only spent a single night under the hill, when you came out again a hundred years might have passed. "Remember that," Zofia said to me. "It doesn't matter how cute a guy is. If he wants you to come back to his place, it isn't a good idea. It's okay to fool around, but don't spend the night."

Every once in a while, a woman from under the hill would marry a man from the village, even though it never ended well. The problem was that the women under the hill were terrible cooks. They couldn't get used to the way time worked in the village, which meant that supper always got burnt, or else it wasn't cooked long enough. But they couldn't stand to be criticized. It hurt their feelings. If their village husband complained, or even if he looked like he wanted to complain, that was it. The woman from under the hill went back to her home, and even if her husband went and begged and pleaded and apologized, it might be three years or thirty years or a few generations before she came back out.

Even the best, happiest marriages between the Baldeziwurle-kistanians and the people under the hill fell apart when the children got old enough to complain about dinner. But everyone in the village had some hill blood in them.

"It's in you," Zofia said, and kissed me on the nose. "Passed down from my grandmother and her mother. It's why we're so beautiful."

When Zofia was nineteen, the shaman-priestess in her village threw the tiles and discovered that something bad was going to happen. A raiding party was coming. There was no point in fighting them. They would burn down everyone's houses and take the young men and women for slaves. And it was even worse than that. There was going to be an earthquake as well, which was bad news because usually, when raiders showed up, the village went down under the hill for a night and when they came out again the raiders would have been gone for months or decades or even a hundred years. But this earthquake was going to split the hill right open.

The people under the hill were in trouble. Their home would be destroyed, and they would be doomed to roam the face of the earth, weeping and lamenting their fate until the sun blew out and the sky cracked and the seas boiled and the people dried up and turned to dust and blew away. So the shaman-priestess went and divined some more, and the people under the hill told her to kill a black dog and skin it and use the skin to make a purse big enough to hold a chicken, an egg, and a cooking pot. So she did, and then the people under the hill made the inside of the purse big enough to hold all of the village and all of the people under the hill and mountains and forests and seas and rivers and lakes and orchards and a sky and stars and spirits and fabulous monsters and sirens and dragons and dryads and mermaids and beasties and all the little gods that the Baldeziwurlekistanians and the people under the hill worshipped.

"Your purse is made out of dog skin?" I said. "That's disgusting!"

"Little dear pet," Zofia said, looking wistful, "dog is delicious. To Baldeziwurlekistanians, dog is a delicacy."

Before the raiding party arrived, the village packed up all of their belongings and moved into the handbag. The clasp was made out of bone. If you opened it one way, then it was just a purse big enough to hold a chicken and an egg and a clay cooking pot, or else a pair of reading glasses and a library book and a pillbox. If you opened the clasp another way, then you found yourself in a little boat floating at the mouth of a river. On either side of you was forest, where the Baldeziwurlekistanian villagers and the people under the hill made their new settlement.

If you opened the handbag the wrong way, though, you found yourself in a dark land that smelled like blood. That's where the guardian of the purse (the dog whose skin had been sewn into a purse) lived. The guardian had no skin. Its howl made blood come out of your ears and nose. It tore apart anyone who turned the clasp in the opposite direction and opened the purse in the wrong way.

"Here is the wrong way to open the handbag," Zofia said. She twisted the clasp, showing me how she did it. She opened the mouth of the purse, but not very wide and held it up to me. "Go ahead, darling, and listen for a second."

I put my head near the handbag, but not too near. I didn't hear anything. "I don't hear anything," I said.

"The poor dog is probably asleep," Zofia said. "Even nightmares have to sleep now and then."

After he got expelled, everybody at school called Jake Houdini instead of Jake. Everybody except for me. I'll explain why, but you have to be patient. It's hard work telling everything in the right order.

Jake is smarter and also taller than most of our teachers. Not quite as tall as me. We've known each other since third grade. Jake has always been in love with me. He says he was in love with me even before third grade, even before we ever met. It took me a while to fall in love with Jake.

In third grade, Jake knew everything already, except how to make friends. He used to follow me around all day long. It made me so mad that I kicked him in the knee. When that didn't work, I threw his backpack out of the window of the school bus. That didn't work either, but the next year Jake took some tests and the school decided that he could skip fourth and fifth grade. Even I felt sorry for Jake then. Sixth grade didn't work out. When the sixth graders wouldn't stop flushing his head down the toilet, he went out and caught a skunk and set it loose in the boy's locker room.

The school was going to suspend him for the rest of the year, but instead Jake took two years off while his mother home-schooled him. He learned Latin and Hebrew and Greek, how to write sestinas, how to make sushi, how to play bridge, and even how to knit. He learned fencing and ballroom dancing. He worked in a soup kitchen and made a Super-8 movie about Civil War reenactors who play extreme croquet in full costume instead of firing off cannons. He started learning how to play guitar. He even wrote a novel. I've never read it—he says it was awful.

When he came back two years later, because his mother had cancer for the first time, the school put him back with our year, in seventh grade. He was still way too smart, but he was finally smart enough to figure out how to fit in. Plus he was good at soccer and he was really cute. Did I mention that he played guitar? Every girl in school had a crush on Jake, but he used to come home after school with me and play Scrabble with Zofia and ask her about Baldeziwurlekistan.

Jake's mom was named Cynthia. She collected ceramic frogs and knock-knock jokes. When we were in ninth grade, she had cancer again. When she died, Jake smashed all of her frogs. That was the first funeral I ever went to. A few months later, Jake's father asked Jake's fencing teacher out on a date. They got married right after the school expelled Jake for his AP project on Houdini. That was the first wedding I ever went to. Jake and I stole a bottle of wine and drank it, and I threw up in the swimming pool at the country club. Jake threw up all over my shoes.

So, anyway, the village and the people under the hill lived happily every after for a few weeks in the handbag, which they had tied around a rock in a dry well which the people under the hill had determined would survive the earthquake. But some of the Baldeziwurlekistanians wanted to come out again and see what was going on in the world. Zofia was one of them. It had been summer when they went into the bag, but when they came out again, and climbed out of the well, snow was falling and their village was ruins and crumbly old rubble. They walked through the snow, Zofia carrying the handbag, until they came to another village, one they'd never seen before. Everyone in that village was packing up their belongings and leaving, which gave Zofia and her friends a bad feeling. It seemed to be just the same as when they went *into* the handbag.

They followed the refugees, who seemed to know where they were going, and finally everyone came to a city. Zofia had never seen such a place. There were trains and electric lights and movie theaters, and there were people shooting each other. Bombs falling. A war was going on. Most of the villagers decided to climb right back inside the handbag, but Zofia volunteered to stay in the world and look after the handbag. She had fallen in love with movies and silk stockings and with a young man, a Russian deserter.

Zofia and the Russian deserter married and had many adventures and finally came to America, where my mother was born. Now and then Zofia would consult the tiles and talk to the people who lived in the handbag and they would tell her how best to avoid trouble and how she and her husband could make some money. Every now and then one of the Baldeziwurlekistanians, or one of the people from under the hill, came out of the handbag and wanted to go grocery shopping, or to a movie or an amusement park to ride on roller coasters, or to the library.

The more advice Zofia gave her husband, the more money they made. Her husband became curious about Zofia's handbag, because he could see that there was something odd about it, but Zofia told him to mind his own business. He began to spy on Zofia, and saw that strange men and women were coming in and out of the house. He became convinced that either Zofia was a spy for the Communists, or that she was having affairs. They fought and he drank more and more, and finally he threw away her divination tiles. "Russians make bad husbands," Zofia told me. Finally, one night while Zofia was sleeping, her husband opened the bone clasp and climbed inside the handbag.

"I thought he'd left me," Zofia said. "For almost twenty years I thought he'd left me and your mother and taken off for California. Not that I minded. I was tired of being married and cooking dinners and cleaning house for someone else. It's better to cook what I want to eat, and clean up when I decide to clean up. It was harder on your mother, not having a father. That was the part that I minded most.

"Then it turned out that he hadn't run away after all. He'd spent one night in the handbag and then come out again twenty years later, exactly as handsome as I remembered, and enough time had passed that I had forgiven him all the quarrels. We made up and it was all very romantic and then, when we had another fight the next morning, he went and kissed your mother, who had slept right through his visit, on the cheek, and climbed right back inside the handbag. I didn't see him again for another twenty years. The last time he showed up, we went to see *Star Wars* and he liked it so much that he went back inside the handbag to tell everyone else about it. In a couple of years they'll all show up and want to see it on DVD and all of the sequels too."

"Tell them not to bother with the prequels," I said.

The thing about Zofia and libraries is that she's always losing library books. She says that she hasn't lost them, and in fact that they aren't even overdue, really. It's just that even one week inside the faery handbag is a lot longer in library-world time. So what is she supposed to do about it? The librarians all hate Zofia. She's banned from using any of the branches in our area. When I was eight, she got me to go to the library for her and check out a bunch of biographies and science books and some Georgette Heyer novels. My mother was livid when she found out, but it was too late. Zofia had already misplaced most of them.

It's really hard to write about somebody as if they're really dead. I still think Zofia must be sitting in her living room, in her house, watching some old horror movie, dropping popcorn into her handbag. She's waiting for me to come over and play Scrabble.

Nobody is ever going to return those library books now.

My mother used to come home from work and roll her eyes. "Have you been telling them your fairy stories?" she'd say. "Genevieve, your grandmother is a horrible liar."

Zofia would fold up the Scrabble board and shrug at me and Jake. "I'm a wonderful liar," she'd say. "I'm the best liar in the world. Promise me you won't believe a single word."

But she wouldn't tell the story of the faery handbag to Jake. Only the old Baldeziwurlekistanian folktales and fairy tales about the people under the hill. She told him about how she and her husband made it all the way across Europe, hiding in haystacks and in barns, and how once, when her husband went off to find food, a farmer found her hiding in his chicken coop and tried to rape her, and how she managed to fight him off. (What she told me was she opened up the faery handbag in the way she'd showed me, and the dog came out and ate the farmer and all his chickens too.)

She was teaching Jake and me how to curse in Baldeziwurleki. I also know how to say I love you, but I'm not going to ever say it to anyone again, except to Jake, when I find him.

When I was eight, I believed everything Zofia told me. By the time I was thirteen, I didn't believe a single word. When I was fifteen, I saw a man come out of her house and get on Zofia's three-speed bicycle and ride down the street. His clothes looked funny. He was a lot younger than my mother and father, and even though I'd never seen him before, he was familiar. I followed him on my bike, all the way to the grocery store. I waited just past the checkout lanes while he bought peanut butter, Jack Daniel's, half a dozen instant cameras, and at least sixty packs of Reese's Peanut Butter Cups, three bags of Hershey's Kisses, a handful of Milky Way bars, and other stuff from the rack of checkout candy. While the checkout clerk was helping him bag up all of that chocolate, he looked up and saw me. "Genevieve?" he said. "That's your name, right?"

I turned and ran out of the store. He grabbed up the bags and ran after me. I don't even think he got his change back. I was still running away, and then one of the straps on my flip-flops popped out of the sole, the way they do, and that made me really angry so I just stopped. I turned around.

"Who are you?" I said.

But I already knew. He looked like he could have been my mom's younger brother. He was really cute. I could see why Zofia had fallen in love with him.

His name was Rustan. Zofia told my parents that he was an expert in Baldeziwurlekistanian folklore who would be staying with her for a few days. She brought him over for dinner. Jake was there too, and I could tell that Jake knew something was up. Everybody except my dad knew something was going on.

"You mean Baldeziwurlekistan is a real place?" my mother asked Rustan. "My mother is telling the truth?"

I could see that Rustan was having a hard time with that one. He obviously wanted to say that his wife was a horrible liar, but then where would he be? Then he couldn't be the person that he was supposed to be.

There were probably a lot of things that he wanted to say. What he said was, "This is really good pizza."

Rustan took a lot of pictures at dinner. The next day I went with him to get the pictures developed. He'd brought back some film with him, with pictures he'd taken inside the faery handbag, but those didn't come out well. Maybe the film was too old. We got doubles of the pictures from dinner so that I could have some too. There's a great picture of Jake, sitting outside on the porch. He's laughing, and he has his hand up to his mouth, like he's going to catch the laugh. I have that picture up on my computer, and also up on my wall over my bed.

I bought a Cadbury Creme Egg for Rustan. Then we shook hands and he kissed me once on each cheek. "Give one of those kisses to your mother," he said, and I thought about how the next time I saw him, I might be Zofia's age, and he would only be a few days older. The next time I saw him, Zofia would be dead. Jake and I might have kids. That was too weird.

I know Rustan tried to get Zofia to go with him, to live in the handbag, but she wouldn't.

"It makes me dizzy in there," she used to tell me. "And they don't have movie theaters. And I have to look after your mother and you. Maybe when you're old enough to look after the handbag, I'll poke my head inside, just long enough for a little visit."

I didn't fall in love with Jake because he was smart. I'm pretty smart myself. I know that smart doesn't mean nice, or even mean that you have a lot of common sense. Look at all the trouble smart people get themselves into.

I didn't fall in love with Jake because he could make maki rolls and had a black belt in fencing, or whatever it is that you get if you're good in fencing. I didn't fall in love with Jake because he plays guitar. He's a better soccer player than he is a guitar player.

Those were the reasons why I went out on a date with Jake. That, and because he asked me. He asked if I wanted to go see a movie, and I asked if I could bring my grandmother and Natalie and Natasha. He said sure and so all five of us sat and watched *Bring It On*, and every once in a while Zofia dropped a couple of Milk Duds or some popcorn into her purse. I don't know if she was feeding the dog, or if she'd opened the purse the right way, and was throwing food at her husband.

I fell in love with Jake because he told stupid knock-knock jokes to Natalie, and told Natasha that he liked her jeans. I fell in love with Jake when he took me and Zofia home. He walked her up to her front door and then he walked me up to mine. I fell in love with Jake when he didn't try to kiss me. The thing is, I was nervous about the whole kissing thing. Most guys think that they're better at it than they really are. Not that I think I'm a real genius at kissing, either, but I don't think kissing should be a competitive sport. It isn't tennis.

Natalie and Natasha and I used to practice kissing with each other. Not that we like each other that way, but just for practice. We got pretty good at it. We could see why kissing was supposed to be fun.

But Jake didn't try to kiss me. Instead he just gave me this really big hug. He put his face in my hair and he sighed. We stood there like that, and then finally I said, "What are you doing?"

"I just wanted to smell your hair," he said.

"Oh," I said. That made me feel weird, but in a good way. I put my nose up to his hair, which is brown and curly, and I smelled it. We stood there and smelled each other's hair, and I felt so good. I felt so happy.

Jake said into my hair, "Do you know that actor John Cusack?"

I said, "Yeah. One of Zofia's favorite movies is *Better Off Dead*. We watch it all the time."

"So he likes to go up to women and smell their armpits."

"Gross!" I said. "That's such a lie! What are you doing now? That tickles."

"I'm smelling your ear," Jake said.

Jake's hair smelled like iced tea with honey in it, after all the ice has melted.

Kissing Jake is like kissing Natalie or Natasha, except that it isn't just for fun. It feels like something there isn't a word for in Scrabble.

The deal with Houdini is that Jake got interested in him during Advanced Placement American History. He and I were both put in tenth grade history. We were doing biography projects. I was studying Joseph McCarthy. My grandmother had all sorts of stories about McCarthy. She hated him for what he did to Hollywood.

Jake didn't turn in his project—instead he told everyone in our AP class except for Mr. Streep (we call him Meryl) to meet him at the gym on Saturday. When we showed up, Jake reenacted one of Houdini's escapes with a laundry bag, handcuffs, a gym locker, bicycle chains, and the school's swimming pool. It took him three and a half minutes to get free, and this guy named Roger took a bunch of photos and then put the photos online. One of the photos ended up in the *Boston Globe*, and Jake got expelled. The really ironic thing was that while his mom was in the hospital, Jake had applied to MIT. He did it for his mom. He thought that way she'd have to stay alive. She was so excited about MIT. A couple of days after he'd been expelled, right after the wedding, while his dad and the fencing instructor were in Bermuda, he got an acceptance letter in the mail and that same afternoon, a phone call from this guy in the admissions office who explained why they had to withdraw the acceptance.

My mother wanted to know why I let Jake wrap himself up in bicycle chains and then watched while Peter and Michael pushed him into the deep end of the school pool. I said that Jake had a backup plan. Ten more seconds and we were all going to jump into the pool and open the locker and get him out of there. I was crying when I said that. Even before he got in the locker, I knew how stupid Jake was being. Afterward, he promised me that he'd never do anything like that again.

That was when I told him about Zofia's husband, Rustan, and about Zofia's handbag. How stupid am I?

So I guess you can figure out what happened next. The problem is that Jake believed me about the handbag. We spent a lot of time over at Zofia's, playing Scrabble. Zofia never let the faery handbag out of her sight. She even took it with her when she went to the bathroom. I think she even slept with it under her pillow.

I didn't tell her that I'd said anything to Jake. I wouldn't ever have told anybody else about it. Not Natasha. Not even Natalie, who is the most responsible person in all of the world. Now, of course, if the handbag turns up and Jake still hasn't come back, I'll have to tell Natalie. Somebody has to keep an eye on the stupid thing while I go find Jake.

What worries me is that maybe one of the Baldeziwurlekistanians or one of the people under the hill or maybe even Rustan popped out of the handbag to run an errand and got worried when Zofia wasn't there. Maybe they'll come looking for her and bring it back. Maybe they know I'm supposed to look after it now. Or maybe they took it and hid it somewhere. Maybe someone turned it in at the lost-and-found at the library and that stupid librarian called the FBI Maybe scientists at the Pentagon are examining the handbag right now. Testing it. If Jake comes out, they'll think he's a spy or a superweapon or an alien or something. They're not going to just let him go.

Everyone thinks Jake ran away, except for my mother, who is convinced that he was trying out another Houdini escape and is probably lying at the bottom of a lake somewhere. She hasn't said that to me, but I can see her thinking it. She keeps making cookies for me.

What happened is that Jake said, "Can I see that for just a second?"

He said it so casually that I think he caught Zofia off guard. She was reaching into the purse for her wallet. We were standing in the lobby of the movie theater on a Monday morning. Jake was behind the snack counter. He'd gotten a job there. He was wearing this stupid red paper hat and some kind of apron-bib thing. He was supposed to ask us if we wanted to supersize our drinks.

He reached over the counter and took Zofia's handbag right out of her hand. He closed it and then he opened it again. I think he opened it the right way. I don't think he ended up in the dark place. He said to me and Zofia, "I'll be right back." And then he wasn't there anymore. It was just me and Zofia and the handbag, lying there on the counter where he'd dropped it.

If I'd been fast enough, I think I could have followed him. But Zofia had been guardian of the faery handbag for a lot longer. She snatched the bag back and glared at me. "He's a very bad boy," she said. She was absolutely furious. "You're better off without him, Genevieve, I think."

"Give me the handbag," I said. "I have to go get him."

"It isn't a toy, Genevieve," she said. "It isn't a game. This isn't Scrabble. He comes back when he comes back. If he comes back."

"Give me the handbag," I said. "Or I'll take it from you."

She held the handbag up high over her head, so that I couldn't reach it. I hate people who are taller than me. "What are you going to do now?" Zofia said. "Are you going to knock me down? Are you going to steal the handbag? Are you going to go away and leave me here to explain to your parents where you've gone? Are you going to say good-bye to your friends? When you come out again, they will have gone to college. They'll have jobs and babies and houses and they won't even recognize you. Your mother will be an old woman and I will be dead."

"I don't care," I said. I sat down on the sticky red carpet in the lobby and started to cry. Someone wearing a little metal name tag came over and asked if we were okay. His name was Missy. Or maybe he was wearing someone else's tag.

"We're fine," Zofia said. "My granddaughter has the flu."

She took my hand and pulled me up. She put her arm around me and we walked out of the theater. We never even got to see the stupid movie. We never got to see another movie together. I don't ever want to go see another movie. The problem is, I don't want to see unhappy endings. And I don't know if I believe in the happy ones.

"I have a plan," Zofia said. "I will go find Jake. You will stay here and look after the handbag."

"You won't come back either," I said. I cried even harder. "Or if you do, I'll be like a hundred years old and Jake will still be sixteen."

"Everything will be okay," Zofia said. I wish I could tell you how beautiful she looked right then. It didn't matter if she was lying or if she actually knew that everything was going to be okay. The important thing was how she looked when she said it. She said, with absolute certainty, or maybe with all the skill of a very skillful liar, "My plan will work. First we go to the library, though. One of the people under the hill just brought back an Agatha Christie mystery, and I need to return it."

"We're going to the library?" I said. "Why don't we just go home and play Scrabble for a while." You probably think I was just being sarcastic here, and I *was* being sarcastic. But Zofia gave me a sharp look. She knew that if I was being sarcastic my brain was working again. She knew that I knew she was stalling for time. She knew that I was coming up with my own plan, which was a lot like Zofia's plan, except that I was the one who went into the handbag. *How* was the part I was working on.

"We could do that," she said. "Remember, when you don't know what to do, it never hurts to play Scrabble. It's like reading the I Ching or tea leaves."

"Can we please just hurry?" I said.

Zofia just looked at me. "Genevieve, we have plenty of time. If you're going to look after the handbag, you have to remember that. You have to be patient. Can you be patient?"

"I can try," I told her. I'm trying, Zofia. I'm trying really hard. But it isn't fair. Jake is off having adventures and talking to talking animals, and who knows, learning how to fly and some beautiful three-thousand-year-old girl from under the hill is teaching him how to speak fluent Baldeziwurleki. I bet she lives in a house that runs around on chicken legs, and she tells Jake that she'd love to hear him play something on the guitar. Maybe you'll kiss her, Jake, because she's put a spell on you. But whatever you do, don't go up into her house. Don't fall asleep in her bed. Come back soon, Jake, and bring the handbag with you.

I hate those movies, those books, where some guy gets to go off and have adventures and meanwhile the girl has to stay home and wait. I'm a feminist. I subscribe to *Bust* magazine, and I watch *Buffy* reruns. I don't believe in that kind of shit.

We hadn't been in the library for five minutes before Zofia picked up a biography of Carl Sagan and dropped it in her purse. She was definitely stalling for time. She was trying to come up with a plan that would counteract the plan that she knew I was planning. I wondered what she thought I was planning. It was probably much better than anything I could come up with.

"Don't do that!" I said.

"Don't worry," Zofia said. "Nobody was watching."

"I don't care if nobody saw! What if Jake's sitting there in the boat, or what if he was coming back and you just dropped it on his head!"

"It doesn't work that way," Zofia said. Then she said, "It would serve him right, anyway."

That was when the librarian came up to us. She had a nametag on as well. I was so sick of people and their stupid nametags. I'm not even going to tell you what her name was. "I saw that," the librarian said.

"Saw what?" Zofia said. She smiled down at the librarian, like she was Queen of the Library, and the librarian were a petitioner.

The librarian stared hard at her. "I know you," she said, almost sounding awed, like she was a weekend birdwatcher who had just seen Bigfoot. "We have your picture on the office wall. You're Ms. Swink. You aren't allowed to check out books here."

"That's ridiculous," Zofia said. She was at least two feet taller than the librarian. I felt a bit sorry for the librarian. After all, Zofia had just stolen a seven-day book. She probably wouldn't return it for a hundred years. My mother has always made it clear that it's my job to protect other people from Zofia. I guess I was Zofia's guardian before I became the guardian of the handbag.

The librarian reached up and grabbed Zofia's handbag. She was small but she was strong. She jerked the handbag and Zofia stumbled and fell back against a work desk. I couldn't believe it. Everyone except for me was getting a look at Zofia's handbag. What kind of guardian was I going to be?

The librarian said, "I saw you put a book in here. Right here." She opened the handbag and peered inside.

"Genevieve," Zofia said. She held my hand very tightly, and I looked at her. She looked wobbly and pale. She said, "I feel very bad about all of this. Tell your mother I said so."

Then she said one last thing, but I think it was in Baldezi-wurleki.

Out of the handbag came a long, lonely, ferocious, utterly hopeless scream of rage. I don't ever want to hear that noise again. Everyone in the library looked up. The librarian made a choking noise and threw Zofia's handbag away from her. A little trickle of blood came out of her nose and a drop fell on the floor. What I thought at first was that it was just plain luck that the handbag was closed when it landed. Later on I was trying to fig-ure out what Zofia said. My Baldeziwurleki isn't very good, but I think she was saying something like "Figures. Stupid librarian. I have to go take care of that damn dog." So maybe that's what happened. Maybe Zofia sent part of herself in there with the skinless dog. Maybe she fought it and won and closed the hand-bag. Maybe she made friends with it. I mean, she used to feed it popcorn at the movies. Maybe she's still in there.

What happened in the library was Zofia sighed a little and closed her eyes. I helped her sit down in a chair, but I don't think she was really there anymore. I rode with her in the ambulance, when the ambulance finally showed up, and I swear I didn't even think about the handbag until my mother showed up. I didn't say a word. I just left her there in the hospital with Zofia, who was on a respirator, and I ran all the way back to the library. But it was closed. So I ran all the way back again, to the hospital, but you already know what happened, right? Zofia died. I hate writing that. My tall, funny, beautiful, book-stealing, Scrabble-playing, story-telling grandmother died.

But you never met her. You're probably wondering about the handbag. What happened to it. I put up signs all over town, like Zofia's handbag was some kind of lost dog, but nobody ever called.

So that's the story so far. Not that I expect you to believe any of it. Last night Natalie and Natasha came over and we played Scrabble. They don't really like Scrabble, but they feel like it's their job to cheer me up. I won. After they went home, I flipped all the tiles upside down and then I started picking them up in groups of seven. I tried to ask a question, but it was hard to pick just one. The words I got weren't so great either, so I decided that they weren't English words. They were Baldeziwurleki words.

Once I decided that, everything became perfectly clear. First I put down "kirif" which means "happy news," and then I got a *b*, an *o*, an *l*, an *e*, an *f*, another *i*, an *s*, and a *z*. So then I could make "kirif" into "bolekirifisz," which could mean "the happy result of a combination of diligent effort and patience."

I would find the faery handbag. The tiles said so. I would work the clasp and go into the handbag and have my own adventures and would rescue Jake. Hardly any time would have gone by before we came back out of the handbag. Maybe I'd even make friends with that poor dog and get to say good-bye, for real, to Zofia. Rustan would show up again and be really sorry that he'd missed Zofia's funeral and this time he would be brave enough to tell my mother the whole story. He would tell her that he was her father. Not that she would believe him. Not that you should believe this story. Promise me that you won't believe a word.

First they played Go Fish, and then they played
Crazy Eights, and then they made the babysitter into
a mummy by putting shaving cream on her arms
and legs, and wrapping her in toilet paper.

The Specialist's Hat

"WHEN YOU'RE DEAD," Samantha says, "you don't have to brush your teeth . . ."

"When you're Dead," Claire says, "you live in a box, and it's always dark, but you're not ever afraid."

Claire and Samantha are identical twins. Their combined age is twenty years, four months, and six days. Claire is better at being Dead than Samantha.

The babysitter yawns, covering up her mouth with a long white hand. "I said to brush your teeth and that it's time for bed," she says. She sits crosslegged on the flowered bedspread between them. She has been teaching them a card game called Pounce, which involves three decks of cards, one for each of them. Samantha's deck is missing the Jack of Spades and the Two of Hearts, and Claire keeps on cheating. The babysitter wins anyway. There are still flecks of dried shaving cream and toilet paper on her arms. It is hard to tell how old she is—at first they thought she must be a grownup, but now she hardly looks older than they. Samantha has forgotten the babysitter's name.

Claire's face is stubborn. "When you're Dead," she says, "you stay up all night long."

"When you're dead," the babysitter snaps, "it's always very cold and damp, and you have to be very, very quiet or else the Specialist will get you."

"This house is haunted," Claire says.

"I know it is," the babysitter says. "I used to live here."

Something is creeping up the stairs,
Something is standing outside the door,
Something is sobbing, sobbing in the dark;
Something is sighing across the floor.

Claire and Samantha are spending the summer with their father, in the house called Eight Chimneys. Their mother is dead. She has been dead for exactly 282 days.

Their father is writing a history of Eight Chimneys and of the poet Charles Cheatham Rash, who lived here at the turn of the century, and who ran away to sea when he was thirteen and returned when he was thirty-eight. He married, fathered a child, wrote three volumes of bad, obscure poetry and an even worse and more obscure novel, *The One Who Is Watching Me Through the Window*, before disappearing again in 1907, this time for good. Samantha and Claire's father says that some of the poetry is actually quite readable and at least the novel isn't very long.

When Samantha asked him why he was writing about Rash, he replied that no one else had and why didn't she and Samantha go play outside. When she pointed out that she was Samantha, he just scowled and said how could he be expected to tell them apart when they both wore blue jeans and flannel shirts, and why couldn't one of them dress all in green and the other in pink?

Claire and Samantha prefer to play inside. Eight Chimneys is as big as a castle, but dustier and darker than Samantha imagines a castle would be. There are more sofas, more china shepherdesses with chipped fingers, fewer suits of armor. No moat.

The house is open to the public, and, during the day, people—families—driving along the Blue Ridge Parkway will stop to tour the grounds and the first story; the third story belongs to Claire and Samantha. Sometimes they play explorers, and sometimes they follow the caretaker as he gives tours to visitors. After a few weeks, they have memorized his lecture, and they mouth it along with him. They help him sell postcards and copies of Rash's poetry to the tourist families who come into the little gift shop.

When the mothers smile at them and say how sweet they are, they stare back and don't say anything at all. The dim light in the house makes the mothers look pale and flickery and tired. They leave Eight Chimneys, mothers and families, looking not quite as real as they did before they paid their admissions, and of course Claire and Samantha will never see them again, so maybe they aren't real. Better to stay inside the house, they want to tell the families, and if you must leave, then go straight to your cars.

The caretaker says the woods aren't safe.

Their father stays in the library on the second story all morning, typing, and in the afternoon he takes long walks. He takes his pocket recorder along with him and a hip flask of Gentleman Jack, but not Samantha and Claire.

The caretaker of Eight Chimneys is Mr. Coeslak. His left leg is noticeably shorter than his right. He wears one stacked heel. Short black hairs grow out of his ears and his nostrils and there is no hair at all on top of his head, but he's given Samantha and Claire permission to explore the whole of the house. It was Mr. Coeslak who told them that there are copperheads in the woods, and that the house is haunted. He says they are all, ghosts and snakes, a pretty bad-tempered lot, and Samantha and Claire should stick to the marked trails, and stay out of the attic.

Mr. Coeslak can tell the twins apart, even if their father can't; Claire's eyes are grey, like a cat's fur, he says, but Samantha's are *gray*, like the ocean when it has been raining.

Samantha and Claire went walking in the woods on the second day that they were at Eight Chimneys. They saw something. Samantha thought it was a woman, but Claire said it was a snake. The staircase that goes up to the attic has been locked. They peeked through the keyhole, but it was too dark to see anything.

And so he had a wife, and they say she was real pretty. There was another man who wanted to go with her, and first she wouldn't, because she was afraid of her husband, and then she did. Her husband found out, and they say he killed a snake and got some of this snake's blood and put it in some whiskey and gave it to her. He had learned this from an island man who had been on a ship with him. And in about six months snakes created in her and they got between her meat and the skin. And they say you could just see them running up and down her legs. They say she was just hollow to the top of her body, and it kept on like that till she died. Now my daddy said he saw it.

—An Oral History of Eight Chimneys

Eight Chimneys is over two hundred years old. It is named for the eight chimneys that are each big enough that Samantha and Claire can both fit in one fireplace. The chimneys are red brick, and on each floor there are eight fireplaces, making a total of twenty-four. Samantha imagines the chimney stacks stretching like stout red tree trunks, all the way up through the slate roof of the house. Beside each fireplace is a black firedog and a set of wrought iron pokers shaped like snakes. Claire and Samantha pretend to duel with the snake-pokers before the fireplace in their bedroom on the third floor. Wind rises up the back of the chimney. When they stick their faces in, they can feel the air rushing damply upwards. The flue smells old and sooty and wet, like stones from a river.

Their bedroom was once the nursery. They sleep together in a poster bed that resembles a ship with four masts. It smells of mothballs, and Claire kicks in her sleep. Charles Cheatham Rash slept here when he was a little boy, and also his daughter. She disappeared when her father did. It might have been gambling debts. They may have moved to New Orleans. She was fourteen years old, Mr. Coeslak said. What was her name, Claire asked. What happened to her mother, Samantha wanted to know. Mr. Coeslak closed his eyes in an almost wink. Mrs. Rash had died the year before her husband and daughter disappeared, he said, of a mysterious wasting disease. He can't remember the name of the poor little girl, he said.

Eight Chimneys has exactly one hundred windows, all still with the original wavery panes of handblown glass. With so many windows, Samantha thinks, Eight Chimneys should always be full of light, but instead the trees press close against the house, so that the rooms on the first and second story—even the third-story rooms—are green and dim, as if Samantha and Claire are living deep under the sea. This is the light that makes the tourists into ghosts. In the morning, and again towards evening, a fog settles in around the house. Sometimes it is grey like Claire's eyes, and sometimes it is gray, like Samantha's eyes.

I met a woman in the wood,
Her lips were two red snakes.
She smiled at me, her eyes were lewd
And burning like a fire.

A few nights ago, the wind was sighing in the nursery chimney. Their father had already tucked them in and turned off the light. Claire dared Samantha to stick her head into the fireplace, in the dark, and so she did. The cold wet air licked at her face and it almost sounded like voices talking low, muttering. She couldn't quite make out what they were saying.

Their father has mostly ignored Claire and Samantha since they arrived at Eight Chimneys. He never mentions their mother. One evening they heard him shouting in the library, and when they came downstairs, there was a large sticky stain on the desk, where a glass of whiskey had been knocked over. It was looking at me, he said, through the window. It had orange eyes.

Samantha and Claire refrained from pointing out that the library is on the second story.

At night, their father's breath has been sweet from drinking, and he is spending more and more time in the woods, and less in the library. At dinner, usually hot dogs and baked beans from a can, which they eat off of paper plates in the first floor dining room, beneath the Austrian chandelier (which has exactly 632 leaded crystals shaped like teardrops) their father recites the poetry of Charles Cheatham Rash, which neither Samantha nor Claire cares for.

He has been reading the ship diaries that Rash kept, and he says he has discovered proof in them that Rash's most famous poem, "The Specialist's Hat," is not a poem at all, and in any case, Rash didn't write it. It is something one of the men on the whaler used to say, to conjure up a whale. Rash simply copied it down and stuck an end on it and said it was his.

The man was from Mulatuppu, which is a place neither Samantha nor Claire has ever heard of. Their father says that the man was supposed to be some sort of magician, but he drowned shortly before Rash came back to Eight Chimneys. Their father says that the other sailors wanted to throw the magician's chest overboard, but Rash persuaded them to let him keep it until he could be put ashore, with the chest, off the coast of North Carolina.

> *The specialist's hat makes a noise like an agouti;*
> *The specialist's hat makes a noise like a collared peccary;*
> *The specialist's hat makes a noise like a white-lipped peccary;*
> *The specialist's hat makes a noise like a tapir;*
> *The specialist's hat makes a noise like a rabbit;*
> *The specialist's hat makes a noise like a squirrel;*
> *The specialist's hat makes a noise like a curassow;*
> *The specialist's hat moans like a whale in the water;*
> *The specialist's hat moans like the wind in my wife's hair;*
> *The specialist's hat makes a noise like a snake;*
> *I have hung the hat of the specialist upon my wall.*

The reason that Claire and Samantha have a babysitter is that their father met a woman in the woods. He is going to see her tonight, and they are going to have a picnic supper and look at the stars. This is the time of year when the Perseids can be seen, falling across the sky on clear nights. Their father said that he has been walking with the woman every afternoon. She is a distant relation of Rash and besides, he said, he needs a night off and some grownup conversation.

Mr. Coeslak won't stay in the house after dark, but he agreed to find someone to look after Samantha and Claire. Then their father couldn't find Mr. Coeslak, but the babysitter showed up precisely at seven o'clock. The babysitter, whose name neither twin quite caught, wears a blue cotton dress with short floaty sleeves. Both Samantha and Claire think she is pretty in an old-fashioned sort of way.

They were in the library with their father, looking up Mulatuppu in the red leather atlas, when she arrived. She didn't knock on the front door, she simply walked in and then up the stairs, as if she knew where to find them.

Their father kissed them good-bye, a hasty smack, told them to be good and he would take them into town on the weekend to see the Disney film. They went to the window to watch as he walked into the woods. Already it was getting dark and there were fireflies, tiny yellow-hot sparks in the air. When their father had entirely disappeared into the trees, they turned around and stared at the babysitter instead. She raised one eyebrow. "Well," she said. "What sort of games do you like to play?"

Widdershins around the chimneys,
Once, twice, again.
The spokes click like a clock on the bicycle;
They tick down the days of the life of a man.

First they played Go Fish, and then they played Crazy Eights, and then they made the babysitter into a mummy by putting shaving cream from their father's bathroom on her arms and legs, and wrapping her in toilet paper. She is the best babysitter they have ever had.

At nine-thirty, she tried to put them to bed. Neither Claire nor Samantha wanted to go to bed, so they began to play the Dead game. The Dead game is a let's pretend that they have been playing every day for 274 days now, but never in front of their father or any other adult. When they are Dead, they are allowed to do anything they want to. They can even fly by jumping off the nursery bed and just waving their arms. Someday this will work, if they practice hard enough.

The Dead game has three rules.

One. Numbers are significant. The twins keep a list of important numbers in a green address book that belonged to their mother. Mr. Coeslak's tour has been a good source of significant amounts and tallies: they are writing a tragical history of numbers.

Two. The twins don't play the Dead game in front of grown-ups. They have been summing up the babysitter, and have decided that she doesn't count. They tell her the rules.

Three is the best and most important rule. When you are Dead, you don't have to be afraid of anything. Samantha and Claire aren't sure who the Specialist is, but they aren't afraid of him.

To become Dead, they hold their breath while counting to 35, which is as high as their mother got, not counting a few days.

"You never lived here," Claire says. "Mr. Coeslak lives here."

"Not at night," says the babysitter. "This was my bedroom when I was little."

"Really?" Samantha says. Claire says, "Prove it."

The babysitter gives Samantha and Claire a look, as if she is measuring them: how old, how smart, how brave, how tall. Then she nods. The wind is in the flue, and in the dim nursery light they can see the milky strands of fog seeping out of the fireplace.

"Go stand in the chimney," she instructs them. "Stick your hand as far up as you can, and there is a little hole on the left side, with a key in it."

Samantha looks at Claire, who says, "Go ahead." Claire is fifteen minutes and some few uncounted seconds older than Samantha, and therefore gets to tell Samantha what to do. Samantha remembers the muttering voices and then reminds herself that she is Dead. She goes over to the fireplace and ducks inside.

When Samantha stands up in the chimney, she can only see the very edge of the room. She can see the fringe of the mothy blue rug, and one bed leg, and beside it, Claire's foot, swinging back and forth like a metronome. Claire's shoelace has come undone and there is a Band-Aid on her ankle. It all looks very pleasant and peaceful from inside the chimney, like a dream, and for a moment she almost wishes she didn't have to be Dead. But it's safer, really.

She sticks her left hand up as far as she can reach, trailing it along the crumbly wall, until she feels an indentation. She thinks about spiders and severed fingers, and rusty razorblades, and then she reaches inside. She keeps her eyes lowered, focused on the corner of the room and Claire's twitchy foot.

Inside the hole, there is a tiny cold key, its teeth facing outward. She pulls it out, and ducks back into the room. "She wasn't lying," she tells Claire.

"Of course I wasn't lying," the babysitter says. "When you're Dead, you're not allowed to tell lies."

"Unless you want to," Claire says.

Dreary and dreadful beats the sea at the shore.
Ghastly and dripping is the mist at the door.
The clock in the hall is chiming one, two, three, four.
The morning comes not, no, never, no more.

Samantha and Claire have gone to camp for three weeks every summer since they were seven. This year their father didn't ask them if they wanted to go back and, after discussing it, they decided that it was just as well. They didn't want to have to explain to all their friends how they were half-orphans now. They are used to being envied, because they are identical twins. They don't want to be pitiful.

It has not even been a year, but Samantha realizes that she is forgetting what her mother looked like. Not her mother's face so much as the way she smelled, which was something like dry hay and something like Chanel No. 5, and like something else too. She can't remember whether her mother had gray eyes, like her, or grey eyes, like Claire. She doesn't dream about her mother anymore, but she does dream about Prince Charming, a bay whom she once rode in the horse show at her camp. In the dream, Prince Charming did not smell like a horse at all. He smelled like Chanel No. 5. When she is Dead, she can have all the horses she wants, and they all smell like Chanel No. 5.

"Where does the key go to?" Samantha says.

The babysitter holds out her hand. "To the attic. You don't really need it, but taking the stairs is easier than the chimney. At least the first time."

"Aren't you going to make us go to bed?" Claire says.

The babysitter ignores Claire. "My father used to lock me in the attic when I was little, but I didn't mind. There was a bicycle up there and I used to ride it around and around the chimneys until my mother let me out again. Do you know how to ride a bicycle?"

"Of course," Claire says.

"If you ride fast enough, the Specialist can't catch you."

"What's the Specialist?" Samantha says. Bicycles are okay, but horses can go faster.

"The Specialist wears a hat," says the babysitter. "The hat makes noises."

She doesn't say anything else.

When you're dead, the grass is greener
Over your grave. The wind is keener.
Your eyes sink in, your flesh decays. You
Grow accustomed to slowness; expect delays.

The attic is somehow bigger and lonelier than Samantha and Claire thought it would be. The babysitter's key opens the locked door at the end of the hallway, revealing a narrow set of stairs. She waves them ahead and upwards.

It isn't as dark in the attic as they had imagined. The oaks that block the light and make the first three stories so dim and green and mysterious during the day don't reach all the way up. Extravagant moonlight, dusty and pale, streams in the angled dormer windows. It lights the length of the attic, which is wide enough to hold a softball game in, and lined with trunks where Samantha imagines people could sit, could be hiding and watching. The ceiling slopes down, impaled upon the eight thick-waisted chimney stacks. The chimneys seem too alive, somehow, to be contained in this empty, neglected place; they thrust almost angrily through the roof and attic floor. In the moonlight they look like they are breathing. "They're so beautiful," she says.

"Which chimney is the nursery chimney?" Claire says.

The babysitter points to the nearest right-hand stack. "That one," she says. "It runs up through the ballroom on the first floor, the library, the nursery."

Hanging from a nail on the nursery chimney is a long black object. It looks lumpy and heavy, as if it were full of things. The babysitter takes it down, twirls it on her finger. There are holes in the black thing and it whistles mournfully as she spins it. "The Specialist's hat," she says.

"That doesn't look like a hat," says Claire. "It doesn't look like anything at all." She goes to look through the boxes and trunks that are stacked against the far wall.

"It's a special hat," the babysitter says. "It's not supposed to look like anything. But it can sound like anything you can imagine. My father made it."

"Our father writes books," Samantha says.

"My father did too." The babysitter hangs the hat back on the nail. It curls blackly against the chimney. Samantha stares at it. It nickers at her. "He was a bad poet, but he was worse at magic."

Last summer, Samantha wished more than anything that she could have a horse. She thought she would have given up anything for one—even being a twin was not as good as having a horse. She still doesn't have a horse, but she doesn't have a mother either, and she can't help wondering if it's her fault. The hat nickers again, or maybe it is the wind in the chimney.

"What happened to him?" Claire asks.

"After he made the hat, the Specialist came and took him away. I hid in the nursery chimney while it was looking for him, and it didn't find me."

"Weren't you scared?"

There is a clattering, shivering, clicking noise. Claire has found the babysitter's bike and is dragging it towards them by the handlebars. The babysitter shrugs. "Rule number three," she says.

Claire snatches the hat off the nail. "I'm the Specialist!" she says, putting the hat on her head. It falls over her eyes, the floppy shapeless brim sewn with little asymmetrical buttons that flash and catch at the moonlight like teeth. Samantha looks again and sees that they are teeth. Without counting, she suddenly knows that there are exactly 52 teeth on the hat, and that they are the teeth of agoutis, of coatimundis, of white-lipped peccaries, and of the wife of Charles Cheatham Rash. The chimneys are moaning, and Claire's voice booms hollowly beneath the hat. "Run away, or I'll catch you. I'll eat you!"

Samantha and the babysitter run away, laughing as Claire mounts the rusty, noisy bicycle and pedals madly after them. She rings the bicycle bell as she rides, and the Specialist's hat bobs up and down on her head. It spits like a cat. The bell is shrill and thin, and the bike wails and shrieks. It leans first towards the right and then to the left. Claire's knobby knees stick out on either side like makeshift counterweights.

Claire weaves in and out between the chimneys, chasing Samantha and the babysitter. Samantha is slow, turning to look behind. As Claire approaches, she keeps one hand on the handlebars and stretches the other hand out towards Samantha. Just as she is about to grab Samantha, the babysitter turns back and plucks the hat off Claire's head.

"Shit!" the babysitter says, and drops it. There is a drop of blood forming on the fleshy part of the babysitter's hand, black in the moonlight, where the Specialist's hat has bitten her.

Claire dismounts, giggling. Samantha watches as the Specialist's hat rolls away. It picks up speed, veering across the attic floor, and disappears, thumping down the stairs. "Go get it," Claire says. "You can be the Specialist this time."

"No," the babysitter says, sucking at her palm. "It's time for bed."

When they go down the stairs, there is no sign of the Specialist's hat. They brush their teeth, climb into the ship-bed, and pull the covers up to their necks. The babysitter sits between their feet. "When you're Dead," Samantha says, "do you still get tired and have to go to sleep? Do you have dreams?"

"When you're Dead," the babysitter says, "everything's a lot easier. You don't have to do anything that you don't want to. You don't have to have a name, you don't have to remember. You don't even have to breathe."

She shows them exactly what she means.

When she has time to think about it (and now she has all the time in the world to think), Samantha realizes with a small pang that she is now stuck indefinitely between ten and eleven years old, stuck with Claire and the babysitter. She considers this. The number 10 is pleasing and round, like a beach ball, but all in all, it hasn't been an easy year. She wonders what 11 would have been like. Sharper, like needles maybe. She has chosen to be Dead, instead. She hopes that she's made the right decision. She wonders if her mother would have decided to be Dead, instead of dead, if she could have.

Last year they were learning fractions in school, when her mother died. Fractions remind Samantha of herds of wild horses, piebalds and pintos and palominos. There are so many of them, and they are, well, fractious and unruly. Just when you think you have one under control, it throws up its head and tosses you off. Claire's favorite number is 4, which she says is a tall, skinny boy. Samantha doesn't care for boys that much. She likes numbers. Take the number 8 for instance, which can be more than one thing at once. Looked at one way, 8 looks like a bent woman with curvy hair. But if you lay it down on its side, it looks like a snake curled with its tail in its mouth. This is sort of like the difference between being Dead, and being dead. Maybe when Samantha is tired of one, she will try the other.

On the lawn, under the oak trees, she hears someone calling her name. Samantha climbs out of bed and goes to the nursery window. She looks out through the wavy glass. It's Mr. Coeslak. "Samantha, Claire!" he calls up to her. "Are you all right? Is your father there?" Samantha can almost see the moonlight shining through him. "They're always locking me in the tool room. Goddamn spooky things," he says. "Are you there, Samantha? Claire? Girls?"

The babysitter comes and stands beside Samantha. The babysitter puts her finger to her lip. Claire's eyes glitter at them from the dark bed. Samantha doesn't say anything, but she waves at Mr. Coeslak. The babysitter waves too. Maybe he can see them waving, because after a little while he stops shouting and goes away. "Be careful," the babysitter says. "*He'll* be coming soon. It will be coming soon."

She takes Samantha's hand and leads her back to the bed, where Claire is waiting. They sit and wait. Time passes, but they don't get tired, they don't get any older.

Who's there?
Just air.

The front door opens on the first floor, and Samantha, Claire, and the babysitter can hear someone creeping, creeping up the stairs. "Be quiet," the babysitter says. "It's the Specialist."

Samantha and Claire are quiet. The nursery is dark and the wind crackles like a fire in the fireplace.

"Claire, Samantha, Samantha, Claire?" The Specialist's voice is blurry and wet. It sounds like their father's voice, but that's because the hat can imitate any noise, any voice. "Are you still awake?"

"Quick," the babysitter says. "It's time to go up to the attic and hide."

Claire and Samantha slip out from under the covers and dress quickly and silently. They follow her. Without speech, without breathing, she pulls them into the safety of the chimney. It is too dark to see, but they understand the babysitter perfectly when she mouths the word, *Up*. She goes first, so they can see where the finger-holds are, the bricks that jut out for their feet. Then Claire. Samantha watches her sister's foot ascend like smoke, the shoelace still untied.

"Claire? Samantha? Goddammit, you're scaring me. Where are you?" The Specialist is standing just outside the half-open door. "Samantha? I think I've been bitten by something. I think I've been bitten by a goddamn snake." Samantha hesitates for only a second. Then she is climbing up, up, up the nursery chimney.

After a while, everyone had become a zombie.
So they went for a swim.

MONSTER

NO ONE IN Bungalow 6 wanted to go camping. It was raining, which meant that you had to wear garbage bags over your backpacks and around the sleeping bags, and even that wouldn't help. The sleeping bags would still get wet. Some of the wet sleeping bags would then smell like pee, and the tents already smelled like mildew, and even if they got the tents up, water would collect on the ground cloths. There would be three boys to a tent, and only the boy in the middle would stay dry. The other two would inevitably end up squashed against the sides of the tent, and wherever you touched the nylon, water would come through from the outside.

Besides, someone in Bungalow 4 had seen a monster in the woods. Bungalow 4 had been telling stories ever since they got back. It was a no-win situation for Bungalow 6. If Bungalow 6 didn't see the monster, Bungalow 4 would keep the upper hand that fate had dealt them. If Bungalow 6 did see a monster—but who wanted to see a monster, even if it meant that you got to tell everyone about it? Not anyone in Bungalow 6, except for James Lorbick, who thought that monsters were awesome. But James Lorbick was a geek and from Chicago and he had a condition that made his feet smell terrible. That was another thing about camping. Someone would have to share a tent with James Lorbick and his smelly feet.

And even if Bungalow 6 did see the monster, well, Bungalow 4 had seen it first, so there was nothing special about that, seeing a monster after Bungalow 4 went and saw it first. And maybe Bungalow 4 had pissed off that monster. Maybe that monster was just waiting for more kids to show up at Honor Lookout where all the pine trees leaned backwards in a circle around the bald hump of the hill in a way that made you feel dizzy when you lay around the fire at night and looked up at them.

"There wasn't any monster," Bryan Jones said, "and anyway if there was a monster, I bet it ran away when it saw Bungalow 4." Everybody nodded. What Bryan Jones said made sense. Everybody knew that the kids in Bungalow 4 were so mean that they had made their counselor cry like a girl. The Bungalow 4 counselor was a twenty-year-old college student named Eric who had terrible acne and wrote poems about the local girls who worked in the kitchen and how their breasts looked lonely but also beautiful, like melted ice cream. The kids in Bungalow 4 had found the poetry and read it out loud at morning assembly in front of everybody, including some of the kitchen girls.

Bungalow 4 had sprayed a bat with insect spray and then set fire to it and almost burned down the whole bungalow.

And there were worse stories about Bungalow 4.

Everyone said that the kids in Bungalow 4 were so mean that

their parents sent them off to camp just so they wouldn't have to see them for a few weeks.

"I heard that the monster had big black wings," Colin Simpson said. "Like a vampire. It flapped around and it had these long fingernails."

"I heard it had lots of teeth."

"I heard it bit Barnhard."

"I heard he tasted so bad that the monster puked after it bit him."

"I saw Barnhard last night at dinner," Colin Simpson's twin brother said. Or maybe it was Colin Simpson who said that and the kid who was talking about flapping and fingernails was the other twin. Everybody had a hard time telling them apart. "He had a Band-Aid on the inside of his arm. He looked kind of weird. Kind of pale."

"Guys," their counselor said. "Hey guys. Enough talk. Let's pack up and get going." The Bungalow 6 counselor was named Terence, but he was pretty cool. All of the kitchen girls hung around Bungalow 6 to talk to Terence, even though he was already going out with a girl from Ohio who was six foot two and played basketball. Sometimes before he turned out the lights, Terence would read them letters that the girl from Ohio had written. There was a picture over Terence's camp bed of this girl sitting on an elephant in Thailand. The girl's name was Darlene. Nobody knew the elephant's name.

"We can't just sit here all day," Terence said. "Chop chop."

Everyone started complaining.

"I know it's raining," Terence said. "But there are only three more days of camp left and if we want our overnight badges, this is our last chance. Besides it could stop raining. And not that you should care, but everyone in Bungalow 4 will say that you got scared and that's why you didn't want to go. And I don't want everyone to think that Bungalow 6 is afraid of some stupid Bungalow 4 story about some stupid monster."

It didn't stop raining. Bungalow 6 didn't exactly hike; they waded. They splashed. They slid down hills. The rain came down in clammy, cold, sticky sheets. One of the Simpson twins put his foot down at the bottom of a trail and the mud went up all the way to his knee and pulled his tennis shoe right off with a loud sucking noise. So they had to stop while Terence lay down in the mud and stuck his arm down, fishing for the Simpson twin's shoe.

Bryan Jones stood next to Terence and held out his shirt so the rain wouldn't fall in Terence's ear. Bryan Jones was from North Carolina. He was a big tall kid with a friendly face, who liked paint guns and BB guns and laser guns and pulling down his pants and mooning people and putting hot sauce on toothbrushes.

Sometimes he'd sit on top of James Lorbick's head and fart, but everybody knew it was just Bryan being funny, except for James Lorbick. James Lorbick hated Bryan even more than he hated the kids in Bungalow 4. Sometimes James pretended that Bryan Jones's parents died in some weird accident while camp was still going on and that no one knew what to say to Bryan and so they avoided him until James came up to Bryan and said exactly the right thing and made Bryan feel better, although of course he wouldn't really feel better, he'd just appreciate what James had said to him, whatever it was that James had said. And of course then Bryan would feel bad about sitting on James's head all those times. And then they'd be friends. Everybody wanted to be friends with Bryan Jones, even James Lorbick.

The first thing that Terence pulled up out of the mud wasn't the Simpson twin's shoe. It was long and round and knobby. When Terence knocked it against the ground, some of the mud slid off.

"Hey. Wow," James Lorbick said. "That looks like a bone."

Everybody stood in the rain and looked at the bone.

"What is that?"

"Is it human?"

"Maybe it's a dinosaur," James Lorbick said. "Like a fossil."

"Probably a cow bone," Terence said. He poked the bone back in the mud and fished around until it got stuck in something that turned out to be the lost shoe. The Simpson twin took the shoe as if he didn't really want it back. He turned it upside down and mud oozed out like lonely, melting soft-serve ice cream.

Half of Terence was now covered in mud, although at least, thanks to Bryan Jones, he didn't have water in his ear. He held the dubious bone as if he was going to toss it off in the bushes, but then he stopped and looked at it again. He put it in the pocket of his rain jacket instead. Half of it stuck out. It didn't look like a cow bone.

By the time they got to Honor Lookout, the rain had stopped. "See?" Terence said. "I told you." He said it as if now they were fine. Now everything would be fine. Water plopped off the needles of the pitiful pine trees that leaned eternally away from the campground on Honor Lookout.

Bungalow 6 gathered wood that would be too wet to use for a fire. They unpacked their tents and tent poles and tent pegs, which descended into the sucking mud and disappeared forever. They laid out their tents on top of ground cloths on top of the sucking, quivering, nearly animate mud. It was like putting a tent up over chocolate pudding. The floor of the tents sank below the level of the mud when they crawled inside. It was hard to imagine sleeping in the tents. You might just keep on sinking.

"Hey," Bryan Jones said, "look out! Snowball fight!" He lobbed a brown mudball which hit James Lorbick just under the chin and splashed up on James's glasses. Then everyone was throwing mudballs, even Terence. James Lorbick even threw one. There was nothing else to do.

When they got hungry, they ate cold hot dogs for lunch while the mud dried and cracked and fell off their arms and legs and faces. They ate graham crackers with marshmallows and chocolate squares and Terence even toasted the marshmallows with a cigarette lighter for anyone who wanted. Since they couldn't make a fire, they made mud sculptures instead. Terence sculpted an elephant and a girl on top. The elephant even looked like an elephant. But then one of the Simpson twins sculpted an atom bomb and dropped it on Terence's elephant and Terence's girlfriend.

"That's okay," Terence said. "That's cool." But it wasn't cool. He went and sat on a muddy rock and looked at his bone.

The twins had made a whole stockpile of atom bombs out of mud. They decided to make a whole city with walls and buildings and everything. Some of the other kids from Bungalow 6 helped with the city so that the twins could bomb the city before it got too dark.

Bryan Jones had put mud in his hair and twisted it up in muddy spikes. There was mud in his eyebrows. He looked like an idiot, but that didn't matter, because he was Bryan Jones and anything that Bryan Jones did wasn't stupid. It was cool. "Hey man," he said to James. "Come and see what I stole off the clothes line at camp."

James Lorbick was muddy and tired and maybe his feet did

smell bad, but he was smarter than most of the kids in Bungalow
6. "Why?" he said.

"Just come on," Bryan said. "I don't want anyone else to see
this yet."

"Okay," James said.

It was a dress. It had big blue flowers on it, and James Lorbick got a bad feeling.

"Why did you steal a dress?" he said.

Bryan shrugged. He was smiling as if the whole idea of a
dress made him happy. It was a big, happy, contagious smile,
but James Lorbick didn't smile back. "Because it will be funny,"
Bryan said. "Put it on and we'll go show everybody."

"No way," James said. He folded his muddy arms over his
muddy chest to show he was serious.

"I *dare* you," Bryan said. "Come on, James, before everybody
comes over here and sees it. Everybody will laugh."

"I know they will," James said. "No."

"Look, I'd put it on, I swear, but it wouldn't fit me. No way
would it fit. So you've got to do it. Just do it, James."

"No," James said.

James Lorbick wasn't sure why his parents had sent him off to
a camp in North Carolina. He hadn't wanted to go. It wasn't
as if there weren't trees in Chicago. It wasn't as if James didn't
have friends in Chicago. Camp just seemed to be one of those
things parents could make you do, like violin lessons, or karate,
except that camp lasted a whole month. Plus, he was supposed to
be thankful about it, like his parents had done him a big favor.
Camp cost money.

So he made leather wallets in arts and crafts, and went swimming every other day, even though the lake smelled funny and

the swim instructor was kind of weird and liked to make the campers stand on the high diving board with their eyes closed. Then he'd creep up and push them into the water. Not that you didn't know he was creeping up. You could feel the board wobbling.

He didn't make friends. But that wasn't true, exactly. James was friendly, but nobody in Bungalow 6 was friendly back. Sometimes right after Terence turned out the lights, someone would say, "James, oh, James, your hair looked really excellent today" or "James, James Lorbick, I wish I were as good at archery as you" or "James, will you let me borrow your water canteen tomorrow?" and then everyone would laugh while James pretended to be asleep, until Terence would flick on the lights and say, "Leave James alone—go to sleep or I'll give everyone five demerits."

James Lorbick knew it could have been worse. He could have been in Bungalow 4 instead of Bungalow 6.

At least the dress wasn't muddy. Bryan let him keep his jeans and T-shirt on. "Let me do your hair," Bryan said. He picked up a handful of mud and pushed it around on James's head until James had sticky mud hair just like Bryan's.

"Come on," Bryan said. "Let's go show everyone."

"Why do I have to do this?" James said. He held his hands out to the side so that he wouldn't have to touch the dress. He looked ridiculous. He felt worse than ridiculous. He felt terrible. He felt so terrible that he didn't even care anymore that he was wearing a dress.

"You didn't have to do this," Bryan said. He sounded like he thought it was a big joke, which it was. "I didn't make you do it, James."

One of the Simpson twins was running around, dropping atom bombs on the sagging, wrinkled tents. He skidded to a stop in front of Bryan and James. "Why are you wearing a dress?" the Simpson twin said. "Hey, James is wearing a dress!"

Bryan gave James a shove. Not hard, but he left a muddy handprint on the dress. "Come on," he said. "Pretend that you're a zombie. Like you're a kitchen girl zombie who's come back to eat the brains of everybody from Bungalow 6, because you're still angry about that time we had the rice pudding fight with Bungalow 4 out on the porch of the dining room. Like you just crawled out of the mud. I'll be a zombie too. Let's go chase people."

"Okay," James Lorbick said. The terrible feeling went away at the thought of being a zombie, and suddenly the flowered dress seemed magical to him. It gave him the strength of a zombie, only faster. He staggered with Bryan along towards the rest of Bungalow 6, holding out his arms. Kids said things like, "Hey, look at James! James is wearing a *dress*!" as if they were making fun of him, but then they got the idea. They realized that James and Bryan were zombies and they ran away. Even Terence.

After a while, everybody had become a zombie. So they went for a swim. Everybody except for James Lorbick, because when he started to take off the dress, Bryan Jones stopped him. Bryan said, "No, wait. Keep it on. I dare you to wear that dress until we get back to camp tomorrow. I dare you. We'll show up at breakfast and say that we saw a monster and it's chasing us, and then you come in the dining room and it will be awesome. You look completely spooky with that dress and all the mud."

"I'll get my sleeping bag all muddy," James said. "I don't want to sleep in a dress. It's dumb."

Everybody in the lake began to yell things.

"Come on, James, wear the dress, okay?"

"Keep the dress on! *Do* it, James!"

"I dare you," said Bryan.

"I dare *you*," James said.

"What?" Bryan said. "What do you dare me to do?"

James thought for a moment. Nothing came to him. "I don't know."

Terence was floating on his back. He lifted his head. "You tell him, James. Don't let Bryan talk you into anything you don't want to do."

"Come on," Bryan said. "It will be so cool. Come on."

So everybody in Bungalow 6 went swimming except for James Lorbick. They splashed around and washed off all the mud and came out of the pond and James Lorbick was the only kid in Bungalow 6 who was still covered in crusty mud. James Lorbick was the only one who still had mud spikes in his hair. James Lorbick was the only one wearing a dress.

The sun was going down. They sat on the ground around the campfire that wouldn't catch. They ate the rest of the hot dogs and the peanut butter sandwiches that the kitchen girls always made up when bungalows went on overnight hikes. They talked about how cool it would be in the morning, when James Lorbick came running into the dining room back at camp, pretending to be a monster.

It got darker. They talked about the monster.

"Maybe it's a werewolf."

"Or a were-skunk."

"Maybe it's from outer space."

"Maybe it's just really lonely," James Lorbick said. He was sitting between Bryan Jones and one of the Simpson twins, and he felt really good, like he was really part of Bungalow 6 at last, and also kind of itchy, because of the mud.

"So how come nobody's ever seen it before?"

"Maybe some people have, but they died and so they couldn't tell anybody."

"No way. They wouldn't let us camp here if somebody died."

"Maybe the camp doesn't want anybody to know about the monster, so they don't say anything."

"You're so paranoid. The monster didn't do anything to Bungalow 4. Besides, Bungalow 4 is a bunch of liars."

"Wait a minute, do you hear that?"

They were quiet, listening. Bryan Jones farted. It was a sinister, brassy fart.

"Oh, man. That's disgusting, Bryan."

"What? It wasn't me."

"If the monster comes, we'll just aim Bryan at it."

"Wait, what's that?"

Something was ringing. "No way," Terence said. "That's my cell phone. No way does it get reception out here. Hello? Hey, Darlene. What's up?" He turned on his flashlight and shone it at Bungalow 6. "Guys. I've gotta go down the hill for a sec. She sounds upset. Something about her car and a chihuahua."

"That's cool."

"Be careful. Don't let the monster sneak up on you."

"Tell Darlene she's too good for you."

They watched Terence pick his way down the muddy path in a little circle of light. The light got smaller and smaller, farther and farther away, until they couldn't see it any more.

"What if it isn't really Darlene?" a kid named Timothy Ferber said.

"What?"

"Like what if it's the monster?"

"No way. That's stupid. How would the monster know Terence's cell phone number?"

"Are there any marshmallows left?"

"No. Just graham crackers."

They ate the graham crackers. Terence didn't come back. They couldn't even hear his voice. They told ghost stories.

"And she puts her hand down and her dog licks it and she thinks everything is okay. Except that then, in the morning, when she looks in the bathtub, her dog is in there and he's dead and there's lots of blood and somebody has written HA HA I REALLY FOOLED YOU with the blood."

"One time my sister was babysitting and this weird guy called and wanted to know if Satan was there and she got really freaked out."

"One time my grandfather was riding on a train and he saw a naked woman standing out in a field."

"Was she a ghost?"

"I don't know. He used to like to tell that story a lot."

"Were there cows in the field?"

"I don't know, how should I know if there were cows?"

"Do you think Terence is going to come back soon?"

"Why? Are you scared?"

"What time is it?"

"It's not even ten thirty. Maybe we could try lighting the fire again."

"It's still too wet. It's not going to catch. Besides, if there was a monster and if the monster was out there and we got the fire lit, then the monster could see us."

"We don't have any marshmallows anyway."

"Wait, I think I know how to get it started. Like Bungalow 4 did with the bat. If I spray it with insecticide, and then—"

Bungalow 6 fell reverently silent.

"Wow. That's awesome, Bryan. They should have a special merit badge for that."

"Yeah, to go with the badge for toxic farts."

"It smells funny," James Lorbick said. But it was nice to have a fire going. It made the darkness seem less dark. Which is what fires are supposed to do, of course.

"You look really weird in the firelight, James. That dress and all the mud. It's kind of funny and kind of creepy."

"Thanks."

"Yeah, James Lorbick should always wear dresses. He's so hot."

"James Lorbick, I think you are so hot. Not."

"Leave James alone," Bryan Jones said.

"I had this weird dream last year," Danny Anderson said. Danny Anderson was from Terre Haute, Indiana. He was taller than anyone else in Bungalow 6 except for Terence. "I dreamed that I came home from school one day and nobody was there except this man. He was sitting in the living room watching TV and so I said, 'Who are you? What are you doing here?' And he looked up and smiled this creepy smile at me and he said, 'Hey, Danny, I'm Angelina Jolie. I'm your new dad.'"

"No way. You dreamed your dad was Angelina Jolie?"

"No," Danny Anderson said. "Shut up. My parents aren't divorced or anything. My dad's got the same name as me. This guy said he was my *new* dad. He *said* he was Angelina Jolie. But he was just some guy."

"That's a dumb dream."

"I know it is," Danny Anderson said. "But I kept having it, like, every night. This guy is always hanging out in the kitchen and talking to me about what we're going to do now that I'm his kid. He's really creepy. And the thing is, I just got a phone call from my mom, and she says that she and my dad are getting divorced and I think maybe she's got a new boyfriend."

"Hey, man. That's tough."

Danny Anderson looked as if he might be about to cry. He said, "So what if this boyfriend turns out to be my new dad? Like in the dream?"

"My stepdad's pretty cool. Sometimes I get along with him better than I get along with my mom."

"One time I had a dream James Lorbick was wearing a dress."

"What's that noise?"

"I didn't hear anything."

"Terence has been gone a long time."

"Maybe he went back to camp. Maybe he left us out here."

"The fire smells really bad."

"It reeks."

"Isn't insect stuff poisonous?"

"Of course not. Otherwise they wouldn't be able to sell it. Because you put it on your skin. They wouldn't let you put poison on your skin."

"Hey, look up. I think I saw a shooting star."

"Maybe it was a space ship."

They all looked up at the sky. The sky was black and clear and full of bright stars. It was like that for a moment and then they noticed how clouds were racing across the blackness, spilling across the sky. The stars disappeared. Maybe if they hadn't looked, the sky would have stayed clear. But they did look. Then snow started to fall, lightly at first, just dusting the muddy ground and the campfire and Bungalow 6 and then there was more snow falling. It fell quietly and thickly. It was going to be the thirteenth of July tomorrow, the next-to-last day of camp, the day that James Lorbick, wearing a dress and a lot of mud, was going to show up and scare everyone in the dining room.

The snow was the weirdest thing that had ever happened to Bungalow 6.

One of the Simpson twins said, "Hey, it's snowing!"

Bryan Jones started laughing. "This is awesome," he said. "Awesome!"

James Lorbick looked up at the sky, which had been so clear a minute ago. Fat snowflakes fell on his upturned face. He wrapped his crumbly mud-covered arms around himself. *"Awesome,"* he repeated.

"Terence! Hey Terence! It's snowing!"

"Nobody is going to believe us."

"Maybe we should go get in our sleeping bags."

"We could build a snow fort."

"No, seriously. What if it gets really cold and we freeze to death? All I brought is my windbreaker."

"No way. It's going to melt right away. It's summer. This is just some kind of weather event. We should take a picture so we can show everybody."

So far they had taken pictures of mud, of people pretending to be mud-covered zombies, of James Lorbick pretending to be a mud-haired, dress-wearing monster. Terence had taken a picture of the bone that wasn't a cow bone. One of the Simpson twins had put a dozen marshmallows in his mouth and someone took a picture of that. Someone had a digital photo of Bryan Jones's big naked butt.

"So why didn't anyone from Bungalow 4 take a picture of the monster?"

"They did. But you couldn't see anything."

"Snow is cooler anyway."

"No way. A monster is way better."

"I think it's weird that Terence hasn't come back up yet."

"Hey, Terence! Terence!"

They all yelled for Terence for a few minutes. The snow kept falling. They did little dances in the snow to keep warm. The fire got thinner and thinner and started to go out. But before it went out, the monster came up the muddy, snowy path. It smiled at them and it came up the path and Danny Anderson shone his flashlight at it and they could all see it was a monster and not Terence pretending to be a monster. No one in Bungalow 6 had ever seen a monster before, but they all knew that a monster was what it was. It had a white face and its hands were red and dripping. It moved very fast.

You can learn a lot of stuff at camp. You learn how to wiggle an arrow so that it comes out of a straw target without the metal tip coming off. You learn how to make something out of yarn and twigs called a skycatcher, because there's a lot of extra yarn and twigs in the world, and someone had to come up with something to do with it. You learn how to jam your feet up into the mattress of the bunk above you, while someone is leaning out of it, so that they fall out of bed. You learn that if you are riding a horse and the horse sees a snake on the trail, the horse will stand on its hind legs. Horses don't like snakes. You find out that tennis rackets are good for chasing bats. You find out what happens if you leave your wet clothes in your trunk for a few days. You learn how to make rockets and you learn how to pretend not to care when someone takes your rocket and stomps on it. You learn to pretend to be asleep when people make fun of you. You learn how to be lonely.

The snow came down and people ran around Honor Lookout. They screamed and waved their arms around and fell down. The monster chased them. It moved so quickly that sometimes it seemed to fly. It was laughing like this was an excellent fun game. The snow was still coming down and it was dark which made it hard to see what the monster did when it caught people. James Lorbick sat still. He pretended that he was asleep or not there. He pretended that he was writing a letter to his best friend in Chicago who was spending the summer playing video games and hanging out at the library and writing and illustrating his own comic book. *Dear Alec, how are you? Camp is almost over, and I am so glad. This has been the worst summer ever. We went on a hike and it rained and my counselor found a bone. This kid made me put on a dress. There was a monster which ate everybody. How is your comic book coming? Did you put in the part I wrote about the superhero who can only fly when he's asleep?*

The monster had one Simpson twin under each arm. The twins were screaming. The monster threw them down the path. Then it bent over Bryan Jones, who was lying half inside one of the tents, half in the snow. There were slurping noises. After a minute it stood up again. It looked back and saw James Lorbick. It waved.

James Lorbick shut his eyes. When he opened them again, the monster was standing over him. It had red eyes. It smelled like rotting fish and kerosene. It wasn't actually all that tall, the way you'd expect a monster to be tall. Except for that, it was even worse than Bungalow 4 had said.

The monster stood and looked down and grinned. "You," it said. It had a voice like a dead tree full of bees: sweet and dripping and buzzing. It poked James on the shoulder with a long black nail. "What are you?"

"I'm James Lorbick," James said. "From Chicago."

The monster laughed. Its teeth were pointed and terrible. There was a smear of red on the dress where it had touched James. "You're the craziest thing I've ever seen. Look at that dress. Look at your hair. It's standing straight up. Is that mud? Why are you covered in mud?"

"I was going to be a monster," James said. He swallowed. "No offense."

"None taken," the monster said. "Wow, maybe I should go visit Chicago. I've never seen anything as funny as you. I could look at you for hours and hours. Whenever I needed a laugh. You've really made my day, James Lorbick."

The snow was still falling. James shivered and shivered. His teeth were clicking together so loudly he thought they might break. "What are you doing here?" he said. "Where's Terence? Did you do something to him?"

"Was he the guy who was down at the bottom of the hill? Talking on a cell phone?"

"Yeah," James said. "Is he okay?"

"He was talking to some girl named Darlene," the monster said. "I tried to talk to her, but she started screaming and it hurt my ears so I hung up. Do you happen to know where she lives?"

"Somewhere in Ohio," James said.

"Thanks," the monster said. He took out a little black notebook and wrote something down.

"What are you?" James said. "Who are you?"

"I'm Angelina Jolie," the monster said. It blinked.

James's heart almost stopped beating. "Really?" he said. "Like in Danny Anderson's dream?"

"No," the monster said. "Just kidding."

"Oh," James said. They sat in silence. The monster used one long fingernail to dig something out between its teeth. It belched a foul, greasy belch. James thought of Bryan. Bryan probably would have belched right back, if he still had a head.

"Are you the monster that Bungalow 4 saw?" James said.

"Were those the kids who were here a few days ago?"

"Yeah," James said.

"We hung out for a while," the monster said. "Were they friends of yours?"

"No," James said. "Those kids are real jerks. Nobody likes them."

"That's a shame," the monster said. Even when it wasn't belching, it smelled worse than anything James had ever smelled before. Fish and kerosene and rotting maple syrup poured over him in waves. He tried not to breathe.

The monster said, "I'm sorry about the rest of your bungalow. Your friends. Your friends who made you wear a dress."

"Are you going to eat me?" James said.

"I don't know," the monster said. "Probably not. There were a lot of you. I'm not actually that hungry anymore. Besides, I would feel silly eating a boy who's wearing a dress. And you're really filthy."

"Why didn't you eat Bungalow 4?" James said. He felt sick to his stomach. If he looked at the monster he felt sick, and if he looked away, there was Danny Anderson, lying facedown under a pine tree with snow on his back, and if he looked somewhere else, there were Bryan Jones's legs poking out of the tent. There was Bryan Jones's head. One of Bryan's shoes had come off and that made James think of the hike, the way Terence lay down in the mud to fish for the Simpson twin's shoe. "Why didn't you eat them? They're mean. They do terrible things and nobody likes them."

"Wow," the monster said. "I didn't know that. I would have eaten them if I'd known, maybe. Although most of the time I can't worry about things like that."

"Maybe you should," James said. "I think you should."

The monster scratched its head. "You think so? I saw you guys eating hot dogs earlier. So do you worry about whether those were good dogs or bad dogs when you're eating them? Do you only eat dogs that were mean? Do you only eat bad dogs?"

"Hot dogs aren't really made from dogs," James said. "People don't eat dogs."

"I never knew that," the monster said. "But see if I worried about that kind of thing, whether the person I was eating was a nice guy or a jerk, I'd never eat anyone. And I get hungry a lot. So to be honest, I don't worry. All I really notice is whether the person I'm chasing is big or small or fast or slow. Or if they have a sense of humor. That's important, you know. A sense of humor. You have to laugh about things. When I was hanging out with Bungalow 4, I was just having some fun. I was just playing around. Bungalow 4 mentioned that you guys were going to show up. I was joking about how I was going to eat them and they said I should eat you guys instead. They said it would be really funny. I have a good sense of humor. I like a good joke."

It reached out and touched James Lorbick's head.

"Don't do that!" James said.

"Sorry," said the monster. "I just wanted to see what the mud spikes felt like. Do you think it would be funny if I wore a dress and put a lot of mud on my head?"

James shook his head. He tried to picture the monster wearing a dress, but all he could picture was somebody climbing up to Honor Lookout. Somebody finding pieces of James scattered everywhere like pink and red confetti. That somebody would wonder what had happened and be glad that it hadn't happened to them. Maybe someday people would tell scary stories about what had happened to Bungalow 6 when they went camping. Nobody would believe the stories. Nobody would understand why one kid had been wearing a dress.

"Are you shivering because you're cold or because you're afraid of me?" the monster said.

"I don't know," James said. "Both. Sorry."

"Maybe we should get up and run around," the monster said. "I could chase you. It might warm you up. Weird weather, isn't it? But it's pretty, too. I love how snow makes everything look nice and clean."

"I want to go home," James said.

"That's Chicago, right?" the monster said. "That's what I wrote down."

"You wrote down where I live?" James said.

"All those guys from the other bungalow," the monster said. "Bungalow 4. I made them write down their addresses. I like to travel. I like to visit people. Besides, if you say that they're jerks, then I should go visit them? Right? It would serve them right."

"Yeah," James said. "It would serve them right. That would be really funny. Ha ha ha."

"Excellent," the monster said. It stood up. "It was great meeting you, James. Are you crying? It looks like you're crying."

"I'm not crying. It's just snow. There's snow on my face. Are you leaving?" James said. "You're going to leave me here? You aren't going to eat me?"

"I don't know," the monster said. It did a little twirl, like it was going to go running off in one direction, and then as if it had changed its mind, as if it was going to come rushing back at

James. James whimpered. "I just can't decide. Maybe I should flip a coin. Do you have a coin I can flip?"

James shook his head.

"Okay," the monster said. "How about this. I'm thinking of a number between one and ten. You say a number and if it's the same number, I won't eat you."

"No," James said.

"Then how about if I only eat you if you say the number that I'm thinking of? I promise I won't cheat. I probably won't cheat."

"No," James said, although he couldn't help thinking of a number. He thought of the number four. It floated there in his head like a big neon sign, blinking on and off and back on. Four, four, four. Bungalow 4. Or six. Bungalow 6. Or was that too obvious? Don't think of a number. He would have bet anything that the monster could read minds. Maybe the monster had put the number four in James's head. Six. James changed the number to six hundred so it wouldn't be a number between one and ten. Don't read my mind, he thought. Don't eat me.

"I'll count to six hundred," the monster said. "And then I'll chase you. That would be funny. If you get back to camp before I catch you, you're safe. Okay? If you get back to camp first, I'll go eat Bungalow 4. Okay? I tell you what. I'll go eat them even if you don't make it back. Okay?"

"But it's dark," James said. "It's snowing. I'm wearing a dress."

The monster looked down at its fingernails. It smiled like James had just told an excellent joke. "One," it said. "Two, three, four. Run, James! Pretend I'm chasing you. Pretend that I'm going to eat you if I catch you. Five, six. Come on, James, run!"

James ran.

Everybody knew what the aliens looked like.

THE SURFER

IN THE DREAM I was being kidnapped by aliens. I was dreaming, and then I woke up.

Where was I? Someplace I wasn't supposed to be, so I decided to stand up and take a look around, but there was no room and I couldn't stand up after all. My legs. And I was strapped in. I was holding on to something. A soccer ball. It slid out of my hands and into the narrow space in front of me, and it took two tries to hook it up again with my feet. The floor kept moving up and down, and my hands were floppy.

"One more pill, Dorn. Oops. Here. Have another one. Want some water?"

I had a sip of water. Swallowed. I was in a little seat. A plane? I was on a plane. And we were way up. The clouds were down. There was a woman who looked like my mother, except she wasn't. "Let me take that," she said. "I'll put it up above for you."

I didn't want to give it to her. Even if she did look like my mother.

"Come on, Dorn." My father again. Wasn't he supposed to be at the hospital today? I'd been at soccer practice. I was in my soccer clothes. Cleats and everything. "Dorn?" I ignored him. He said to the woman, "Sorry. He took some medication earlier. He's a bad flier."

"I'm not," I said. "A bad flier." I was having a hard time with my mouth. I tried to remember some things. My father had come by in his car. And I'd gone to see what he wanted. He was going to drive me home even though practice wasn't. Wasn't over. I drank something he gave me. Gatorade. That had been a mistake.

I said, "I'm not on a plane. This isn't a plane and you're not my mother." I didn't sound like me.

"Poor kid," the woman said. The floor bounced. If this was a plane, then she was a something. A flight attendant. "Wouldn't he be more comfortable if I stowed that up above for him?"

"I think he'll be fine." My father again. I kept my arms around my. My soccer ball. Keeping my shoulders forward. Hunched so nobody could take it. From me. Nobody ever got a soccer ball away from me.

"You gave me Gatorade," I said. The Gatorade had had something. In it. Everything I ought to know was broken up. Fast and liquid and too close up and then slow like an instant. Replay. My lips felt mushy and warm, and the flight attendant just looked at me like I was drooling. I think I was.

"Dorn," my father said. "It's going to be okay."

"Saturday," I said. Our first big match and I was missing practice. My head went forward and hit the soccer ball. I felt the flight attendant's fingers on my forehead.

"Poor kid," she said.

I lifted up my head. Tried as hard as I could. To make her understand me. "Where. This flight. Is it going."

"Costa Rica," the flight attendant said.

"You," I said to my father. "I. Will never. Forgive. You." The floor tilted and I went down.

When I woke up we were in Costa Rica, and I remembered exactly what my father had done to me. But it was too late to do anything about it. By then everything had changed because of a new flu scare. Costa Rica could have turned the plane around, but I guess by that point we couldn't have gotten back into the States. They'd shut down all the airports, everywhere. We went straight into quarantine. Me, my father, the flight attendant who didn't look anything like my mother, after all, and all the other people on the plane.

There were guards wearing N95 masks and carrying machine guns to make sure we all got on a bus. Once we were seated, a man who really needed a shave boarded and stood at the front. He wore an N95 mask with a shiny, tiny mike-pen clipped to it. He held up his gloved hands for silence. Sunlight melted his rubbery fingers into lozenges of pink taffy.

People put down their cells and their googlies. I'd checked my cell and discovered three missed calls, all from my coach, Sorken. I didn't check the messages. I didn't even want to know.

In the silence you could hear birds and not a lot else. No planes taking off. No planes landing. You could smell panic and antibacterial potions. Some people had been traveling with disposable masks, and they were wearing them now. My father always said those didn't really do much.

The official waited a few more seconds. The skin under his eyes was grayish and pouched. He said, "It's too bad, these precautions that we must take, but it can't be helped. You will be our guests for a short period of observation. Without this precaution, there will be unnecessary sickness. Deaths that could be prevented. You will be given care if you become ill. Food and drink and beds. And in a few days, when all have been given a clean bill of health, we will let you continue with your business, your homecoming, your further travel arrangements. You have questions, but I have no time for them. Excuse me. Please do not attempt to leave this bus or to go away. The guards will shoot you if you cannot be sensible."

Then he said the whole speech all over again in Spanish. It was a longer speech this time. Nobody protested when he disembarked and our bus started off to wherever they were taking us.

"Did you understand any of that? The Spanish?" my father asked. And that was the first thing he said to me, except for what he'd said on the plane, when it landed. He'd said, "Dorn, wake up. Dorn, we're here." He'd been so excited that his voice broke when he said *here*.

"If I did," I said. "Why would I tell you?" But I hadn't. I was taking Japanese as my second language.

"Well," he said. "Don't worry. We'll be fine. And don't worry too much about the machine guns. They have the safeties on."

"What do you know about machine guns?" I said. "Never mind. You got us into this situation. You *kidnapped* me."

"What was I supposed to do, Dorn," he said. "Leave you behind?"

"I have a very important match tomorrow," I said. "*Today*. In Glenside." I had my soccer ball wedged between my knees and the back of the seat in front of me. I was wearing my cleats and soccer clothes from the day before. For some reason that made me even more furious.

"Don't worry about the match," my father said. "Nobody is going to be playing soccer today. Or anytime soon."

"You knew about this, didn't you?" I said. I knew that doctors talked to each other.

"Keep your voice down," my father said. "Of course I didn't."

There was a girl across the aisle from us. She kept looking over, probably wondering if I had this new flu. She was about my height and at least twice my weight. A few years older. Bleached white hair and a round face. Cat's-eye glasses. Her skin was very tan, and she wasn't wearing a disposable mask. Her lips were pursed up and her eyebrows slanted down. I looked away from her and out the window.

Everything outside the bus was saturated with color. The asphalt deep purplish brown. The sky such a thick, wet blue you expected it to come off on the bus and the buildings. A lizard the size of my forearm, posed like a hood ornament on the top of a Dumpster, shining in the sun like it had been wrought of beaten silver, and its scales emeralds and topazes, gemstone parings. Off in the distance were bright feathery trees, some fancy skyscrapers, the kind you see on souvenir postcards, mountains on either side of us, cloud-colored, looking like special effects.

I couldn't tell if it was the drugs my father had given me, or if this was just what Costa Rica looked like. I looked around the bus at the other passengers in their livid tropical prints and their blank, white, disposable masks, at the red filaments of stubble on my father's face, pushing out of his skin like pinprick worms. So okay. It was the drugs. I felt like someone in one of my father's Philip K. Dick paperback science fiction novels. Kidnapped? Check. In a strange environment and unable to trust the people that you ought to be able to rely on, say, your own father? Check.

On some kind of hallucinogenic medication? Check. Any minute now I would realize that I was really a robot. Or God.

Our bus stopped and the driver got out to have a conversation with two woman soldiers holding machine guns. There was a series of hangar buildings a few hundred yards in front of us. One of the soldiers got onto the bus and looked us over. She lifted up her N95 mask and said, "Patience, patience." She smiled and shrugged. Then she sat down on the rail at the front of the bus with her mask on again. Everyone on the bus clicked on their cell phones again. It didn't seem as if we were going anywhere soon.

There was a clammy breeze, and it smelled like some place I'd never been to before, and where I didn't want to be. I wanted to lie down. I wanted a bathroom and a sink and a toothbrush. And I was hungry. I wanted a bowl of cereal. And a peanut-butter sandwich.

That girl was still looking at me.

I leaned across and said, "I'm not sick or anything, okay? My father gave me a roofie. I was at soccer practice, and he kidnapped me. I'm a goalie. I don't even speak Spanish." Even as I said it, I knew I wasn't making much sense.

The girl looked at my father. He said, "True, more or less. But, as usual, Adorno is oversimplifying things."

The girl said, "You're here for the aliens."

My father's eyebrows shot up.

The fat girl said, "Well, you don't look like UCR students. You don't look wealthy enough to be tourists. Besides, tourist visas are hard to come by unless you've got a lot of money, and no offense but I don't think so. So either you're here because you work in the software industry or because of the aliens. And no offense, but you look more like the latter than the former."

I said, "So which are you? Aliens or software?"

"Software," she said, sounding a little annoyed. "Second year, full scholarship to UCR."

About three decades ago, a software zillionaire in Taiwan had died and left all his money to the University of Costa Rica to fund a progressive institute of technology. He left them his patents, his stocks, and controlling shares in the dozen or so companies that he'd owned. Why? They'd given him an honorary degree or something. All the techie kids at my school dreamed about getting into one of the UCR programs, or else just getting lucky in the visa lottery and coming out to Costa Rica after college to work for one of the new start-ups.

"I'm Dr. Yoder," my father said. "General practice. We're on our way out to join Hans Bliss's Star Friend community, as it happens. Their last doctor packed up and left two weeks ago. I've been in contact with Hans for a few years. We're here at his invitation."

Which was what he'd told me in the car when he picked me up at practice. After I drank the Gatorade he'd brought me.

"Amazing how easy it is for some rich lunatic like Bliss to get visas. I bet there are twenty people on this bus who are headed out to join Bliss's group," the girl said. "What I've never figured out is why everybody is so convinced that if the aliens come back, they're going to show up to see Bliss. No offense, but I've seen him online. I watched the movie. He's an idiot."

My father opened his mouth and shut it again. A woman in the seat behind us leaned forward and said, "Hans Bliss is a great man. We heard him speak in Atlanta and we just knew we had to come out here. The aliens came to him because he's a great man. A *good* man."

I had gone with my father to see Hans Bliss talk at the

Franklin Institute in Philadelphia last year. I had my own opinions.

The girl didn't even turn around. She said, "Hans Bliss is just some surfer who happened to be one of a dozen people stupid enough to be out on an isolated beach during a Category 3 hurricane. It was just dumb luck that he was the one the aliens scooped up. If he's so great, then why did they put him back down on the beach again and just take off? Why didn't they take him along if he's so amazing? In my opinion, you don't get points just for being the first human ever to talk with aliens. Especially if the conversation only lasts about seven minutes by everyone else's count. I don't care how long he says he was out there. Furthermore, you *lose* points if the aliens go away after talking to you and don't ever come back again. How long has it been? Six years? Seven?"

Now the whole bus was listening, even the bus driver and the soldier with the gun. The woman behind us was probably twenty years older than my father; she had frizzy gray hair and impressive biceps. She said to the girl, "Can't you see that people like you are the reason that the aliens haven't come back yet? They told Bliss that they would return in the fullness of time."

"Sure," the girl said. You could tell she was enjoying herself. "Right after we make Bliss president of the whole wide world and learn to love each other and not feel ashamed of our bodies. When Bliss achieves world peace and we're all comfortable walking around in the nude, even the people who are fat, like me, the aliens will come back. And they'll squash us like bugs, or harvest us to make delicious people-burgers, or cure cancer, or bring us cool new toys. Or whatever Hans Bliss says that they're going to do. I love Hans Bliss, okay? I love the fact that he fell in love with some aliens who swooped down one stormy afternoon and scooped him up into the sky and less than an hour later dropped him off, naked, in front of about eighteen news crews, disaster-bloggers, and gawkers, and now he's going to wait for the rest of his life for them to come back, when clearly it was just some weird kind of one-night stand for them. It's just so sweet."

The woman said, "You ignorant little—"

People at the front of the bus were getting up. A man said something in Spanish, and the girl who didn't like Bliss said, "Time to go." She stood up.

My father said, "What's your name?"

The soldier with the machine gun was out on the asphalt, waving us off the bus. People around us grabbed carry-on bags. The angry woman's mouth was still working. A guy put his hand on her arm. "It's not worth it, Paula," he said. Neither of them were wearing face masks. He had the same frizzy hair, and a big nose, and those were his good features. You could see why he was hoping the aliens might come back. Nobody on Earth was ever going to fall in love with him.

"My name's Naomi," the girl said.

"Nice to meet you, Naomi," my father said. "You're clearly very smart and very opinionated. Maybe we can talk about this some more."

"Whatever," Naomi said. Then she seemed to decide that she had been rude enough. "Sure. I mean, we're going to be stuck with each other for a while, right?"

My father motioned for her to step out in front of us. He said, "Okay, Naomi, so once I tell the people in charge here that I'm a doctor, I'm going to be busy. I'd appreciate it if you and Adorno kept an eye on each other. Okay? Okay."

I didn't have the energy to protest that I didn't need a baby-sitter. I could hardly stand up. Those drugs were still doing things to my balance. My eyes were raw, and my mouth was dry. I smelled bad, too. I stopped when we got out of the bus, just to look around, and there was the hangar in front of us and my father pushed me forward and we funneled into the hangar where there were more soldiers with guns, standing back as if they weren't really making us do anything. Go anywhere. As if the hangar was our decision. Sun came down through oily windows high above us, and somehow it was exactly the sort of sunlight that ought to fall on you on a movie set or in a commercial while you pretend to sit on a white, sandy beach. But the hangar was vast and empty. Someone had forgotten to truck in that white sand and the palm trees and the beautiful painted background. Nobody was saying much. We just came into the hangar and stood there, looking around. The walls were cinderblock, and a warm wind came in under the corrugated roof, rattling and popping it like a steel drum. The floor was whispery with grit.

There were stacks of lightweight cots folded up with plastic mattresses inside the frames. Foil blankets in tiny packets. So the next thing involved a lot of rushing around and grabbing, until it became clear that there were more than enough cots and blankets, and plenty of space to spread out in. My father and I carried two cots over toward the wall farthest away from the soldiers. Naomi stuck near us. She seemed suddenly shy. She set up her cot and then flopped down on her stomach and rolled over, turned away.

"Stay here," my father said. I watched him make his way over to a heap of old tires where people stood talking. An Asian woman with long twists of blue and blond hair took two tires, rolling them all the way back to her cot. She stacked them, and then she had a chair. She sat down in it, pulled out a tiny palmtop computer, and began to type, just like she was in an office somewhere. Other people started grabbing tires. There was some screaming and jumping around when some of the tires turned out to contain wildlife. Spiders and lizards. Kids started chasing lizards, stomping spiders.

My father came back with two tires. Then he went and got another two tires. I thought they were for me but instead he rolled them over to Naomi. He tapped her on the shoulder and she turned over, saw the tires, and made a funny little face, almost as if she were irritated with my father for trying to be nice. I knew how she felt. "Thanks," she said.

"I'm going to go find out where the bathroom is." I put the soccer ball down on my bed, thought about it, and picked it up again. Put it down.

"I'll come," my father said.

"Me, too." Naomi. She bounced a little, like she really needed the toilet.

I put my soccer ball down on the gritty concrete. Began to guide it across the hangar with my feet and my knees. My balance wasn't great, but I still looked pretty good. Soccer is what I was made to do. Passengers in white masks, soldiers with guns turned their heads to watch me go by.

The October after I turned fourteen I became first goalie for not one but two soccer teams: the club team that I'd belonged to for four years, and the state soccer team, which I had tried out for three days after my birthday. Only a few months later, and during state matches I was on the field more than I sat out. I had my own coach, Eduardo Sorken, a sour, bad-tempered man who was displeased when I played poorly and offered only grudging acknowledgment when I played well. Sorken had played in the

World Cup for Bolivia, and when he was hard on me, I paid attention, telling myself that one day I would not only play in the World Cup but play for a winning team, which Sorken had not.

There was a smudgy black figure on the outside wall of the ranch house back in Philadelphia where I lived with my father. I'd stood up against the house and traced around my own outline with a piece of charcoal brick. I'd painted the outline in. When my father noticed, he wasn't angry. He never got angry. He just nodded and said, "When they dropped the atom bomb on Hiroshima, you could see the shapes of people who'd died against the buildings." Like that's what I'd been thinking about when I'd stood there and blackened my shape in. What I was thinking about was soccer.

When I kicked the ball, I aimed for that black silhouette of me as hard as I could. I liked the sound that the ball made against the house. If I'd knocked the house down, that would have been okay, too.

I had two expectations regarding my future, both reasonable. The first, that I would one day be taller. The other, that I would be recruited by one of the top international professional leagues. I favored Italy or Japan. Which was why I was studying Japanese. Nothing made me happier than the idea of a future in which, like the present, I spent as much time as possible on a soccer field in front of a goal, doing my best to stop everything that came at me.

A pretty girl in a mask sat cross-legged on the floor of the hangar, tapping at her googly, earplugs plugged in. She stopped typing and watched me go by. I popped the ball up, let it ride up one shoulder, around my neck, and down the other arm. During flu season, up in the bleachers, during matches, everyone wore masks like hers, bumping them up to yell or knock back a drink. But our fans painted their masks with our team colors or wrote slogans on them. There were always girls who wrote DORN on the mask, and so I'd look up and see my name right there, over their mouths. It was kind of a turn-on.

Sometimes there was a scout up in the bleachers. I figured another year or two, another inch or two, and I'd slip right into that bright, deserved future. I *was* the future. You can't stop the future, right? Not unless you're a better goalie than me.

I went in a circle, came back around, making the ball spin in place. "Hey," I said.

She gave me a little wave. I couldn't tell whether or not she was smiling, because of the mask. But I bet you she was.

I was magic out on a field. In front of a goal. I stopped everything. I was always exactly where I needed to be. When I came forward, nobody ever got around me. I put out my hands and the ball came to me like I was yanking it through the air. I could jump straight up, so high it didn't matter how short I was. I had a certain arrangement with gravity. I didn't get in its way, and it didn't get in mine. When I was asleep I dreamed about the field, the goal, the ball sailing toward me. I didn't dream about anything else. This year, on the weekends, I'd been wearing that black silhouette away.

I stood a few feet away from the girl, letting her see how I could keep the ball up in the air, adjusting its position first with one knee, then the other, then my left foot, then my right foot, then catching it between my knees. Maybe she was a soccer fan, maybe not. But I knew I looked pretty good.

I was already a bit taller than that silhouette I'd painted. If you measure yourself in the morning, you're always a few centimeters taller. I'm named after my mother's father. (Italian American, but you probably guessed that. Her mother was Japanese American. My father, if you're curious, is African American.) I never met my grandfather, although one time I'd asked my mother how tall he was. He wasn't. I wish they'd named me after someone taller. My father is six foot three.

I circled back one more time, went wide around my father and Naomi. The little lizard-chasing, spider-stomping kids were still running around in the hangar. Some of them were now wearing the foil blankets like capes. I kicked the ball to a little girl and she sent it right back. Not too bad. I was feeling much better. Also angrier.

You could have gotten half a dozen soccer matches going all at once in the hangar. According to my watch it was less than two hours until the start of the match back in Glenside. Sorken, my coach, would be wondering what had happened to me. Or he would have been, except for the flu. Matches were always being canceled because of flu or civil unrest or terror alerts. Maybe I'd be home before anyone even realized what had happened to me.

Or maybe I'd get the flu and die like my mother and brother had. That would show my father.

Along the wall closest to the hangar doors where we'd come in were the soldiers who were still guarding us. Whenever people tried to approach them, the guards waved them back again with their machine guns. The N95 masks gave them a sinister look, but they didn't seem particularly annoyed. It was more like, *Yeah, yeah, leave us alone. Scram.*

The makeshift latrines were just outside the hangar. People went in and out of the hangar, got in line, or squatted on the tarmac to read their googlies.

"So you're pretty good with that thing," Naomi said. She got in line behind me.

"Want my autograph?" I said. "It will be worth something someday."

There was a half-wall of corrugated tin divided up with more tin sheets into four stalls. Black plastic hung up for doors. Holes in the ground, and you could tell that they had been dug recently. There was a line. There were covered plastic barrels of water and dippers and more black plastic curtains so that you could take a sponge bath in private.

I tucked my soccer ball under my arm, took a piss, then dunked my hands into a bucket of antiseptic wash.

Back inside the hangar, airline passengers sorted through cardboard boxes full of tissue packs, packets of surgical masks, bottled water, hotel soaps and shampoos, toothbrushes. A man with an enormous mustache came up to my father with a group of people and said, "Miike says you're a doctor?"

"Yes," my father said. "Carl Yoder. This is my son, Dorn. I'm a G.P., but I have some experience with flu. I'll need a translator, though. I've started learning Spanish recently, but I'm still not proficient."

"We can find a translator," the man said. "I'm Rafe Zuleta-Arango. Hotel management. You've already met Anya Miike"—the woman who'd made the chair out of old tires. "Tom Laudermilk. Works for a law firm in New New York. Simon Purdy, the pilot on the flight down." My father nodded at the others. "We've been talking about how we ought to handle this. Almost everyone has been able to make contact with their families, to let them know the situation."

My father said, "How bad is it? A real pandemic or just another political scare? Any reports of flu here? I couldn't get through to my hospital. Just got a pretty vague official statement on voice mail."

Zuleta-Arango shrugged. Miike said, "Rumors. Who knows? There are riots ongoing in the States. Calexico has shut down its borders. Potlatch Territories, too. Lots of religious nuts making the usual statements online about the will of God. According to some of the other passengers, there's already a rumor about a new vaccine, and not enough to go around. People have started laying siege to hospitals."

"Just like last time," my father said. Last time had been three years ago. "Has anybody talked to the guys with the guns? I thought Costa Rica didn't have an army. Who are these guys?"

"Volunteers," Zuleta-Arango said. "Mostly teachers, believe it or not. There was a quarantine situation here four months ago. Small outbreak of blue plague. Lasted about a week, and it didn't turn into anything serious. But they know the drill. Simon and I went over and asked them a few questions. They don't anticipate keeping us here longer than a week. As soon as someone at the terminal has sorted through the luggage, they'll get it out here. They just need to check first for guns and contraband."

"My kit's in my luggage," my father said. "I'll set up a clinic when it shows. What about food?"

"We'll be getting breakfast soon," Purdy, the pilot, said. "I've gotten the flight crew together to set up a mess table over by the far wall. Looks like we've got two kerosene grills and

basic staples. Hope you like beans. We'll make an announcement about the clinic when everyone sits down to eat."

I'd been caught in a quarantine once before, during a trip to
the mall. Hadn't turned out to be anything serious, just a college student with a rash. During the really bad flu, three years
ago, I'd stayed home and played video games. My father had
been stuck over at the hospital, but our refrigerator is pretty well
stocked with frozen pizzas. My father stays over at the hospital
all the time. I can take care of myself. When I got the e-mail
about my mother and my brother, I didn't even page him. It's not
like he could have done anything anyway. I just waited until he
got home and told him then.

Lots of people died from that flu. Famous actors and former presidents and seven teachers at my school. Two kids on my
soccer team. A girl named Corinne with white-blond hair who
used to say, "Hey, Dorn" to me whenever I saw her in the hall at
school. She came to all my games.

Our first meal in the hangar, served from a series of the largest
pots I'd ever seen: reconstituted eggs and fried potatoes and lots
and lots of beans. That was our second meal, too, and every meal
after that, as long as we were in the hangar. Be glad that you've
never had to live in a hangar with eighty-four people eating beans
for breakfast, lunch, and dinner. For variety, there were little fat
yellow-green bananas and industrial-size jars of these rubbery,
slippery cylinders that Naomi said were hearts of palm.

My father said a couple of things to me. I ignored him. So he
started talking to Naomi instead, about aliens and Costa Rica.

After breakfast I went back and lay down on my cot and
thought about how I was going to get home. I had made it as
far as some weird place where everyone was running around,

setting fires to these inflatable germ-proof houses, when I woke up, face and arms and legs stuck to the plastic mattress with sweat, confused and overheated and pissed off. I didn't know where I was or why and then, when I did, it didn't make me any happier. The girl Naomi was sitting on the floor beside her cot. She was reading a beat-up old paperback. I figured I knew who she'd borrowed it from.

"You missed the excitement," she said. "Some executive type got all worked up and tried to pick a fight with the guards. He said something about how they couldn't do this to him because he's a U.S. citizen and he has rights. I thought we gave up those years ago. Zuleta-Arango and some of the others held him down while your father stuck him with a muscle relaxant.

"Have you read this?" she said. "I haven't seen one of these in years. Me, reading a book. I feel so very historical. We got our luggage back, so that's one good thing, although they've taken our passports away. I've never even heard of Olaf Stapleton. He's pretty good. Your dad doesn't exactly travel light. He's got like a hundred more actual books in his luggage. And you snore."

"I do not. Where is he?"

"Over there. In the office he set up. Taking temperatures and talking to hypochondriacs."

"Look," I said. "Before he comes back, we need to get something straight. You're not my babysitter, okay?"

"Of course I'm not," she said. "Aren't you a little old for a babysitter? How old are you? Sixteen?"

"Fourteen," I said. "Okay, good. That's settled. The other thing we need to straighten out is Hans Bliss. I'm with you. He's a loser, and I don't want to be here. As soon as they lift quarantine, I'm calling my soccer coach back in Philadelphia so he can buy me a ticket and get me out of here."

"Sure," she said. "Good luck with that. It would be terrible if a global flu epidemic meant the end of your soccer career."

"Pandemic," I said. "If it's global, it's a pandemic. And they're working on a vaccine right now. Couple of days and a couple of jabs and things will go back to normal, more or less, and I'll go home."

"This *is* home," Naomi said. "For me."

While she read Stapleton, I went through the luggage to see what my father had packed. The things he hadn't: my trophies, my soccer magazines, the knitted wool hat that a girl named Tanya gave me last year, when we were sort of going out. I liked that hat.

What he had packed bothered me even more than what he hadn't, because you could tell how much time he'd spent planning this. He'd brought maybe a third of his collection of paperback SF. And in my duffel bag were my World Cup T-shirts, my palmtop, my sleeping bag, my toothbrush, two more soccer balls. An envelope of photos of my mother and of my brother, Stephen. The little glass bottle with nothing inside it that my mother gave me the last time I saw her. I wonder what my father thought when he found that glass bottle in my dresser drawer. It was the first thing he ever gave my mother. She liked to tell me that story. It didn't work out between them, but they didn't hate each other after the divorce, the way some parents do. Whenever they talked on the phone they laughed and gossiped about people as if they were still friends. And she never threw away that bottle of nothing. So I couldn't, either.

My father collects books, mostly sci-fi, mostly paperbacks. Most people keep their books on a googly or a flex, but my father likes paper. I read one of his books every once in a while when I got bored. Sometimes my father had written in the margins and on the blank pages, making notes about whether these were hopeful portraits of the future, or realistic, or about other stories he was reminded of. Sometimes he doodled pictures of blobby or feathery aliens or spaceships or women whose faces looked kind of like my mother's face, except with tentacles coming out of their heads or with insect eyes, standing on pointy rocks with their arms akimbo, or sitting and holding hands with men in space suits. My father read his paperbacks over and over again, and so sometimes I left my own comments for him to find. He'd packed two suitcases for himself, and one was mostly books. I pulled out Ray Bradbury's *R Is for Rocket* and wrote on the first page of the first story, down in the bottom margin, "I HATE YOU." Then I dated it and put it back in the suitcase.

One of the two small offices in the hangar became my father's clinic. He spent most of the day there—among the passengers on our flight there were seven diabetics, one weak heart, two pregnancies (eight months, and five months), a dozen asthmatics, a migraine sufferer, three methadone users, one prostate cancer, one guy on anti-psychotic medication, and two children with dry coughs. My father set up cots in the second office for the children and their parents, reassuring them that this was only a precaution. In fact, they ought to think of it as a privilege. Everyone else was going to be camping out in the hangar.

He came back smelling of hand sanitizer and B.O. "Feeling better?" he said to me.

I'd changed T-shirts and put on some jeans, but I probably smelled just as bad. I said, "Better than what, exactly?"

"Dinner's at seven," Naomi said. "They divided us into meal groups while you were asleep, Dorn. Meal groups with cute names. The Two-toed Sloths—*Perezosos de dos Dedos*—and the *Mono Congos*, howler monkeys to you, and the *Tucancillos*. That's us. Us *Tucancillos* get dinner first tonight. We're rotating dinner slots and chores. We do the dishes tonight, too. The *Mono Congos* are on latrine duty. I am really not looking forward to that."

It was beans and rice and eggs again, along with some kind of pungent, fibrous sausage. Chorizo. I loaded so much food on my plate that Naomi called me a pig. But there was plenty of food for everybody. After dinner, Naomi and I went out to wash dishes in the area that had been rigged for bathing. After I'd rinsed several stacks of smeary plates and sprayed them with disinfectant, I poured a dipper of water over my own head.

I was washing dishes at a barrel next to the girl that I'd showed off for earlier. Not an accident, of course. Even with her mask on, she was better than pretty this close up. "American?" she said.

"Yeah," I said. "From Philadelphia. Liberty Bell, Declaration of Independence, AOL Cable Access Riots of 2012. Are you Costa Rican?"

"Tica," she said. "I'm a Tica. That's what you say here." She had long, shiny hair and these enormous baby-animal eyes, like a heroine in an anime. She was taller than me, but I was used to girls who were taller than me. I liked her accent, too. *"Me llamo Lara."*

"I'm Dorn," I told her. "This is Naomi. We met on the bus."

"Hola," Naomi said. "I'm at UCR. Dorn is here with his father because of Hans Bliss and the aliens. Because, you know, Hans Bliss said that the aliens are going to show up again real soon and this time he knows what he's talking about. Not like all those other times when he said the aliens were coming back."

Several *Tucancillos* stopped washing dishes.

"Hans Bliss is a big deal here," Lara said.

I glared at Naomi. "I'm not really interested in this guy Bliss. I'm here because my father kidnapped me."

My father had got out of dish duty when Zuleta-Arango announced some kind of committee meeting. Figures. First he kidnapped me, and now I was stuck doing his dishes.

"Hans Bliss can kiss my fat ass," Naomi said. Now some of our fellow *Tucancillos* were beginning to seem really irritated. I recognized the woman from the bus, Paula, the one that Naomi had already gotten riled up. The younger guy who had grabbed Paula's arm, back on the bus, was—I saw now—wearing a SHARE THE BLISS, HANS BLISS FOR WORLD PRESIDENT T-shirt. He gave Naomi a meaningful look, the kind of look that said he felt sorry for her.

"Let's get out of here," I said.

"Cool," Naomi said. "*Porta a mi.* Wait a minute, look over there. Is that an alien? Does it want to say something to us?"

Everyone looked, of course, but it was just a huge, disgusting bug. "Whoops," Naomi said. "Just a roach. But I hear our friends the roaches love Hans Bliss, too. Just like everyone else."

The woman Paula said, "I'm going to punch her right in that smug little mouth! If she says one more word!"

"Paula," the big-nosed guy said. "She isn't worth it. Okay?"

Naomi turned around and said, loudly, "I am too worth it. You have no idea how worth it I am."

The guy just smiled. Naomi gave him the finger. Then we were out of there.

While we were walking back, Lara said, "*Tengala adentro.* Naomi, I am not saying that I am a big fan of Bliss, but do you think that he was lying about his encounter with these aliens? Because I have seen the footage and read the eyewitness accounts, and my mother knows a man who was there. I don't believe it can all be a hoax."

Naomi shrugged. Back in the hangar, people were sorting through their suitcases, talking on cell phones, tapping away furiously at their peeties and googlies. We ended up back at the wall where our cots were, and Lara and I sat on the floor. Naomi hunkered down on her tires.

"I believe there were aliens," she said. "I just resent the fact that the first credible recorded contact with an extraterrestrial species was made by an idiot like Bliss. People who decide to go surfing in a Category 3 hurricane ought to be up for the Darwin Award, not considered representative of the human race. Well, not considered representative of the best the human race has to offer. And we only have Bliss's story about what the aliens said to him. I just don't buy that an intelligent race, the first we've ever come into contact with, would casually drop by to tell us to be happy and naked and polyamorous and vegetarian and oh yeah, *destroy all nuclear stockpiles*. All of those are good things, don't get me wrong. But they're exactly the kind of things you expect a retro-hippie surfer like Bliss to say. And the result? What's left of the United States, not to mention Greater Korea, Indonesia, and most of the Stans, are all stockpiling weapons faster than ever, because they've decided it's suspicious that aliens apparently want us to destroy all nuclear weapons. Which kind of puts this whole flu thing into perspective, you know? If Bliss's aliens come back, there are going to be a lot of missiles pointed right at them, a lot of fingers hovering on those special fingerprint-sensitive keypads."

"And a lot of naked people lined up on beaches everywhere, singing 'Kumbaya' and throwing flowers," I said.

"Including you?" Naomi asked. Lara giggled.

"No way," I said. "I've got better things to do."

"Like what?" Lara said. I started to think she was flirting with me. "What kind of things are you into, Dorn?"

"I'm a soccer player," I said. "A pretty good one. I'm not bragging or anything. I really am good. You saw me, right? I'm a goalie. And I'm kind of feeling like an idiot right now. I mean, if I'd known my father was planning to kidnap me and bring me down here, I would have at least learned to say some stuff in Spanish. Like, *This man is kidnapping me.* How do you say that? I don't know anything about Costa Rica except the usual stuff. Like there are a lot of beaches down here, right? And software. And iguana farms? I know a kid down the street whose father lost his job, and his father keeps saying he's going to raise iguanas in the basement under special lights and sell the meat online. Or else raise llamas in his backyard. He hasn't made up his mind. His kid said iguana tastes like chicken. More or less."

"I'm a vegetarian," Lara said. "It's okay that you don't know Spanish. You'll learn."

"I hope we're out of here soon," Naomi said, "because I have exams coming up. Is your phone working, Lara? My googlie keeps crashing when I try to get on. I just want to know if they've shut the university down."

Lara thumbed her phone. "My battery is almost dead," she said at last. "But I know the situation of the schools. They're closed for the indefinite future. My mother spoke to her cousin a few hours ago. Still no outbreak of this flu in San Jose or any other place in Costa Rica, but the government is asking people to stay at home except in situations of emergency. Just for a few days. All of the cruise ships are anchored offshore. My cousin runs a cruise-supply company, which is how she knows. The army is dropping food and supplies onto the decks of the boats.

I've never been on a cruise. I wish I were on a boat instead of in here. On the talk shows, they are talking about the flu. How perhaps it was manufactured and then released accidentally or even on purpose."

"They say that every time," I said. "My father says sure, it's possible, but you'd have to be really stupid to do something like that. And anyway, all we have to do is sit here and wait. Wait and see if anyone here is sick. Wait and see if anyone out there comes up with a vaccine. Once they get a vaccine cultured, they get it distributed pretty quickly. The question is, what do we do for fun in the meantime?"

"No point in studying if we're doomed," Naomi said, sounding nonchalant. "Maybe I should wait and see how bad this flu really is."

"We're safer in here than almost anywhere else," I said. At dinner, my father had made some announcements. He'd said clinic hours would run every day from eight A.M. until four P.M., and that if anyone began to feel achy or as if they had an elevated temperature, they should come talk to him at once. He said the odds that someone in the hangar would have the flu were minimal. He'd already talked with everyone who'd been on the flight and there was no one coming from Calexico or from anywhere farther west than Cincinnati. Our plane had started out the previous morning in Costa Rica and there hadn't been any changes of crew, except a flight attendant who got on in Miami after spending her day off at home, with her daughter. He explained that if we got sick at all, it would probably be some kind of stomach bug or mild cold, the kind of stuff you usually got when you traveled. Anya Miike had stood next to him, translating everything he said into Spanish and then into Japanese for these two guys from Osaka.

People had set up card games in the hangar. They'd brought out duty-free gins or tequilas or marijuana or those little bottles of Bailey's. Kids were drawing with smart crayons right on the concrete floor of the hangar, or watching the anime *Brave Hortense*, which someone had loaded onto a googly with a fancy bubble screen. Big, fat tears were plopping out of Brave Hortense's eyes, faster and faster, and the evil kitten who had made her cry began to build a raft, looking worried. A few feet away from us, a man was streaming a Spanish-language news program. The newsfeed became a Spanish-language song set to a languid beat. Elsewhere you could still hear news coming from tinny or expensive little speakers. There was good news and there was bad news. Mostly flu news. Flu in North America, and also in London and Rome. None in Costa Rica. The music made a nice change.

"I love this song," Naomi said. "It's on all the time, but I don't care. I could listen to it all day long."

"Lola Rollercoaster," Lara said. "She always sings about love."

"*¡Qué tuanis!* What else is there to sing about?" Naomi said.

I rolled my eyes.

People sprawled on their tires and talked in Spanish and English and Japanese and German and watched the guards who were watching them. A man and woman began dancing to the Lola Rollercoaster song; others joined them. Mostly older people. They danced close to each other without quite touching. I didn't see the point in that. If someone in here came down with the flu, dancing two inches apart wasn't going to be much of a prophylactic. Lara looked like she wanted to say something, and I wondered if she'd ask me to dance. But it turned out that her mother, a not-bad-looking woman in a pair of expensive cornsilk jeans, was waving her back over to where they'd set up cots.

"I'll see you later," Lara said. *"Buenas noches,* Naomi, Dorn."

"Buenas noches." And then, "I think she likes me," I said, when she got out of earshot. "Girls usually like me. I'm not bragging or anything. It's just a fact."

"Yeah, well, that's probably why her mother's calling her back over," Naomi said. "An American boy like you is no catch, even if you do have a wicked nice smile and nice green eyes."

"What do you mean?" I said.

"Everybody knows that American boyfriends and girlfriends only want one thing. Costa Rican citizenship. Look over there. See that *macha,* that blond girl? The one flirting with the cute Tico?"

I looked where Naomi was pointing. "Yeah," I said.

"She probably came down here on a tourist visa, hoping to meet guys just like him," Naomi said. "This is a real stroke of luck for her. We're going to be in here for at least five or six days. Lots of time for flirting. If I looked like her, I'd be trying to pull off the same thing while I'm at UCR. I'd rather cut off my legs than have to go back and live in the States. At least here they can grow you a new pair."

"It's not that bad," I said.

"Really?" Naomi said. "If girls seem to like you, Dorn, realize that it's probably not for your brains or your keen grasp of socio-political-economic issues. Tell me what you like best about our country. Is it the blatantly rigged elections, the lack of access to abortion, the shitty educational system? Is it the fact that most of the states where anyone would ever actually want to live would secede like Calexico and Potlatch, if they had someone like Canada or Mexico to back them up? Is it the health care, the most expensive and least effective health-care system in the world, the national debt so impressive it takes almost two whole pages of little tiny zeros to write it out? Tell me about your job prospects, Dorn. Who would you just kill to work for? Wal-Mart, McDisneyUniverse, or some prison franchise? Or were you going to join the army and go off to one of the Stans or Bads because you've always wanted to get gassed or shot at or dissolved into goo when your experimental weapon malfunctions?"

"Professional soccer," I said. "Preferably in Japan or Italy. Whoever offers the best money."

Naomi blinked, opened her mouth, and then closed it again. She pulled out a bar of chocolate and broke off a piece still in the wrapper and gave it to me. We pushed our masks up and chewed. "This is good," I said.

"Yeah," she said. "Even the chocolate is, like, ten times better down here. Oh boy. Look over there."

I turned around. It was that woman again. Paula. She was standing in a row of about two dozen other women and men and she was taking off all her clothes. Then she was standing there naked. They were all taking off their clothes. The homely guy who'd been wearing the HANS BLISS FOR PRESIDENT T-shirt turned out to have a full-color portrait of Hans Bliss—on his surfboard, on a towering wave, about to be lifted up by the aliens—tattooed across his chest. It was pretty well done. Lots of detail. But I didn't spend too much time looking at him. There were more interesting things to look at.

"These are the people that my dad wants to go hang out with?" I said. I thought about getting out my camera. There were other people with the same idea, holding out their cells, clicking pics.

"Look, a priest," Naomi said. "Of course there would be a priest. A Church-of-the-Second-Reformation priest, too, by the look of him. And Dorn? Try not to drool. Surely you've seen naked women before."

"Only on the Internet," I said. "This is better."

A guy in a black suit and a priest's collar was striding over toward the protestors, yelling some things in Spanish. A naked man, so hairy that he was hardly naked at all, really, stepped out of the line with his arms out wide. Hans Bliss's Star Friends believed in embracing all of mankind. Preferably in the nude. (Or as nude as you can get when you're still wearing your stupid little face mask.)

The priest had apparently had run-ins with Star Friends before. He picked up a tennis racket beside someone's suitcase and commenced swinging it ferociously.

"What's he saying?" I asked Naomi.

"Lots of stuff. Put on your clothes. Have you no shame. There are decent people here. Do you call that nothing a penis. I've seen bigger equipment on a housecat."

"Did he really say that?"

"No," Naomi said. "Just the stuff about decency. Et cetera. Now he's saying that he's going to beat the shit out of this guy if he doesn't put his clothes back on. We'll see who's tougher. God or the aliens. My money's on God. Does your father really buy into all this? The nudity? The peace, love, and Bliss *über alles*?"

"I don't think so," I said. "He just really wants to get a chance to see aliens. Up close."

"Not me," Naomi said. "Maybe I've just seen too many animes where the aliens turn out to be, you know, alien. Not like us. I am really, really tired of these Bliss people. Can I borrow another sci-fi book? Do women ever write this stuff? A story with some romance in it would be nice. Something with fewer annotations."

"Connie Willis is fun," I said. "Or there's this book *Snow Crash*. Or you could read some Tiptree or Joanna Russ or Octavia Butler. Something nice and grim."

The priest continued to shout at the naked Star Friends and make menacing, swatting motions with the tennis racket. Other passengers got involved, like this was a spectator sport, yelling things, or whistling, or shouting. My father and Zuleta-Arango and the rest of the committee were walking over. The guards watched from their station by the hangar entrance. Clearly they had no plans to get involved.

It was twilight. The sky through the high windows was lilac and gold, like a special effect. There were strings of lights looped along the walls, and a few worklights that people had found in one of the offices and set up strategically around the hangar, which made it look even more like a movie set. You could see the blue-white glow of googly screens everywhere. And then there were the bats. I don't know who noticed the bats first, but they were hard to miss, once the yelling started.

The bats seemed almost as surprised as we were. They poured into the hangar, looking like blackish, dried-up, flappy leaves, making long, erratic passes back and forth, skimming low and then winking up and away. People ducked down, covered their heads with their hands. The Hans Bliss people put their clothes back on—score one for the bats—and yet the priest was swinging his tennis racket at the bats now, just as viciously as he had the nudists. A bat dipped down and I ducked. "Go away!"

It went.

"They have vampire bats down here," Naomi said. She didn't seem bothered at all. "In case you're wondering. They come into people's houses and make little incisions in the legs or toes and then drink your blood. Hence the name. But I don't think these are vampire bats. These look more like fruit bats. They probably live up in the roof where those folds in the steel are. Relax, Dorn. Bats are a good thing. They eat mosquitoes. They've never been a vector for flu. Rabies, maybe, but not flu. We love bats."

"Except for the ones who drink blood," I said. "Those are big bats. They look thirsty to me."

"Calm down," Naomi said. "They're fruit bats. Or something."

I don't know how many bats there were. It's hard to count bats when they're agitated. At least two hundred, probably a lot more than that. But as the people in the hangar got more and more upset, the bats seemed to get calmer. They really weren't that interested in us. One or two still went scissoring through the air every now and then, but the others were somewhere up in the roof now, hanging down above us, glaring down at us with their malevolent, fiery little eyes. I imagined them licking their pointy little fangs. The man with the music turned it off. No more sad love songs. No more dancing. The card parties and conversations broke up.

My father and Zuleta-Arango walked up and down the makeshift aisles of the hangar, talking to the other passengers. Probably explaining about bats. People turned off the worklights, lay down on their cots, pulling silver foil emergency blankets and makeshift covers over themselves: jackets, dresses, beach towels. Some began to make up beds under the cots, where they would be safe from bats if not the spiders, lizards, and cockroaches that were, of course, also sharing our temporary quarters.

Half a soccer field away, Lara sat on a cot leaning back against her mother as her mother brushed her hair. She'd taken off her mask. She was even better looking than I'd thought she'd be. Possibly even out of my league.

Naomi was looking, too. She said, "Your parents are divorced, right? That's why your father kidnapped you? Have you called your mom? Does she know where you are now?"

"She's dead," I said. "She and my brother lived out on a dude ranch in Colorado. They caught that flu three years ago when it jumped from horses."

"Oh," Naomi said. "Sorry."

"Why be sorry? You didn't know," I said. "I'm fine now." My father was headed our way. I took off my mask and lay down on my cot and pulled the foil blanket over my head. I didn't take off my clothes, not even my shoes. Just in case the bats turned out not to be fruit bats.

All night long, people talked, listened to newsfeeds, got up to go to the bathroom, dreamed the kind of dreams that woke them up and other people, too. Children woke up crying. Naomi snored. I don't think that my father ever went to sleep at all. Whenever I looked over, he was lying on his cot, thumbing through a paperback. An Alfred Bester collection, I think.

We settled into certain routines quickly. Zuleta-Arango's committee set up a schedule for recharging googlies and palmtops and cell phones from the limited number of outlets in the hangar. After some discussion, the Hans Bliss people rigged up a kind of symbolic wall out of foil blankets and extra cot frames. That was the area where you went if you wanted to hang out in the nude and talk about aliens. Of course you could just wander by and get an eyeful and an earful, but after a while nude people just don't seem that interesting. Really.

My dad spent some of the day in the clinic and some of his time with Zuleta-Arango. He hung out with the Hans Bliss people, and he and Naomi sat around and argued about Hans Bliss and aliens. Somebody started an English/Spanish-language discussion group, and he got involved in that. He set up a lending library, passing out his sci-fi books, taking down the names of people who'd borrowed them. There were plenty of movies and digests that people were swapping around on their googlies, but the paperbacks had novelty appeal. Science fiction is always good for taking your mind off how bad things are.

I still wasn't speaking to my father, of course, unless it was absolutely necessary. He didn't really notice. He was too excited about having made it this far, impatient to get on with the next stage of his journey. He was afraid that while we were quarantined, the thing he'd been waiting for would arrive, and he'd be stuck in a hangar less than a hundred miles away. So close, and yet he couldn't get any closer until the quarantine period was over.

I figured it served him right.

Most of the passengers in quarantine were returning to Costa Rica. The foreign passengers were almost all in Costa Rica because of tech industry stuff or the aliens. Mostly aliens. Because of Hans Bliss. Some of them had waited years to get a visa. There were close to a thousand Star Friends in Costa Rica, citizens of almost every nation, true believers, currently living down along the Pacific coastline, right next to Manuel Antonio National Park; Lara had been to Manuel Antonio a few times on camping trips with friends. She said it was a lot nicer than camping in a hangar.

The first day, the Star Friends quarantined in the hangar got through, on their cells and on e-mail, to friends already out with Hans Bliss. My father even managed to speak to Hans Bliss himself for a few minutes, to explain that he had made it as far as San Jose. The Star Friends community was under quarantine as well, of course, and Hans Bliss was somewhat put out that his doctor was stuck at the airport. Preparations for the imminent return of the aliens were being hampered by the quarantine.

Like I said, I saw Hans Bliss speak in Philadelphia once. He was this tall, good-looking blond guy with a German accent. He was painfully sincere. So sincere he hardly ever blinked, which was kind of hypnotic. When he stood on the stage and described the feeling of understanding and joy and compassion that had descended upon him and lifted him up as he stood out on that beach, in the middle of that ferocious storm, I sat there gripping the sides of my chair, because I was afraid that otherwise I might get up and run toward the stage, toward the thing that he was promising. Other people in the audience did exactly that. When he talked about finding himself back on that beach again, abandoned and forsaken and confused and utterly alone, the man sitting next to me started to cry. Everyone was crying. I couldn't stand it. I looked up at my father and he was looking down at me, like what I thought mattered to him.

"What are we doing here?" I whispered. "Why are we here?"

He said, "I don't like this any better than you do, Dorn. But I have to believe. I have to believe at least some of what he's saying. I have to believe that they'll come back."

Then he stood up and asked the crying man to excuse us. "What were they like?" someone yelled at Bliss. "What did the aliens look like?"

Everybody knew what the aliens looked like. We'd all seen the footage hundreds of times. We'd heard Bliss describe the aliens on news shows and in documentaries and on online interviews and casts. But my father stopped in the aisle and turned back to the stage and so did I. You would have, too.

Hans Bliss held out his arms as if he were going to embrace

the audience, all of us, all at once. As if he were going to heal us of a sickness we didn't even know that we had, as if rays of energy and light and power and love were suddenly going to shoot out of his chest. The usual agents and government types and media who followed Hans Bliss everywhere he went looked bored. They'd seen this show a hundred times before. "They were beautiful," Hans Bliss said. People said it along with him. It was the punch line to one of the most famous stories ever. There had even been a movie in which Hans Bliss played himself.

Beautiful.

My father started up the aisle again. We walked out and I thought that was that. He never said anything else about Hans Bliss or Costa Rica or the aliens until he picked me up at soccer practice.

I put on my running shoes. I stretched out on the concrete floor and ran laps around and around the hangar. There were other people doing the same thing. After breakfast, I went over to an area where no one had set up a bed and started messing around, kicking the ball and catching it on the rebound. Nice and high. Some people came over and we played keep-away. When there were enough players, we took two cots and made them goals. We picked teams. Little kids came and sat and watched and chased down the ball when it went out-of-bounds. Even Naomi came to watch. When I asked her if she was going to play, she just looked at me like I was an idiot. "I'm not into being athletic," she said. "I'm too competitive. The last time I played organized sports, I broke someone's nose. It was only kind of an accident."

Lara came up behind me and tapped me on the back of the head. "*¿Cómo está ci arroz?* What's up?"

"You ever play soccer?" I said.

She ended up on my team. I was pretty excited about that, even before I saw her play. She was super fast. She put up her hair in a ponytail, took off her mask, and zipped up and down the floor. Our team won the first match, 3–0. We swapped some players around, and my team won again, 7–0, this time.

At lunch, people came by the table where I was sitting and nodded to me. They said things in Spanish, gave me the thumbs-up. Lara translated. Apparently they could tell how good I was, even though I was being careful on the concrete. I didn't want to strain or smash anything. This was just for fun.

After dinner there was some excitement when the bats woke up. Apparently nobody had really been paying attention that first night, but this time we saw them go. They bled out into the twilight in a thin, black slick, off to do bat things. Eat bugs. Sharpen their fangs. Nobody was happy to see them come back, either, except some of the little kids, and Naomi, of course. This whole one corner of the hangar floor was totally covered in bat guano. My dad said it wasn't a health risk, but as a matter of fact, one of the joggers slipped on it the next day and sprained an ankle.

The next day: more of the same. Wake up, run, play soccer. Listen to Naomi rant about stuff. Listen to people talk about the flu. Flirt with Lara. Ignore my father. I still wasn't ready to check in with Sorken, or to check e-mail. I didn't want to know.

That afternoon we had our second invasion. Land crabs, this time, the size of silver-dollar pancakes, the color of old scabs, and they smelled like rotting garbage. There were hundreds of them, thousands of hairy, armored legs, all dragging and scratching and clicking. They went sideways, their pincers held up and forward. Everybody stood on their cots or tires and took pictures. When the crabs got to the far wall, they spread out until they found the little cracks and gaps where they could squeeze through. A boy used his shirt to catch three or four crabs; some of the kids had started a petting zoo.

"What was that about?" I said to Naomi.

"Land migration," she said. "They do that when they're mating. Or is it molting? That's why they're so stinky right now."

"How do you know so much about all this?" I said. "Bats and crabs and stuff?"

"I don't date much," she said. "I stay home and watch the nature feeds online."

By lunch that second day we knew about outbreaks of flu in New New York, Copenhagen, Houston, Berlin, plenty of other places. The World Health Organization had issued the report my father had been predicting, saying that was a full-on pandemic, killing the young and the healthy, not just the very young and the very elderly. We knew there were hopeful indications in India and in Taiwan with a couple of modified vaccines. The mood in the hangar was pretty unhappy. People were getting calls and e-mails about family members or friends back in the States. Not good news. On the other hand, we appeared to be in good shape here. My father said that in another two or three days, Costa Rican health officials would probably send a doctor out to sign off that we were officially flu-free. The two children with the dry coughs turned out just to have allergies. Besides that, the most pressing health issues in the hangar were some cases of cabin fever, diarrhea, and the fact that we were going through our supply of toilet paper too fast.

On the third day in the hangar we built better goals. Not quite regulation, but you'd be surprised what you can do with some expensive fishing gear and the frames from a couple of cots.

Then practice drills. I sat out the first quarter of the first game, and a Tico with muscle-y legs took the goal. We still won.

The hangar guards changed over every twelve hours or so. After a while they were kind of like the bats. You didn't even notice them most of the time. But I liked watching them watch us when we played soccer. They were into soccer. They took turns coming over to watch, and whistled through their teeth whenever I blocked a goal. They placed bets. On the third day a guard came over to me during a time-out, and pushed up his N95 mask. *"¡Que cache!"* He made enthusiastic hand gestures. *"¡Pura vida!"* I understood that. He was a young guy, athletic. He was talking fast, and Naomi and Lara weren't around to translate, but I thought I had a pretty good idea what he was saying. He was trying to give me some advice about keeping goal. I just nodded, like I understood what he was saying and appreciated it. Finally he clapped me on the shoulders and went back over to his wall like he'd finally remembered that he was a guard.

Naomi was working her way through Roger Zelazny and Kage Baker. She was a pretty fast reader. First a Baker novel, then Zelazny. Then Baker again. I kept catching her reading the endings first. "What's the point of doing that?" I said. "If you cheat and read the end of the book first, why even bother reading the rest?"

"I'm antsy," she said. "I need to know how certain things turn out." She turned over so she was facing the wall, and said something else in Spanish.

"Fine," I said. I wasn't really all that invested. I was rereading some Fritz Leiber.

About fifteen minutes later, Lara came over and sat down on the cot next to Naomi. She picked up the stack of books that

Naomi had already read, commenting in Spanish on the covers. Naomi laughed every time she said something. It was annoying, but I smiled like I understood. Finally Lara said, in English, "All of these girls have the large breasts. I did not know science fiction was about the breasts. I like the real stories. Stories about real astronauts, or scientific books."

"My father doesn't really go in for nonfiction," I said. I didn't see what was so bad about breasts, really.

"It makes for depressing reading," Naomi said. "Look at the space program in the old disunited States. Millionaires signing up for outer space field trips. The occasional unmanned flight that conks out somewhere just past Venus. SETI enthusiasts running analysis programs on their personal computers, because some guys blew up the Very Large Array, and guess what, when the real aliens show up, some guy named Hans Bliss says something and they go away again. Poof."

"Our space program is state of the art," Lara said. "Not to brag, like Dorn is always saying. But we will be sending a manned flight to Mars in the next five years. Ten years tops. If I keep my grades up and if I am chosen, I will be on that flight. That is my personal goal. My dream."

You want to go to Mars?" I said. I'm sure I looked surprised.

"Mars, to begin with," Lara said. "Then who knows? I'm in an accelerated science and physical education course at my school. Many of the graduates go into the program for astronauts."

"There are advanced classes at UCR doing some work with your space program," Naomi said. "I don't know much about it, except that it all sounds pretty cool."

"We sent a manned flight to the moon last year," Lara said. "I met one of the astronauts. She came and spoke at my school."

"Yeah, I remember that flight," I said. "We did that, like, last century." I was just joking, but Lara didn't get that.

"And what have you done since?" she asked me.

I shrugged. It wasn't really anything I was interested in. "What's the point," I said. "I mean, the aliens showed up and then they left again. Not even Hans Bliss is saying that we ought to go around chasing after them. He says that they'll come back when the time is right. Costa Rica getting all involved in a space program, is, I don't know, it's like my father deciding to leave everything behind, our whole life, just to come down here, even though Hans Bliss is just some surfer who started a cult. I don't see the point."

"The point is to go to space," Lara said. She looked at Naomi, not at me, as if I were too stupid to understand. "To go to space. It was a good thing when the aliens came to Costa Rica. They made us think about the universe, about what might be out there. Not everybody wants to sit on a beach and wait with your Hans Bliss to see if the aliens will come back."

"Okay," I said. "But not everybody gets a chance to go to Mars on a spaceship, either. Maybe not even you."

I was just being reasonable, but Lara didn't see it that way. She made this noise of exasperation, then said, emphatically, like she was making a point except that she was saying it in Spanish and really fast, so it didn't really tell me anything: *"¡Turista estúpido! ¡Usted no es hermoso como usted piensa usted es!"*

"Sorry?" I said.

But she just got up and left.

"What? What did she say?" I asked Naomi.

Naomi put down her paperback, *The Doors of His Face, the Lamp of His Mouth*. She said, "You can be kind of a jerk, Dorn. Some advice? *Hazme caso*—pay attention. I've seen you play soccer and you're pretty good. Maybe you'll get back to the States and get discovered and maybe one day you'll save some goal for some team and it will turn out to be the block that wins the World Cup. I'll go out to a bar and get drunk to celebrate when that happens. But my money's on Lara. I bet you anything Lara gets her chance and goes to Mars. I don't know if you've noticed, but when she isn't playing soccer or hanging out with us, she's studying for her classes or talking with the pilots about what it's like to fly commercial jets. And she also knows how to get along with people, Dorn. Maybe you don't have to be a nice guy to do well in team sports, but does it hurt?"

"I am a nice guy," I said.

"Stupid me," Naomi said. "Here I was thinking that you were arrogant, and, um, stupid, and what was the other thing? Oh yeah, *short.*" And then she picked up the Zelazny again and ignored me.

Lara didn't speak to me for the rest of the day. She didn't come back when we played soccer in the afternoon, and even though it was the Tucancillos' turn to do the dishes, she didn't turn up.

We still had plenty of surgical masks, but by the fourth day hardly anybody was wearing them. Just the sticklers and the guards in their N95s. I think everybody else was using the remaining supply for toilet paper. I wore one like a headband during soccer. I kind of needed a haircut. I couldn't do anything about that, but I did have a bath on the fourth night, after dinner, in one of the makeshift bathing stalls. Some of the people on the flight didn't have a lot of clothes in their suitcases, and so some borrowing had been going on, and there were clothes and various species of underwear draped over tires. I leaned against the outside wall of the hangar, away from the latrines, and admired the sunset for a bit. Not that I was a huge fan of sunsets, but the ones here were bigger, or something. And it smelled better out here. Not that you noticed how bad it smelled in the hangar most of the time, but once you came outside you realized you didn't want to go back in, not immediately, at least.

And the guards didn't seem to mind. There wasn't really anywhere for us to go. Just asphalt and runways. Still no planes coming in. Nobody to watch the sunset with me, which was an odd thing to think, since I'm usually pretty comfortable being alone. Even out on the field, during the game, the goalie is alone more often than not. Lara wasn't talking to me. I wasn't talking to my dad. Naomi and I weren't talking to each other. The sun went down fast, regardless of how I felt about the whole thing, and yeah, I know that's a melodramatic way to think about a sunset, but so what? Universe 1, Dorn 0.

When I came back into the hangar, Lara was over in the petting zoo, just sitting there. A dog was curled up on her legs and she was thumping its belly, softly, like a drum.

The petting zoo was an ongoing project. There were the three smelly crabs and a skinny brownish snake in a plastic makeup case that the kids fed beetles to. Some girl had caught it when she went out to use the bathroom. There were lizards in recycled food containers and a smallish iguana one of the guards had donated. There were even two dogs who got spoiled rotten.

I wandered over, trying to come up with something interesting to say. "What's up?" was all I came up with.

She looked up at me, then down again. Petted the dog.

"Watching the iguana," she said.

"What's it doing?" I said.

"Not much."

I sat down next to her. We didn't say anything else for a while. Finally I said, "Naomi says I shouldn't be such a jerk. And also that I'm short."

"I like Naomi," Lara said. "She's pretty."

Really? I thought. (But I knew better than to say that out loud.)

"What about me?"

Lara said, "I like watching you play soccer. It's like watching the soccer on television."

"Naomi's pretty brutal, but she's honest," I said. "I may never get tall enough to be a world-class goalie."

"You'll be taller. Your father is tall. Sometimes I have a temper," she said. "I shouldn't have said what I said to you."

"What did you say exactly?" I asked.

"Learn Spanish," she said. "Then when I say the awful things to you, you'll understand." Then she said, "And I am going to go up one day."

"Up?" I said.

"To Mars."

She wasn't wearing her mask. She was smiling. I don't know if she was smiling at me or at the idea of Mars, but I didn't care all that much. Mars was far away. I was a lot closer.

My father was on his cell phone. "Yes," he said. "Okay. I'll talk to him." He hung up. He said, "Dorn, come sit down for a minute."

I didn't say anything to him. I just sat down on my cot.

I realized that I was looking around, as if something had happened. Naomi was over against the wall, talking to the HANS BLISS FOR WORLD PRESIDENT guy, the one with the big nose. He was a lot taller than Naomi. Did Naomi mind being short?

My father said, "Your coach. He wanted to talk to you."

"Sorken called?" I said. I felt kind of sick to my stomach already, even though I wasn't sure why. I should have listened to those messages.

"No," my father said. "I'm sorry, Dorn. It was Coach Turner. He was calling about Sorken."

And I understood the difference immediately. "Sorken's dead."

My father nodded.

"Is everybody else okay? On the team?"

"I really don't know," my father said. "Mr. Turner hasn't been able to reach everyone. A lot of people around Philadelphia came down with flu, just like everywhere else. If I'd had more time to plan, I don't think I would have booked that flight. You were right, you know. I got an e-mail from a colleague out in Potlatch who thought something was coming, and meanwhile I'd been in touch with Hans Bliss off and on, and the visas had just come, and it seemed like a minor risk, getting us onto the flight, getting us through the airport. I thought if we didn't leave right then, who knew when we'd get here?"

I didn't say anything. I was remembering how Sorken used to come down on me when I was being a showoff or not paying enough attention to what was happening, on the field, during practice. Sorken wasn't like my dad. If you weren't paying attention to him or you were sulking, he'd throw a soccer ball at your head. Or one of his shoes. But I'd just left those messages from him on the phone. I didn't even know where my phone was right now.

I'd never really thought about Sorken getting the flu and dying, but it had always seemed like there was a good chance that my father would catch something. A lot of hospital workers died during the last pandemic.

My father said, "Dorn? Are you okay?"

I nodded.

"I'm sorry about Sorken," he said. "I never really sat down and talked to him."

"He didn't have much time for people who didn't play soccer," I said.

"It always looked like he was riding you pretty hard."

"I don't think he liked me," I said. "I didn't like him most of the time. But he was a good coach. He wasn't ever harder on me than he should have been."

"I told Coach Turner that you wouldn't be back for a while," my father said. "To be honest with you, I don't know what we'll do. If we'll be allowed to stay. There's been some talk in the hangar. Rumors that our government is responsible. That we were targeting Calexico. It doesn't seem likely to me, but we weren't going to be very popular down here, Dorn, even before people starting making up stories like that. And I'm not going to be much more popular back in Philadelphia. I checked in with my team. Dr. Willis yelled for about five minutes and then she just hung up. I skipped out even though I knew they were going to need me."

"Maybe you would have gotten sick if we'd stayed," I said. "Or maybe I would have gotten sick."

My father studied his hands. "Who knows? I was planning to tell you about the visas. Give you a choice. But then I just couldn't leave you. You know, in case." He stopped and swallowed. "I was talking to Paula and some of the other Hans Bliss people. As of this morning they haven't been able to get hold of anyone out that way. At the colony. They've been under quarantine, too, remember? And no doctor. Just two OB-GYNs and a chiropractor."

"Everything will be fine," I said. I was a regular cheerleader. But I couldn't help looking around again, and this time I could see all the things that I'd been trying not to see. All around us, other people were having, had been having, conversations just like this one. About people who had died. About what had been going on while we were trapped in here.

I said, "The aliens are coming back to see Hans Bliss, remember? So there's no way that Hans Bliss can just keel over dead from something like flu. Those aliens probably vaccinated him or something. Remember how he said he didn't ever get sick anymore?"

"Good point," my father said. "If you're gullible enough to buy all the things that Hans Bliss says."

"Hey, you two," Naomi said. She looked flushed and happy, as if she'd gotten the last word again with the Hans Bliss guy. She didn't seem to be annoyed with me. And I couldn't really be annoyed with her, either. Everything she'd said was true, more or less. I hadn't known her very long, but I already knew that that was the terrible thing about Naomi.

My father took the soccer ball out of my hands. I don't even know when I'd picked it up, but it felt right to let go of it. He put it down on the floor, sat down beside me on the cot, and patted my leg. "It will all be fine," he said, and I nodded.

My brother Stephen was older than me by four years. He didn't like me. According to my father, when I was a baby Stephen used to unfasten my seatbelt and also the strap that held my baby seat in. When I was five, he pushed me down a flight of stairs. I broke my wrist. My mother saw him do it, and so once a week for the next two years Stephen went to see a counselor named Ms. Blair in downtown Philadelphia; I remember I was jealous.

When our parents got divorced, Stephen was ten and I was six, and they decided they would each take custody of one child. Stephen thought that this was a great idea. His goal had always been to become an only child.

My mother went back home to Dalton, Colorado, where she took over the bookkeeping at her family's fancy dude ranch and spa. Whenever I flew out to visit, Stephen made sure I understood that it was all his. His house, his horses—all of them—his mom, his grandparents, his uncles, aunts, cousins. He came back east to stay with us once, and then he developed an inner-ear condition that made it impossible for him to fly. So he didn't ever have to come visit again. He didn't like my father much either.

The last time I saw my mom and Stephen, Stephen was applying to colleges. He didn't seem to loathe me as much as usual. He was practically an adult. I was just a kid. I was athletic, which he wasn't, but my grades were pitiful. I was small for my age. He could tell how annoyed I was that he was tall and I wasn't, and somehow it made things better. He had a girlfriend, a massage therapist at the spa, and he didn't even care that she made a point of being nice to me. I had a pretty good time on that trip. My mother and I rode out and went camping down in the canyons. Stephen's girlfriend cooked dinner for us when we got home. It was almost like we were a family. Stephen showed us a movie he'd made to send along with his college applications. When I said I liked it, he was pleased. We got into arguments the way we always did, but this time I realized something, that Stephen liked a good fight. Maybe he always had, or maybe he'd just grown up. If you stood up to him, it made him happy. I had never tried standing up to him before. He was applying for a visa so he could go study at a big-deal film school in Calexico.

A few months later, the horses at the dude ranch started

dying. My mother e-mailed and said my uncle had brought the local vet in. They were putting the sick horses down. When we talked on the phone, she sounded terrible. My mother loved horses. Then people on the ranch started dying, too. Sometimes a flu will jump from one species to another. That's why a lot of people don't keep cats or birds as pets anymore.

I talked to my mother two more times the next day. Then things got worse, real fast. My father was staying over at the hospital, and lots of people were dying. My mother got the flu. She died. Stephen died. The girlfriend got sick, and then she got better again. She sent one e-mail before she got sick and one after she got better, which is how I found out what had happened. Her first e-mail said that Stephen had wanted her to tell us how much he loved us. But he probably died in quarantine. He probably felt like he was getting a cold, and then I bet his temperature shot up until he was delirious or completely unconscious and couldn't say anything to anyone. My dad said that their kind of flu was fast. So you didn't suffer or anything. I think the girlfriend was just making all that up, about Stephen and what he supposedly said. She was a nice person. I don't think he'd ever said anything to her about how much he disliked me. About how he used to try to kill me. You want the people you like to think that you get along with your family.

It was the hardest thing I ever had to do, telling my father when he finally came home. And we haven't talked about it much since then. I don't know why it's easier for some people to talk about aliens than to talk about death. Aliens only happen to some people. Death happens to everyone.

That night in the hangar, I dreamed about Sorken. He was standing in front of the goal, instead of me, and he was talking at me in Spanish, like the Costa Rican guard. I knew that if I could only understand what he was saying, he'd be satisfied, and then I could take the goal again. I wanted to say I was sorry that he was dead, and that I was sorry that I was in Costa Rica, and that I was sorry I hadn't ever called him back when he left all those messages, but he couldn't understand what I was saying because I couldn't speak Spanish. I kept hoping that Lara would show up.

Instead the aliens came. They came down just like Hans Bliss had said, in this wave of feeling: joy and love and perfect acceptance and knowingness, so that it didn't matter anymore that Sorken didn't remember how to speak English and I didn't know Spanish. For the first time we just understood each other. Then the aliens scooped up Sorken and took him away.

I grabbed onto the frame of the soccer goal and held on as hard as I could, because I was sure they were going to come back for me. I didn't want to go wherever it was, even though it was beautiful, so beautiful; they were even more beautiful than Hans Bliss had said. A wave of warm, alien ecstasy poured over me, and then I woke up because Naomi was hitting me on the shoulder. She had a plate of food with her. Breakfast.

"Stop moaning about how beautiful it is," she said. "Please? Whatever it is, it's really, really beautiful. I get that, totally. Oh shit, Dorn, were you having a wet dream? I am so very embarrassed. Oh yuck. Let me go somewhere far away now and not eat my breakfast."

I wanted to die. But instead I got changed under the foil blanket and then went and got my own breakfast and came back. Naomi had her nose in a book. I said, "I don't see what the big deal is. It's just something that happens to guys, okay?"

"It happens to girls, too," Naomi said. "Not that I want to

be having some sex-education discussion with you. Although you probably need it, from what I hear about American schools nowadays."

"Like you had it so much better," I said. "And my dad's a doctor, remember? I know everything I need to know and lots of other stuff, too. And what were you doing last night? You woke me up when you came to bed. I don't even know when it was. It was late."

"My parents homeschooled me," Naomi said. "They wanted me to have every advantage." Her eyes were all red.

"What?" I said. "Are you sick? Is everything okay?"

"I think so," Naomi said. She scraped her nose with a sterile wipe. "I talked to my mom last night. She says that Vermont is still under martial law, so she can't get out to see my grandmother. She can't get her on the phone either. That's probably bad, right?"

"It might not be," I said.

Naomi didn't say anything.

"At least your mom and dad are all right," I said.

She nodded.

"Here," I said. "Let's get a book for you. Something cheerful. How about Naomi Novik?"

We sat and she read and I thought about stuff. Sorken. My father. My mother. My brother Stephen. I thought about how the kind of thing that Stephen thought was funny when he was alive wasn't really anything that I thought was funny. For example, when he pushed me down the stairs. I remember he was giggling. The last time I was out visiting my mother, it was different. He laughed at some of the things that I said, and not like it was because he thought I was an idiot. We got into one of those arguments about something really stupid, and then I said something and he just started laughing. I wish I could remember what I said, what we were arguing about.

Naomi looked up and saw me looking at her. "What?" she said.

"Nothing," I said.

"Hey," she said. "Do you surf?"

"No," I said. "Why?"

"Not much to do out there on the beach with Hans Bliss," she said. "Not a lot of soccer players. Everybody goes surfing. You know that Hans Bliss guy? Philip? The one with the tattoo and the mother. Paula." The one with the big nose. "He was telling me this story about a guy he knew, a surfer. One day this surfer guy was out in the water and he got knocked under by this really big wave. He went down and his board shot out from under him, really sliced him. But he didn't realize what had happened until he got out of the water, because the water was really cold, but when he got out of the water and pulled his suit down, it turned out that the fin on his board had cut his ball sac right open, and he hadn't felt it because the water was so cold. When he pulled his suit down, his testicle fell out and was just hanging there, way down on his leg on, like, this string. Like a yo-yo."

"So?" I said. "Are you trying to gross me out or something? My dad's a doctor, remember? I hear stories like this all the time."

Naomi looked nonplussed. "Just be careful," she said. "What's up? Bad news?"

I'd found my cell phone, and I was trying to decide whether or not to listen to Sorken's messages. But in the end I just deleted them. Then I went and got some people together to play soccer.

It was the fifth day, if you're counting, and nobody in the hangar had the flu, which was good news, but my father still had his hands full. There was the pregnant woman from Switzerland who had come over to join Hans Bliss. A couple of days in quarantine, and she decided that she'd had enough. She threw this major tantrum, said she was going into labor. The best part: she took off all her clothes before she threw the tantrum. So you had this angry, naked, pregnant woman yelling stuff in German and French and English and stomping her foot like Gojiro. It totally broke up the soccer game. We all stopped to watch.

My father went and sat on the floor next to her. I went and stood nearby, just in case she got dangerous. Someone needed to look out for my father. He said that he'd be happy to examine her, if she liked, but she probably wouldn't go into labor for another months, at least, and we weren't going to be stuck in here that long. And anyway, he'd delivered babies before. All you really needed was boiling water and lots of towels. I think he was kidding about that.

Just a few hours later, a Tico doctor showed up with a full mobile clinic. By that point we were just kind of kicking the ball around. I was showing off some for Lara. The doctor's name was Meñoz, and it was all pretty much like my father had said it was going to be. My father and Dr. Meñoz talked first, and then they looked at the clinic records my father had been keeping. I hung around for a bit, hoping that Dr. Meñoz would just go ahead and tell us that we were free to go, but it seemed like it was going to take a while. So Lara and I went around and got one last soccer match together. A lot of people came and watched.

That guard who'd talked to me a few times was, like, my biggest fan now. Whenever we were playing he yelled and clapped his hands, and he'd dance around when I stopped a goal. All the guards came over to watch this time, not just him, as if they knew that the rules didn't really matter now. So much for quarantine.

Before we started for real, something strange happened. My guard put down his gun. He talked to his friends, and they gave him a high five. Then he came out onto the field. He even took off his N95 mask. He smiled at me. "I play, too," he said. He seemed proud of having this much English. Well, it was more English than I had Spanish.

I shrugged. "Sure," I said. I waved at the other team, the one Lara was on. "Play for those guys. They need all the help they can get."

It was around three in the afternoon, and it was warm, but there was a breeze coming in through the vents up in the tin roof and through the big metal doors. Like always, there was music playing on someone's googly, and the little kids were having a conference over in the petting zoo, probably figuring out what to do with all of the freaky little animals they'd collected. I was almost enjoying being here. I was almost feeling nostalgic. It wasn't like I had a lot of friends in the hangar, but most people knew me well enough to say hi. When I wanted to get a match going, there were always enough people to play, and nobody got all that upset about the fact that my team won most of the time. Whatever happened next, I didn't think I'd be spending a lot of time playing soccer. Wherever we ended up, nobody was going to know much about me, about what I could do in a soccer game. I'd just be some American kid whose dad was a doctor who had wanted to see aliens.

Naomi, who had decided she enjoyed refereeing a match every once in a while, threw the ball in, and that hangar guard was on it immediately, before anyone else even thought about moving. He was amazing. He was better than amazing. He went up and down the concrete as if no one else was on the floor. And he put the ball past me every single time, no matter what I did. And every time, when I failed to stop him, he just grinned and said, "Good try. Good try."

The worst part is that he did it without even taking advantage of my height. He didn't go over me. He just went around. The way he did it was so good it was like a bad dream. Like science fiction. Like I was Superman and he was Kryptonite. He seemed to know what I was going to do before I did. He knew all about me, like he'd been taking notes during all those other games.

After a while both teams stopped playing and they just watched while he did all sorts of interesting stuff. If I came forward, he skimmed around and behind me. Score. If I hung back in front of the goal, it didn't matter. He put the ball where I wasn't. I didn't give up, though. I finally stopped a goal. I felt good about that, until I realized that he'd *let* me have the save. I hadn't really stopped anything.

And that was the last straw. There he was, grinning at me, like this had just been for fun. He wasn't even breathing hard. I made myself grin back. He didn't realize I knew he'd let me save that last goal. He didn't even think I was that smart. He clapped for me. I clapped for him. Everyone who had been watching was clapping and yelling. Even Lara. So I just walked away.

I didn't feel angry or upset or anything. I just felt as if I'd found out something important. I wasn't as good as I thought I was. I'd thought I was amazing, but I wasn't. Some guy who'd spent five days standing against a wall holding a gun could walk in and prove in about ten minutes that I wasn't anything special. So that was that. I know you'll think that I was being melodramatic, but I wasn't. I was being realistic. I gave up on soccer right then.

For some reason, I was thinking about the little empty glass bottle that my father gave my mother, that my mother gave me. I wondered what Sorken would think when I told him I was quitting soccer, and then I remembered Sorken was dead. So I didn't have to worry what he thought.

Something was going on with the Hans Bliss group. They'd disassembled their modesty wall. Actually, they'd just kicked it over. They were huddled together, looking really bad. Utterly hopeless. I could sympathize. My father and Zuleta-Arango and Dr. Meñoz were there too, so I went over. My father said, "Dr. Meñoz had some news about the Star Friends community."

"Not good news," I said.

"No," my father said. He didn't sound particularly upset, but that's my father. He doesn't ever seem particularly anything. "One of the last arrivals came in from Calexico, and he had the flu. They weren't being very careful in the community. Hans Bliss didn't believe they were in any real danger. Lots of physical contact. Communal eating. They didn't have good protocols in place. No doctor. They had no doctor."

"It might not have made any difference," Zuleta-Arango said. "There were deaths on one of the cruise ships, too. And in a few neighborhoods of San Jose, a few cities, they have set up additional quarantine zones. There are deaths. But the mobile units are being supplied with vaccines, which Dr. Meñoz says will do the trick. It isn't as bad as it's been in the States. We have been lucky here."

"Not all of us," my father said. "Hans Bliss is dead."

The pregnant woman began to wail. Lots of other people were crying. "The remaining community is in bad shape. As soon as quarantine is lifted here, I'll go out to see how I can help, if they'll let me."

Dr. Meñoz popped his cell phone closed and struck up a

conversation in rapid Spanish with Zuleta-Arango, Miike, and Purdy. The Hans Bliss people were still standing there. They looked like they'd been pithed. That guy Philip, the one with the surfer friend, the one that Naomi seemed to like, blew his nose hard. He said to my father, "We'll all go out. There will be things that they'll need us to do."

"What about me?" I asked.

"Yes," my father said. "What about you? I can't send you home."

Dr. Meñoz said, "As of right now, I'm authorized to lift quarantine here. This news is good, at least? There will be a bus outside the hangar within the hour. It will transport all of you into San Jose, to a center for displaced travelers. They are arranging for the necessary series of vaccinations there. Shall I make the announcement or would you prefer to do it?"

Zuleta-Arango made the announcement. There was something anticlimactic about it. Everyone already knew what he was about to say. And what he said wasn't really the thing that we needed to know. What we didn't know was what was going to happen next. Where we would be sent. What would happen in the next few weeks. When the flight ban would be lifted. Where the flu had come from. Whether or not the people that we loved would be okay. What we would find when we got home.

Naomi had already packed up her duffel bag. She said, "Lots of people have been coming by, bringing back your father's books. I finished the last Kim Stanley Robinson. I guess there are still a couple of short-story collections. I heard about Bliss. That really sucks. Now I feel bad about calling him an idiot."

"He was an idiot," I said. "That's why he's dead."

"I guess," Naomi said. "What's in that bottle?"

Like I said, the glass bottle with nothing inside it was the first present that my father ever gave my mother. He told her that there was a genie in the bottle. That he'd bought it at a magic shop. A *real* magic shop. He said that he'd already made two wishes. The first wish had been to meet a beautiful girl. That was my mother. The second wish was that she would fall in love with him, but not just because of the wish. That she would really fall in love with him. So already you can see the problem, right? You wouldn't fall for some guy who was telling you this. Because if you fall in love with someone because of a wish, how can it not be the wish that makes you fall in love? I said that to my mother one time and she said that I was being too literal minded. I said that actually, no, I was just saying that my father's made-up story was kind of stupid.

My mother always said that she'd never used that last wish. And I didn't understand that either. Why didn't she use it when they were getting divorced? Why didn't she use it to make Stephen like having a little brother better? I used to think that if I had the bottle I'd wish for Stephen not to hate me so much. For him to like me. Just a little. The way that older brothers are supposed to like younger brothers. There were other wishes. I mean, I've made lists and lists of all the wishes I could make, like being the best goalie there has ever been. Like getting taller by a few inches. Other stuff that's too embarrassing to talk about. I could come up with wishes all day long. That it wouldn't rain. That I'd suddenly be a genius at math. That my parents would get back together.

I hadn't ever made any of those wishes, not even the soccer wish, because I don't believe in wishes. Also because it would be like cheating, because when I was a famous goalie I'd always wonder if I were really the best soccer player in the world, or whether I'd just wished it true. I could wish that I were taller, but maybe one day I will be. Everyone says that I will be. I guess if I were Paula or one of the Star Friends, I'd wish that Hans Bliss had been smarter. That he hadn't died. Or I'd wish that the aliens would come back. I don't know which of those I'd wish for.

I gave the bottle to Lara when she came over to say goodbye. I didn't really mean anything by it.

She said, "Dorn, what is this?"

"It's a genie in a bottle," Naomi said. "Like a fairy tale. Dorn says that there's one wish left in there. I said that if he gave it to me, I'd wish for world peace, but he's giving it to you instead. Can you believe it?"

Lara shook the glass bottle.

"Don't do that," I said. "How would you like to be shaken if you were an invisible genie who's been trapped in a bottle for hundreds of years?"

"I don't believe in wishes," Lara said. "But it is very sweet of you, Dorn, to give it to me."

"It belonged to my mother," I said.

"His *dead* mother," Naomi said. "It's a precious family heirloom."

"Then I can't keep it," Lara said. She tried to give it back.

I put my hands behind me.

"Never mind then," Lara said. She looked a little annoyed, actually. As if I were being silly. I realized something: Lara wasn't particularly romantic. And maybe I am. She said, "I'll keep it safe for you, Dorn. But I have something important to tell you."

"I know," I said. "You were watching the guard walk all over me. During that last game. You want to tell me to pick a new career."

"No, Dorn," Lara said. Even more annoyed now. "Stop talking, okay? That guard isn't just a guard, you know? He was on the team for Costa Rica. The team that was supposed to go to the World Cup three years ago, before the last influenza."

"What?" I said.

"His name is Olivas," Lara said. "He got into a fight this summer and they kicked him off the team for a while. He sounds like you, Dorn, don't you think? Not very bright. But never mind. He says you are good. Talented."

"If I were any good, he wouldn't have been able to walk past me like that, over and over again," I said. But I started to feel a little better. He wasn't just a guard with a gun. He was a professional soccer player.

"No, Dorn," Lara said again. "You are *good*, but he is *very good*. There is a difference, you know?"

"Apparently," I said, "there is a difference. I just hadn't realized how big. I didn't know he was, like, a soccer superstar. I thought that maybe he was just average for Costa Rica. I was thinking that I ought to quit soccer and take up scuba diving or something."

"I hadn't realized that you were a quitter," Lara said. She still sounded very disapproving. Her eyebrows were knit together, and her lower lip stuck out. She looked even prettier, and it was because she was disappointed in me. Interesting.

"Maybe you ought to get to know him better," Naomi said, looking at me looking at Lara like she knew what I was thinking. "Dorn needs to pack. You two will have plenty of time to talk on the bus. It's not like you're never going to see each other again. At least, not yet. Lara, *pele el ojo*. Your mother is coming this way."

"*Es un chingue*," Lara said. "*¡Que tigra!*" She sighed and kissed me right on the mouth. She had to dip her head down. Then she dashed off. Zip. When I thought about it, I wasn't looking forward to getting to know her mother, and her mother sure wasn't looking forward to getting to know me.

"So," Naomi said. She was grinning. "You know what Lara told me a few days ago? That she wasn't ever planning on having boyfriends. You can't get serious about boys if you want to go to Mars. So much for that. Not that you'll care, but you aren't the only one who got lucky."

"What," I said. "Did that blond girl come over to show you her engagement ring or something?"

"No," Naomi said. She waggled her eyebrows like crazy. "*I* got lucky. Me. That cute guy, Philip? Remember him?"

"We're not thinking about the same guy," I said. "He's not cute. I know cute. I *am* cute."

"He's nice," Naomi said. "And he's funny. And smart."

I didn't know so much about nice. Or smart. I finished packing my suitcase, and started in on my father's. I wished I hadn't given away that little glass bottle. I could have given Lara a paperback instead. "You must have a lot to talk about."

"I suppose," Naomi said. "You know the best part?"

"What?" I said. I looked around for my father and finally spotted him. He was sitting on a cot beside the pregnant woman, who probably had a name but I'd never bothered to find out. She was sobbing against his shoulder, her mouth still open in that wail. Her face was all shiny with snot. I was betting that if her baby was a boy, she'd name him Hans. Maybe Bliss if it was a girl.

A girl walked by, dragging an iguana behind her on a homemade leash. Were they going to let her bring the iguana on the bus?

Naomi said, "The best part is he has dual citizenship. His father's from Costa Rica. And he likes smart, fat, big-mouthed chicks."

"Who doesn't," I said.

"Don't be so sarcastic," Naomi said. "It's an unattractive quality in someone your size. Want a hand with the suitcases?"

"You take the one with all the books in it," I said.

People were still packing up their stuff. Some people were talking on their cell phones, transmitting good news, getting good news and bad news in return. Over by the big doors to the hangar, I ran into the guard. Olivas. I was beginning to think I recognized his name. He nodded and smiled and handed me a piece of paper with a number on it. He said something in Spanish.

Naomi said, "He says you ought to come see him practice next month, when he's back on his team again."

"Okay," I said. "*Gracias.* Thank you. *Bueno. Bueno.*" I smiled at Olivas and tucked his phone number into my shirt pocket. I was thinking, One day, I'll be better than you are. You won't get a thing past me. I'll know Spanish, too. So I'll know exactly what you're saying, and not just stand here looking like an idiot. I'll be six inches taller. And when I get scouted, let's say I'm still living down here, and let's say I end up on the same team as you, I won't get kicked off, not for fighting. Fighting is for idiots.

Naomi and I went out onto the cracked tarmac and sat on our luggage. Costa Rican sunlight felt even more luxurious when you were out of quarantine, I decided. I could get used to this kind of sunlight. Lara was over with her mother and some other women, all of them speaking a mile a minute. Lara looked over at me and then looked away again. Her eyebrows were doing that thing. I was pretty sure we weren't going to end up sitting next to each other on the bus. Off in the distance, you could see somewhere that might have been San Jose, where we were going. The sky was blue, and there were still no planes in it. They were all lined up along the runways. Our transportation wasn't in sight yet, so I went to use the latrines one last time. That's where I was when the aliens came. I was pissing into a hole in the ground. And my father was still sitting inside the hangar, his arm around an inconsolable, enormously pregnant, somewhat gullible Swiss woman, hoping that she would eventually stop crying on his T-shirt.

It was kind of like the bats. They were there, and after a while you noticed them. Only it wasn't like the bats at all and I don't really mean to say that it was. The aliens' ships were lustrous and dark and flexible; something like sharks, if sharks were a hundred feet long and hung in the air, moving just a little, as if breathing. There were three of the ships, about 150 feet up. They were so very close. I yanked up my pants and pushed the latrine curtain aside, stumbled out. Naomi and that guy Philip were standing there on the tarmac, looking up, holding hands. The priest crossing himself. The kid with her iguana. Lara and her mother and the other passengers all looking up, silently. Nobody saying anything yet. When I turned toward San Jose, I could see more spacecraft, lots more. Of course, you already know all this. Everyone saw them. You saw them. You saw the aliens hovering over the melting ice floes of Antarctica, too, and over New New York and Paris and Mexico City, and Angkor Wat and all those other places. Unless you were blind or dead or the kind of person who always manages to miss seeing what everybody else sees. Like aliens showing up. What I want to know is did they come back because they knew that Hans Bliss was dead? People still argue about that, too. Poor Hans Bliss. That's what I was thinking: Poor, stupid, lucky, unlucky Hans Bliss.

I ran inside the hangar, past Olivas and the other guards and Dr. Meñoz and Zuleta-Arango, and two kids spinning around in circles, making themselves dizzy on purpose.

"Dad," I said. "Dad! Everyone! The aliens! They're here. They're just outside! Lots of them!"

My father got up. The pregnant woman stopped crying. She stood up, too. They were walking toward me and then they were running right past me.

Me, I couldn't make up my mind. It seemed as if I had a choice to make, which was stupid, I know. What choice? I wasn't sure. Outside the hangar were the aliens and the future. Inside the hangar it was just me, a couple hundred horrible bats sleeping up in the roof, the remains of a petting zoo, and all of the rest of the mess we were leaving behind. The cots. Our trash. All the squashed water bottles and crumpled foil blankets and the used surgical masks and no-longer-sterile wipes. The makeshift soccer field. I had this strange urge, like I ought to go over to the field and tidy it up. Stand in front of one of the cobbled-together goals. Guard it. Easier to guard it, of course, now that Olivas wasn't around. I know it sounds stupid, I know that you're wondering why aliens show up and I'm still in here, in the empty hangar, doing nothing. I can't explain it to you. Maybe you can explain it to me. But I stood there feeling empty and lost and ashamed and alone until I heard my father's voice. He was saying, "Dorn! Adorno, where are you? Adorno, get out here! They're beautiful, they're even more beautiful than that idiot said. Come on out, come and see!"

So I went to see.

The devils were full of little spiky bones.
Zilla ate two.

THE CONSTABLE OF ABAL

THEY LEFT ABAL in a hurry, after Ozma's mother killed the constable. It was a shame, too, because business had been good. Ozma's mother had invitations almost every night to one party or another in the finest homes of Abal. Rich gentlemen admired Ozma's mother, Zilla, for her beauty, and their wives were eager to have their fortunes told. Ozma, in her shiny, stiff, black-ribboned dress, was petted and given rolls and hot chocolate. The charms and trinkets on the ends of the ribbons that Ozma and her mother wore (little porcelain and brass ships, skulls, dolls, crowns, and cups) were to attract the attention of the spirit world, but fashionable ladies in Abal had begun to wear them, too. The plague had passed through Abal a few months before Ozma and her mother came. Death was fashionable.

Thanks to Ozma's mother, every wellborn lady of Abal strolled about town for a time in a cloud of ghosts—a cloud of ghosts that only Ozma and her mother could see. Zilla made a great deal of money, first selling the ribbons and charms and then instructing the buyer on the company she now kept. Some ghosts were more desirable than others of course, just as some addresses will always be more desirable, more sought after. But if you didn't like your ghosts, well then, Ozma's mother could banish the ones you had and sell you new charms, new ghosts. A rich woman could change ghosts just as easily as changing her dress and to greater fashionable effect.

Ozma was small for her age. Her voice was soft, and her limbs were delicate as a doll's. She bound her breasts with a cloth. She didn't mind the hot chocolate, although she would have preferred wine. But wine might have made her sleepy or clumsy, and it was hard enough carefully and quietly slipping in and out of bedrooms and dressing rooms and studies unnoticed when hundreds of ghost charms were dangling like fishing weights from your collar, your bodice, your seams, your hem. It was a surprise, really, that Ozma could move at all.

Zilla called her daughter Princess Monkey, but Ozma felt more like a beast of burden, a tricked-up pony that her mother had laden down with secrets and more secrets. Among Ozma's ghost charms were skeleton keys and tiny chisels. There was no magic about how Ozma got into and out of locked desks and boudoirs. And if she were seen, it was easy enough to explain what she was looking for. One of her ghosts, you see, was playing a little game. The observer saw only a small solemn girl chasing after her invisible friend.

Zilla was not greedy. She was a scrupulous blackmailer. She did not bleed her clients dry; she milked them. You could even say she did it out of kindness. What good is a secret without someone to know it? When one cannot afford a scandal, a blackmailer is an excellent bargain. Ozma and Zilla assembled the evidence of love affairs, ill-considered attachments, stillbirths, stolen inheritances, and murders. They were as vigilant as any biographer, solicitous as any confidante. Zilla fed gobbets of tragedy, romance, comedy to the ghosts who dangled so hungrily at the end of their ribbons. One has to feed a ghost something delicious, and there is only so much blood a grown woman and a smallish girl have to spare.

The constable had been full of blood: a young man, quite pretty to look at, ambitious, and in the pay of one Lady V——. Zilla had been careless, or Lady V—— was cleverer than she looked. For certain, she was more clever than she was beautiful, Zilla said, in a rage. Zilla stabbed the constable in the neck with a demon needle. Blood sprayed out through the hollow needle like red ink. All of Ozma's ghosts began to tug at their ribbons in a terrible frenzy as if, Ozma thought, they were children and she were a maypole.

First the constable was a young man, full of promise and juice, and then he was a dead man in a puddle of his own blood, and then he was a ghost, small enough that Zilla could have clapped him between her two hands and burst him like a pastry bag, had he any real substance. He clutched at one of Zilla's ribbon charms as if it were a life rope. The look of surprise on his face was comical.

Ozma thought he made a handsome ghost. She winked at him, but then there was a great deal of work to do. There was the body to take care of, and Zilla's clothes and books and jewelry to be packed, and all of the exceedingly fragile ghost tackle to wrap up in cotton and rags.

Zilla was in a filthy temper. She kicked the body of the constable. She paced and drank while Ozma worked. She rolled out maps and rolled them back up again.

"Where are we going this time?" Ozma said.

"Home," Zilla said. She blew her nose on a map. Zilla had terrible allergies in summer. "We're going home."

On the seventh day of their journey, outlaws shot and killed Neren, Zilla's manservant, as he watered the horses from a stream. From inside the coach, Zilla drew her gun. She waited until the outlaws were within range and then she shot them both in the head. Zilla's aim was excellent.

By the time Ozma had the horses calmed down, Neren's ghost had drifted downstream, and she had no ribbons with which to collect trash like the outlaws anyway. Zilla had made her leave most of her ghosts and ribbons at home. Too many ghosts made travel difficult: they frightened horses and drew unwelcome attention. And besides, it was easy enough to embroider new ribbons and collect new ghosts when one arrived in a new place. Ozma had kept only three favorites: an angry old empress, a young boy whose ghost was convinced it was actually a kitten, and the constable. But neither the empress nor the little boy said much anymore. Nothing stirred them. And there was something more vivid about the constable, or perhaps it was just the memory of his surprised look and his bright, bright blood.

She's a monster, the constable said to Ozma. He was looking at Zilla with something like admiration. Ozma felt a twinge of jealousy, of possessive pride.

"She's killed a hundred men and women," Ozma told him. "She has a little list of their names in her book. We light candles for them in the temple."

I don't remember my name, the constable said. *Did I perhaps introduce myself to you and your mother, before she killed me?*

"It was something like Stamp or Anvil," Ozma said. "Or Cobble."

"Ozma," Zilla said. "Stop talking to that ghost. Come and help with Neren."

Ozma and Neren had not liked each other. Neren had liked to pinch and tease Ozma when Zilla wasn't looking. He'd put his hand on the flat place where her breasts were bound. Sometimes he picked her up by her hair to show how strong he was, how little and helpless Ozma was.

They wrapped his body in a red sheet and wedged it between the branches of a tree, winding the sheet around and around the branches. It was what you did for the dead when you were in a hurry. If it had been up to Ozma, they'd have left Neren for dogs to eat. She would have stayed to watch.

I'm hungry, said the constable's ghost. Ozma gave him a little bowl of blood and dirt, scraped from the ground where Neren had died.

After that, they traveled faster. The horses were afraid of Ozma's mother, although she did not use the whips as often as Neren had.

Ozma sat in the carriage and played I Spy with the constable's ghost. *I spy with my little eye*, said the constable.

"A cloud," Ozma said. "A man in a field."

The view was monotonous. There were fields brown with blight, and the air was foul with dust. There had been a disease of the wheat this year, as well as plague. There *were* no clouds. The man in the field was a broken stalk in a clearing, tied with small dirty flags, left as a piece of field magic. A field god to mark the place where someone had drawn the white stone.

Not a man, the constable said. *A woman. A sad girl with brown hair. She looks a little like you.*

"Is she pretty?" Ozma said.

Are you pretty? the constable said.

Ozma tossed her hair. "The ladies of Abal called me a pretty poppet," she said. "They said my hair was the color of honey."

Your mother is very beautiful, the constable said. Out on the coachman's seat, Zilla was singing a song about black birds pecking at someone's eyes and fingers. Zilla loved sad songs.

"I will be even more beautiful when I grow up," Ozma said. "Zilla says so."

How old are you? said the constable.

"Sixteen," Ozma said, although this was only a guess. She'd begun to bleed the year before. Zilla had not been pleased.

Why do you bind your breasts? said the constable.

When they traveled, Ozma dressed in boy's clothes and she tied her hair back in a simple queue. But she still bound her breasts every day. "One day," she said, "Zilla will find a husband for me. A rich old man with an estate. Or a foolish young man with an inheritance. But until then, until I'm too tall, I'm more useful as a child. Zilla's Princess Monkey."

I'll never get any older, the constable said, mourning.

"I spy with my little eye," Ozma said.

A cloud, the constable said. *A wheel of fire.* The dead did not like to say the name of the sun.

"A little mouse," Ozma said. "It ran under the wheels of the carriage."

Where are we going? the constable said. He asked over and over again.

"Home," Ozma said.

Where is home? said the constable.

"I don't know," Ozma said.

Ozma's father was, according to Zilla, a prince of the Under-world, a diplomat from distant Torlal, a spy, a man with a knife in an alley in Benin. Neren had been a small man, and he'd had snapping black eyes like Ozma, but Neren had not been Ozma's father. If he'd been her father, she would have fished in the stream with a ribbon for his ghost.

They made camp in a field of white flowers. Ozma fed and watered the horses. She picked flowers with the idea that perhaps she could gather enough to make a bed of petals for Zilla. She had a small heap almost as high as her knee before she grew tired of picking them. Zilla made a fire and drank wine. She did not say anything about Neren or about home or about the white petals, but after the sun went down she taught Ozma easy conjure tricks: how to set fire dancing on the backs of the green beetles that ran about the camp; how to summon the little devils that lived in trees and shrubs and rocks.

Zilla and the rock devils talked for a while in a guttural, snappish language that Ozma could almost understand. Then Zilla leaned forward, caught up a devil by its tail, and snapped its long neck. The other devils ran away and Zilla chased after them, grinning. There was something wolfish about her: she dashed across the field on all fours, darting back and forth. She caught two more devils while Ozma and the ghosts sat and watched, and then came strolling back to the camp looking flushed and pink and pleased, the devils dangling from her hand. She sharpened sticks and cooked them over the campfire as if they had been quail. By the time they were ready to eat, she was quite drunk. She didn't offer to share the wine with Ozma.

The devils were full of little spiky bones. Zilla ate two. Ozma nibbled at a haunch, wishing she had real silverware, the kind they'd left behind in Abal. All she had was a tobacco knife. Her devil's gummy boiled eyes stared up at her reproachfully. She closed her own eyes and tore off its head. But there were still the little hands, the toes. It was like trying to eat a baby.

"Ozma," Zilla said. "Eat. I need you to stay healthy. Next time it will be your turn to conjure up supper."

Zilla slept in the carriage. Ozma lay with her head on the little pile of white petals, and the constable and the empress and the kitten boy curled up in her hair.

All night long the green beetles scurried around the camp, carrying fire on their backs. It didn't seem to upset them, and it was very beautiful. Whenever Ozma woke in the night, the ground was alive with little moving green lights. That was the thing about magic. Sometimes it was beautiful and sometimes it seemed to Ozma that it was as wicked as the priests claimed. You could kill a man and you could lie and steal as Zilla had done, and if you lit enough candles at the temples, you could be forgiven. But someone who ate little devils and caught ghosts with ribbons and charms was a witch, and witches were damned. It had always seemed to Ozma that in all the world there was only Zilla for Ozma, only Ozma for Zilla.

Ozma thought that Zilla was looking for something. It was four days since Neren had died, and the horses were getting skinny. There was very little grazing. The streambeds were mostly dry. They abandoned the carriage, and Zilla walked while Ozma rode one of the horses (the horses would not carry Zilla) and the other horse carried Zilla's maps and boxes. They went north, and there were no villages, no towns where Zilla could tell fortunes or sell charms. There were only abandoned farms and woods that Zilla said were full of outlaws or worse.

There was no more wine. Zilla had finished it. They drank muddy water out of the same streams where they watered their horses.

At night Ozma pricked her finger and squeezed the blood into the dirt for her ghosts. In Abal, there had been servants to give the blood to the ghosts. You did not need much blood for one ghost, but in Abal they'd had many, many ghosts. It made Ozma feel a bit sick to see the empress's lips smeared with her blood, to see the kitten boy lapping at the clotted dirt. The constable ate daintily, as if he were still alive.

Ozma's legs ached at night, as if they were growing furiously. She forgot to bind her breasts. Zilla didn't seem to notice. At night, she walked out from the camp, leaving Ozma alone. Sometimes she did not come back until morning.

I spy with my little eye, the constable said.

"A horse's ass," Ozma said. "My mother's skirts, dragging in the dirt."

A young lady, the constable said. *A young lady full of blood and vitality.*

Ozma stared at him. The dead did not flirt with the living, but there was a glint in the constable's dead eye. The empress laughed silently.

Ahead of them, Zilla stopped. "There," she said. "Ahead of us, do you see?"

"Are we home?" Ozma said. "Have we come home?" The road behind them was empty and broken. Far ahead, she could see something that might be a town. As they got closer, there were buildings, but the buildings were not resplendent. The roofs were not tiled with gold. There was no city wall, no orchards full of fruit, only brown fields and ricks of rotted hay.

"This is Brid," Zilla said. "There's something I need here. Come here, Ozma. Help me with the packhorse."

They pulled out Ozma's best dress, the green one with silver embroidery. But when Ozma tried to put on her dress, it would not fasten across her back. The shot-silk cuffs no longer came down over her wrists.

"Well," Zilla said. "My little girl is getting bigger."

"I didn't mean to!" Ozma said.

"No," Zilla said. "I suppose you didn't. It isn't your fault, Ozma. My magic can only do so much. Everyone gets older, no matter how much magic their mothers have. A young woman is trouble, though, and we have no time for trouble. Perhaps you should be a boy. I'll cut your hair."

Ozma backed away. She was proud of her hair.

"Come here, Ozma," Zilla said. She had a knife in her hand. "It will grow back, I promise."

Ozma waited with the horses and the ghosts outside the town. She was too proud to cry about her hair. Boys came and threw rocks at her and she glared at them until they ran away. They came and threw rocks again. She imagined conjuring fire and setting it on their backs and watching them scurry like the beetles. She was wicked to think such a thing. Zilla was probably at the temple, lighting candles, but surely there weren't enough candles in the world to save them both. Ozma prayed that Zilla would save herself.

Why have we come here? the constable said.

"We need things," Ozma said. "Home is farther away than I thought it was. Zilla will bring back a new carriage and a new manservant and wine and food. She's probably gone to the mayor's house, to tell his fortune. He'll give her gold. She'll come back with gold and ribbons full of ghosts and we'll go to the mayor's house and eat roast beef on silver plates."

The town is full of people, and the people are full of blood, the constable said. *Why must we stay here outside?*

"Wait, and Zilla will come back," Ozma said. There was a hot breeze, and it blew against her neck. Cut hair pricked where it was caught between her shirt and her skin. She picked up the constable on his ribbon and held him cupped in her hands. "Am I still beautiful?" she said.

You have dirt on your face, the constable said.

The sun was high in the sky when Zilla came back. She was wearing a modest gray dress, and a white kerchief covered her hair. There was a man with her. He paid no attention to Ozma. Instead he went over to the horses and ran his hands over them. He picked up their feet and rapped thoughtfully on their hooves.

"Come along," Zilla said to Ozma. "Help me with the bags. Leave the horses with this man."

"Where are we going?" Ozma said. "Did the mayor give you gold?"

"I took a position in service," Zilla said. "You are my son, and your name is Eren. Your father is dead, and we have come here from Nablos. We are respectable people. I'm to cook and keep house."

"I thought we were going home," Ozma said. "This isn't home."

"Leave your ghosts here," Zilla said. "Decent people like we are going to be have nothing to do with ghosts."

The man took the reins of the horses and led them away. Ozma took out her pocketknife and cut off her last three ribbons. In one of the saddlebags, there was a kite that a lady of Abal had given her. She tied the empress and the kitten boy to it by their ribbons, and then she threw the kite up so the wind caught it. The string ran through her hand, and the two ghosts sailed away over the houses of Brid.

What are you doing? the constable said.

"Be quiet," Ozma said. She tied a knot in the third ribbon and stuck the constable in her pocket. Then she picked up a saddlebag and followed her mother into Brid.

Her mother walked along as if she had lived in Brid all her life. They stopped in a temple and Zilla bought a hundred candles. Ozma helped her light them all, while the priest dozed, stretched out on a prayer bench. Couldn't he tell how wicked they were? Ozma wondered. Only wicked, wicked people would need to light so many candles.

But Zilla, kneeling in front of the altar steps, lighting candle after candle, looked like a saint in her gray dress. The air was thick with incense. Zilla sneezed, and the priest woke up with a snort. This would be a very dull game, Ozma thought. She wished that Zilla had charmed the constable instead of killing him. She had not been at all tired of their life in Abal.

Zilla led Ozma through a public square where women were drawing water from a well, and down a narrow street. The gutters smelled of human sewage. In Abal the finest houses had been outfitted with modern plumbing. There had been taps and running water and hot baths. And a public bath—even if Brid had such a thing, Ozma realized—would be out of the question, as long as she was a boy.

"Here," Zilla said. She went up to the door of a two-story stone house. It did not compare to the house they had lived in, in Abal. When Zilla knocked, a woman in a housemaid's cap opened the door. "You're to go around to the back," the woman said. "Don't you know anything?" Then she relented. "Come in quickly, quickly."

There was a vestibule and a front hall with a mosaic set in the floor. The blue and yellow tiles were set in a spiralling pattern, and Ozma thought she saw dragons, but the mosaic was cracked and some of the tiles were missing. Light fell down through a vaulted skylight. There were statues standing in paneled niches in the wall, gods and goddesses looking as if they had been waiting for a long time for someone to bring their coats and hats. They looked dowdier than the gods in Abal did, less haughty, less high. There were ghosts everywhere, Ozma saw. Somehow it made her miss Abal less. At least Brid was like Abal in this one way.

She didn't care for gods. When she thought of them at all, she imagined them catching people the way that Zilla caught ghosts, with charms and ribbons. Who would want to dangle along after one of these household gods, with their painted eyes and their chipped fingers?

"Come along, come along," said the housemaid. "My name's Jemma. I'm to show you your room and then I'll take you back down to the parlor. What's your name, boy?"

Zilla poked Ozma. "Oz—Ozen," Ozma said. "Ozen."

"That's a foreign name," Jemma said. She sounded disapproving. Ozma stared down. Jemma had thick ankles. Her shoes looked as if they pinched. As she hurried them along, little eddies of ghosts swirled around her skirts. Zilla sneezed.

Jemma led them through a door and then up and up a winding staircase. Ghosts drifted after them lazily. Zilla pretended they were not there and so Ozma did the same.

At the top of the stairs was a hall with a door on either side.

Their room had a sloped roof, so there was barely room to stand up. There were two narrow beds, a chair, a basin on a small table, and a window with a pane missing.

"I see there's a fireplace," Zilla said. She sank down into the chair.

"Get up, get up," Jemma said. "Oh please, Miss Zilla, get up. I'm to show you down to the parlor and then I must get back to the kitchen to start dinner. It's a mercy that you've come. It's just been the two of us, me and my da. The house is filthy and I'm no cook."

"Go on," Zilla said. "I'll find the parlor. And then I'll come find you in the kitchen. We'll see what we can do for dinner."

"Yes, Miss Zilla," Jemma said, and made a little bob.

Ozma listened to Jemma thumping down the stairs again as if she were a whole herd of maids. Some of the ghosts went with her, but most remained, crowding around Zilla. Zilla sat in the chair, her eyes shut tightly.

"What are we doing here?" Ozma said. "How could there be anything in this place that we need? Who are we to be?"

Zilla did not open her eyes. "Good people," she said. "Respectable people."

The constable wriggled like a fish in Ozma's pocket. *Good liars*, he said quietly. *Respectable murderers.*

There was water in the basin so that Zilla and Ozma could wash their hands and faces. Zilla had a packet of secondhand clothing for Ozma, which Ozma laid out on the bed. Boy's clothing. It seemed terrible to her, not only that she should have to be a boy and wear boy's clothing but that she should have to wear clothes bought from a store in Brid. In Abal and in the city before Abal, she'd had the most beautiful dresses and gloves and cloaks, and shoes made of the softest leather. It was one thing to dress as a boy on the road, when there was no one to admire her. She slipped the constable out of the pocket of her old clothes and into the pocket of her shirt.

"Stop sulking or I'll sell you to the priests," Zilla said. She was standing at the window, looking out at the street below. Ozma imagined Brid below them: dull, dull, dull.

Ozma waited just outside the door of the parlor. Really, the house was full of ghosts. Perhaps she and Zilla could start a business here in Brid and export fine ghosts to Abal. When Zilla said, "Come in, son," she stepped in.

"Close the door quickly!" said the ugly old man who stood beside Zilla. Perhaps he would fall in love with Zilla and beg her to marry him. Something flew past Ozma's ear: the room was full of songbirds. Now she could hear them as well. There were cages everywhere, hanging from the roof and from stands, and all of the cage doors standing open. The birds were anxious. They flew around and around the room, settling on chairs and chandeliers. There was a nest on the mantelpiece and another inside the harpsichord. There were long streaks of bird shit on the furniture, on the floor, and on the old man's clothes. "They don't like your mother very much," he said.

This was not quite right, Ozma saw. It was the ghosts that followed Zilla and Ozma that the birds did not like.

"This is Lady Rosa Fralix," Zilla said.

So it was an ugly old woman. Ozma remembered to bow instead of curtsy.

"What is your name, child?" said Lady Fralix.

"Ozen," Ozma said.

"Ozen," Lady Fralix said. "What a handsome boy he is, Zilla."

Zilla sneezed sharply. "If it meets with your approval, Lady Fralix, dinner will be served in the small dining room at eight. Tomorrow Ozen and Jemma and I will begin to put your house in order. Shall we begin here?"

"If Ozen will agree to help me cage my friends," Lady Fralix said. "We can go over the schedule tomorrow morning after breakfast. I'm afraid there's been too much work for poor Jemma. There are one or two rooms, though, that I would prefer that you leave alone."

"Very well, madam," Zilla said in her most disinterested voice, and *aha!* thought Ozma. There were birds perched on Lady Fralix's head and shoulders. They pulled at her thin white hair. No wonder she was nearly bald.

Zilla was a good if unimaginative cook. She prepared an urchin stew, a filet of sole, and because Jemma said Lady Fralix's teeth were not good, she made a bread pudding with fresh goat's milk and honey. Ozma helped her carry the dishes into the dining room, which was smaller and less elegant than the dining rooms of Abal, where ladies in beautiful dresses had given Ozma morsels from their own plates. The dining room was without distinction. It was not particularly well appointed. And it was full of ghosts. Everywhere you stepped there were ghosts. The empty wineglasses and the silver tureen in the center of the table were full of them.

Zilla stayed to serve Lady Fralix. Ozma ate in the kitchen with Jemma and Jemma's da, a large man who ate plate after plate of stew and said nothing at all. Jemma said a great deal, but very little of it was interesting. Lady Rosa Fralix had never married as far as anyone knew. She was a scholar and a collector of holy relics and antiquities. She had traveled a great deal in her youth. She had no heir.

Ozma went up the stairs to bed. Zilla was acting as lady's maid to Lady Fralix, or rifling through secret drawers, or most likely of all, had gone back to the temple to light candles again. Jemma had started a fire in the grate in the dark little bedroom. Ozma was grudgingly grateful. She used the chamber pot and then bathed as best she could in front of the fire with a sponge and water from the basin. She did all of this behind a screen so that she was hidden from the constable, although she hadn't been so modest while they were traveling.

The constable did not have much to say, and Ozma did not feel much like talking, either. She thought of a thousand questions to ask Zilla, if only she were brave enough. When she woke in the night, there were strange cracking sounds and the fire in the grate was shooting out long green tongues of flame. Zilla was crouched before it, adding things to the blaze. She was burning her ghost tackle—the long needles and the black silk thread, the tubes and ointments and all of her notebooks. "Go back to sleep, Ozma," Zilla said, without turning around.

Ozma closed her eyes.

Zilla woke her in the morning. "What time is it?" Ozma said. A thin gray light was dribbling through the window.

"Five in the morning. Time to wake and dress and wash your face," Zilla said. "There's work to do."

Zilla made a porridge with raisins and dates while Ozma located a broom, a brush, a dustpan, and cloths. "First of all," Zilla said, "we'll get rid of the vermin."

She opened the front door and began to sweep ghosts out of the front hall, through the vestibule, down the front steps and into the street. They tumbled in front of her broom in white, astonished clouds. "What are you doing?" Ozma said.

"This is a respectable house," Zilla said. "And we are respectable people. An infestation of this kind is disgraceful."

"In Abal," Ozma said, "fashionable homes were full of ghosts. You made it the fashion. What is different about Brid? What are we doing here?"

"Sweeping," Zilla said and handed Ozma a brush and a dustpan.

They went through the smaller dining room and the larger dining room and the breakfast room and two sitting rooms, which seemed to Ozma pleasant at best. Everywhere there were souvenirs of Lady Fralix's travels: seashells, souvenir paperweights, music boxes, and umbrella stands made from the legs of very strange animals. They all seethed with ghosts. There was a ballroom where the ghosts rinsed around their ankles in a misty, heatless boil. Ozma's fingers itched for her ribbons and her charms. "Why are there so many?" she said.

But Zilla shook her head. When the clocks began to strike eight o'clock, at last she stopped and said, "That will do for now. After Lady Fralix has dressed and I've brought her a tray, she wants your help in the front parlor to catch the birds."

But Lady Fralix caught the birds easily. They came and sat on her finger, and she fed them crumbs of toast. Then she shut them in their cages. She didn't need Ozma at all. Ozma sat on the piano bench and watched. Her hands were red and blistered from sweeping ghosts.

"They need fresh water," Lady Fralix said finally.

So Ozma carried little dishes of water back and forth from the kitchen to the parlor. Then she helped Lady Fralix drape the heavy velvet covers over the cages. "Why do you have so many birds?" she said.

"Why do you have a ghost in your pocket?" Lady Fralix said.

"Does your mother know you have him? She doesn't seem to care for ghosts."

"How do you know I have a ghost?" Ozma said. "Can you see ghosts, too? Why is your house so full of ghosts? In Abal, we caught them for ladies to wear on their dresses, but the ladies only pretended that they could see their ghosts. It was fashionable."

"Let me take a look at yours," Lady Fralix said. Ozma took the constable out of her pocket. She did it reluctantly.

The constable bowed to Lady Fralix. *My lady*, he said.

"Oh, he's charming," said Lady Fralix. "I see why you couldn't give him up. Would you like me to keep him safe for you?"

"No!" Ozma said. She quickly put the constable back in her pocket. She said, "When I first saw you I thought you were an ugly old man."

Lady Fralix laughed. Her laugh was clear and quick and warm. "And when I saw you, Ozen, I thought you were a beautiful young woman."

After lunch, which was rice and chicken seasoned with mint and almonds, Zilla gave Ozma a pail of soapy water and a pile of clean rags. She left her in the vestibule. Ozma washed the gods first. She hoped they were grateful, but they didn't seem to be. When she was finished, they had the same sort of look that Zilla wore when she was bamboozling someone: distant, charming, untrustworthy.

Ozma's back and arms ached. Twice she'd almost dropped the constable in the pail of water, thinking he was a clean rag.

Zilla appeared in the vestibule. She reached up and touched the robe of one of the gods, a woman with a wolf's head. She left her hand there for a moment, and Ozma felt a terrible jealousy. Zilla rarely touched Ozma so gently.

"Be careful with the tiles," Zilla said. She did not look particularly dirty or tired, although she and Jemma had been beating bird shit out of the carpets and upholstery all afternoon.

Lady Fralix came and watched from the balcony while Ozma cleaned the mosaic. "Your mother says she will try to find tiles to replace the ones that have been broken," she said.

Ozma said nothing.

"The artist was a man from the continent of Gid," Lady Fralix said. "I met him when I was looking for a famous temple to the god Addaman. His congregation had dwindled, and in a fit of temper Addaman drowned his congregation, priests, temple and all, in a storm that lasted for three years. There's a lake there now. I went swimming in it and found all kinds of things. I brought the mosaic artist back with me. I always meant to go back. The water was meant to cure heartsickness. Or maybe it was the pox. I have a vial of it somewhere, or maybe that was the vial that Jemma thought was my eyedrops. It's so important to label things legibly."

Ozma wrung dirty water out of a rag. "Your mother is very religious," Lady Fralix said. "She seems to know a great deal about the gods."

"She likes to light candles," Ozma said.

"For your father?" Lady Fralix said.

Ozma said nothing.

"If your ghost needs blood," Lady Fralix said, "you should go to the butcher's stall in the market. I'll tell your mother that I sent you to buy seeds for the birds."

There was nothing to do in Brid. There was no theater, no opera, no chocolate maker. Only temples and more temples. Zilla visited them all and lit hundreds of candles each day. She gave away the dresses that she had brought with her from Abal. She gave away all her jewels to beggars in the street. Zilla did not explain to Ozma about home or what she was planning or why they were masquerading in Brid as a devout, respectable housekeeper and her son. Zilla used only the most harmless of magics: to make the bread rise, to judge whether or not it was a good day to hang up the washing in the courtyard.

She made up simple potions for the other servants who worked in the houses on the street where Lady Fralix lived. She told fortunes. But she only told happy fortunes. The love potions were mostly honey and sugar dissolved in wine. Zilla didn't charge for them. Neighborhood servants sat around the kitchen table and gossiped. They told stories of how the mayor of Brid had been made a fool of, all for love; of accidental poisonings; who had supposedly stuffed their mattresses with bags of gold coins; which babies had been dropped on their heads by nurse-maids who drank. Zilla did not seem to pay any attention.

"Lady Fralix is a good woman," Jemma said. "She was wild in her youth. She talked to the gods. She wasn't afraid of anything. Then she came to Brid to see the temples and she bought this house on a whim because, she said, she'd never been in a town that was so full of sleepy gods. She claims that it's restful. Well, I don't know about that. I've never lived anywhere else."

"There's something about Brid," Zilla said. She looked cross, as if the word *Brid* tasted bad. "Something that drew me to Brid, but I don't know what. I don't know that I'd call it peaceful. Ozen finds it dull, I'm afraid."

Ozma said, "I want to go *home*." But she said it quietly, so that Jemma wouldn't hear. Zilla looked away as if she hadn't heard either.

Ozma developed calluses on her hands. It was a good thing

that there was nothing to do in Brid. She spent all her time mopping and dusting and carrying firewood and beating upholstery. Zilla's nose was always pink from sneezing. The constable grew bored. *This was not what I expected death to be like,* he said.

"What is death like?" Ozma said. She always asked the ghosts this, but they never gave satisfactory answers.

How do I know? the constable said. *I'm carried around all day in a young girl's pocket. I drink the stale blood of market cattle. I thought there would be clouds of glory, or beautiful lecherous devils with velvet bosoms, or a courtroom full of gods to judge me.*

"It will be different when Zilla has done what she needs to do," Ozma said. "Then we'll go home. There will be clouds of glory, and my pockets will be lined with lavender and silk. Everyone will know Zilla, and they'll bow to her when we drive by in our carriage. Mothers will frighten their children with stories about Zilla, and kings will come and beg her to give them kisses. But she will only love *me.*"

You think your mother is a blackmailer and a thief and a murderer, the constable said. *You admire her for what you think she is.*

"I know she is!" Ozma said. "I know what she is!"

The constable said nothing. He only smirked. For several days they did not speak to each other until Ozma relented and gave him her own blood to drink as a peace offering. It was only a drop or two, and she was almost flattered to think that he preferred it.

It was hard work keeping Lady Fralix's house free of ghosts. Ozma said so when she brought Lady Fralix's breakfast up one morning. Zilla and Jemma had gone to a temple where there was a god who, according to his priests, had recently opened his painted mouth and complained about the weather. This was supposed to be a miracle.

"Your mother wants me to let my birds go free," Lady Fralix said. "First the ghosts, now the birds. She says it's cruel to keep things trapped in cages."

This did not sound at all like Zilla. Ozma was beginning to grow tired of this new Zilla. It was one thing to *pretend* to be respectable; it was another entirely to *be* respectable.

Lady Fralix said, "It's considered holy in some places to release birds. People free them on holy days because it pleases the gods. Perhaps I should. Perhaps your mother is right to ask."

"Why do the ghosts come back again and again?" Ozma said. She was far more interested in ghosts than in birds. All birds did was eat and shit and make noise. "What do you want to wear today?"

"The pink dressing gown," Lady Fralix said. "If you let me keep your ghost in my pocket today, I'll give you one of my dresses. Any dress you like."

"Zilla would take it away and give it to the poor," Ozma said. Then: "How did you know I'm a girl?"

"I'm old but I'm not blind," Lady Fralix said. "I see all sorts of things. Ghosts and girls. Little lost things. You shouldn't keep dressing as a boy, my dear. Someone as shifty as you needs some truth now and then."

"I'll be a boy if I want to be a boy," Ozma said. She realized that she didn't really think of herself as Ozma anymore. She had become Ozen, who strutted and flirted with the maids fetching water, whose legs were longer, whose breasts did not need to be bound.

Be a girl, said the constable, muffled, from inside her pocket. *Your hips are too bony as a boy. And I don't like how your voice is changing. You had a nicer singing voice before.*

"Oh, be quiet," Ozma said. She was exasperated. "I've never heard so much nonsense in all my life!"

"You're an insolent child, but my offer stands," Lady Fralix said. "When you're ready to be a girl again. Now. Let's go down and do some work in my collection. I need someone with clever fingers. My old hands shake too much. Will you help me?"

"If you want me to," Ozma said, ungraciously. She helped Lady Fralix out of bed and into a dressing gown and then she combed what was left of Lady Fralix's hair. "How old are you?"

"Not as old as your mother," Lady Fralix said, and laughed at Ozma's look of disbelief.

There was no door to the room in which Lady Fralix kept her collection, but Ozma felt sure she had never noticed this room before. There were four or five ghosts brushing against the door that wasn't there. They stayed on the threshold as if tethered there. "What are they doing?" Ozma said.

"They want to go inside," Lady Fralix said. "But they're afraid. Something draws them. They want it and they don't know why. Poor little things."

The room was very strange. It was the size of a proper ball-room in Abal, only it was full of paintings on stands, altars, and tables piled high with reliquaries and holy books and icons. Along the far wall there were gods as large as wardrobes and little brass gods and gods of ivory and gold and jade gods and fat goddesses giving birth to other gods and goddesses. There were bells hanging from the ceiling with long silk ropes, bells resting on the floor so big that Ozma could have hidden under them, and there were robes stiff with embroidery, hung about with bells no bigger than a fingernail.

Where are we? said the constable.

Lady Fralix had stepped inside the room. She beckoned to Ozma. But when Ozma put her foot down on the wooden floor, the board beneath her foot gave a terrible shriek.

What is that noise? said the constable.

"The floor—" Ozma said.

"Oh," Lady Fralix said. "Your ghost. You had better tie him up outside. He won't want to come in here."

The constable trembled in Ozma's hand. He looked about wildly, ignoring her at first. She tied him to the leg of an occasional table in the hallway. *Don't leave me here,* the constable said. *There's something in that room that I need. Bring it to me, boy.*

"Boy!" Ozma said.

Please, boy, said the constable. *Ozma, please. I beg you on my death.*

Ozma ignored him. She stepped into the room again. And again, with each step, the floor shrieked and groaned and squeaked. Lady Fralix clapped her hands. "It's almost as good as going to see the orchestra in Oldun," she said. She walked in a quick odd pattern toward an altar carved in the shape of a winged fish.

"Why don't you make any sound when you walk?" Ozma said.

"I know where to place my foot," Lady Fralix said. "I keep my most precious relics here. All the things that belong to gods. There. Put your foot down there. There's a pattern to it. Let me teach you."

She showed Ozma how to navigate the room. It was a little like waltzing. "Isn't this fun?" said Lady Fralix. "An adept can play the floor like a musical instrument. It comes from a temple in Nal. There's an emerald somewhere, too. The eye of a god. From the same temple. Here, look at this."

There was a tree growing out of an old stone altar. The tree had almost split the altar in two. There was fruit on it, and Lady Fralix bent a branch down. "Not ripe yet," she said. "I've been waiting almost twenty years and it's still not ripe."

"I suppose you want me to dust everything," Ozma said.

"Perhaps you could just help me go through the books," said Lady Fralix. "I left a novel in here last summer. I was only halfway through reading it. The beautiful gypsy had just been kidnapped by a lord disguised as a narwhal."

"Here it is," Ozma said, after they had hunted for a while in companionable silence. When she looked up, she felt strange, as if the room had begun to spin around her. The gods and their altars all seemed very bright, and the bells were tolling, although without any sound. Even Lady Fralix seemed to shimmer a little, as if she were moving and standing still at the same time.

"You're quite pale," Lady Fralix said. "I'd have thought you wouldn't be susceptible."

"To what?" Ozma said.

"To the gods," Lady Fralix said. "Some people have a hard time. It's a bit like being up in the mountains. Some people don't seem to notice."

"I don't care for gods," Ozma said. "They're nothing to me. I hate Brid. I hate this place. I hate the gods."

"Let's go and have some tea," Lady Fralix said. She did not sound in the least bit perturbed to hear that Ozma was a heretic.

In the hallway, the constable was tugging at his ribbon, as if the room were full of blood.

"What is it?" Ozma said. "There's nothing in that room, just boring old gods."

I need it, the constable said. *Be kind, be kind. Give me the thing I need.*

"Don't be tiresome," Ozma said. Her head ached.

Before Ozma could put him in her pocket, Lady Fralix took hold of her wrist. She picked up the constable by his ribbon.

"Very curious," Lady Fralix said. "He's so lively, such a darling. Not the usual sort of ghost. Do you know how he died?"

"He ate a bad piece of cheese," Ozma said. "Or maybe he fell off a cliff. I don't remember. Give him back."

"It's a good thing," Lady Fralix said, "that most people can't see or talk to ghosts. Watching them scurry around, it makes you dread the thought of death, and yet what else is there to do when you die? Will some careless child carry me around in her pocket?"

Ozma shrugged. She was young. She wouldn't die for years and years. She tried not to think of the handsome young constable in her pocket, who had once thought much the same thing.

By the time Zilla and Jemma returned from the temple, Lady Fralix had made up her mind to let the birds go, as soon as possible.

"I only kept them because the house seemed so empty," she said. "Brid is too quiet. In the city of Tuk, the god houses are full of red and green birds who fly back and forth carrying holy messages."

Zilla and Jemma and Ozma carried cage after cage out onto the street. The birds fussed and chattered. Lady Fralix watched from her bedroom window. It was starting to rain.

Once the birds were free, they seemed more confused than liberated. They didn't burst into joyful songs or even fly away. Ozma had to shoo them out of their cages. They flew around the house and beat their wings against the windows. Lady Fralix closed her curtains. One bird flew against a window so hard that it broke its neck.

Ozma picked up its body. The beak was open.

"The poor little things," Jemma said. Jemma was terribly tenderhearted. She wiped rain off her face with her apron. There were feathers sticking out of her hair.

"Where do the ghosts of birds and animals go?" Ozma said quietly to Zilla. "Why don't we see them?"

Zilla looked at her. Her eyes glittered and her color was high. "I see them," she said. "I can see them plain as anything. It's good that you can't see them, Ozen. It's more respectable not to see any kind of ghosts."

"Lady Fralix knows I'm a girl," Ozma said. Jemma was chasing the birds away from the house, flapping her own arms and her sodden apron. The rain fell harder and harder but Zilla didn't seem to notice. "She said something about how I ought to be careful. I think that perhaps I'm becoming a boy. I think she may be right. I stand up when I piss now. I'm shaped differently. I have something down there that I didn't have before."

"Let me take a look at you," Zilla said. "Turn around. Yes, I see. Well, it has nothing to do with me. You must be doing it yourself somehow. How enterprising you've become. How inconvenient."

"Actually," Ozma said, "it's more convenient. I like standing up when I piss."

"It won't do," Zilla said. "It's not very respectable, that's for certain. We'll take care of it tonight."

I liked you better as a girl, the constable said. *You were a nice girl. That girl would have given me what I wanted. She would have found what I needed in that room.*

"I wasn't a nice girl!" Ozma said. She stood naked in the attic room. She wished she had a mirror. The thing between her legs was very strange. She didn't know how long it had been here.

Ever since we came to this house, the constable said. He was sitting in the corner of the grate on a little heap of ashes. He looked very gloomy. *Ever since your mother told you to be a boy. Why do you always do what your mother tells you?*

"I don't," Ozma said. "I kept you. I keep you secret. If she knew about you, she'd sweep you right out of the house."

Don't tell her then, the constable said. *I want to stay with you, Ozma. I forgive you for letting her kill me.*

"Be quiet," Ozma said. "Here she comes."

Zilla was carrying a small folded pile of clothes. She stared at Ozma. "Get dressed," she said. "I've seen all that before. It doesn't particularly suit you, although it does explain why the housemaids next door have been mooning and swanning around in their best dresses."

"Because of me?" Ozma said. She began to pull her trousers back on.

"No, not those. Here. Lady Fralix has lent you a dress. I've made something up, although only a liar as good as I am could pull off such a ridiculous story. I fed Jemma some confection about how you've been dressing as a boy as penance. Because a young man had fallen in love with you and committed suicide. You're handsome enough as a boy," Zilla said. "But I don't know what you were thinking. I never cared much for that shape. It's too distracting. And people are always wanting to quarrel with you."

"You've been a man?" Ozma said. The dress felt very strange, very confining. The thing between her legs was still there. And she didn't like the way the petticoats rubbed against her legs. They scratched.

"Not for years and years," Zilla said. "Gods, I don't even know how long. It's one thing to dress as a man, Ozma, but you mustn't let yourself forget who you are."

"But I don't know who I am," Ozma said. "Why are we different from other people? Why do we see ghosts? Why did I change into a boy? You said we were going home, but Brid isn't home, I know it isn't. Where is our home? Why did we come here? Why are you acting so strangely?"

Zilla sighed. She snapped her fingers, and there was a little green flame resting on the back of her hand. She stroked it with her other hand, coaxing it until it grew larger. She sat down on one of the narrow beds and patted the space beside her. Ozma sat down. "There's something that I need to find," Zilla said. "Something in Brid. I can't go home without it. When Neren died—"

"Neren!" Ozma said. She didn't want to talk about Neren.

Zilla gave her a terrible look. "If those men had killed you instead of Neren . . ." she said. Her voice trailed off. The green flame dwindled down to a spark and went out. "There was something that I was supposed to do for him. Something that I knew how to do once. Something I've forgotten."

"I don't understand," Ozma said. "We buried him in the tree. What else could we have done?"

"I don't know," Zilla said. "I go to the temples every day and I humble myself and I light enough candles to burn down a city, but the gods won't talk to me. I'm too wicked. I've done terrible things. I think I used to know how to talk to the gods. I need to talk to them again. I need to talk to them before I go home. I need them to tell me what I've forgotten."

"Before *we* go home," Ozma said. "You wouldn't leave me here, would you? You wouldn't. Tell me about home, oh please, tell me about home."

"I can't remember," Zilla said. She stood up. "I don't remember. Stop fussing at me, Ozma. Don't come downstairs again until you're a girl."

Ozma had terrible dreams. She dreamed that Lady Fralix's birds had come back home again and they were pecking at her head. Peck, peck, peck. Peck, peck. They were going to pull out all of her hair because she had been a terrible daughter. Neren had sent them. She was under one of Lady Fralix's bells in the darkness because she was hiding from the birds. The constable was kissing her under the bell. His mouth was full of dead birds.

Someone was shaking her. "Ozma," Zilla said. "Ozma, wake up. Ozma, tell me what you are dreaming about."

"The birds," Ozma said. "I'm in the room where Lady Fralix keeps her collection. I'm hiding from the birds."

"What room?" Zilla said. Her hand was still on Ozma's shoulder, but she was only a dark shape against darkness.

"The room full of bells and altars," Ozma said. "The room that the ghosts won't go in. She wanted me to find a book for her this afternoon. The floor is from a temple in Nal. You have to walk on it a certain way. It made me feel dizzy."

"Show me this room," Zilla said. "I'll fetch a new candle. You've burned this one down to the stub. Meet me downstairs."

Ozma got out of bed. She went and squatted over the chamber pot.

So you're a girl again, the constable said from behind the grate.

"Oh, be quiet," Ozma said. "It's none of your business."

It is my business, the constable said. *You'll go and fetch the thing that your mother needs, but you won't help me. I thought you loved me.*

"You?" Ozma said. "How could I love you? How could I love

a ghost? How could I love something that I have to keep hidden in my pocket?"

She picked up the constable. "You're filthy," she said.

You're lovely, Ozma, the constable said. *You're ripe as a peach. I've never wanted anything as much as I want just a drop of your blood, except there's something in that room that I want even more. If you bring it to me, I'll promise to be true to you. No one will ever have such a faithful lover.*

"I don't want a lover," Ozma said. "I want to go home."

She put the constable in the pocket of her nightgown and went down the dark stairs in her bare feet. Her mother was in the vestibule, where all the gods were waiting for dawn. The flame from the candle lit Zilla's face and made her look beautiful and wicked and pitiless. "Hurry, Ozma. Show me the room."

"It's just along here," Ozma said. It was as if they were back in Abal and nothing had changed. She felt like dancing.

"I don't understand," Zilla said. "How could it be here under my nose all this time and I couldn't even see it?"

"See what?" Ozma said. "Look, here's the room." As before, there were ghosts underfoot, everywhere, even more than there had been before.

"Filthy things," Zilla said. She sneezed. "Why won't they leave me alone?" She didn't seem to see the room at all.

Ozma took the candle from Zilla and held it up so that they could both see the entrance to the room. "Here," she said. "Here, look. Here's the room I was telling you about."

Zilla was silent. Then she said, "It makes me feel ill. As if something terrible is calling my name over and over again. Perhaps it's a god. Perhaps a god is telling me not to go in."

"The room is full of gods!" Ozma said. "There are gods and gods and altars and relics and sacred stones, and you can't go in there or else the floorboards will make so much noise that everyone in the house will wake up."

Bring me the thing I need! shouted the constable. *I will kill you all if you don't bring me the thing I need!*

"Ozma," Zilla said. She sounded like the old Zilla again, queenly and sly, used to being obeyed. "Who is that in your pocket? Who thinks that he is mightier than I?"

"It's only the constable of Abal," Ozma said. She took the constable out of her pocket and held him behind her back.

Let me go, the constable said. *Let me go or I will bite you. Go fetch me the thing that I need and I will let you live.*

"Give him to me," Zilla said.

"Will you keep him safe while I go in there?" Ozma said. "I know how to walk without making the floor sing. The ghosts won't go in there, but I could go in. What am I looking for?"

"I don't know," Zilla said. "I don't know, but you will know it when you see it. I promise. Bring me the thing that I'm looking for. Give me your ghost."

Don't give me to her, the constable said. *I have a bad feeling about this. Besides, there's something in that room that I need. You'll be sorry if you help her and not me.*

Zilla held out her hand. Ozma gave her the constable. "I'm sorry," Ozma said to the constable. Then she went into the room.

She was instantly dizzy. It was worse than before. She concentrated on the light falling from the candle, and the wax that dripped down onto her hand. She put each foot down with care. The ropes from stolen temple bells slithered across her shoulders like dead snakes. The altars and tables were absolutely heaped with things, and all of it was undoubtedly valuable, and it was far too dark. How in the world did Zilla expect her to come out again with the exact thing that was needed? Perhaps Ozma should just carry out as much as she could. There was a little wax god on the table nearest her. She held up the hem of her nightgown like an apron and dropped the god inside. There was a book covered in gold leaf. She picked it up. Too heavy. She put it back down again. She picked up a smaller book. She put it in her nightgown.

There was a little mortar and pestle for grinding incense. They didn't feel right. She put them down. Here was a table piled with boxes, and the boxes were full of eyes. Sapphire eyes and ruby eyes and pearls and onyx and emeralds. She didn't like how they looked at her.

As she searched, she began to feel as if something was pulling at her. She realized that it had been pulling at her all this time, and that she had been doing her best to ignore it, without even noticing. She began to walk toward the thing pulling at her, but even this was hard. The pattern she had to walk was complicated. She seemed to be moving away from the thing she needed, the closer she tried to get. She put more things in the scoop of her nightgown: a bundle of sticks tied with strips of silk; a little bottle with something sloshing inside of it; a carving of a fish. The heavier her nightgown grew, the easier it became to make her way toward the thing that was calling her. Her candle was much shorter than it had been. She wondered how long she'd been in the room. Surely not very long.

The thing that had been calling her was a goddess. She felt strangely annoyed by this, especially when she saw which goddess it was. It was the same wolf-headed goddess who stood in the vestibule. It seemed to be laughing wolfishly and silently at her, as if she, Ozma, was small and insignificant and silly. "I don't even know your name," Ozma said, feeling as if this proved something. The goddess said nothing.

There was a clay cup on the palm of the goddess's hands. She held it as if she were offering a drink to Ozma, but the cup was empty. Ozma took it. It was old and ugly and fragile. Surely it was the least precious thing in the entire room.

As she made her way back toward the hall, she began to smell something that was both sweet and astringent, a fragrance nothing like Brid. Brid smelled of cobblestones and horses and soap and candles. This fragrance was more agreeable than anything she had ever known. It reminded her of the perfumed oils that the fashionable ladies of Abal wore, the way their coiled, jeweled hair smelled when the ladies bent down like saplings over her and told her what a lovely child she was, how lovely she was. A drowsy, pearly light was beginning to come through the high windows. It settled on the glossy curves of the hanging bells and the sitting bells, like water. The two halves of the stone altar and the tree that had split them were in front of her.

All the leaves of that strange, stubborn tree were moving, as if in a wind. She wondered if it was a god moving through the room, but the room felt hushed and still, as if she were utterly alone. Her head was clearer now. She bent down a branch and there was a fruit on it. It looked something like a plum. She picked it.

When she came out of the room, Zilla was pacing in the hallway. "You were in there for hours," Zilla said. "Do you have it? Let me have it."

The plum was in Ozma's pocket and she didn't take it out. She pulled the things from Lady Fralix's room out of the gathered hem of her nightgown and put them on the floor. Zilla knelt down. "Not this," she said, rifling through the book. "Not this either. This is nothing. This is less than nothing. A forgery. A cheap souvenir. Nothing. You've brought me trash and junk. A marble. A fish. A clay cup. What were you thinking, Ozma?"

"Where is the constable of Abal?" Ozma said. She picked up the clay cup and held it out to Zilla. "This is the thing you wanted, I know it is. You said I would know it. Give me the constable and I'll give you the cup."

"What have you got in your pocket?" Zilla said. "What are you keeping from me? What do I want with an old clay cup?"

"Tell me what you did with the constable," Ozma said, still holding out the empty cup.

"She swept him out the door with all the other ghosts," said Lady Fralix. She stood in the hallway, blinking and yawning. All her hair stood out from her head in tufts, like an owl. Her feet were bare, just like Ozma's feet. They were long and bony.

"You did what?" Ozma said. Zilla made a gesture. Nothing, the gesture said. The constable was nothing. A bit of trash.

"You shouldn't have left him with her," Lady Fralix said. "You should have known better."

"Give it to me," Zilla said. "Give me the thing in your pocket, Ozma, and we'll leave here. We'll go home. We'll be able to go home."

A terrible wave of grief came down on Ozma. It threatened to sweep her away forever, like the ghost of the constable of Abal. "You killed him. You murdered him! You're a murderer and I hate you!" she said.

There was something in her hand and she flung it at Zilla as hard as she could. Zilla caught the cup easily. She dashed it at the floor, and it broke into dozens of pieces. The nothingness that had been in the cup spilled out and splashed up over Zilla's legs and skirts. The empty cup had not been empty after all, or rather, it had been full of emptiness. There seemed to be a great deal of it.

Ozma put her hands over her face. She couldn't bear to see the look of contempt on her mother's face.

"Oh, look!" Lady Fralix said. "Look what you've done, Ozma," she said again, gently. "Look how beautiful she is."

Ozma peeked through her fingers. Zilla's hair was loose around her shoulders. She was so beautiful that it was hard to look at her directly. She still wore her gray housekeeper's uniform, but the dress shone like cloth of silver where the emptiness, the *nothing*, had soaked it. "Oh," Zilla said. And "oh" again.

Ozma's hands curled into fists. She stared at the floor. She was thinking of the constable. How he had promised to love her faithfully and forever. She saw him again, as he was dying in Zilla's parlor in Abal. How surprised he had looked. How his ghost had clung to Zilla's ribbon so he would not be swept away.

"Ozma," Zilla said. "Look at me." She sneezed and then sneezed again. "I have not been myself, but I am myself again. You did this, Ozma. You brought me the thing that I needed, Ozma, I have been asleep for all this time, and you have woken me! Ozma!"

Ozma did not look up. She began to cry instead. The hallway was as bright as if someone had lit a thousand candles, all burning with a cool and silver light. "Little Princess Monkey," Zilla said. "Ozma. Look at me, daughter."

Ozma would not. She felt Zilla's cool hand on her burning cheek. Someone sighed. There was a sound like a bell ringing, very far away. The cool silver light went out.

Lady Fralix said, "She's gone, you stubborn girl. And a good thing, too. I think the house might have come down on us if she'd stayed any longer."

"What? Where has she gone? Why didn't she take me with her?" Ozma said. "What did I do to her?" She wiped at her eyes.

Where Zilla had stood, there was only the broken clay cup. Lady Fralix bent over and picked up the pieces as if they were precious. She wrapped them in a handkerchief and put them in one of her pockets. Then she held out her hand to Ozma and helped her stand up.

"She's gone home," Lady Fralix said. "She's remembered who she is."

"Who *is* she? What do you mean, 'who she is'? Why doesn't anyone ever explain anything to me?" Ozma said. She felt thick with rage and unhappiness and something like dread. "Am I too stupid to understand? Am I a stupid child?"

"Your mother is a goddess," Lady Fralix said. "I knew it as soon as she applied to be my housekeeper. I've had to put up with a great deal of tidying and dusting and mopping and spring-cleaning, and I must say I'm glad to be done with it all. There's something that tests the nerves, knowing that there's a goddess beating your rugs and cooking your dinner and burning your dresses with an iron."

"Zilla isn't a goddess," Ozma said. She felt like throwing more things. Like stamping her foot until the floor gave way and the house fell down. "She's my mother."

"Yes," Lady Fralix said. "Your mother is a goddess."

"My mother is a liar and a thief and a murderer," Ozma said.

"Yes," Lady Fralix said. "She was all of those things and worse. Gods don't make very good people. They get bored too easily. And they're cruel when they're bored. The worse she behaved, the more she forgot herself. To think of a god of the dead scheming like a common quack and charlatan, leading ghosts around on strings, blackmailing silly rich women, teaching her daughter how to pick locks and cheat at cards."

"Zilla is a god of the dead?" Ozma said. She was shivering. The floor was cold. The morning air was colder, somehow, than the night had seemed. "That's ridiculous. Just because we can see ghosts. You can see ghosts, too, and I can see ghosts. It doesn't mean anything. Zilla doesn't even like ghosts. She was never kind to them, even when we were in Abal."

"Of course she didn't like them," Lady Fralix said. "They reminded her of what she ought to be doing, except she couldn't remember what to do." She chafed Ozma's arms. "You're freezing, child. Let me get you a blanket and some slippers."

"I'm not a child," Ozma said.

"No," Lady Fralix said. "I see you're a young woman now. Very sensible. Here. Look what I have for you." She took something out of her pocket.

It was the constable. He said, *Did you bring me what I need?*

Ozma looked at Lady Fralix. "The fruit you picked from the tree," Lady Fralix said. "I see it ripened for you, not for me. Well, that means something. If you gave it to me, I would eat it. But I suppose you ought to give it to him."

"What does the fruit do?" Ozma said.

"It would make me young again," Lady Fralix said. "I would enjoy that, I think. It gives back life. I don't know that it would do much for one of the other ghosts, but your ghost is really only half a ghost. Yes, I think you ought to give it to him."

"Why?" Ozma said. "What will happen?"

"You've been giving him your blood to drink," Lady Fralix said. "Powerful stuff, your blood. The blood of a goddess runs in your veins. That's what makes your constable so charming, so unusual. So lively. You've kept him from drifting any further away from life. Give him the fruit."

Give me what I need, the constable said. *Just one bite. Just one taste of that delicious thing.*

Ozma took the ghost of the constable from Lady Fralix. She untied him from Zilla's ribbon. She gave him the fruit from the tree and then she set him down on the floor.

"Oh yes," Lady Fralix said wistfully. They watched the constable eat the fruit. Juice ran down his chin. "I was so looking forward to trying that fruit. I hope your constable appreciates it."

He did. He ate the fruit as if he were starving. Color came back into his face. He was taller than either Ozma or Lady Fralix and perhaps he wasn't as handsome as he had been, when he was a ghost. But otherwise, he was still the same constable whom Ozma had carried around in her pocket for months. He put his hand to his neck, as if he were remembering his death. And then he put his hand down again. It was strange, Ozma thought, that death could be undone so easily. As if death was only a cheat, another one of Zilla's tricks.

"Ozma," the constable said.

Ozma blushed. Her nightgown seemed very thin, and she wondered if he could see through it. She crossed her arms over her breasts. It was odd to have breasts again. "What is your name?" she said.

"Cotter Lemp," said the constable. He looked amused, as if it were funny to think that Ozma had never known his name. "So this is Brid."

"This is the house of Lady Fralix," Ozma said. The constable bowed to Lady Fralix, and Lady Fralix made a curtsy. But the constable kept his eyes on Ozma all the time, as if she were a felon, a known criminal who might suddenly bolt. Or as if she were something rare and precious that might suddenly vanish into thin air. Ozma thought of Zilla.

"I have no home," Ozma said. She didn't even know she had said it aloud.

"Ozma, child," Lady Fralix said. "This is your home now."

"But I don't like Brid," Ozma said.

"Then we'll travel," Lady Fralix said. "But Brid is our home. We will always come back to Brid. Everyone needs a home, Ozma, even you."

Cotter Lemp said, "We can go wherever you like, Ozma. If you find Brid too respectable, there are other towns."

"Will I see her again?" Ozma said.

And so, while the sun was rising over the roofs of the houses of the city of Brid, before Jemma had even come downstairs to stoke the kitchen stove and fetch the water to make her morning tea, Lady Fralix and the constable Cotter Lemp went with Ozma to the temple to see her mother.

"Not just the ocean!" Clementine said.
"The things in it. There might be, you know, sharks.
Or mermaids. The world is full of things and nobody
ever sees them! Nobody except for you and me."

PRETTY MONSTERS

THE WORLD WAS still dark. Windows were blue-black rectangles nailed up on black walls. Her parents' door was shut; the interrogative snores and snorts from their bedroom were the sounds of a beast snuffling about in a cave. Clementine Cleary went down the hallway with her hands outstretched, then down the stairs, avoiding the ones that complained. She had been dreaming, and it seemed to her still part of her dream when she opened the front door and left her parents' house. Wet confetti ends of grass, cut the day before, stuck to the soles of her bare feet. The partial thumbprint of a moon lingered in the sky even as the sun came up and she rode her bike down to Hog Beach.

Bathing suits and towels belonging to college students and families from Charlotte and Atlanta and Greenville hung like snakeskins from the railings and balconies of rented beach houses. Far down the shoreline, two dogs ran up and down as the surf came in, went out. A surfer ascended the watery, silver curl of the horizon; on the pier, a fisherman in a yellow slicker cast out his line. His back was to Clementine.

She left her bike in the dunes and waded out into the ocean until her pajamas were wet to her knees. The water was warmer than the air. How to explain the thing that she was doing? She was awake or she was dreaming. It was all the same impulse: to climb out of bed in the dark; to leave her house and ride her bike down to Hog Beach; to walk, without thinking, into the water. Even the rip current as it caught her up seemed part of her waking dream, the dream that she had never stopped dreaming.

It was as if her dream were carrying her out to sea.

Clementine was already a quarter of a mile out when she came fully awake, choking on salt water and paddling hard. Already the current had dragged her past the pier where in a few hours her grandfather would join the other old men to smoke cigarettes and complain about fish, or perhaps by then her parents would have found her empty bed, her bike abandoned on the beach.

Clementine thought: I'm going to drown. The thought was so enormous she forgot everything her parents had ever told her about riptides. Thrashing, she went under, and then under again. She imagined her mother, waking up now, going down to the kitchen to make coffee and cut up oranges. In a while she would call Clementine for breakfast. Clementine willed herself back into her own bed, tried to see the ceiling fan lazily sieving the air above her, the heaped clothes in the hamper against the wall, on the desk, the library books she'd meant to return two weeks ago.

Instead she saw her first-grade classroom and the first-grade reading hut with its latched port window and shelves crowded with I Can Read books, the low, dark ceiling made from salvaged boat planks and studded with seashells, the floor lined with pillows smelling of mildew. Although she was twelve now, Clementine clung to the smell of those cushions as if cushions and the smell of mildew could keep her afloat.

The waves grew taller, stacks and columns of jade-colored water that caved in, rose up in jellied walls, rolling Clementine in one direction and then another as if shaping a blob of dough. She could no longer tell if she was swimming toward shore.

And then someone wrapped a hand around and under her armpit and pulled her up, across a surfboard.

"Breathe," they said.

Clementine sobbed for air. Her hair hung in a wet rag over her eyes. Her body had no bones. Water eddied over the lip of the board, sucked at her fingers.

Her rescuer said, "You got caught in the rip. It'll dump us down by Headless Point." Which was what everyone called the place where a woman's headless body had washed up, years ago. Supposedly she crawled up and down the dunes after dark, running her fingers through the sand, looking for a head. Anyone's head would do. She wasn't picky. "What's your name?"

Clementine said, "Clementine Cleary." She looked up and knew her rescuer immediately. He was in the high school. She walked by his house every day on the way to school, even though it wasn't on the way.

"I know your mom," the boy with his arm around Clementine said. "She's a teller at the bank."

"I know you from school," Clementine said. "You built a reading hut. When I was in first grade."

"Y'all still remember that?" Cabell Meadows said. His white-blond hair, longer than Clementine's, was pulled back into a ponytail. Waves spilled over Cabell Meadows's arm, then Clementine's. She brought her knees up against the board.

In first grade, the girls had fought over who was going to marry Cabell Meadows when they grew up. Clementine had carved his initials next to her own on the underside of the bottom shelf of the reading hut. Put them in a heart. "You saved my life," Clementine said.

The fine hairs on Cabell Meadows's arm were white-blond, too, and there was an old bruise that was turning colors. A woven leather bracelet around his wrist that she knew some girl had made for him.

"What were you doing?" Cabell said. "Going for a swim in your pajamas? Sleepwalking?"

Clementine said, "I don't know." What she thought was, it was you. I woke and I came down to the beach and I almost drowned because of you. I didn't know it, but it was all because of you.

"I tried to put myself down the laundry chute once while I was asleep," Cabell said.

Clementine was too shy to look at his face.

"Here," he said. "If you can climb up and sit on the board— yeah, like that. Like a boogie board. I'll paddle kick. Anyway, the tide's bringing us back in. You just hang on."

When the water was shallow enough, they waded ashore. Clementine's pajamas dried as they walked the mile and a half back through the dunes to Hog Beach where Clementine's mother waited on the pier for the Coast Guard to return with her husband, to tell her whether or not her daughter was drowned.

Every time Clementine saw Cabell in the hall, once school had started, he said hey. When she smiled at him and he smiled back, it meant they had a secret. Two secrets. One, that no matter how far out you go, eventually you come home again. And two, whether or not he fully understood this yet, Clementine and Cabell Meadows were meant to be together.

Lee, who has both a driver's license and her mother's van, gets coffees and doughnuts at the gas station, then picks up everyone else. Czigany's house is, of course, the last stop.

It's just after eight. Mr. Khulhat has already left for his train. Mr. Khulhat is a diplomat, although Czigany, his daughter, refers to him instead as the automat. Mrs. Khulhat, who works at the hospital, has gone to drop Czigany's younger sister, Parci, off at the pool where she will swim laps for an hour before school begins. Parci specializes in the backstroke. The four girls in the van know this because they've taken turns staking out the Khulhats' house. No element of Czigany's Ordeal has been left to chance.

Lee and Bad wait in the van while Nikki and Maureen knock on the front door. When Czigany opens the door, Bad high-fives Lee as Maureen grabs Czigany's arm and Nikki ties the blindfold around her eyes. They have a pair of handcuffs borrowed from Maureen's mother's chest of drawers, the same place they found the blindfold. Among other things that Maureen has described to them in disgusting detail.

This is when things go seriously wrong. Czigany is talking and waving her hands around. The handcuffs dangle off one wrist. Next Maureen and Nikki and Czigany go inside the Khulhats' house. The door closes.

"Not good," Bad says.

"Maybe Czigany needs the bathroom," Lee says.

"Or Nikki," Bad says. "That girl pees every five minutes."

"If they're not back out again in three minutes, we go get them," Lee says. She pulls out her book as if she might actually start reading it.

"What's that?" Bad asks her.

"A book," Lee says. Lee always likes to have a book with her, just in case. She sticks it back into her purse.

"Really?" Bad says. "I thought it was a zeppelin."

"It's supposed to be kind of a romance," Lee says. "You know. With werewolves and stuff."

"Any vampires?"

"No vampires," Lee says. "In fact there aren't even any werewolves yet."

"That you know of," Bad says. "So is it sexy?"

"Um, no," Lee says. "The heroine's twelve years old right now."

Bad says, "She almost drowns, right? I've read this. That's the first story, the werewolf one? The werewolf story is definitely the best, although the werewolves don't actually show up un-til—"

"La la la, Spoiler Girl!" Lee sings loudly, covering her ears. "Not listening!"

"Here they come," Bad says. And then, "Uh-oh."

Czigany has her blindfold on. And the handcuffs. Nikki has her arm on Czigany's shoulder, guiding her. Then Maureen. Then Czigany's sister Parci.

"What's she doing here?" Bad says to Maureen and Nikki when everyone's in the car.

"Hey," Czigany says. Her mouth is unhappy, under the blindfold. "Great timing, people."

"I have an ear infection," Parci says. She looks around the van with great interest, as if she's expecting to see a black folder, somewhere, labeled CZIGANY'S ORDEAL. "I'm supposed to stay home from school today."

"So why aren't you?" Bad says.

"Are you kidding me?" Parci says. "You're kidnapping Czigany and taking her off on some adventure and you want me to stay home?"

"She said she'd call her mom if we didn't let her come, too," Maureen says. "We were going to tie her up and leave her in a closet, but Czigany wouldn't let us."

"Whatever," Czigany says. "Let me just say it again. Your timing is just perfect. If Parci and I are not home by five o'clock tonight, my mother is going to really freak out. I mean, call the police, call the president, send in the marines, summon all the powers of hell freak out. Can I take this freaking blindfold off now?"

"We'll have you home before five," Lee says, crossing her fingers down below the seat, where she hopes Parci, in the backseat, can't see her do it.

"The blindfold stays on," Maureen says sternly, then spoils the effect by sneezing three times in a row. "It's part of the deal. The Ordeal. Why does the van suddenly smell like the pound? I'm allergic to dogs. You're covered in dog hair, Czigany."

"So sue me," Czigany says. "We have a dog. You're not really going to take Parci. Seriously? This is such a bad idea. I promise she won't tell on us. Come on."

"I will too tell. And I want a blindfold," Parci says. Lee and Nikki and Maureen and Bad look at each other and shrug.

"Okay," Maureen says, sneezing again. She gets Lee's gym bag and pulls a shirt out of it. "We can use this."

"A real blindfold," Parci says. Her eyes are shiny with excitement. "I don't want to be blindfolded with a smelly shirt."

"Don't do this, guys," Czigany whines. "Please, please don't do this." She starts to sit up, and Nikki, who is sitting next to her, pushes her back into the seat and buckles her in.

"Don't worry," Lee says. She reverses out of the Khulhats' driveway. "The shirt's clean. I don't actually go to gym. I have a doctor's pass."

"Her mom's a doctor, like yours," Bad explains to Parci. "Lee stole a pass from her mother's partner's office. It says Lee has an enlarged heart or something. So she gets to sit in the bleachers and knit while we run around."

Lee really does have a bad heart. But she's told everyone that the pass is a fake. It's easier than having everyone be sorry for her all the time.

"I have a condition," Parci says, importantly. "So does Czigany. That's why we have to be home by five. We have to take all of these disgusting pills with weird names."

"Parci," Czigany says. "Shut up! They don't want to know about any conditions."

"I wasn't going to say anything else," Parci says sullenly. With their blindfolds on, it's remarkable how much the sisters look alike. They have the same thick, black hair and heavy, slanting eyebrows. The same scowls; narrow shoulders; thin, downy wrists.

"Home by five," Czigany says. Her voice is more serious than it ought to be. Deep and ominous, like the voiceover in a movie trailer. "Or the doom falls on all of us."

"Home by five," Maureen says. Lee accelerates onto the onramp of 295.

They're barely past Teaneck, heading towards the wilds of

upstate New York, an hour into what all of them think of as CZIGANY'S ORDEAL, folder or no folder, just like that, with all caps in some fancy gothic font, when Maureen pokes Lee in the shoulder and says, "Roll down the windows."

"It's too cold," Lee says. They've already stopped, once, so Maureen could pee and buy Claritin. Bad is driving, and Lee is sitting in the passenger seat, reading her romance. Still no werewolves.

"Roll down the windows, please," Maureen says. "Or pull over. I'm carsick."

"Switch with Bad. You can drive."

"No way," Bad says. "I get carsicker. You switch with her."

Lee compromises. She rolls down the windows an inch.

"More," Maureen says. "I'm in hell. This is hell. It's like it's my Ordeal, not Czigany's. When we get to your aunt's place, I bet it turns out I'm allergic to goats, too."

"Maureen, shut up!" Lee says.

"Don't worry," Maureen says. "They're asleep. So is Nikki. Parci's drooling on your upholstery. Can I say how much I love being an only child?"

"So does this change our plans?" Lee asks the other two. She can't help it: she whispers.

"What? Parci?" Bad says. "No way. Ear infection, my sweet curvy ass. Maybe her mom buys that act, but I don't. Look, Lee, it's not like we're going to let them get hurt or anything. We give them cab money and drop them off at the movies at midnight. At the latest. So they'll have to take some pills a couple of hours late. So their parents freak out just a little. Czigany's parents could use a wake-up call, you know? They act like they own her. It isn't natural and anyway, it's not like Czigany's going to tell on us."

Maureen says, "Parci won't tell on us, either."

"How do you know?" Lee says.

"I told her we'd spread it around the school that Czigany hit on Bad. That she tried to feel Bad up in the locker room even though she knows Bad already has a serious girlfriend, and that when Bad told her to back the hell off, Czigany asked if she was into threesomes."

"Nice touch," Bad says. "I'm flattered. Look, Lee. Parci is into this, okay? You can tell. And it makes it more of a real Ordeal for Czigany to have her little sister along."

"For my Ordeal all they did was make me wear a sandwich board for a day," Lee says.

"Yeah, a sandwich board, at the mall, that said PEOPLE I HAVE THOUGHT ABOUT MAKING OUT WITH. Listing all the names they'd coaxed out of you at a party and then made you sign."

"It was a short list!" Lee says.

"Steve Buscemi?" Bad says.

Maureen says, "Don't forget Al Gore, Gandhi, and Hillary Clinton. Not to mention John Boyd and Eric Park. That went all over the school."

"I didn't know what it was for," Lee says. "I didn't want to be rude! Besides, Eric asked me out the next day."

Bad says, "Only because he felt sorry for you. The point is, it's not like we don't like Czigany, you know? The accent is cool. She's been all over the world. She's met the Pope—wasn't he on your list, Lee? Whatever. The point is we're going to give Czigany the coolest, most legendary Ordeal ever. But the girl is weird. Admit it."

"It's her parents," Lee says. "The whole overprotective thing. She told me once that they had to have a bodyguard when they lived in the Ukraine or somewhere like that. Because of kidnappers."

"Funny," Bad says. "Considering. They probably make her pee in a cup, too, after she hangs out with us. Mom the doctor totally gave me the stink eye the last time I ran into her. Like she wanted to shred me into little pieces."

"She hates you for sure," says Maureen.

"Just because Czigany was, like, thirty minutes late for dinner? On a weekend night? No. I think it's because they know I'm a lesbian. I mean, your mom gets kind of freaked out, too, Lee, but she totally compensates by trying to be extra nice and making me cappuccinos and stuff."

"The Khulhats will go insane when they get home and they can't find Czigany and Parci," Lee predicts. She realizes something. The Ordeal was Bad's idea. And it isn't just Czigany's Ordeal, either. You don't ever want to get on Bad's bad side, which is what Mrs. Khulhat has done.

"Yeah, well," Bad says. She gives Lee what Lee thinks of as the invisible smile. That is, Bad isn't smiling at all, and yet you can tell how very pleased Bad is with herself. As if she is holding the perfect poker hand and all of your money is already on the table, and the smile will cost extra.

"Turn on the radio," Maureen says. Maureen is full of the kind of reasonable demands that Lee always wants, most unreasonably, to refuse. Friendships of long standing are defined by feelings of this kind perhaps more often than they are by feelings of harmonious accord. "A road trip's no good without a soundtrack."

"This isn't a road trip," says Bad, who has known Maureen just as long as Lee has. Bad never tries to be reasonable when she can be perverse. "It's a kidnapping. And it's already all messed up. Just like in the movies. It will end up with Lee shooting all of us and then having to dispose of the bodies in a wood chipper."

"It's not a kidnapping," Lee says. "It's an Ordeal." She turns on the radio. Opens up her book again.

The next time Cabell Meadows saved Clementine Cleary's life, Clementine was fifteen and Cabell was twenty-one. The occasion was the wedding of John Cleary, Clementine's mother's younger brother, who was getting married for the second time around, this time to a local girl, Dancy Meadows. Cabell's nineteen-year-old sister.

That Dancy Meadows and John Cleary met in the first place had been Clementine's fault. Dancy Meadows managed the T-Shurt Yurt down along the strip and, knowing this, when Clementine was fourteen she lied about her age in order to get a job at the Yurt. She planned to befriend Dancy, who was just out of high school herself. This turned out not to be as easy as getting the job had been, but even before John Cleary made his entrance, Clementine had managed to steal a picture of Cabell out of Dancy's wallet. And once Dancy mentioned with loathing her brother's habit of sleeping in the nude and how, during a sleepover in seventh grade, she'd charged her friends ten bucks each for the chance to sneak into his bedroom in the middle of the night to see, by the light of the full moon, for themselves.

Clementine's uncle, who had already married one girl straight out of high school, came into the Yurt on a Thursday afternoon looking for a gag gift for Clementine's grandfather's eighty-first birthday. Finding Clementine behind the counter, he used this as an excuse to spend the rest of the day in the T-Shurt Yurt, telling jokes and flirting with Dancy. Some of the jokes were pretty funny. Even Clementine had to admit that much.

And she could tell that the flirting was working, too, because Dancy began to act as if she and Clementine were very best friends, even when John Cleary wasn't around. Dancy told Clementine the story about Cabell's evil first girlfriend, and how Cabell had cried for three days when she dumped him just before Valentine's Day and then kept the diamond pendant anyway, and then how he'd cried for a whole week when their dad had accidentally stepped on Buffy (his pet tarantula), getting out of the shower.

Dancy showed Clementine how the senior girls put on eyeliner. And explained what boys liked. Clementine didn't believe all of it, but some of what Dancy said must have been true because by Christmas Dancy was pregnant, and Clementine's aunt was divorcing John Cleary and moving down to Charleston. Out of the frying pan and into the next frying pan, Clementine's mother said.

By this point, Clementine wasn't quite sure how she felt about Dancy. She was Cabell's sister, which was a point in her favor. They had the same eyes. She seemed to know every one of Cabell's secrets, too. Clementine kept a file on her computer in which she put down every single thing Dancy said, with annotations where she felt Dancy was being unfair. Once Dancy and Uncle John were engaged, Clementine spent some sleepless nights thinking about the fact that she was going to be Dancy's niece. It might be awkward if she ended up being Dancy's sister-in-law as well. And if she was Dancy's niece, then what would Cabell be? An uncle-in-law? Some sort of second cousin? There wasn't really anyone that she could ask for advice, either, because she'd stopped talking to her two best friends. That was because of Cabell.

Cabell had visited Clementine's tenth-grade biology class in May. He'd been tracking black bears along the Blue Ridge Trail over Chapel Hill's spring break, part of an independent study. Clementine went up to say hey before class started, while Cabell was setting up his slides. She'd wondered, sometimes, where Cabell would have sat in Mr. Kurtz's biology class. Stupid, stupid. Her heart was somewhere down at the bottom of her stomach, but she said, "Hey, Cabell. Remember me?"

Mr. Kurtz said, "Clementine? Did you have a question for Mr. Meadows?"

Cabell squinted. He said, "The sleepswimmer? No way!" He said she'd changed a lot, which was true. She had. It turned out, no surprise, that Cabell was an excellent public speaker. Clementine smiled whenever he looked in her direction. He finished by telling Clementine's class a story about a girl in California who went and had her hair permed and then, the same day, went hiking and got knocked unconscious.

"When she woke up," Cabell said, "she was way out in the middle of the woods, off the path and under a tree, and she put her hand up on her hair, and it was all wet and foamy." That seemed to be the end of the story. He grinned out at the class. Clementine smiled back until her face hurt.

Madeline, who lived down the street from Clementine and had wet the bed until they were both in fifth grade, raised her hand. Mr. Kurtz said, "Yes, Madeline?"

Madeline said, "I don't understand. What happened to her? Why was her hair wet?"

Cabell said, "Oops. Sorry. I guess I left that part out. It was a bear? It was attracted by the smell of the chemicals in her perm? So it hit her over the head, knocked her unconscious, dragged her off the path and into the woods. Then it licked all the perm out of her hair."

"That's disgusting!" Madeline said. Other kids were laughing. Someone said, "It liked the taste of the *sperm* in her hair?" It worried Clementine, because it wasn't clear whom they were laughing at: Madeline, Cabell, or the girl with the perm.

"She was lucky," Cabell said. "Not that it licked her head," he explained, in case Clementine's class was particularly stupid. Which, in Clementine's opinion, they were. "Lucky that it didn't eat her."

After all of that, Clementine couldn't even manage to ask any questions. Even though she'd spent the whole night before coming up with questions that Cabell might be impressed by. At lunch she said, "So he's pretty amazing, isn't he?" She couldn't keep it in any longer.

Madeline and Grace, who was going through an awkward phase, according to Clementine's mother—although this was just being kind; Grace had been awkward since the second grade— just stared at her. Finally Madeline said, "Who?" Madeline was annoying that way. You had to explain everything to her.

"Cabell," Clementine said. Madeline and Grace continued to stare at her as if she had something in her teeth. "Cabell Meadows?"

"Very funny," Grace said. "You're joking, right?"

They looked at Clementine and saw that she was not joking. Clementine saw that they were astonished. Cabell Meadows, she said to herself. Cabell Meadows.

"Cabell Meadows doesn't wear deodorant," Madeline said.

"That's because of bears." It was like the perm. Bears were sensitive to manmade smells that way. Clementine said this, hoping to reason with them. They were best friends. They liked the same movies. They borrowed each other's clothes. When they went out for pizza, they never ordered pizza with onions because Grace hated onions.

"Let's put it this way," Madeline, former bedwetter, said. "Even if he did wear deodorant, he could wear all the deodorant in the world and I still wouldn't lick him. Anywhere. His eyes are close together. He has weird hands. They're all veiny, Clementine! And his hair! Even when he was still in school here, he wasn't exactly prime real estate, okay? He was a smelly hippie. And it's worse now! Much, much worse!"

She stopped speaking in order to wipe the spit away from the corners of her mouth. Madeline was a sprayer when she got excited. Most likely, Clementine thought, Madeline still wet the bed sometimes, too. Leaky, squeaky Madeline.

Grace took over, as if she and Madeline were training for the Olympics in the freestyle unsolicited advice relay. She said, "It's kind of romantic, Clementine. I mean, you must have been in love with him for a long time? I remember how you used to talk about him when we were just little kids. But you've grown up, Clementine, and he hasn't, okay? At a certain age, for guys, it comes down to robots or girls. Superheroes in tights or girls. Online porn or real girls. Bears or girls . . . although that's not one I've run into before. The point is that this guy has already made the choice, Clementine. If you were all hairy and ran around in the forest maybe you'd have a chance, but you're not and you don't. If Cabell Meadows is the big secret crush you've been hiding all of these years, God help you. Because I sure can't."

Madeline said, "I agree with everything she just said."

No big surprise there. Madeline and Grace were both big fans of personality quizzes and advice columns and self-help books. They could spend hours agreeing with each other about what some boy had meant when he walked by at lunch and said, "Ladies."

Clementine thought about stabbing Madeline with a spork.

The only thing stopping her, really, was that she knew Grace and Madeline would get a lot of mileage out of analyzing that, too. Like how it was a cry for help because what else could you ever hope to achieve by attacking someone with a plastic utensil? The reasons they had plastic utensils was because kids did that sometimes. Once someone had stabbed a teacher in the arm. Lawyers had claimed it was the hormones in the hamburger meat. Cabell was a vegetarian. Clementine had learned that in Mr. Kurtz's class. She thought about what her mother would say when Clementine came home and said she was a vegetarian, too. Maybe she could sell it as a diet. Or a school project.

Clementine realized that she was still gripping her spork defensively. She put it down and saw that Madeline and Grace were once again staring at her. Clementine had been somewhere else, and now they knew *who* that somewhere else was.

Clementine said, "He saved my life."

"Let *me* save you from the biggest *mistake* of your life," Madeline said. Her voice took on a thrilling intensity, as if she was about to impart the secrets of the universe to Clementine. Madeline's father was a preacher. He was a spitter, too. Nobody liked to sit in the first pew. "Cabell Meadows is not hot. Cabell Meadows is at least six years older than you and he still doesn't know that tube socks are not a good look with Birkenstocks. Cabell Meadows voluntarily came to a high-school biology class to talk about how he spent his spring break shooting bears in the butt with tranquilizer darts. Cabell Meadows is an epic, epic loser."

Clementine put down her spork. She got up and left the table, and for the rest of the year she avoided Grace and Madeline whenever possible. When they began to go out with boys, she would have liked to say something to them about standards and hypocrisy and losers. But what was the point? It was clearly just the way the world worked when it came to friends and love and sex and self-help books and boys. First you're an expert and then you go out into the field with your tranquilizer guns to get some practical experience.

Clementine found Cabell's LiveJournal, "TrueBaloo," after some research online. He had about two hundred friends, mostly girls with names like ElectricKittyEyes and FurElise who went to Chapel Hill, too, and came from San Francisco and D.C. and Cleveland and lots of other places that Clementine had never been to. She got a LiveJournal account and friended Cabell. She sent an e-mail that said "Remember me, the dumb girl u saved from drowning? Just, thanx 4 that & 4 coming to talk about bears. ;)" Cabell friended her back. Asked how school was going and then never wrote again, even after Dancy broke up Clementine's uncle's marriage, and even after Clementine wrote and said everybody had missed him at the engagement party. Which was okay, because Cabell was probably busy with classes, or maybe he was off watching bears again. Or maybe he thought Clementine was upset about the whole thing with Dancy. So Clementine wasn't all that bothered. What mattered was that he'd friended her back. It was a bit like him and the bears, like she and Cabell had tagged each other.

Clementine loaded up her iPod with all the music that Cabell had ever mentioned online. One day they might get a chance to talk about music.

Most Chapel Hill students came back for parties, or to do laundry once in a while, but not Cabell. Not for Christmas, not for spring break (which was understandable, Clementine knew: if you grew up an hour away from Myrtle Beach, you'd officially had all the spring break you'd ever need). He'd shown up to talk about bears, but he didn't show up at Dancy's engagement party, not even to denounce John Cleary for being a sleazy, cradle-robbing son of a bitch. Which he was. Even Clementine's grandfather said so. Ex–star quarterback, which was all that anyone needed to say, really.

Clementine had to be grateful about her uncle and Dancy—except for the wedding, who knew when Cabell would have come home.

Dancy had talked John Cleary into getting married down on the beach, near enough to Headless Point that it felt like a good omen to Clementine. She went running along the beach at Headless Point some mornings, remembering how she and Cabell had walked back through the dunes when everyone else in the world who cared about Clementine had thought she was dead. Drowned. Only Cabell and she had known otherwise.

She begged out of being one of Dancy's bridesmaids because she wasn't going to be wearing discount lemon-custard chiffon when Cabell saw her for the first time in a year. Instead she spent three hundred dollars of T-Shurt Yurt paychecks in a boutique down in Myrtle Beach for a sea-green dress with rhinestone straps. She found a pair of worn-once designer pumps with stiletto heels on eBay and only paid eight bucks for them. Dancy's maid of honor, who'd been an infamous slut back in high school, swore up and down that Clementine looked at least eighteen.

Two weeks before the wedding, Clementine went to Myrtle Beach with her youth choir; on the bus ride home, she sat in the last row and made out with a boy named Alistair. She'd read enough romance novels and spent enough time talking to Dancy to have some general idea of what you were supposed to do, but nothing substitutes for experience in the field.

Having achieved limited success under difficult circumstances (wrong boy, wrong mouth, sticky bus floor, lingering aroma of someone's forgotten banana, two girls—Miranda and Amy—not even bothering to pretend not to watch over the back of the next seat), Clementine felt adequately prepared for the real thing.

"Are we there yet?" It's Parci who's asking. Just as if this is a family vacation and not an Ordeal. She's taken off her blindfold at some point in the last few minutes, but that's okay because they're off the highway now and bumping along the rutted road that winds up the mountain. It's all gloomy thick stands of pine trees and fir trees and under them the remains of old stone walls. Once, a long time ago, there was a French settlement. Farms and orchards. Archeologists arrive every summer, to camp and have romances and dig. Lee's aunt, Dodo, says that it's nice to have some company besides her goats, and the relationship dramas are better than anything on television.

Czigany is either still sleeping, or else pretending. Bad and Nikki are singing along with the radio at the top of their lungs, so most likely it's the latter. Maureen is texting some new boyfriend. Judging by how fast and hard her thumbs are hitting the keys, it's a fight.

"Don't be surprised when you lose your signal," Lee tells Maureen. "There aren't a lot of cell towers up here."

"To be continued," Maureen says, and bites her lip. "Oh, yeah."

Here is the turnoff, and here, another mile down, is Dodo's secret kingdom. Lee directs Bad down the dirt road into a meadow surrounded by mountains, a stream running through it. A two-story farmhouse that Dodo has painted Pepto-Bismol pink. (Paint rescued from some Dumpster. The trim is canary yellow for no good reason.) Only the barn looks the way a barn should: red and white and with a weathervane; a nanny goat standing upon a wheel of cheese. Only when you get closer do you see that instead of painting the barn, Dodo has cut open and tacked up hundreds and hundreds of Coca-Cola cans to the wooden boards.

Peaceable Kingdom was never much of a tourist attraction. There was a snack stand, a petting zoo, a go-cart track, a carousel, and a smallish Ferris wheel. The go-cart track is overgrown with grass and the beginnings of a bamboo thatch that Dodo's goats keep close-cropped. Goats play king of the hill on the collapsed wooden platform of the carousel, whose roof blew away years ago. Dodo, who purchased Peaceable Kingdom in its declining years, long ago sold off the carousel horses, one by one, to buy her goats.

Over the years, Peaceable Kingdom's Ferris wheel has peaceably sunk into the marshy ground of the goat meadow. Lightning strikes it when there are storms, and at least once every summer there is the morning when Dodo discovers, going out to milk the goats, a broken-hearted archeologist crumpled in sleep after a night of solitary drinking, in the bottommost chair where the mice build their nests. Lee herself likes to sit and read and rock gently in the cracked, lime-green vinyl bucket seat where a Pygmy goat now stands sentinel, front legs propped up on the rusty safety bar, listening to Bad honk the horn in delight at what she is seeing.

Goats are eating the green sea of grass and the creeping trumpet vine that would otherwise pull down the tilted wheel.

Others kneel or perch upon the boulders jutting out of the scrubby pasture.

"Your aunt lives here?" Maureen says. Nikki is taking pictures with her cell phone.

Dodo is Lee's mother's older sister. She's a former anarchist who served nine years in a high-security women's prison. Now she makes cheese instead of bombs. When she set up her herd at Peaceable Kingdom, she invested in six Toggenburgs. Over time she's swapped, bartered, adopted, and bought increasingly more esoteric breeds. The current herd numbers somewhere around thirty goats, including Booted Goats, Nubian Blacks, Nigerian Dwarfs, Pygmy Goats, and four Tennessee Fainting Goats. Dodo spent her years in prison doing coursework in animal husbandry. Goats, she likes to say, are the ultimate anarchists.

Bad parks beside the pink farmhouse. "Let me guess," Maureen says. "I bet there's a composting toilet."

"It's an outhouse, actually," Lee tells her, even as Dodo appears on the front porch where three goats loiter, hoping, no doubt, to get into the house where there are interesting things to chew. She's wearing pink camouflage waders that come halfway up to her hips. Her hair, too, has been colored to match the house.

"Nice boots," Bad says. The others are still gaping at Dodo, the pink house, the shining Coca-Cola barn, the goats, the Ferris wheel. Even Czigany's posture has changed subtly, as if, still pretending to sleep, she is listening very, very hard.

"Take off the blindfold," Lee tells Nikki. "And her handcuffs." And then, to everyone, "I told you my aunt was eccentric. And her feelings get hurt kind of easy. When you try the cheese, pretend you like it even if you don't. Okay?"

"Czigany," Parci shouts. She bounces on the seat. "Wake up! Your Ordeal is about to begin!"

Czigany sits up. She yawns hugely and fakely. "Hey, guys. Sorry about that. I had a late night last night."

"Boy, did we," Parci says.

When the blindfold is off, Czigany's big eyes get bigger. "Where are we?"

"That's for us to know," Nikki says.

"I need to say something before we get out of the van," Bad says. "The rules of the Ordeal are in effect. For both of you, Parci. *Both* of you have to do whatever we say. Okay?"

"Okay," Czigany says. Parci nods vigorously. She is visibly trembling with excitement. Czigany, too, is alert, and Lee thinks that just as Czigany was pretending to be asleep, she is still play-acting, concealing some other, deeper reflex.

Lee and Bad and Nikki and Maureen have lived all of their lives on Long Island. The school that they attend is small: in all, their graduating class will be nineteen girls, if Meg Finnerton manages the miraculous and passes Advanced Algebra.

The Khulhats move from country to country whenever Czigany and Parci's father is reassigned to a new embassy. Czigany has lived, for two years or less, in the following places: Bosnia, Albania, England, Israel, and Ukraine, and Lee is undoubtedly forgetting one or two others.

When Czigany moves again, in another year or two, what will she remember? Lee hopes with all of her heart that the Ordeal, at least this part of it, will be something that Czigany remembers for all of her life. Dodo and her farm are the best, most *secret* secret Lee knows. She has been sure since the first time her mother took her to visit Dodo that there isn't anywhere in the world as magical as Peaceable Kingdom with the pink house and the Ferris wheel and Dodo's goats, so smart they know how to open the front door when Dodo forgets to lock it. But perhaps it will be nothing to Czigany. Lee thinks this, and then wonders why it matters so much that Czigany is impressed.

Lee looks from Czigany's shuttered face to Bad.

Bad says, "Go for it, Lee."

The wedding was a disaster from the beginning. After the hurricane warning, they had to take down the wedding tent and the dinner tents up on the bluff and relocate to the pavilion beside the parking lot where kids went in the summer to play Ping-Pong and eat ice-cream sandwiches. When it came to weather, you had to be sensible, even though most warnings came to nothing. Clementine's parents' house had been flooded so many times they'd given up trying to qualify for insurance policies. Instead they just kept everything valuable on the second floor of the house.

The hurricane turned out to be not even a baby hurricane. Not even a tropical storm. Instead it just rained so hard that the caterers couldn't get the fire going in the pits where they were supposed to set up their clambake.

Dancy didn't look pregnant until you saw her from the side, but Mrs. Meadows had had to let the dress out that morning. Clementine had helped decorate the ladies' room on the beach with orange blossoms and crape myrtle the night before. An hour before the ceremony was supposed to begin, Mrs. Meadows had sent her off to dig through the trunk of the maid of honor's car for tit tape. Clementine came back in triumph and was immediately sent off again, this time for ginger ale and soda crackers. Dancy's face, all afternoon, had been the color of Clementine's sea-foam dress. Meanwhile, John Cleary had lain down in his tuxedo in the sand under the pier with all of his old high-school friends standing over him. Nobody could persuade him to stand up again; he was still hungover from his bachelor party the night before. Clementine and her father had a bet going over who would puke first, the bride or the groom.

When the bagpipes started up—no Cleary had ever managed to make it down the aisle without a lot of wailing and woe to make it clear that marriage, like going into battle, was serious business—Clementine was standing beside her mother on the damp concrete floor of the pavilion, trying not to slap at her legs. Beach weddings rapidly became less romantic once the sand fleas found you. Wet seeped down through rotted places in the roof. Her mother leaned over and said into Clementine's ear, "Don't you ever do this to me."

"Do what?" Clementine said.

"You know what," her mother said.

"Get married?"

"Not until you're at least thirty-five."

It had always been clear to Clementine that her mother found marriage to be something of a trial, although why, exactly, was less clear. Clementine's father chewed with his mouth shut, never left the toilet seat up, and all of his hair was his own. The previous year on her birthday he had given his wife an emerald-cut diamond pendant and taken her to the nicest Italian restaurant in Myrtle Beach. The following morning Clementine heard her complaining on the phone to some friend that her husband didn't have a romantic bone in his body and she might as well have married a wooden post.

"Swear to God," Clementine said, but her mother only sighed.

Cabell stood with the rest of the wedding party, wearing the same purple plaid bow tie Dancy had made all the groomsmen wear. He was tall and he was blond and tan and his hair was only a little bit long around the ears. There was something about the way he wore his tuxedo that seemed both natural and also unnatural, as if he was only wearing it in order to disappear into his surroundings. As if weddings and black bears were both things that required you to get as close as possible without anyone ever realizing that you were there at all. When she'd bought her dress, Clementine had imagined it was something like the color of Cabell's eyes. It wasn't. Why had he stayed away for so long?

John Cleary and Dancy Meadows were making the kinds of promises that hardly anyone ever manages to keep. Clementine strained to catch every single word, moved despite knowing Dancy had picked Headless Point for her wedding because Headless Point was where she and Clementine's uncle had first had drunken, unprotected, sand-in-underwear sex under a tipped canoe. Dancy had given Clementine all the details. It wasn't the way things would go with Cabell.

No bagpipes. No caterers. No sand fleas or tit tape or mutant bow ties. When, looking at Dancy, Clementine tried to visualize this mysterious future of togetherness with Cabell, it was like that first time on the surfboard. Only this time, instead of wading in to Headless Point, Cabell and Clementine floated out to sea and never came back.

Dancy and John Cleary kissed. They mashed their lips together so hard Clementine expected to see blood afterwards. But instead Dancy laughed. She threw her bouquet straight up so that it hit the roof of the pavilion. "Now there's an omen for you," Clementine's mother said. She picked a clump of baby's breath out of Clementine's hair.

When the bagpipes started up again, Clementine for the first time in her life felt in need of a stiff drink. Then she would go and find Cabell. They'd dance. Or sit in a car and talk until the rain stopped and the sun came up over the ocean.

Dancy had once said that vodka was practically tasteless, and just outside the pavilion was the ten-gallon cooler Clementine had helped fill with ice and soft drinks and beer. She'd seen a bottle of Smirnoff, too.

She found a can of Coke and poured half of it out. Poured vodka in. It was almost as not-bad as everyone had said. As long as she was borrowing things, she decided, she might as well take the golf umbrella someone had left propped against the pavilion and the towel on top of the cooler. Well supplied, she crept off with the Coke and the rest of the Smirnoff to hide in the dunes.

Eventually all the Coke was gone, and because she wasn't entirely sure whether or not she was drunk yet, Clementine stayed put, sipping from the Smirnoff bottle. Her butt, on the towel, got wetter and wetter. Down below the dunes the Ping-Pong pavilion seemed as far away as a dream. Slowly, as the last heavy gray light evaporated, she became aware of little breathless yips, shadows rustling the coarse, rain-beaten tubes of dune grass. Wild dogs, or even coyotes, six or seven, perhaps: she guessed they were hunting mice or frogs. They ignored Clementine, miserably invisible beneath her umbrella. Now running, now halted; backs hunched, muzzles down, paws tearing at the caked gray sand. There were bats dipping down, as if unzipping the rain, and the dogs in the dunes chased them, too, empty jaws snapping like porcelain traps.

When Clementine stood up at last, they looked at her as if she were a party crasher. She shook the umbrella and the dogs fled. Later it was clear that this was the good part of the evening, where she'd managed to get drunk and not be eaten by wild dogs.

Things went downhill after that. There was the trip to the bathroom where Clementine saw what had happened to her hair and her makeup. Where she tore the hem of her dress on the plywood door of the bathroom stall. When she found Cabell, he was dancing with slutty Lizzy York, the maid of honor.

It didn't matter. Not even the hideous, antiquated music mattered. "Hey, Cabell," Clementine yelled.

"Hey, Clementine," Cabell yelled back. He executed a dance move. "Your mom was looking for you. What's up?".

"Sorry, Lizzy," Clementine said. "I need to show Cabell something. We'll be right back. Promise."

Lizzy gave Clementine the finger; Clementine shrugged and smiled and pulled Cabell through the dancers, out into the rain. She'd left the umbrella somewhere, but never mind. The rain fizzed on her skin.

"What did you want to show me?" her sweet love said.

They walked along the tidemark. Tiny, ghostly crabs did mysterious things to the wet sand. They were writing the story of Clementine's life. Cabell Meadows, Cabell Meadows. Clementine loves Cabell.

"Clementine? What did you want me to see?"

She waved her arm. "The ocean!"

Cabell laughed, and Clementine decided that this was a good thing. She was amusing.

"Not just the ocean!" she said. "The things in it. There might be, you know, sharks. Or mermaids. Like the wild dogs in the dunes. The world is full of things and nobody ever sees them! Nobody except for you and me." Her hair stuck in wet coils to her neck. Maybe she looked like a mermaid.

"Do you think I look like a mermaid?" she asked her love.

"Clementine, sweetheart," Cabell said. "I think you look drunk. And we're both soaked. Let's go back."

"It's romantic here, isn't it?" Clementine said. "If you wanted to kiss me, I'd understand."

No stars, only rain. She wanted more than anything to get rid of her hose, but first she had to take off her pumps. Perhaps it had been a mistake to wear stilettos to a beach wedding. Every step Clementine had taken, all night long, she'd left a little hole in the poor, blameless sand.

"Don't think I don't appreciate the offer, Clementine," Cabell said, "but hell, no."

"Oh shit," Clementine said. "You're gay?"

"No!" Cabell said. "And stop taking off your clothes, okay? I'm not gay, I'm just not interested. Not to be an asshole, but you're not my type."

"I'm not taking off my clothes," Clementine said. "Just my shoes. And my pantyhose. And what do you care? Dancy said you sleep in the nude. Do you still sleep in the nude? There's sand in my pantyhose. And what do you mean I'm not your type? What type am I?"

"Underage," Cabell said. "Unlike your uncle, I don't go for babies." And having offered up this retort, which could have come straight out of one of Clementine's romance novels, he turned and walked away and left Clementine all alone in the rain with one shoe off and her pantyhose down around both ankles.

When Clementine finally got the damn stilettos off, she pretended that the ocean was the whole stupid wedding, balled up the hose, and threw them at it. Then the stilettos. On the way back to the pavilion, she took a shortcut through the parking lot and sliced her left foot so badly on a broken beer bottle that she ended up needing sixteen stitches and four pints of blood. They also pumped her stomach, just in case. Want to know who found her passed out and gushing blood and called the ambulance?

Go on. Three guesses.

❦ L ❦

Dodo gives them a lunch of goat cheese and apples and dark, chewy bread in the kitchen. There is a hard cheese and a soft, runny cheese, and a cheese-and-herb spread. Dodo tells them about her life as an anarchist, while a chorus of goats bleats threats through the screen door. How she blew up a bank. "It was three in the morning, and I know it was stupid to stay, but I wanted to see what all that money and paperwork would look like, raining down in the air. Instead, minutes before the explosives were wired to go off, there was this flood of rats and cockroaches, all pouring out of the building and across the street where I was standing in an alley behind a Dumpster. It was like they knew it was going to happen. I took off, too. Not because of the bomb, but because of the cockroaches. I can't stand roaches. It was even worse finding out that they have ESP."

She tells them how she has been shot with rubber bullets, sprayed with hoses, pistol-whipped by a D.C. cop. Look, here's the scar on her cheek. Here's the sexy mermaid tattoo another inmate gave Dodo with a ballpoint pen and a sharpened toothbrush. Bad is smitten. The others giggle nervously whenever Dodo swears, which is often.

After lunch, Dodo gives the girls the tour. She shows them the cheese-making room and the cheese cave. She takes them down to the goat barn with its threadbare brocade armchairs and hairy, goat-eaten couches where every evening she and the goats watch movies on her old projection screen. She passes out handfuls of corn to feed the goats and explains why Tennessee Fainting Goats faint. The goats are alternately curious and standoffish. Sometimes crowding around the girls, sometimes going off to confer, noisily, among themselves.

They take the corn daintily from Lee's palm but ignore the hand that Parci holds out.

"Funny little bastards," Dodo says fondly. "They just don't get along with some people."

Parci throws her corn into the grass, and still the goats won't go near it.

"This is my Ordeal? To come and feed goats and listen to your aunt talk about how to make bombs?" Czigany says to Lee.

"It's too bad you have to be home so early," Lee says, testing. "We could spend the night here. Sleep in the barn. Watch old movies."

"Or we could get home before five, like you promised, and then my parents won't murder Parci and me. I am not kidding, Lee." Czigany watches Lee carefully as she says this, as if she is waiting for Lee to give away the secret of the Ordeal.

Bad is allowing a Toggenburg to chew the fringes off her ratty sweater. She says, "Hey, Lee? Dodo says she's going to show us a midden heap. We're going to go look for arrowheads."

"You should go check it out, Czigany," Lee says. "Once Dodo found a piece of pottery down there and it turned out it wasn't pottery after all, it was a piece of skull."

Czigany gives Lee one last look and then follows the others. The goats lag behind, having no interest in arrowheads. Lee, who has her own rituals when she comes to Peaceable Kingdom, goes to visit the Ferris wheel. She climbs inside the bottommost carriage and opens up her book.

When Clementine's mother was angry, she didn't throw things or shout. Instead she began to talk slowly, as if words had lots of extra syllables that only got used when you were in real trouble.

The morning after Dancy's wedding, Clementine woke up and discovered her mother looking through her drawers. Not quietly, either.

Clementine lay on her bed wanting to die, watching her mother look for whatever it was that she was looking for. Her head, her stomach, her throat, her foot were blobs of raw sensation. There was a hole in her arm where someone had put the blood back into her, and an orange band around her wrist. She was too weak to pull it off.

Her mother said, "Everybody in town heard you yelling down on the beach last night about how much you love that Meadows boy."

"Was I yelling?" Clementine said. She gave up wishing she could die and began to wish, instead, that she had never been born. Her mouth tasted like vomit. "I don't remember. I think I was drunk."

"Which makes it all better," her mother said. "Is Cabell why you went to Myrtle Beach and bought a six-hundred-dollar dress?"

"Three hundred," Clementine said. "It was on sale. Some of the rhinestones were missing. Are you spying on me?"

"As if I would spy on my own child," her mother said. "The very idea. Geraldine Turkle happened to be picking up some Clinique foundation at Lord & Taylor's. When she saw you over in the designer dresses, she thought she ought to keep an eye on you."

"She thought I was shoplifting," Clementine said.

"She didn't say that," her mother said, equivocating. "You remember her daughter, Robin, bless her heart, who got caught on camera in the CVS with five hundred dollars' worth of Sudafed? You can hardly blame her for being concerned. And stop trying to change the subject. What's going on with you and Dancy Meadows's brother? He's a grown man and you're a little girl!"

"Nothing, nothing, nothing is going on! I can't talk about this right now. Can I have some Advil? What's wrong with my foot?"

Her mother said, "You sliced up your tendon. You would have bled to death in the parking lot if Cabell Meadows hadn't called 911. And not even a baby aspirin until you tell me the truth. Did that boy give you alcohol?"

"Nothing is going on and I'm *telling* you the truth! I just like him, okay? He saved my life. And I didn't know I was drinking alcohol. I thought I was drinking Coke, okay? Somebody must've put something in it. *Not* Cabell. You can ground me if you want. But stop asking me about Cabell Meadows. Okay? This is so embarrassing. I wish I were dead." At which point Clementine forced a couple of tears from her eyes. It wasn't hard.

Her mother went away. She came back with ginger ale and three Advil. She said, "Dancy has asked me to pass on how much she appreciates you ruining her wedding. Not to mention ruining Cabell's rented tuxedo. They've tried everything but they don't think they can get the blood out. And Clementine? Here's something to think about. Every time you and Cabell meet up, you almost die. Does that sound like a healthy relationship to you?"

"Every time we meet up he saves my life," Clementine said.

Her mother said, "Clementine. He's nothing special. He's just some boy."

DARLINGSEA: u saved my life again

TRUEBALOO: dont mention it

DARLINGSEA: you saved my life 2X now. u didnt take advantage. u know, even tho I was drunk and obnoxious and sed that u were gay. ;)

TRUEBALOO: clementine, its ok. really dont mention it. ok?

DARLINGSEA: your not, right? i mean your not gay r u? even if your not im sorry about the tux. did the blood come out?

TRUEBALOO: not last time i checked

TRUEBALOO: dont worry about the tux

DARLINGSEA: my dress got ruined 2. mom found out how much it cost & shes madder about that than me being drunk

TRUEBALOO: hope your foot is ok

DARLINGSEA: its fine

DARLINGSEA: so i know your all busy with classes but i just wanted to say thanx. for being a gentleman when i was a total idiot & for saving my life

DARLINGSEA: also can i ask u some things about chapel hill? because im thinking about applying. mrs padlow in ap chemistry talks about u all the time & chapel hill

DARLINGSEA: she went there

DARLINGSEA: she said she saw your picture in the paper from the lab animal protests & i think thats so cool, that your doing something

TRUEBALOO: tell mrs p hey for me

DARLINGSEA: so r u coming home when dancy has the baby? she says i can watch if i want but i dont think mom will let me

TRUEBALOO: maybe

TRUEBALOO: look, c, gotta run, got lab, stay off the booze, okay

 **L**

"What are you reading?" someone says.

Lee looks up. It's Parci. "Just some book. You know."

"Is it good?" Parci says.

"I don't know. It's a love story. Kind of."

"Then I wouldn't like it," Parci says. "I like stories about animals. Do you have a boyfriend? Because Czigany isn't allowed to date. Neither am I."

"Your parents are kind of strict," Lee says. "There's this boy I run into sometimes when I buy comic books. He asked me out to the movies once, but it was a horror movie. I don't like horror movies."

Parci says, "Nobody found any arrowheads. Just a dead vole. So is this Czigany's Ordeal?"

Czigany and the others are back up in the barn. Probably Dodo is showing them how to make cheese. Or pipe bombs. Lee can hear them shouting and laughing.

"This is the part of the Ordeal that I'm in charge of," Lee says, evading Parci's question as gracefully as she can.

"I thought it would be something really embarrassing. Or dangerous. Or disgusting. Not that this isn't kind of awesome." But Parci sounds almost disappointed. "Everybody in my grade talks all the time about the Ordeal. How scared they are. But you can tell they're really into it."

"It's just this tradition," Lee says. "Girls' schools have all kinds of weird traditions. Normally you have your Ordeal when you're a freshman—you know, a rite of passage or something. But we think Czigany is great, and so a couple of weeks ago we asked her if she wanted one because otherwise you don't really fit in. You'll see. When your class goes through their Ordeals."

"We won't be here," Parci says. "We have to move a lot."

DARLINGSEA: hey, cabell, dancys baby is really ugly. no kidding. first i thought all kids must be that ugly when theyre born, but my mom said lucinda larkin cleary is in her own special category

TRUEBALOO: ha ha

DARLINGSEA: u really need to come see her quick. shes got hair all over her body & she also had teeth

TRUEBALOO: r u @ the hospital? tried to call but dancys phone is off

DARLINGSEA: when she was born! & a big caul that your mom went & buried somewhere in the yard. last year in biology we read that when a fetus grows inside the mother its like it goes through different species on its way to being human

DARLINGSEA: yeah im here in the waiting room

DARLINGSEA: so maybe baby lucinda got stuck somewhere around the wolverine stage. just kidding! do you remember dancys wedding when i got completely wasted? how i asked if i looked like a mermaid because of my dress which is why i bought it in the first place

DARLINGSEA: because it looked like something a mermaid would wear. but what i was wondering is do you think there really are mermaids? or vampires?

TRUEBALOO: how is dancy? tell her im psyched to be an uncle

DARLINGSEA: shes great shes on lots of drugs. i brought her this book

DARLINGSEA: about a girl who falls in love with a vampire. it was kind of bad except i also kind of enjoyed it

DARLINGSEA: anyway dont know if dancy told u, but im going out with a guy. hes got a widows peek just like a vampire might have

TRUEBALOO: good for you, c

DARLINGSEA: dancy says u have a serious girlfriend. so i didnt want u to think i still had some weird crush

DARLINGSEA: on u

TRUEBALOO: youre a sweet kid

DARLINGSEA: bcause i did have a crush on u when i was 12 & u saved me from drowning

TRUEBALOO: tell her i can't wait to see the new kid. next time u need your life saved u know where to find me ok?

 L

Lee dog-ears the page and checks her cell phone. Time to get going. Time for part two of Czigany's Ordeal. But she doesn't move.

There are birds' nests tufted with goat hair and candy-bar wrappers discarded by broken-hearted archeologists, or relics, perhaps, of Lee's childhood, high in the spokes of the Ferris wheel. Trees crowd the pasture, guarding Peaceable Kingdom or else threatening it, Lee is never sure which. The air is scented with sweet meadow grass and the Christmas smell of the stands of pine. If only the Ferris wheel would turn again, down would come the birds' nests and up would go Lee, to be the queen of all she surveys: goats, pine trees, barn, pink house, arrowheads, Maureen on her way to the outhouse to pee one last time, Bad and Nikki escorting Parci and Czigany back to the van.

As if she really were queen, an official delegation—Aunt Dodo and the goats—is headed in Lee's direction. "Nice of you to come see me," Dodo hollers.

"Sorry," Lee says. "It's just that I wanted to get to the end of this story. And this is my favorite reading spot in the world. Sometimes I think the only time I'm ever completely happy is when I'm here. Or am I being melodramatic?"

"It's the only place I've ever been happy," Dodo says. "So remind me again. You'll be back in an hour or so?"

"Is that still okay?" Lee says.

"Just keep an eye on your friends. Caught Bad trying to sneak up on my Tennessee girls and make them faint. What kind of name is that anyway?"

"Her real name is Patricia. And I used to do that, too," Lee reminds her.

"When you were eight. Glad you're not eight anymore. You were a real punk." Dodo says this without a drop of fondness.

"So what am I now?" Lee says, teasing.

Dodo sighs. Gives Lee a hard look. "A monster. You and your friends, all of you. Pretty monsters. It's a stage all girls go through. If you're lucky you get through it without doing any permanent damage to yourself or anyone else. You sure you really want to do this to your friend? It's cruel, Lee. She'll be frightened. Parci, too."

"Parci made us bring her along," Lee says. "Parci's tough. We won't leave them alone for more than a few hours. All they have to do is stay put. And Nikki is going to go up the tree before they get there. So if they get loose and wander off, she can deal with it."

"Something bad happens to Czigany and Parci and it's back to prison for me," Dodo says. "Or if Nikki falls out of the tree. You ever think about that?"

"You think we shouldn't do it?"

Bad is gesturing for Lee to come on. Aunt Dodo is frowning down at her. "I'm not sure I'm the one to ask," she says finally. "I've made some terrible mistakes. Not the bank. I don't regret blowing up the bank. But I did some dumb things before that and goddess knows I did some dumb things afterwards, too. So now everything seems like it might be a mistake, which is why I don't leave Peaceable Kingdom very often. It's a long way back down the mountain if something goes wrong, Lee."

"Hey, Lee!" Bad yells. "Let's get this show on the road!"

"It'll be fine," Lee tells Dodo. "Bad and Maureen will kill me if I mess up the next part. That's the only thing I'm worried about."

"So don't," Dodo says, and gives Lee a hug. The goats all look surprised. Dodo isn't a hugger.

Bad has plugged in her iPod and is playing some yodelly crap. Czigany and Parci are blindfolded and Nikki has handcuffed the sisters wrist to wrist.

"We're going home now, right?" Czigany says.

"Home?" Nikki says. "What, no Ordeal?"

Czigany says, "Having to use an outhouse wasn't Ordeal enough?"

Parci says, "I think we need to go home. My ear is kind of achy?"

"Don't worry," Bad says. "We just have one stop first. Then home."

Clementine was seventeen when Cabell came home. He'd been kicked out of graduate school for breaking into a research lab in

Durham and liberating the test animals. Dogs, monkeys, rats, and cats. Clementine watched it all on Fox, with her mother and Lucinda Larkin. "See that man?" Clementine said to Lucinda Larkin. "That's your uncle! He's sleeping in your basement!" The news anchor informed them that when security caught up with Cabell on the lawn of the research building, he'd had an octopus with him, sloshing around in a two-gallon bucket.

Lucinda Larkin didn't seem particularly impressed. She went on playing with Clementine's hair. Clementine's mother said, "Dancy looked fit to kill when she dropped Lucinda Larkin off. Said something about John's computer. Some e-mail account she's come across."

Clementine's mother and Dancy had become quite close despite the difference in their ages. Their favorite topics of conversation were their respective marriages, Clementine, and, of course, John Cleary.

"Lucky Cabell," Clementine said. "Hope he remembered his earplugs. And lucky me!" She squeezed Lucinda Larkin. "I get a slumber party with my favorite little girl."

When she drove Lucinda Larkin over the next afternoon to pick up a change of clothes, Dancy wasn't home. Cabell was napping on the couch in the basement.

"So what were you going to do with that octopus?" Clementine said.

"The octopus?" Cabell said. He had on a pair of old flannel pajamas and there was a duffel bag beside the couch. His hair had gotten long again. "I don't know. Elope with it, run off to the Gulf of Mexico?"

"You remember me, right?" Clementine said.

"How could I forget?" Cabell said. "What time is it?"

"Two," Clementine said. "Where's Dancy?"

"Uh, I think she said something about yoga," Cabell said. "She and John were up pretty late last night. You know, talking?"

"Those two sure like to talk," Clementine said.

Cabell smiled in the direction of Clementine's knee, where Lucinda Larkin was lurking. "I don't think she likes me."

"Dancy is raising her to hate all men," Clementine said. "To be their doom. Isn't that right, Lucinda Larkin?"

"Daddy's a bad man," Lucinda Larkin said.

Cabell said, "That's the first thing I've heard her say since I got here."

Clementine sat down on the floor opposite Cabell and pulled Lucinda Larkin into her lap. Lucinda Larkin held on hard, like any minute the airlock doors would open and she'd be sucked away into the blackness of the void. Clementine knew exactly how she felt. "Are they really making you sleep on that thing?"

Cabell pulled a T-shirt out of the duffel bag. "Yes. Why?"

"Because that couch used to belong to Uncle John's fraternity," Clementine said. "He bought it off them when he graduated because he'd gotten lucky on it so many times. Dancy tried to set it on fire last New Year's. Because it doesn't go with her décor, but Uncle John won't let her get rid of it."

Cabell said, "After all the, um, *talk* last night, I was afraid your uncle was going to come down and ask if there was room on the couch."

Clementine put her hands over Lucinda Larkin's ears. "Dancy's been sleeping on your niece's top bunk for at least a week. So you should be safe. Speaking of true love, are you still going out with that girl? The one Dancy told me about at Christmas? Because I have a boyfriend now, but it isn't serious. Not really. Lucinda Larkin, let go of my arm. You are going to leave bruises. Want a Coke, Cabell? If you don't want a Coke, I know where Dancy hides all the booze. So how are things, anyway?"

"I'll take a Coke," Cabell said. "And how things are, more or less, is I just got kicked out of a graduate-school program that I still owe at least eight thousand dollars' tuition on. I'm stuck living in the basement of my kid sister's house for the foreseeable future because my mother's yard is full of reporters. I can't even go down to the beach with my surfboard without running into a million people who've known me my whole life, who know all about my life, who want to tell me what I should do with my life. I'm pretty sure getting it on with some high-school kid isn't going to turn things around for me at this stage, if that's what you were so delicately offering. All I need is your mother chasing after me with a bread knife."

"My mother warned you off?" Clementine said.

"Yeah," Cabell said. "Not directly. She talked to Dancy and then Dancy sat down and had a talk with me. Like Dancy ought to be giving anyone advice. Not that I was planning to take advantage of what is obviously some unfortunate quirk of your otherwise undoubtedly mature and capable personality. Your mother says you have straight As and a chance at a four-year scholarship at Queens."

"Don't worry," Clementine said. "I'm not still hung up on you or anything. I just owe you. For, you know, saving my life. Twice. And I need a good excuse to break up with my boyfriend. Want to play Resident Evil on Uncle John's Wii? Or would you rather help me help Dancy figure out if Uncle John is cheating on her? There's this Web site she wants to check out."

"I hate zombies," Cabell said. "Hey, Lucinda Larkin, let's go spy on your daddy."

"Those pajamas belong to Momma," Lucinda Larkin said to Clementine as they went up the stairs. "He had to borrow them because he doesn't have any pajamas and all of Daddy's were dirty."

Clementine said, "I had a pair of pajamas like that once. I went swimming in them and your Uncle Cabell had to fish me out. Otherwise I would have drowned. That was when I was a little girl just like you."

"Cut it out, Clementine," Cabell said. "I mean it." But he sounded friendly. As if they were friends, teasing each other.

"You were just a kid, too," Clementine said. It was weird to think about. "I'm older now than you were then." They'd both been so young then. She went and got two of Dancy's wine coolers out of the fridge and a sippy cup with chocolate milk. Lucinda Larkin followed Cabell into her parents' bedroom, turned on the television, and popped *Beauty and the Beast* into the DVD player.

"Need a password," Cabell said. He had Uncle John's laptop out already.

"Dancy says it's zero-L-D-S-K-zero-zero-one underscore sixty-nine."

"Got it. What are we looking for?"

"I have this address she saved. It was in his history. She put it in Favorites. Okay. Here's the Web site. Sexy Russians. Sexy surfer girls. Sexy man-girls. That would be the best. You think he's into man-girls? Mail-order brides?"

"All of the above, no doubt," Cabell said. He took the laptop back. "Just a minute. Let me open up another window. Want to check my e-mail. Okay." He clicked back to the sexy Russian Web site. "If Dancy and your uncle get divorced, you think she'll get the house?"

"Cabell, she'll get everything she wants. Including the couch. You want to make her real happy? Let's go look on Craigslist to see if we can find her a new couch."

The next hour was the best hour of Clementine's life. Two months earlier she'd persuaded tenor David Ledbetter that it would be really, really special if they broke into the elementary school in the middle of the night. One thing had led to another and they'd lost their virginity together in the first-grade reading hut, and even though the whole thing had been kind of a catastrophe, ever since then David Ledbetter seemed to have this idea that in order to keep Clementine happy he had to come up with new and better locations. It was making Clementine crazy.

She and Cabell didn't even kiss. Nobody saved anybody's life, and Lucinda Larkin began to scream halfway through *Beauty and the Beast* because Clementine hadn't remembered to fast-forward through the scene where the singing candlestick did something scary that Lucinda Larkin had never been able to explain. They had to make her promise not to tell Dancy.

Clementine's choir group left for Hawaii a week later. Everyone said Cabell was going to get a job as a lifeguard and stick around at least through the end of the summer. Clementine sent a postcard to Lucinda Larkin. She sent one to Cabell, too. She went swimming. David Ledbetter gave her a lei. (No jokes, please.) When she came home a week later, Dancy had kicked Uncle John out of the house. Cabell had left the country. Her mother related all of this to her in the car on the way home from the airport.

Clementine said, "Cabell did what?"

"Nobody really knows," my mother said. "He's in Romania. Apparently he got offered some job with a conservation group tracking wolf populations."

"I thought he had a court date!" Clementine said. "Didn't he have to post bail or something? Can you just do that, just leave the country like that when you're wanted for stealing an octopus?"

"Why are you so all het up?" her mother said, cutting a look at her.

Clementine said nothing.

"Clementine," her mother said. "Someday you'll find someone who will make you happy. For a while. If you're lucky. But for the sake of my blood pressure, would you please stop mooning and making yourself miserable over a boy who can't even manage to take some dogs out for a walk without getting himself on Fox News!"

Clementine waited to see if she was finished. She wasn't. "Just look at your face! You look like someone ran over your daddy. You have been nothing but trouble since the day you were born. Don't give me that look! I swear if you decide to swallow a bottle of aspirin or run away to Atlanta or get knocked up by that peaky-faced tenor just to make some damn point, I *will* make your life a living hell."

"I can do what I want to!" Clementine said.

"Not in my house, you can't," her mother said. "And not in anybody else's house, either, not unless you want me to come after you with a two-by-four. You are going to finish your senior year, graduate with honors, and go off to Duke or Chapel Hill or Queens College or, God forbid, UNC-Wilmington, and have a good life. Are we clear on that?"

Clementine said nothing.

"I said, are we clear?"

"Yes, ma'am," Clementine said.

Nobody heard anything from Cabell. Clementine broke

up with David Ledbetter. She and Madeline and Grace, friends again, all went to prom stag. Everyone had boy trouble.

The Saturday before graduation, Clementine went over to help Dancy throw all of John Cleary's trash out. He was living down in Myrtle Beach with some girl who had three piercings in her lip and one bad-tempered pit bull. Dancy wouldn't let Lucinda Larkin sleep over there, which meant Clementine was babysitting almost every Wednesday, Thursday, and Friday night while Dancy waitressed at the Bad Oyster.

"I don't know what I'm going to do when you go off to Queens," Dancy said. "Lucinda Larkin is going to miss you so much! Aren't you, baby?"

"No," Lucinda Larkin said.

Clementine gave Lucinda Larkin a squeeze. "I'll come home every weekend," she said. "You know, to do laundry."

Dancy dumped out a box. "College essays," she said. "John used to brag about how he didn't write any of these. Just got his girlfriends to write them for him. It's like serial killers, how they keep souvenirs."

"At least you didn't meet him until later," Clementine said. "You didn't have to write about the theme of loneliness in the poetry of Rudyard Kipling. Or compare and contrast Helen of Troy with Hester Prynne."

"Like giving birth to Lucinda Larkin was so much easier," Dancy said. She held up a photograph of John Cleary and some girl. Another photograph of John Cleary and another girl. "You know what I wish? I wish I'd never met him."

Clementine said, "Sorry about that."

"Yeah, well, I'm sorry about my brother. That he ran off to Romania to count wolves. I kind of thought maybe one day you and he—"

Clementine waited. When Dancy didn't say anything else, she said, "You thought maybe one day what?"

Dancy said, "That he might ask you out. When you were out of high school. He said you were a funny kid. You made him laugh. That would have been nice, don't you think, if one day you and I had ended up being sisters-in-law?"

"That would have been weird," Clementine said. "At least it would have been weird if you were also still technically my aunt. We would have had a hard time explaining it all to Lucinda Larkin."

"You won't have a hard time meeting guys in college," Dancy said. "If I were a guy, I'd totally hook up with you."

"Thanks," Clementine said, not sure whether she ought to feel flattered or creeped out. "I feel the same way. Are you going to answer your phone?"

"It's either going to be the Bad Oyster or you-know-who. And if it's you-know-who calling to say he can't take you-know-who for a couple of hours tomorrow, I'm going to you-know-what him with a set of nail clippers," Dancy said. "Hello?" Her voice changed immediately. "Cabell? Where are you?" Pause. "What time is it there? That late? Are you coming home? We miss you so much!" Her face changed. She looked over at Clementine, and Clementine made her face as blank as she possibly could.

Dancy said, "Married? For real? You're not pulling my leg?"

When she could speak, Clementine said, "Hey, Lucinda Larkin, you want an ice-cream sandwich? Let me go get you an ice-cream sandwich. You stay here with your momma."

She went into the bathroom first. Looked at herself in the mirror. She could still hear Dancy's voice, going on and on about something, and so she went into the kitchen and opened the refrigerator door. Stared into it, wondering why Dancy had so many grapefruits and hardly anything else. She bent over the kitchen sink and splashed water on the back of her neck. On her face. When she came back, Dancy was still talking and Lucinda Larkin said, "We don't have any more ice-cream sandwiches?"

Clementine said, "No. They're all gone. Sorry about that."

Lucinda Larkin said, "Can I sleep at your house tonight?"

"Not tonight," Clementine said. "Maybe tomorrow?"

Dancy was saying something. She said, "Hey, Cabell? Clementine's here. She's helping me pack up all John's crap. We were just talking about you." She put the phone down and said to Clementine, "He's married. He got married a week ago. He's going to live in a castle. It's like a Disney movie or something. Do you want to talk to him?"

Clementine said, "Tell him congratulations."

"Clementine says congratulations. He says thank you, Clementine. Here," Dancy said. "I'll put him on speakerphone."

Cabell was saying, ". . . because it's exactly like here. I mean, like home. Everybody knows everybody's business. There's the castle, where Lenuta and her sisters and her family live, and then there's the village, and then there's not much else. Hardly even a road. Lots of forest and mountain. So it's really hard for Lenuta and her sisters to meet guys, and all the locals are really superstitious, and it's not like Lenuta and her sisters can travel very far."

"Why not?" Dancy said.

"Two of her sisters are practically babies. Nine years old and eleven years old. They don't go to school. Lenuta home-schools them. Plus their family has got this whole deal going with the wolf population. They're really involved in habitat conservation."

"So will you come home for Christmas?" Dancy said.

"Can't," Cabell said. "You know. Lenuta's English isn't that great. She'd have a terrible time. You know how Mom gets. I'm going to give her some time to cool down. You know, about this marriage thing. Besides, I skipped out on bail. Not very cool, you know?"

"Hey, Cabell," Clementine said. She swallowed.

"Clementine! How's school?"

"I graduate next week," Clementine said. "Lucinda Larkin really misses you. She cries all the time."

"Tell Lucinda Larkin I'm not worth it," Cabell said. "Hey, Dancy? I'll call back later. I'm down at the townie bar and the last bus is about to head back up the mountain. There's no phone at the castle. Get this. I have to go all the way to Râmnicu Vâlcea if I want Internet access. It's like the Middle Ages here. I love it. I left a message on Mom's cell phone. Tell her I'll send an address where she can mail the rest of my clothes and things as soon as I can. Tell everyone not to worry about wedding gifts. Lenuta's got all this family silverware and monogrammed linen and stuff."

"Don't go yet!" Dancy said. "Cabell?"

"I think he hung up," Clementine said. She wanted to howl like a dog.

Dancy pushed a pile of her husband's clothes off the bed. She sat down and bounced. "This is so weird, all of this! I mean, here I am getting divorced and he goes and gets married? To some girl he just met? And he wants me to tell Mom and Dad? I can't stand it. Come here, baby," Dancy said. "Somebody give me a hug." She was laughing, but when Clementine looked she saw that Dancy was crying, too. "It's crazy, right?" Dancy said.

Clementine sat down beside Dancy and put her head in Dancy's lap. She couldn't help it. She sobbed. Dancy cried even harder.

Lucinda Larkin gave them a look like they were both crazy. She came over and hit Clementine on the nose with the remote. She wasn't at an age where she understood about sharing.

❧ L ❧

Twenty minutes, and Lee parks the van at the very top of Peaceable Mountain. There isn't much of a view. Just trees and more trees.

"Why are we stopping?" Czigany demands. "What's going on?"

Parci says, "Shut up, Czigany! You'll fail the Ordeal."

Bad gets out and slides open the passenger door and Nikki starts up the trailhead. During their planning sessions, Lee has described the place where she is to stop: the old stone wall, the historical marker, the tree struck by lightning where they will leave Czigany and Parci.

It takes Maureen and Bad and Lee a while longer to get there, guiding the blindfolded, handcuffed Khulhat sisters. "Watch out here," Lee says. "It goes down. Be careful where you put your foot. Okay, good job."

Parci keeps on laughing. Czigany is saying, "You have to call my mom. Come on, Lee. If we're not home by five she's going to go crazy. At least tell her where we are, okay?"

"Don't worry," Lee says. "It's going to be fine. We're almost there. You're almost done."

"It is not going to be okay," Czigany says. "Let me call my mother. So she can come get Parci? Bad, listen to me. If we're not home to take our pills, it's serious. Remember how Parci told you we both have a condition? It's like epilepsy. Take the blindfold off. I need to talk to you." Her hand clutches Lee's forearm with terrible strength, but Lee says nothing. She is sure she will find the marks of Czigany's fingers there later.

"It is not!" Parci yells. "We don't have epilepsy. It's something completely different."

"Shut up, Parci," Czigany says. "We have to tell them."

"You shut up," Parci says. "You say anything else and Mom will seriously kill you."

"Shut up both of you," Bad says. "Save your breath. There's a steep bit here."

At last they are at the summit. They are all panting. Czigany's breath comes in sobs. When she jerks at the handcuffs, Parci stumbles. "Quit it," Parci says. "Just quit it!"

Here is the tree, and here is Nikki, up in the branches. She grins at Lee and gives her the thumbs-up. She has her iPod, loaded up with several hours' worth of *Project Runway*, her yarn and plastic needles, her Thermos and a sandwich.

Maureen says, "Czigany, you can stop. You and Parci sit down here."

She helps the two sisters sit down with their backs to the tree.

While Maureen winds the rope around and around Czigany, Parci, the tree, Bad explains. "Most Ordeals are kind of lame. For mine, they put a personal ad on Craigslist and I had to go sit at Rosie's Strong Brew, wearing a rose in my hair, and meet all of these ancient guys. The last three, it turned out, had all been told to show up at the same time, and I wasn't allowed to explain, either. The creepy thing was how none of them were surprised that I was a fifteen-year-old lesbian. So the ad must have mentioned that. Whatever. My point is that I wanted this to be different. So I went and did some research on Ordeals and what I found out is that you used to have one if you were going to be a knight. You had to go into a church and kneel on the stone floor all night long and stay awake to pray, and if you did, they made you a knight."

"We checked the weather," Maureen says. Maureen's Ordeal was so humiliating that she refuses to talk about it at all. "It's not supposed to get down past forty degrees tonight. Thank you, global warming. The church thing wasn't going to work, but when we talked about it, Lee said that we could come here."

"You can't leave us here all night!" Czigany says.

"We'll be back to get you in the morning," Bad says. "And, just in case, someone is going to be keeping an eye on you. You know. So don't try to get loose. It's a long way down the mountain."

"Call my mom," Czigany says. "Just call her and tell her what's happening. I can't believe you guys are doing this to me! You said we were going home. You said we were going home!"

When no one says anything, she begins to thrash, horribly. She throws herself against the rope at her chest as if she means to cut herself in half. This is not how the Ordeal is supposed to go. Lee's stomach hurts as if she is the one caught in the ropes.

"Ow, ow, ow," Parci says. "Quit it, Czigany. You're making it really tight."

Czigany says, "Take off the blindfolds. At least take off our blindfolds!"

"Stop whining," Bad says. She sounds exasperated, as if she can't believe how ungrateful Czigany is being. "The whole point of an Ordeal is that it sucks. The blindfolds are just part of the suckiness."

"Am I going to be a knight, too?" Parci says. "Or whatever? Because it isn't fair otherwise."

Bad says, "Hear that? Your little sister's a badass, Czigany."

Czigany's shirt has ridden up as she wriggles in the ropes. Lee bends over to pull it back down. As she bends over, she says, as quietly as she can, "Czigany? Don't worry. We'll be back sooner than you think. Okay?"

"You lied to me," Czigany says.

"I know," Lee whispers. "I'm sorry."

"I'm sorry, too," Czigany says. And presses her lips together tightly.

"Don't worry about us," Parci says. "We'll be fine." She's grinning like a mad fiend.

No one says anything on the way back to the van until Maureen says, finally, "Maybe we should call the Khulhats. Just in case. Czigany was really freaking out."

"You would, too, if you had her mom," Bad says.

Lee says, "Good luck getting a signal. My aunt has Skype, but we can't call from her account. I don't want her to get in trouble. Maureen, you made Czigany leave the note, right? What did she say?"

"We had to improvise because of Parci. Something about needing space. And wanting a chance to do some sister bonding. I had Czigany say they might take the train into the city to see a matinee."

"Solid," Bad says. "It's like you've been kidnapping people for years."

"Yeah, well, next time let's kidnap somebody who isn't such an ungrateful freak," Maureen says.

"That's not fair," Lee says.

"Like the Ordeal is supposed to be about fairness?" Maureen says. She's practically yelling. "Like *my* Ordeal was cake and roses and champagne? Czigany has no idea. No idea whatsoever. It's like she thinks this is all about her."

"I've got a rash on my arm," Bad says. "It had better not be poison ivy, is all I'm saying."

"Probably just goat saliva," Maureen says, calming down. "They ate one of my tennis shoe laces. They're cute, you know, but they're kind of a pain in the ass, too. Like boyfriends."

It's three thirty when they get back to Peaceable Kingdom, and Maureen complains about boyfriends the whole way down. Dodo is boiling water for pasta salad. "How did it go?" she says.

"That depends on who you ask," Lee says. "Czigany isn't very happy. Her parents are pretty strict."

Dodo chops scallions and doesn't ask anything else. When Lee first asked her if they could bring Czigany to Peaceable Kingdom for her Ordeal, Dodo had a lot of questions. What will your mom say? What about missing classes? What's the point of the Ordeal anyway? After Lee described some of the Ordeals she'd heard about, Dodo sighed and said she guessed Lee and the others had everything all figured out.

"I thought you guys might want to go for a hike," Dodo says. "I thought we'd have an early dinner, then make a lot of popcorn and take it out to the goat barn. We could watch a couple of movies. You guys like Jackie Chan movies?"

Lee says, "We have to be back up there around eight. I want to get back just a little early, to be on the safe side."

"Four hours isn't much of an Ordeal," Bad grouses. She's still annoyed that no one else was willing to go along with the full knightly Ordeal, her original plan.

"The real Ordeal will be when they get home," Lee says.

"It's going to be kind of an Ordeal for us, too," Maureen says. "We have to ride back with them. Czigany's kind of scary when she's mad. Dibs on the front seat. You get to sit next to Czigany, Bad."

"Does anyone ever refuse to go along with this Ordeal business?" Dodo asks.

They all stare at her.

"Never mind," Dodo says. "Clearly I am out of my mind for asking."

Maureen and Bad opt for the hike. Lee guesses Maureen wants to complain about the new boyfriend. Lee sits in the kitchen with Dodo for a while, telling her about school. She wonders if Czigany is still trying to wriggle free. Nikki is under strict orders to document the part they are missing.

Eventually Lee heads back to the Ferris wheel with her book. She isn't sure she understands Clementine, why Clementine keeps hoping Cabell will finally notice her. Lee's never felt that way about anyone, and she's not sure she wants to, either. She reads until it's time to go and call the goats to dinner. Bad and Maureen come back from their hike still talking about Maureen's difficulties with the new boyfriend. Sometimes Lee wonders if Bad has a crush on Maureen. It's how Bad looks at Maureen sometimes. Not that Maureen would ever notice.

Dodo has made plenty of pasta salad, and garlic bread with goat butter, and iced tea. After the dishes are washed and dried, they all help make popcorn, which it turns out is not for them. It's for the goats.

After browsing through Dodo's limited selection of movies, they decide on *Lawrence of Arabia*. Dodo says, "But it's four hours long. You won't be able to see all of it!"

"We've seen it before," Bad says. "Like four times. It's okay if we don't get to the end. And it seems like the right kind of movie to watch with a herd of goats. The only thing that would be better would be if you had camels."

"It's not like it's a happy ending anyway," Lee says, and Maureen nods in agreement.

The goats are done with the popcorn before the theme music has even started. They pick their way from couch to couch, never setting foot on the floor of the barn, talking loudly. There's a reason why movie theaters don't encourage people to bring their goats. Dodo has left the barn doors open so that the goats can come and go. "They're always a bit mad when the moon is full," Dodo says. "Little terrors. Little monsters."

"Hey! Don't eat that!" Lee says, holding her book up and out of reach. The Nubian gives her a haughty look.

"Good book?" Dodo says.

"Not sure yet," Lee says. "I'm not finished. Bad's read it."

Bad grunts. She is pulling clumps of hair from the sides of a very pregnant LaMancha. "It was so-so. You know. There's this girl and she's crazy about this guy and does all these stupid things and then at the end—"

Lee says, "Shut up! I haven't gotten to the end yet!"

"I'm going to get more popcorn," Dodo says. "Anybody want anything?" The goats all go trailing after her.

"This is nice, isn't it?" Maureen says. She comes and leans over Lee's couch, gives Lee a voluptuous hug. "Being here. How come you never brought us here before?"

Lee says, "I don't know. We're here now, aren't we?"

"Can we come back?" Maureen says. "Could we come back sometime with Nikki? I feel bad for her, stuck up there by herself. Missing *Lawrence of Arabia*."

"Now in stereo with goats!" Bad says. She's lying on the next couch over, and Lee can't see Bad's expression. Only the back of her head.

"What about Czigany and Parci?" Lee says. Maureen rests her chin on Lee's shoulder. She blows on Lee's hair, garlic and goat cheese. "Quit it, Maureen!"

Bad says, "Not the same as goats. But sure. There are two of them, so I guess it's in stereo."

Maureen says, "They're just so weird. I didn't like the way their house smelled."

"I don't like the way your breath smells," Lee says.

"It's just, we went to a lot of trouble to set this up for Czigany, and I don't think she appreciates it at all. We could have done something really mean, but instead Bad had this cool idea, and I just think it's wasted on Czigany. And I wish it was just us here. You and me and Bad and Nikki. That's all." Maureen stands up and begins to play with Lee's hair.

Over on the other couch, a voice says, "What Maureen said."

"What'd I miss?" Dodo says, coming back into the barn. Goats stream after her, bleating and shoving.

"T. E. Lawrence just drove his motorcycle off the road and died," Bad says. "Then he went to Cairo."

Maureen, who enjoys complaining as much as she enjoys everything else, says with great satisfaction, "What a very epic day this has been." Peter O'Toole's insanely gorgeous face is filling the screen.

Nobody ever got an e-mail from Cabell. Or a phone call. After six months his parents put in a request with the American embassy in Bucharest. The embassy put out a bulletin, but if anyone had seen Cabell they were keeping it to themselves. Dancy and Clementine cried a lot every time Clementine went over to babysit, and then Dancy met a guy online and she and Lucinda Larkin moved out to Seattle.

To Clementine's surprise, this was even worse than Cabell. Somehow Seattle seemed a lot farther away than Romania. In her heart of hearts she was still convinced that someday she would see Cabell again.

After her freshman year at Queens, Clementine worked at a local veterinary clinic until she had enough money for a plane ticket and a Eurail Pass. By then there was the boyfriend, a guy with family money who had dropped out of Duke in order to play poker online. The boyfriend and Clementine went to Rome together. And Dublin. And Prague. And Bucharest, because Clementine told the boyfriend that she wanted to try to find an old family friend.

The best clue she had was that Cabell had married someone named Lenuta who lived in a castle that wasn't very close to Râmnicu Vâlcea. So they went to Râmnicu Vâlcea and rented a car. They began to ask about wolves. The boyfriend was into the whole quest thing. He had a phrasebook. He seemed to like playing detective.

It was difficult, sometimes, to figure out what was up with the boyfriend. It was a good thing he had money. Otherwise you would never have heard a single word he said.

They stayed in a pensione in Râmnicu Vâlcea and went to the springs to bathe. The room in the pensione was stuffy and hot, the window painted shut. All night long, Clementine dreamed of Cabell. She sat on a surfboard, looking toward the shore. When she turned to look over her shoulder, she saw Cabell, running toward her at an astonishing speed, over the top of the waves.

They had decided to drive all the way to Sfântu Gheorghe, but first they came to a town that wasn't on the map. It was hardly a town at all. But there was a gas station and a bus stop, and at the bus stop was a woman who spoke a little English.

She told them there was a castle up in the forest above the town. There was a family up there with many daughters. One of them had an American husband. The boyfriend consulted the phrasebook over and over again. When he and Clementine tried to ask her about wolves, the woman at the bus stop made the sign of the cross. Which really made the boyfriend's day.

In Clementine's guidebook, there was no mention of a castle. The forest got a couple of paragraphs. It wasn't clear which road they were looking for, and there were no signs. Then again, there seemed to be only one road that went up the mountain. They went up it, and after twenty minutes, the boyfriend suggested a picnic, perhaps a bit of a walk. They could scout things out first, rather than just driving up to the castle, if there was a castle. It was only eleven in the morning. Better to show up after lunch. People were usually in a better mood after lunch, right? (said the boyfriend.) Clementine agreed.

All day long, every time the boyfriend opened his mouth she'd wanted to burst out laughing. She was afraid the boyfriend would notice she was behaving strangely and wonder why. She was convinced he would read her mind and at last ditch her. Go back to Bucharest without her. Leave her all alone to find Cabell. Or not find Cabell, which seemed more likely. Except it didn't. She knew she'd find Cabell. She'd woken up in Râmnicu Vâlcea knowing that she would find him.

The boyfriend was an idiot and Clementine was an idiot, too. She wished she could have figured out how to dump the boyfriend before they'd got to Bucharest.

The road went over a stone bridge. What about here? the boyfriend said. We can follow the stream.

They left the car beside the road.

Raspberry canes grew up along the bridge. The boyfriend picked a handful and then threw them away. Sour, he said. I don't think we should drink the water. It's probably snow melt, but you never know.

When they stepped under the trees, Clementine held her breath. She felt that she was listening for something.

So he saved your life when you were a kid, the boyfriend said. Everything that he said came filtered through a great cone of silence.

"Twice," Clementine said. "Can you believe it?" She could not tell if she were whispering or shouting.

If you save someone's life you're responsible for it ever after. So the reason you wanted to come find him is to save him? Because nobody's heard anything from him in years?

"I don't know," Clementine said. "It's just that we're over here. It just seemed like maybe I'd run into him somehow. And you seemed like you were into it."

Yeah. I was. Hey, do you think that's the castle up there? Through the trees? We're on some kind of trail. Maybe if we just keep on going?

"Yeah. I see it. I think I see it. Are you sure it's really a castle? It might just be a rock formation."

No, it's a castle. I think it's a castle. It's not very big, the boyfriend said. How do they decide what's a castle and what's not? Like, how do you decide that something's a castle? Just because it's made out of stone and because it's old?

"I don't know," Clementine said.

Maybe we should stop and have lunch first, the boyfriend said. Then go back to the car? And drive up? I don't know if we're trespassing or not.

Far above, the canopy of leaves was shaken and shivered by a wind, but under the trees the air was heavy and cool and unmoved. The leaves underfoot smelled richly of rot. Little white mushrooms clustered in rings.

In his backpack the boyfriend was carrying the bread and cheese and beer they'd bought at the gas station. There's a clearing up ahead, he said. We can stop and eat there.

But when they came into the clearing, the boyfriend halted so abruptly that Clementine walked into him. The boyfriend stumbled forward.

Less than a yard away, two preadolescent girls lay half under a thorny bush with their arms around each other. There was blood smeared around their mouths. They were naked.

What the hell is going on here? The boyfriend put down his backpack and took his camera out. Are they okay?

There was something about the two girls that made Clementine think of Lucinda Larkin. She could see their narrow chests rising and falling. How their legs twitched, as if they were running in their dreams. Closer, much closer, here, almost at her feet, under a tree, was Cabell. He was naked and so was the woman beside him. They lay sprawled as if they had fallen from a great height. There was blood on their faces and on their bodies and there was blood matting the woman's dark hair, but she was still very beautiful.

"There's been some kind of accident," Clementine said. She couldn't imagine what had happened here, but what she felt was a kind of joy. Here was Cabell, bloodied and unconscious and alive, and here she was to rescue him. This time she would rescue him. Whatever had happened, she was meant to be here.

Clementine? the boyfriend said. He had his hands out, as if to stop from falling into the thing in front of him. A deer, she realized. Its hide peeled back in strips, the ribcage forced apart, blood and bits of entrails sticking to dirt and leaves.

Cabell's eyes opened. Clementine could have bent down and put her hand on his long, tangled hair. The bark on the tree above him was silver. It hung down in tattered flags. The woman beside

Cabell, Cabell's *wife*, flung her arm out, as if to catch something.

It wasn't their blood after all.

Clementine said to the boyfriend, "Did you ever have an idea of how your life was supposed to go, except that you were wrong about everything?"

Clementine, the boyfriend said. He'd put his camera down at last. Clementine, I think we're in real trouble here.

Lee turns the page, but that's the end of the story about Clementine. Not an end at all. Although you can guess what's about to happen to Clementine. Or maybe, Lee thinks, she's wrong. Maybe Cabell will save Clementine again.

Lee puts the book down for one of the goats to eat.

She thinks: It's like watching one of those horror movies, where you know the person is doing something stupid and you can't stop them from doing it, you just have to go on watching them do it. Where you know that the monster is about to show up, but the person acts as if nothing is wrong. As if there is no monster.

Peter O'Toole is blowing up trains. Which makes him a bad guy even though he's a good guy, too, right? Out in the night the full moon is caught in the black spokes of the Ferris wheel. It leaches all the meadow to silver. All the goats are staring in the same direction as Lee. As if even they think the moon is beautiful. Or maybe they're wondering how to climb the Ferris wheel so they can eat the moon.

Maureen says, "I have to go to the bathroom."

"You know where it is," Lee says.

"Someone needs to go with me. It's too far away."

Dodo says, "There's a flashlight up on the wall over there."

"Bad?" Maureen says.

"Sure," Bad says. "I'll go." And if that isn't true love, Lee thinks, it's true friendship, which is probably something better.

Dodo says, "Lee? When they get back you'd better head out."

"Is it that late already?" Lee says.

"It's almost nine." Dodo shoves a goat off the couch and stands up. "I thought you knew. I'll go make some coffee. I'll put some of the pasta salad in a container. For the way back."

"Thanks," Lee says. Once again, she feels a strange reluctance to get up, as if when she leaves Peaceable Kingdom she won't be coming back for a long time. The book has put her in a strange mood. She wishes she hadn't read it. She almost wishes she hadn't brought Bad and the others here.

The goats are sneezing emphatically.

"Bless you," Lee says. "Bless you bless you bless you too."

Dodo grunts. "There must be a coyote out there."

"A what?" Lee says. "Your goats are allergic to coyotes?"

"It's like an alarm system. Goats sneeze like dogs bark," Dodo says. "Haven't I taught you anything about goats? They think there's something out there."

"You're kidding me," Lee says.

"Well," Dodo says, "sometimes they're playing around. If it's not playing around, it's probably coyotes. If it's coyotes, I go out and shoot the rifle and they take off. Hear that?"

"Hear what?" Lee says, but then she hears it. A howl, melancholy and terrible and not particularly far away.

"Hey!" someone yells from far off. Is it Maureen or Bad? Lee can't tell. "There's something out here. We're in the outhouse. It's scratching like crazy to get in. Lee? Dodo?"

"Hang on," Dodo yells back. "I'll be there in a sec."

"I'll come with you," Lee says.

"No," Dodo says. "Stay here." She kneels down and sticks her arm under the sofa where Lee is sitting. She pulls out a shotgun and a box of shells. She adds, "Don't worry. I just use the shotgun to warn them off. It's just buckshot."

Lee and the goats follow Dodo to the barn doors. "I'm going to shut these," Dodo says. "Just to keep the goats inside."

Neither Lee nor the goats are happy about this, but Dodo shuts them in anyway.

"Is someone coming?" Definitely Bad this time. "There's something out here. It's making a lot of noise."

"Hold on, ladies," Dodo calls. "I'll be there in a minute."

The goats are sneezing like crazy. "Bless you," Lee says again. She stands by the barn doors and listens. She can hear Dodo walking away from the barn. Now she hears something padding stealthily along the side of the barn. Not two feet. Four feet. Something whines and scratches at the wall, its nails clicking and catching on the flattened Coke cans.

"Dodo?" Lee yells. Her chest feels funny. Her hands are cold. Once or twice a year she has to take a pill. When she gets overexcited. Her prescription bottle is in her purse in Dodo's kitchen.

She hears Dodo say, "Shoo! Get away." There is the sound of things hitting the ground and Lee realizes that Dodo is throwing rocks. Something growls and Dodo curses. "Get away from the door, Lee, or else I can't shoot. Get the goats away from the door."

"I can't, " Lee calls. "They won't go." All of the goats are now standing at the door, bleating and sneezing and calling excitedly for Dodo to come back. They take little runs and butt at the door with their heads. "What is it?"

"Not a coyote," Dodo says. "A wolf. Between me and the barn now. There's another one here as well. Trying to sneak up on me."

"What should I do?" Lee says. Bad and Maureen yell something about coming out of the outhouse.

"Everybody stay where they are!" Dodo says loudly.

The thing at the side of the barn is scratching and pawing and digging now. Lee can hear its excited breath. There is a loud report from outside, Dodo has pulled the trigger, and inside the barn all four Tennessee Fainting Goats fall over. If only Bad were there to see them. There is a snarling and growling, a bereaved, furious howling.

"I don't like this part," the girl on the bed says. Her sister, sitting in the chair beside the window, stops reading and puts down the book.

Let's call the girl on the bed by an initial. L. Let's call the other girl C. They're sisters and they are also best friends, possibly because they don't have many opportunities to meet other girls their age.

There isn't much to do here, except walk in the woods and then read to each other in that space between twilight and when the moon rises. They order a package of books every month from an online bookseller. They spend a lot of time choosing the books. This book they chose for the cover.

Except you can't judge a book by its cover. Whether or not this story has a happy ending depends, of course, on who is reading it. Whether you are a wolf or a girl. A girl or a monster or both. Not everyone in a story gets a happy ending. Not everyone who reads a story feels the same way about how it ends. And if you go back to the beginning and read it again, you may discover it isn't the same story you thought you'd read. Stories shift their shape.

The two sisters are waiting for the moon to come up, which is not the same thing as waiting for the sun to go down. Not at all.

"It's not like you don't know what happens," C tells L. It's the third time they've read this story. C yawns so widely it seems her mouth will crack open. The tip of a long tongue pokes out between the teeth when her yawn is done. "If you don't like the ending, then why do you always ask me to read the same story?"

"It's not the ending," L says. "It's the part where I don't know who Dodo shot. I like the ending okay. I just don't like this one part."

"We don't have time to finish it tonight anyway," C says.

"If it were my ending, they would all stay friends," L says wistfully. "Czigany and Parci and Lee and everyone else. They would leave the goat farm right after lunch, and Czigany and Parci would get home in plenty of time for dinner and the moon wouldn't come up until everything was all prepared. That would be a better story."

"That wouldn't be much of a story at all. Why do you care what happens to Lee?" C says. C prefers Czigany because she is an older sister, too. "I thought you were worried about Parci getting shot, although I still don't understand why you were ever worried about it in the first place. Even when we read it the first time. It's just buckshot. It's not like Dodo's got a rocket launcher or an ax or silver bullets. I mean, come on. The only thing Dodo gets right is when she tells Lee that it's Lee and her friends who are the monsters. They are! They aren't any better than Czigany and Parci."

L thinks about this. She scratches at her arm, ruthlessly and without pleasure, as if she is itchy underneath her skin in a way that cannot be helped. "But I like Lee! And I kind of like Bad, too. Even if they are totally irresponsible. Even if they totally screw up Czigany's life."

C is out of her chair, stretching toward the open window as if she can reach out and touch the moon. L watches, feeling the change come over her, now, too. It's agony and relief all at once, itchiness so unbearable it is as if you must shrug off your whole self. Once they set up a movie camera, but their mother found it afterwards and there was terrible trouble.

"What I really hate," C pants. "Are those damn goats. Goats are vicious." C was kicked by a goat once.

Thinking of goats, L begins to salivate uncontrollably. She licks her chops. Finds whiskers. How embarrassing. What would Lee think? But there is no Lee, of course, no stupid girl named Lee. No girl named Clementine. No unhappy endings for anyone. Not yet.

There were two girls in a room. They were reading a book. Now there are two wolves. The window is open and the moon is in it. Look again, and the room is empty. The end of the story will have to wait.

KELLY LINK is the author of two collections, *Stranger Things Happen* and *Magic for Beginners*. Her short stories have won three Nebulas, a Hugo, and a World Fantasy Award. She was born in Miami, Florida, and once won a free trip around the world by answering the question "Why do you want to go around the world?" ("Because you can't go through it.")

Link lives in Northampton, Massachusetts, where she and her husband, Gavin J. Grant, run Small Beer Press, co-edit the fantasy half of *The Year's Best Fantasy and Horror*, and play Ping-Pong. In 1996 they started the occasional zine *Lady Churchill's Rosebud Wristlet*.

Her Web site is www.kellylink.net.

SHAUN TAN grew up in the northern suburbs of Perth, Western Australia. He graduated from the University of Western Australia in 1995 with joint honors in Fine Arts and English Literature.

Shaun began drawing and painting images for science fiction and horror stories in small-press magazines as a teenager, and has since become best known for illustrated books that deal with social, political, and historical subjects through surreal, dream-like imagery. Shaun's most recent book is *The Arrival*, a wordless story about a migrant traveling to a strange new country. In addition to receiving multiple starred reviews, it won an Honorable Mention at the Bologna International Book Fair and a World Fantasy Award, and was a *New York Times* Top Ten Illustrated Book, as well as a *Times* Best Seller.

Shaun Tan lives in Melbourne, Australia, with his partner Inari Kiuru and a small yellow parrot. His Web site is www.shauntan.net.

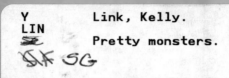